Paul Mendelson began writing at school, wrote and directed on the London fringe theatre circuit, and in 1986 at the age of twenty-one became the then-youngest playwright to be performed at the National Theatre with *You're Quite Safe With Me* at the Cottesloe. A dalliance with TV writing resulted, including work on *The Bill*, followed by eleven nonfiction books, a weekly column in the *Financial Times*, many magazine articles, and numerous monologues and short pieces for the theatre. Paul lives with Gareth and Katy in London and Cape Town. *The First Rule of Survival* is his first novel.

You can discover more about the author at www.paulmendelson.co.uk

THE FIRST RULE OF SURVIVAL

Seven years ago in Cape Town, three young South African schoolboys were abducted in broad daylight on consecutive days. They were never seen again. Now, a new case for the unorthodox Colonel Vaughn de Vries casts a light on the original enquiry, which he is convinced was a personal failure on his part; the abductions have haunted him for those seven years, costing him his marriage and peace of mind. Struggling in a mire of departmental and racial rivalry, de Vries seeks the whole truth and unravels a complex history of abuse, deception and murder — and in the process discovers he is no longer sure who his friends and enemies are . . .

PAUL MENDELSON

THE FIRST RULE OF SURVIVAL

Complete and Unabridged

CHARNWOOD
Leicester

First published in Great Britain in 2014 by
C&R Crime
an imprint of
Constable & Robinson Ltd
London

First Charnwood Edition
published 2016
by arrangement with
Constable & Robinson Ltd
Little, Brown Book Group
London

A catalogue record for this book is available from the British Library.

ISBN 978–1–4448–2855–9

Published by
F. A. Thorpe (Publishing)
Anstey, Leicestershire

Set by Words & Graphics Ltd.
Anstey, Leicestershire
Printed and bound in Great Britain by
T. J. International Ltd., Padstow, Cornwall

Author's Note

In South Africa, even in 2014, it is still commonplace to identify oneself as Black, White or Coloured (sometimes 'so-called Coloured' by those rejecting the identity and describing themselves as Black), Asian, Oriental, etc. Within the general terminology of Black Africans there are many tribal distinctions which, in this book, are not defined.

In 1994 Nelson Mandela was overwhelmingly elected as President of South Africa. Since that time, many positive discrimination policies have sought to equalize status within the country. Unsurprisingly in such a diverse country, this has not been welcomed universally.

In 2010, the South African Police Service (SAPS) reverted from standard police ranks to military-style ranks, strangely harking back to the police of the apartheid era. Some in the SAPS would say that this has made their task of being accepted and respected by all SA citizens even harder.

A few of the names used may also appear strange:

Colonel Vaughn de Vries would pronounce his surname as DeFrees.

Director (or Brigadier) du Toit would pronounce his as DuToy.

Colonel Wertner as Vertner.

Prologue

Almost in the shadow of the Hex River Mountains, where lifeless scrub meets the valley plains of saturated agriculture, the landscape of low hills rolls like gathering waves in mid-Atlantic, stretching endlessly beneath the vast skies of the Western Cape. Fast-moving clouds send shadows scudding across the sandy-grey palette of patchwork fields, giving them a few moments' respite from the white sunlight.

The Toyota double-cab shatters the silence, its dark fumes whipped from the rear-pipe. It stutters, steam billowing from the failing engine. The man jumps from the cab, cursing. He calls his dog from the open rear compartment, walks to a small stand of blue gum trees, props himself against the papery, shedding bark of the thickest trunk. He reaches for his cigarettes, growls for his dog to come away from the vehicle. He tries three times to light his cigarette, hears the sound of the flint grating, the lighter firing, the hollow pop of the flame extinguished in the wind.

The cigarette finally ignites; he inserts the drug between his lips and turns back to his stalled, steaming vehicle. He looks towards the sun, estimates the time: if it comes to it, he can walk. It will be dark before he arrives, but it will not be late. He cannot replace the car; he can barely afford for a mechanic to see it. Without it, he is twenty kilometres from the nearest town — no way for him to sell his produce, no way for him to live.

He begins to stride along the dirt track, his dog following, her head still down, ears back. In a lull in the gusts, he hears a wailing cry. It stops him dead: he holds his breath. It is a human scream. He strains to listen again, frowning at the wind in the crackling scrub. Distantly, there is a man's voice, shouting; then, the scream again. He jogs towards a low peak ahead of him. He is out of breath, sweating, but he is at the top. Two sharp gunshots follow, the sound invisible. He scans his surroundings, swallows hard, his throat gritty. His dog raises her head from the ground and howls into the wind.

PART ONE

Across the gravelled car park of MacNeil's Cape farm-stall, Colonel Vaughn de Vries strides towards him. Don February starts talking the moment he is in range.

'Two bodies, both Caucasian, probably teenagers, looks like they have been shot, possibly in the last forty-eight hours. Dog found them at the bottom of a skip outside the kitchens at the back. Scene sealed as soon as we got here.'

'Good. Trouble from the locals?' De Vries doesn't break step.

'The officer on call is a friend of mine, Ritesh. When he saw what it was, he put the call through to our department immediately. He told me what he saw and then he left. They all knew we were coming.'

'They knew I was coming,' de Vries chuckles. 'I only used to piss off one single department, now I can fuck them over the entire province.'

Warrant Officer February waits for him to finish, then continues, 'I did the paperwork with him. They have a heavy workload already. He seemed relieved.'

'I don't care either way.'

'No, sir.'

'He stamp about the place, touching everything?'

'I doubt it. We were at the Academy together. He is a sound officer.'

'Well, I'd better not find his big feet all over my crime scene.'

Don February looks up at de Vries, almost half a metre taller, looks at his mouth, wonders whether he should wait for more, or continue his report. De Vries looks down at him.

'Everyone present is in the farm-stall shop,' Warrant Officer February resumes. 'We will check details, ask the basic questions.'

De Vries jerks a thumb at the lines of parked cars as he moves towards the scene. 'Looks like there'll be a lot of them.'

'There are — and the chances are that none of them have any idea about two bodies. They could have been dumped in that skip any time, but we got lucky, sir: I checked with the owner and it only gets swapped weekly. The last took place yesterday morning, approximately eight a.m.'

'So we have a definite window?'

Warrant Officer February does not look at de Vries again, eyes never leaving his notepad.

'Close to. The owner did not check the skip, but he says that the drivers would have seen what was in it, and they said nothing. In any case, there is a load of material under the bodies, so that would suggest they were dumped after it started being filled again by the kitchens here.'

'Check with the skip company.'

Don February makes a note, then looks at him, concludes: 'I think we can place the arrival of the two bodies between eight a.m. yesterday morning and seven a.m. this morning: twenty-three hours.'

'Good,' de Vries tells him. 'We got enough men on this?'

'The moment you were assigned, I called for the full team.'

De Vries nods smugly. 'Serious crime. Two murders.'

Don February stops. 'Two *white* boys murdered is a serious crime. Yes, sir. Seems for that, the mountain really does come to Mohammed.'

De Vries moves on, shouts behind him, 'Why do you think I'm here?' He waits until his Warrant Officer has caught up with him. 'The locals think I screw them right up the arse, but that's what we're here for.'

He looks at Don February, wonders how the younger man can cope in the dry autumn heat in his thick baggy suit, loose on his skinny frame. It makes him feel claustrophobic, just to look at him. He loosens his tie and unbuttons his collar.

'What use am I investigating another drug murder in a fucking squatter-camp shebeen? I'm a middle-class white guy; I understand white crime. Let it be politically incorrect — we'll get the job done better.'

Don looks pretty disgusted.

De Vries tells him, conspiratorially, 'You're a fucking find, Don. But don't forget who saved you from the jaws of the Internal Investigation Bureau and that nice David Wertner.' Don laughs. This is not an original routine. 'That's why we cut you a little slack and let you have one moment, every day, for . . . propaganda. And today, Warrant Officer, you've just had it.' Colonel de Vries is only half joking.

7

They walk to the far edge of the low buildings, turn the corner, face the yard. De Vries stands stock still, listens to the near-silence in the rectangular space ahead of him; hears the low hum of an extractor fan, cars accelerating across the plain at the top of Sir Lowry's Pass, the corrugated-tin roof crack in the heat of the morning sun. He traces the boundaries of the crime scene with his eyes, in his head marking everything off into sections, studying their contents. He stares at the battered yellow skip in what is his twenty-fourth section, turns back and puts the scene into the context of the entire farm-stall complex.

Don February stands silently at his side. This is what de Vries likes about this man: he has stillness, the capacity to discriminate between a time to act and talk, and a time to think. He has never known a black police officer like him.

'Lab guys still not here?'

'Nothing yet.'

'That's bad. Scene's deteriorating by the minute in this heat. Tell them to hurry. And then, Don, go over to that farm-stall and take charge. Get the people processed and on their way — but keep your eyes open. You never know.'

Don February bows almost imperceptibly, backs up a few steps, then turns and ambles away. De Vries calls over an officer to give him plastic gloves; stops the officer putting on his own gloves.

'I want no more contamination of this scene by any other officer, do you understand? Only me. When the lab guys arrive, they have to take prints of everyone who's been in there.'

The officer looks mildly embarrassed, struggling to get the right-hand glove off his fingers. He looks up and sees de Vries watching him, mumbles: 'Yes, sir.'

De Vries takes off his suit jacket, hands it to the officer, tucks his tie inside his shirt, pushes up his sleeves. He looks down at the ground and takes a breath.

He starts to walk slowly around the boundary of the scene, scanning the ground, looking above, in vain, for a security camera. He stares at the back wall of the farm-stall, where he knows the kitchen is located. There are two extractor outlets, but only one long narrow window, high up on the wall, and de Vries estimates that no one could see out of it. He calls to the officer.

'These two doors. Do they both lead to the kitchen?'

The officer calls back from behind the tape he himself has put in place.

'The left-hand door leads into the kitchen utility area. The right-hand door is for a storeroom, no access. I checked it: just spare gas bottles for the stoves.'

De Vries realizes that no one would see onto this yard unless they were in it themselves. He looks back to the corner of the farm-stall, around which the bodies must have been carried, or driven, to reach the skip, under the dark overhang of the windblown trees.

When de Vries reaches the skip, he is aware that his senses are at their peak, attuned to anything that might correspond with his training, research and twenty years as a detective.

He knows immediately that it will be almost impossible to find anything of use in the surroundings of the skip. It is an area of heavy traffic: delivery and refuse vehicles, and people running from the kitchen to the four different coloured recycling bins. The skip itself, however, might yield something. He approaches it carefully, climbs the grassy bank at its far side and, holding his breath, he peers in. Amidst the piles of plastic packaging and cardboard the two naked bodies lie twisted, wrapped in thin layers of polythene. Aside from blotches of blood red, the bodies seem very white, very thin. De Vries shudders. One is clearly male, but it is impossible to tell much about the other, and he wonders how Don February knew that he was also a teenage boy.

He turns his back on the skip, lets out his breath, and walks smartly away. He begins to breathe again, but the smell of decay is lodged in his nostrils; it both stimulates and repels him.

The Scene of Crime team arrive and he beckons them through the tape. As they hurry past him, he notes that the team-leader is a man he knows and trusts to do a thorough job. They nod at each other wordlessly; each is moving along his own path and neither hesitates.

De Vries walks slowly from the yard behind the buildings, around the corner of the car park; beyond it, the vista of endless fruit trees, straight lines leading to dark rolling mountains. He imagines a process in reverse: the bodies brought up onto the mountain plain via one of the passes at either end, the drive through thick forest and verdant farmland, and turning into the farm-stall, down the approach track and through the car park; the car driving from a previous point to this place . . . what might have happened there; what led to their deaths. He knows that it is a journey that he will take until he reaches the source.

He walks briskly around the end of the low thatched building to the entrance of the farm-stall, climbs the wide brick steps. There is still a crowd of people, but there is a semblance of order; a cooler, shaded calm. He finds Don February, turns him away from the people, says quietly, 'Good work, Don. I think it's worthless 'cos those bodies have been in there for hours, at least. Looks like condensation inside the wrapping, so that suggests overnight.'

'We are trying to keep it brief.'

'Good. Next, who told you that the two bodies were both boys?'

Don is concerned. 'The owner. Is he wrong?'

'Probably not, but he would have had to move stuff to know. Did he tell you he'd touched them?'

'No. But I was waiting for an official interview. I did not ask much. He is in his office back there.'

De Vries nods quickly and trots towards the door at the end of the food counter. He knocks, enters immediately.

A broad, ginger-haired man is on his cellphone. The moment he sees de Vries he hangs up, stands, wipes his hands on his check shirt and offers his right hand.

11

'Tom MacNeil. It's my place.'

Vaughn introduces himself, asks: 'Did you touch the bodies, or get into the skip to identify them?'

MacNeil hesitates.

De Vries says: 'Whatever you did, it doesn't matter. I just have to know.'

MacNeil sits back down and looks up at de Vries.

'I was an idiot. I saw them. I know I should just have called you guys — but I thought, If I'm wrong, if this isn't what it seems . . . Anyway, one of them was at the top, almost clear of all that shit, and the other was half in. So I pulled him out by his arm, and then . . . then I could see. I knew . . . '

De Vries can't imagine why anyone would do this, but he's satisfied that MacNeil is telling him the truth — that he's stupid, not involved.

'Why did you look in the skip this morning, Mr MacNeil?'

The owner seems relieved that he has not been chastised; uncrosses his arms, his legs.

'My dog just went mad. She was in there, and she just barked and barked. I had to go and see what it was about.'

'So your dog was in the skip?'

He swallows. 'Yes, in the skip. I called her out immediately though.'

De Vries is trying to stay calm. There is a knock at the door. He spins around and opens it. It is one of his men.

'Sir, the lab guys want to move the bodies. They're checking in with you.'

'All right, tell them to wait until I'm there just now.'

The officer leaves and de Vries turns to MacNeil. 'How busy is that yard during the day?'

'Not very.' MacNeil shrugs. 'When we've unpacked stock we might go out there to the recycling, cardboard and stuff . . . and mid-afternoon, when we're emptying the kitchen bins after lunch, but we're not back and forth.'

'What about the door to the kitchen. Is it ever left open?'

'Nah. There'd be flies everywhere, and it's a matter of security too.'

'Locked?'

'From the outside, yes. It's a fire exit — with a bar, you know? You push to release it.'

'And the gas cylinders. How often are they changed?'

'I dunno.' He thinks about it. 'Probably one each week. We have three cooking areas here. Something like that.'

'So, it's quiet out there. Anybody ever park there?'

'Maybe a few delivery vans, but they'd be early in the morning. People use it to turn round if the car park's busy. Otherwise, no.'

'One more thing. When you close, is your car park still open?'

'The gate should be closed. I usually do it myself. First in, last out. You know how it is.'

'You lock it last night?'

MacNeil takes a breath, squeezes his eyes shut. De Vries looks at the wide freckled face on a thick neck, knows that these gestures are only for show.

'Ja. I think so.'

'How often don't you lock it, Mr MacNeil? Let's be quite clear here.'

MacNeil avoids de Vries' eye.

'I locked up last night,' he mutters. 'For sure.'

De Vries stares at him. The expression on MacNeil's face is open: the man apparently believes what he has just said. Everything sounds right; nothing is helping.

'Stay here. My Warrant Officer will be with you now.'

MacNeil asks him plaintively, 'My business. When will I be able to open again?'

Two dead kids.

'Maybe tomorrow,' de Vries answers bitterly.

'Tomorrow?'

'Maybe.'

★ ★ ★

London is dark and grey, the Thames cow-dung dirty. The entire city is blurred through the dense misty rain. John Marantz turns away from the porthole; the view makes him feel depressed. He has been airborne for eleven hours and has another six hours to wait before the next half of his journey. It will be the first time he has been back on native soil for five years.

In the airport lounge, his cellphone rings and a number he has almost forgotten appears on the screen. On answering, the voice is just as he remembers it.

'You don't look well.'

'See me on the cameras?'

14

'Saw you in Vegas. We can see anyone, any time. Are you drinking?'

'Not for three years.'

'What are you on?'

'Seroxat and cannabis. What about you: claret and Prozac?'

A momentary pause, then: 'Who are you seeing?'

'Sexually or psychologically?'

'Either.'

'Neither.'

'That's a pity.'

'How did you know I was here?'

'You're an asset. I know where you are all the time.'

John Marantz likes no part of that sentence.

'I need to know you are all right, John.'

'Why?'

'Because of what happened. Because of what we did.'

'For that,' Marantz says slowly, 'you deserve nothing.'

★　★　★

De Vries walks back to his car with the Scene of Crime team-leader. Most of the vehicles have left the car park now, and there is an officer at the driveway entrance, turning away disappointed customers. MacNeil's farm-stall seems to be a thriving business, and de Vries knows this will mean that with a steady through-flow of customers, staff will be unlikely to identify anyone who might normally have stood out.

'One night outside? That your view too?' de

15

Vries says, lighting a cigarette carefully, shielding his lighter from the breeze, not looking at his colleague.

'Until the coroner confirms time of death, yes. But based on what I've seen, I'd think twenty-four hours tops since they were dumped. Preliminary observations only, Vaughn, but there's no spatter, almost no blood. I'd say you're looking at an alternate crime scene.'

'No IDs?'

'Not on them, obviously. And nothing that we've found so far in the skip or around the site. I'm guessing we won't find anything. Whoever killed them stripped them. He knew that would make identification harder.'

'Time of death?'

'I'll give you my guess: forty-eight, seventy-two hours perhaps. I want the coroner to open the wrapping. Until then, you can't see much.'

'How stacked up are they at the labs?'

'Same old. You'll get prioritized, but I can't promise you anything from my guys for at least forty-eight hours.'

De Vries shakes his head. 'That's why they haven't made *CSI: Cape Town*,' he says. 'They wouldn't have the lab results from the first crime till the series ended.'

Dryly: 'Nice one.'

'How long will you be here?'

'Should finish up before it gets dark. If the bodies were just dumped, there'll not be much outside the immediate scene — though we'll look, of course. After that, as far as I'm concerned, we can reopen everything. Unless

16

you have any objection?'

'Your call now. I'm done here.'

The coroner's van passes them, heading back towards Cape Town.

'I'll have the preliminaries for you by first thing tomorrow.'

'Good.'

De Vries stands by his car, lost in thought. Something at the corner of his brain, his memory, is plaguing him.

'Vaughn?'

He exhales two lungfuls of smoke, sputters: 'Sorry. Was on another planet . . . '

'I was just asking: this scene — are you a policeman who rejoices because this is what you do and it is all about to begin under your charge, or do you despair because there's so much death in our country?'

De Vries hadn't taken his colleague to be a philosopher, not when all he does, week in, week out, is study the detritus of death. He looks over to him, his face blank.

'Neither.' He shrugs. 'Or both?'

★   ★   ★

The pathology suite is not lit by recessed LEDs, a soothing blue mist of light; nor are the benches gleaming and new — but even if they were, you would not be able to see them for the bodies. There are no banks of slim wide-screen computer monitors. You do not enter through swishing, automatic sliding doors . . .

At 6 p.m., Vaughn de Vries and Don February

17

push through the slatted, grey-blue plastic curtain into the large, white-tiled mortuary. Five fluorescent tubes hang on chains from the grey ceiling. The only moderately blue light comes from the ultraviolet fly traps on the wall. Their zapping punctuates the stench of death as it lodges in the men's sinuses.

At the far end of the room, a burly, thick-set man in protective, spatter-resistant clothing is hunched over a table. As they walk past the other benches, de Vries looks at each body. They are all young black men. At the final table, the skinny body in the sickly light is very white.

De Vries, his voice loud in the hush, asks: 'Where's the other one?'

The pathologist looks up at de Vries. 'Good evening, Harry. Thanks for jumping the queue for me. I owe you a beer — '

De Vries baulks. 'Sorry, Harry. Thank you — and, yes . . . Beer.' Vaughn grimaces. 'I'm dog-tired and the adrenalin just kicked in again. I want to get this going. Sorry.'

'Body A has already been processed and is now back in storage. As you can see, we have a backlog.' Harry Kleinman glances back up the room. 'These all need attending to before I go home.' He sighs, looks back at the body on his table, and then back at de Vries. 'I'm finished here. You want what I have?'

'Ja. Any clue to identities?'

Kleinman peels off thick gloves and disposes of them.

'Assuming no one is claiming them, no, not unless we have records on characteristics for

18

missing persons.' He reaches for two clipboards proffered by an assistant, switches spectacles, balances the bottom of the boards on the top of his small, round beer belly. He glances at the first one.

'Body A is a Caucasian male, aged between fourteen and sixteen. Shot once through the chest. Clean through and through — that is to say, the heart exploded but the bullet continued on its way. No traces of munition found, but the wound is consistent with that of a high-powered rifle — a hunting rifle, perhaps. I estimate time of death as between noon and six p.m. on Sunday.'

'That wide?'

'Impossible to judge accurately. Ambient temperatures are all over the place — the wrapping distorts any normal measures. But,' Kleinman adds, 'the wrapping was not done straight after the boys were shot.'

De Vries counts back: the boy died about forty-eight hours ago. The bodies must have been kept for a night, then wrapped in polythene and transported to the farm-stall the following day. They then spent one night out of doors in the skip.

'Anything on the wrapping?'

'Nothing yet, but it's at the lab.' He looks up at de Vries over his glasses. 'Heard the *CSI Cape Town* gag. Very droll, Vaughn.'

'How long were they wrapped for?' de Vries asks, ignoring Kleinman's comment.

'I would say,' the pathologist begins, looking down to open a chocolate bar, 'that both boys would have been dead for at least twelve hours before wrapping. I've already heard the theory

19

that they spent one night in the open whilst wrapped, and I'm inclined to concur. But I can't be definite on that. There are some small areas of post-mortem bruising, possibly from being transported from the original crime scene.'

'Pre-mortem? Signs of struggle?'

'No. I wouldn't expect signs of struggle in a shooting case. However, the wounds indicate that the shooter was standing no more than twenty metres from his targets, and this second boy has classic defensive wounds. He was probably also shot only once, but this bullet made more of a mess. Firstly, it looks like it took the fourth finger of his left hand off. It's possible that this is a separate shot, but I'm inclined towards the theory that it is the same one. Then it punctures his left lung, before ricocheting through him. If the first boy took twenty seconds to die, this one, it was about as instantaneous as it gets.'

'Facing the shooter?'

'It seems so.'

'Moving towards him?'

'I can't tell, but this victim certainly had his hands raised. If I'm right about the same shot taking his finger and piercing his lung, then his hands were more in front of him than up in surrender. I'm merely speculating here, piecing what I have into some kind of a working theory.'

'The boys are definitely from the same scene?'

'Judge for yourself. Body B, here, is also a Caucasian male, as you can see — probably a little older, sixteen to seventeen years. Also, the single shot. Although we don't have the ammunition, it seems pretty clear that it is the same gun.

Same estimate of time of death.'

De Vries interrupts him. 'Can we say, with any certainty, that they were shot at the same time by the same gun?'

Kleinman smiles at him. 'I know you want me to say that, and I concur that it is highly likely. The evidence all points that way, but it is not conclusive yet, not in a scientifically proven sense.'

De Vries feels the first small steps being taken.

'But we can work on that assumption. What else?'

'The contents of their stomachs reveal identical eating patterns leading up to their deaths: both had eaten only one meal, I estimate almost eighteen hours previously, and it appears to be identical: pasta, tomato sauce and carrots. They had drunk only water.'

Kleinman refers again to the boards.

'I noticed a similarity in their builds. Both are lacking muscle for their general development, and carry excess weight in the stomach region. Both display very poorly maintained teeth, with both boys having large amounts of dental decay, which would surely have been causing discomfort, if not pain. You want to see?'

De Vries shakes his head, rotates his hand to restart Harry Kleinman.

'We've run preliminary blood samples and there is no indication that these boys are related.'

'Unrelated, yet showing similar signs of upbringing; recent behaviour?'

'The diet, yes, but they may simply have eaten the same meal on this occasion. The lack of exercise, leading to muscle deterioration, the similar dental patterns, the overall . . . physiognomy of these boys, suggests that they have been living similar lives for many years.'

'Living rough?'

'No. At least, I certainly doubt it. Look how pale his body is. This is a boy who spends very little time outdoors. Palms and soles of feet smooth. Same on Body A.'

'Any forensic interest?'

'One more thing. Both boys display signs of homosexual activity, over a period of years, and seemingly relatively recently also. It's difficult to say, but I tend to think that it was not consensual. I can't identify whether the activity took place between them, or whether it was perpetrated by a third party — or more than one other party. Instinctively I'd say it suggests sexual attack or even sustained abuse.'

There is a silence, interrupted only by a shocking zap from the fly-killer on the wall. Vaughn and Don turn towards the noise, see a narrow wisp of brown smoke rise towards a stained patch on the ceiling.

'However, I can't tell you whether there was a sexual element to the attack which resulted in them being shot. It seems unlikely. And the weapon used, if I'm right, suggests an outdoor scene.'

'Because it is a hunting weapon . . . ?'

'And also that it would be an unwieldy gun to carry around or use indoors.'

Vaughn notices that Kleinman is still staring at the body on the table. 'Forensics?' he asks.

'One substance on the body, looks post-mortem. Both bodies are pretty clean, underneath all of that. Body A has something on his heel. Not sure what it is. Probably from when his body was dragged to where it was wrapped. It's in the lab already.' He looks back down at his clipboards. 'I retrieved samples from beneath their fingernails and particles from their hair, which may come from the original crime scene, and particulate from their throats and lungs.'

'What was that?'

'I can't tell. It might simply be from dust from whatever area they were confined in, but there is a build-up over time.'

Don February asks, 'What do you mean, 'confined', Doctor?'

De Vries smiles to himself, glances at his Warrant Officer: rarely speaks, but misses nothing.

Kleinman turns to Don. 'You're quite right; that was conjecture. It seems to me that these boys have been confined together, probably without proper exercise, possibly for a long period of time. They have been subject to similar routines and, at least recently, a similar diet. This suggests to me a prison — a children's correctional centre? An overbearing, perhaps abusive family, where both, though unrelated, are living?'

In the silence that follows, de Vries begins to hear his heart pumping inside his head, deep and sickly.

He stutters, 'Show me a picture of the other boy, Body A.'

Kleinman gestures at his assistant, who passes him a file.

'Just the face. I only need to see the face.' De Vries is very pale. He feels a fever hit his groin, his stomach, begin to move its way upwards through his body. His legs feel wet with sweat. He grits his teeth and wills these sensations away.

Kleinman pins a picture of the face of Body A to the illuminated board. De Vries looks at it and shuts his eyes. Then he opens them and studies it more closely. He looks up, tries to swallow away the bile that is rising in his throat. His eyes dart from side to side.

Kleinman puts his hand on Vaughn's shoulder.

'What is it, man? You know this victim?'

'It's worse than you can possibly imagine.'

'Who is it then?' Kleinman stares at de Vries, uncomprehending.

'Those boys,' de Vries murmurs. 'All these years, I thought they were dead.'

2007

The Area squad room is packed with detectives, uniformed police officers, now even off-duty officers, chattering in low voices. Expectation is rife. Vaughn de Vries watches the men stand loosely to attention as Senior Superintendent Henrik du Toit weaves through the room towards De Vries' office.

De Vries waits at his door, shakes hands and ushers his commanding officer to his desk. He then turns back to the squad room, announcing: 'Inspector Russell will brief you on the background, so that everyone knows exactly where we are. Then we will assess our reaction and assign officers. It's going to be a long night, so make your excuses to your families, grab a pie and get ready.'

He goes back inside his office, hides his disconcertment that Du Toit is sitting in his chair behind his desk, sits opposite him in one of his deliberately uncomfortable guest chairs.

'There's discontent brewing, Vaughn,' Superintendent du Toit starts, loudly as ever, 'that you weren't at the Annual Family Day.'

De Vries sits up, immediately indignant. 'I have a possible double abduction, and they think I should be braaing with the wives?'

'No, I meant that you weren't at the scene immediately.' Du Toit shakes his head despairingly. 'Anyway, relax Vaughn, I put them straight. But you must understand, if Toby Henderson is really missing — if he doesn't turn up somewhere, really soon — then this could be the third. Three in three days — a serial abduction case. The moment the media get hold of this, that will be it: the floodgates will open. So we need to move fast, and get results. Bring me up to speed with the first two.'

De Vries is downcast.

'There's fuck-all, frankly. Steven Lawson, aged seven years four months, presumed abducted from Rondebosch Common area, Thursday the eighth between 1500 and 1530 hours, walking home from Rondebosch Boys' Prep School to Peacock Lane. Ten-minute walk; safe area. We believe he was seen crossing Campground Road, heading towards the common. He's usually accompanied by a neighbour's son who, that day, was absent from school due to emergency dental work. We've stuck signage in the locale, stopping school-run cars yesterday. We've knocked on

25

everyone's doors: nothing. Absolute blanks.'

Du Toit shakes his head again. De Vries wishes he would stop. He clears his throat.

'Robert Eames, usually called Bobby, eight years, eight months, disappeared from Main Road between Mowbray and Observatory yesterday afternoon, Friday ninth between 1545 and 1615 hours. He was on his way from school to meet his father, who owns the used-car dealership opposite the Shell garage just past Groote Schuur Hospital. His dad called us at 1830 yesterday, having checked with his wife and friends that Bobby had not gone anywhere else.'

Du Toit looks bleak. 'My God. One a day. I can't believe this.'

'We've had officers on the street all this afternoon,' de Vries says. 'As you know, I took them off leave for Family Day. Again nothing. We assume the suspect is in a car. The boy gets in, the car drives away. So far, there are no known connections between the boys, or their friends. Early days still. Why do they get into the car with this guy? Why does nobody see anything?' He tilts his head, like a nervous tic.

Du Toit urges: 'Somebody saw. Maybe they don't even know it. We have to find them.'

'And then, sir, this afternoon, as you know, Toby Henderson goes missing following our own SAPS Family Day.'

'Where's Trevor Henderson now?'

'God knows.' De Vries holds his head. 'Must be going out of his mind. Last I heard, he was still talking with Toby's friends, trying to see if anyone knows anything. Jesus, for this to happen

26

in broad daylight, at the police's own event, for Christ's sake.'

Du Toit nods again, this time remains mute. A silent acknowledgement: Toby Henderson, son of SAPS Inspector Trevor Henderson, is today missing, surely now abducted. They imagine how the scene must have unfolded. A perfect late-summer's afternoon. The cricket club sports ground, an idyllic occasion: the match in play, officers, wives and families, girlfriends, all at tables around the pitch, a running buffet up at the pavilion, braais smoking, filling the air with sweet meat-scented smoke, a cake-stall under bunting. Around the corner, a playground for the kids, a golf speed-gun for the guys, measuring the longest drive in the force. Between cricket sessions, the divisional jazz band playing on the pavilion balcony.

When, thinks de Vries, was the critical moment? In the midst of the afternoon, when the game was in full flow, the party beginning to swing as the effects of long, cold beers on a hot, dry afternoon begin to take hold. One moment when everything is as it should be . . . the next, when you become aware of a low whine of hysteria beginning to disturb the calm — and then that second when everything breaks down. The match stops, the players' formation disintegrates. Policemen congregate, begin to splay out through the crowds, imparting the news, satiating the increasing need to know. And then mothers calling children, older siblings running towards the play area, desperate to claim their own.

A child is missing.

'Everyone cooperating?'

'As you'd expect, sir. None of the men are going home. Uniformed guys are passing through all neighbouring streets to the cricket club, with Toby Henderson's picture, and Steven Lawson's and Bobby Eames' too. I worked through last night and I'll do it again if we have even the slightest chance of finding Toby — not to mention the other boys.'

'And you'll instruct Trevor, how?'

'I'm not going to be the officer calling him off the team, sir.' The 'sir' emphasizing who is of higher rank, who makes decisions. 'If this were my son, nothing on earth would keep me from being right in the middle of the action.'

Du Toit approves.

'Keep an eye on him. We don't want to compromise a prosecution, or the safety of the other abducted boys. You happy I handle the press, leave you alone?'

'Absolutely.'

'But expect a call, Vaughn. They're going to want to talk to you too.'

He looks out towards the now-dark city. 'You think we can issue a warning of some kind?'

De Vries snorts. 'The moment this breaks, there won't be a parent in Cape Town letting go of their child's hand.'

2014

To support power-saving, the SAPS hierarchy have decreed that at the SAPS central building after dark, all non-essential lights are switched off. De Vries, glad to be rid of the pervading

28

fluorescence, has only one small Anglepoise lamp illuminating his office and conference room. He sits, head in hands, nose low over a large beaker of whisky. He's meditating — something he would never do consciously. Steven . . . Bobby . . . Toby . . . : mug-shots, school photographs, headlines, bylines, memories, the file cover closing over them.

From the squad room, Don February has watched him like this for the last fifteen minutes; he is thinking, too. Dr Harry Kleinman enters the squad room and knocks briskly at de Vries' door. Don gets up and follows him into the office, staring at the coroner's thick bare legs in shorts and his short-sleeved pilot's shirt with epaulettes.

De Vries looks up, gestures them to sit down, but Kleinman starts talking immediately.

'It's pretty much confirmed, Vaughn. I went back through the records. Toby Henderson sustained a multiple break in his left ankle, aged six years, seven months. That matches exactly with what I can see.'

De Vries shuts his eyes. Steven . . . Bobby . . . Toby . . .

'I've viewed the case photographs at the time of their abduction, and I believe that the other boy is extremely likely to be Steven Lawson. I've cross-checked the blood type, and that's a match. His group's AB, which is less than five per cent of the population, so it's strong, but certainly not conclusive. We should be able to DNA a confirmation from a hairbrush, or something that his family have kept. In any case, the age, physical features, all seem right.'

29

'Jesus Christ. What do I tell their parents? After seven fucking years, we've found your son; he was alive until forty-eight hours ago, and now you have to come identify your lost, dead child. I fucking hate this job.'

Harry Kleinman slumps down in the chair directly opposite de Vries, his voice weary but soothing.

'In my experience, Vaughn, however traumatic the news, in the long run, the parents of missing children just want to know what happened. They can bury their sons, grieve properly, find closure.'

'I hate that fucking word,' de Vries spits, looking up from his desk.

Kleinman continues smoothly, 'This is what we do, Vaughn. We find out what happened to them. We tell the parents, we catch the bad guy.'

'If I'd caught him seven years ago — Jesus, any time in the last seven years — those boys would still be alive. I should have revisited the files more often.'

Don February asks: 'The third boy . . . '

Kleinman says, 'Bobby Eames.'

'Surely this means that *he* could still be alive? Two bodies, but three abductions.'

De Vries looks at his Warrant Officer. A tiny light illuminates inside his consciousness.

'One boy unaccounted for,' Don says quietly. 'One to be saved.'

Vaughn sits up, focus coming slowly to his eyes.

'Listen, both of you,' he says. 'This goes far deeper than either of you know. You see the name of the Superintendent back in 07, Harry?'

Kleinman looks at his sheets.

'Don't bother,' de Vries tells him. 'It's du Toit. That means we have our Director back in the headlines for the one big case that nearly screwed his career.'

'He's a grown man.'

'He's in a dog-fight,' de Vries retorts. 'So am I. That slimy little shit, David Wertner, at the new Internal Investigations Bureau, is on my back, and he's looking to pay back some old favours to our almighty General. Discrediting me, and ousting du Toit; we're top of his list.'

'And that means?'

'I don't know,' de Vries replies, losing momentum. He frowns, takes a deep breath, counts his decisions off his fingers. 'Nobody hears about this until the morning. I want to brief du Toit personally and hear from him how he wants to proceed. There's going to be a shitstorm in the press, everyone will be watching us and this time, no matter what, we have to find Bobby Eames.'

'And the parents?'

'Jesus, I don't even know what happened to Trevor Henderson. He spent every working moment hunting for his kid, we scarcely saw him for months; he took all his leave. Everyone turned a blind eye when he missed shifts; frankly, he wasn't much use. When he was told that the case was unsolved, he resigned, carried on searching. Last time I heard, he was in some drink, drug rehab place in Wilderness. I know his wife took their daughter back to England. He was English police, Mounted Division originally. Came to the Cape, fell in love with it, and brought his family out here. Good man. I think his wife filed for divorce the moment the plane hit the tarmac. Don't think they even talk. She never wanted to come to Africa, I know that.'

De Vries sighs, sadly. 'I'm pretty certain that the Lawsons are still here, though. I see the father sometimes in Claremont. I fucking hide. Can't bear to face him.' He bows his head, fights tears.

Don February says: 'I will find out what I can about them — their current addresses. And regarding the whereabouts of the Eames family, I will give you what I have. Are you staying here?'

De Vries nods.

'I will find you.' Don struggles out of the low guest chair and stumbles out of the office.

Kleinman gestures back at the closed door. 'I like him.'

De Vries says: 'Don't tell him.'

'There is carrot as well as stick, man.'

De Vries snorts.

Kleinman leans forward. 'February is a Cape Coloured name, isn't it? Your man looks pure black African to me.'

'He told me it's his mother's name; says no one could ever pronounce his African name. I'm trying not to see him for his colour.'

'Perhaps that is what he is hoping. Anyway, if you've found a good man there, what does it matter? He seems to be able to cope with you, anyway.'

'Do I need to be coped with?'

Kleinman raises his eyebrows. He smiles, goes on: 'You know, back in 07, I wasn't here. At that time I was living in Durban — spent three years

32

there. I heard about it, of course. This is one out of nowhere.'

De Vries picks up the whisky bottle, pours a second glass when Kleinman nods, topping up his own.

'All these years, Harry, all this time, those boys have haunted me. You realize what this looks like? Those kids were taken, held hostage in secret: ill-treated, abused, imprisoned for seven long fucking years. How can that happen? How can nobody see, nobody know?'

'I find myself saying it more and more: it is unbelievable.'

'You have a murder, you do all you can to find the bastard responsible. There's a focus, but these boys — we didn't know anything. Weeks went by, and nothing. Complete, total blank. We reckoned pretty quickly they were dead. No ransom demands, no more abductions: three in three days, and then nothing. Never heard of a case like it. These sick fucks start, they go on, never stop until they're caught. But those three. Shit knows how many man-hours we all put in, every one of us, but not one shred. Never seen a case with no evidence like that.'

Kleinman lowers his voice. 'Assuming you did your best, you have to focus only on what happened today. You can't afford to dwell on an investigation that is seven years old.'

'Maybe the answer was there, all the time.'

'No, Vaughn. If it was there, you would have found it.'

'Maybe I missed something. I don't know. Whatever, this guy is still around.'

33

Kleinman leans forward, his big head casting de Vries in shadow from the feeble lamp.

'You have your murders now. And big questions: after seven years, why kill them? He's hidden them perfectly. Why dump the bodies where they could easily be found? Not my department, but I'd say your man just made his first mistake, and that'll be what leads you to him. All this time, a seemingly perfect crime, and now something surely unplanned: to leave the bodies there. Find the man who did this; find Bobby Eames. It's all you can do.'

De Vries nods, thinking ahead.

'And I'll do it too. I fucking swear I will. But, Jesus Christ, what a night ahead.'

'I'll be down below for the next few hours. You want to bounce anything off me, if du Toit wants me, just call me up.'

'Thanks.'

Kleinman takes a couple of breaths. Then he asks: 'What made you think of those boys back in the lab?'

De Vries doesn't look up.

'I never stop thinking about them.'

Harry Kleinman heaves himself up, pats Vaughn's shoulder and stomps off down the grey corridor which leads past the squad room to the elevators. Vaughn hears his heavy footsteps get fainter, one by one, until he is alone, in silence.

2007

Inspector Dean Russell says, 'I've spoken with the last two people to see Toby Henderson: his

34

friends Jacob Oland and Bryan Hollander. Talked to their folks too. Seems they were round the back of the old pavilion, smoking.'

'Smoking at ten years old?' de Vries says. 'Jesus. I was twelve before I started.'

'I got the feeling it was grass.'

De Vries snorts. 'Christ. They're smoking ganja before they're teenagers and they pick a spot behind a field packed with policemen.' He looks back up at Russell. 'You sure they didn't see, hear anything?'

'Toby Henderson told them he felt sick, wandered off towards the trees. They waited for him, looked for him. Nothing. We're still canvassing the neighbouring homes for unusual cars, people, but with SAPS Family Day, the area was packed with strange faces.'

'Shit. All right, keep on with all the usual stuff.'

'He knew,' Russell says. 'He knew that with all those people he could just blend in and take Toby, and nobody would see him.'

'Seems like it.'

'That shows a fuckload of confidence though, doesn't it?'

2014

Don February watches light grey silhouettes posture and dance through the frosted-glass window of de Vries' office, which is next to the dark conference room in which he waits. He knows that he is witnessing the professional agonies of two men, history clawing its way up

35

through the floors, the walls enclosing them, to strangle them with their memories. Everyone who works this job has them; it's endemic. You just pray that you have a chance to solve the cases one day, resolve your unending painful curiosity.

Don, too, keeps his mind moving, zig-zagging to evade demons; he remembers the three-year-old girl, raped and tortured. The wall of silence in the squatter camp, no one breaking. He recalls his anger, the unbearable frustration that he could persuade none of them to talk. Would no one identify her parents? Her relatives? Days of it, unending. Don became convinced that she had been brought to the outskirts of Cape Town from far away with one sole intention: to torture and kill her. And then, six sleepless nights after that revelation, another case came up, and Don could not be spared. The docket was marked unsolved and stored. Don still remembers her nameless tattered corpse; still remembers that somewhere a baby girl is missing, taken to an alien place, from a village far away.

The door to de Vries' office opens.

'Come in, Don.'

Don gets up, walks gingerly into the office; he had no idea they knew he was in there.

'Warrant Officer.' Du Toit shakes Don's hand. 'I'm pleased you are involved in this at this point.'

Don bows politely.

'I gather that Colonel de Vries has already run through with you why this is going to be such a big case. When these boys disappeared seven years ago, it was media saturation for weeks, so the public, the press, everyone will be scrutinizing us. Whether we like it or not, there are always politics in an organization. We have some bloody-minded people on our backs. You were completely uninvolved in the original inquiry. I think it's absolutely right that we add a man unfamiliar with the emotional history of this case.'

Exhausted, but still able to appreciate his superior's talent for saying nothing at length, de Vries smiles to himself.

Du Toit snaps his fingers.

'Notification to the families will be undertaken by me personally tomorrow morning, after which I will hold a press conference.' He turns to Vaughn, who is having trouble keeping his eyes open. 'Assuming that the man who abducted these boys is the same man who killed them, we now have a unique opportunity to catch him. That's what I want emphasized to the press. In fact, there is only one sensible way to play . . . describe this . . . There is now a chance, hitherto thought impossible, of finding Robert Eames alive, and of arresting whoever this monster turns out to be. This is a whole new case, ultimately a completely different case to the original presumed abductions.'

De Vries realizes how that would sound, the way it could influence, even manipulate, how the papers cover the story. He is too tired to be angry, but he knows that this man, whom he has followed up through the ranks, cares less about the victims than how things appear in the media.

De Vries is not like this. He stands up, a new wave of adrenalin hitting him.

'There are some things I want to check.' He looks over to du Toit. 'If we're done here, sir?'

'All right, Vaughn. At seven a.m. tomorrow morning, I am visiting Steven Lawson's parents, then Mr and Mrs Eames. Finally, if no one can find out what the hell's happened to Trevor Henderson, I'll be calling Mrs Henderson in the UK. Then, I give a press conference.' He turns to de Vries. 'Make sure I have something to tell them.'

★ ★ ★

This crime lab is only for the specialized units in town, but it is still open, two men and a woman bent over benches, faces illuminated by bulky computer monitors. The Crime Scene leader stands before de Vries, bleary-eyed. Vaughn still can't remember the man's name.

'Don't expect anything till the morning. Yes, first thing, I know. We'll work it all night.' He gestures to the technicians, but they do not look up. 'Blown the month's overtime in one go.'

De Vries thanks him, strides out of the laboratory and takes the lift back up to his office. It is 2 a.m., and he knows that he cannot progress without forensic evidence. He sits in the low, comfortable chair, wondering why he has never discovered its charms before now, takes off his shoes and lies back. His mind is filled with images of the three abducted boys, the gaunt, hopeless looks on the faces of their families, for

38

seven years an investigation without end — until now.

★   ★   ★

Don February waits until 7 a.m. exactly before waking de Vries. He has managed a few hours dozing on the floor of the shared Warrant Officers' offices, drunk some tepid, weak coffee, and washed inadequately in the dirty toilets. None of it as demeaning as hearing his wife tell him all the ways her life is not matching up to her dreams; bitter, biting into him. His promotion sought only for her, now resented and despised.

'I am paying for our house,' he tells her, his voice echoing back to him from his cellphone.

Don checks his appearance in the mirror, exits the bathrooms and heads to de Vries' office, where he finds him slumped in his chair, his mouth open, gaping to the right, as if he has suffered a stroke.

He taps de Vries on the shoulder, and then a second time.

De Vries is disorientated, then snaps to.

'Forensics?' he asks immediately.

'Thirty minutes from now,' Don tells him. 'In the lab.'

'Jesus. Didn't think I'd drop off.' He looks at Don. 'You all right?'

'Unpopular at home, undervalued at work.'

'At least someone notices you're not there.'

De Vries gets up, brushes himself down, combs his salt and pepper hair; wonders why there is so much more salt than pepper. He puts

39

on a faded tie, looks down at it, murmurs, 'My 'Big Day' tie.'

Don holds open de Vries' office door. Vaughn stops as he passes through.

'The Scene of Crime leader's name?'

'Steve Ulton.'

De Vries nods and walks away.

★ ★ ★

De Vries bursts through the plastic curtains, strides towards him.

'Morning, Steve.'

Ulton looks a bit taken aback, hesitates until Don joins them. Then he delivers the results, the two boys laid out on wheeled stretchers either side of him. De Vries props himself up against a workbench, the almost silent lab emphasizing the sound of throbbing in his right temple.

Unbidden, Ulton starts reading from his report.

'Starting off. The scene itself is devoid of useful physical evidence. There are tyre-tracks from over twenty different vehicles. With the weather as it's been, most of the track is just blowing away, so there's no way we'll get anything there. We searched every inch of the skip and its contents, and there's nothing there either. Finally, to confirm: there were no cameras or other surveillance at MacNeil's farm-stall. They sometimes employ a car-guard, but not so late in the season.'

'Nothing on anything then?' de Vries murmurs.

Ulton doesn't know whether he was meant to hear the aside, but he goes on: 'Some stuff, but mainly negatives. No fingerprint evidence on either side of the polythene wrapping. We have found two small hairs, probably eyebrows, on the inside of the polythene. It is possible that these come from Dr Kleinman or either of the two technicians processing these bodies and their wrapping. They could belong to the boys themselves. However, we will await DNA tests. Otherwise, there are no obvious DNA tags from which we can seek a match. We can assume that whoever wrapped them was wearing gloves, possibly protective clothing. From the state of the blood found inside the polythene, we estimate that between eight and twelve hours passed between the shooting of the victims and the wrapping of the bodies.'

He swallows, takes a couple of breaths. 'The polythene wrapping is odd. It's old and was around from the 1950s through to the late 1970s, possibly, here, the 1980s, when new chemical formulas were developed which made the products lighter, thinner and stronger, also cheaper and with less pollution. In its time, it would probably have been used by warehouse-men, distributors, transport companies, for binding units together securely for transit.'

'Heavy-duty shrinkwrap?'

'The precursor to it, yes.'

'So someone had access to, or had saved, some packing material that hasn't been around since the 1980s?' de Vries queries.

'Apparently, yes. To my knowledge, this product hasn't been made anywhere for thirty, forty years. It's obsolete.'

De Vries nods; it is clear information, but it

41

means nothing. 'I'm sorry, go on.'

Ulton turns a page. 'We haven't been able to retrieve anything from the boys' bodies, but there was particulate in their hair. Grass seeds, and a predominance of leaf and seed matter from *Triticum aestivum* — wheat. They probably fell in a field, or close to a wheat-field. There are corresponding findings: the stomach contents of both boys showed that they had ingested water containing a high level of Atrazine. That's an agricultural pesticide, used mainly on arable crops such as wheat and corn. That might suggest that the boys had drunk water obtained from a borehole, somewhere in the countryside, where arable farming takes place.' He turns another page. 'This ties in with Dr Kleinman's observations of residual damage to the heart and liver of both boys — a likely long-term symptom, after many years of ingesting water contaminated in this way.'

'Seven years?'

'Perhaps. I don't know.'

'Okay.' De Vries turns to Don. 'Let's assume that these boys were held in the countryside, and they were killed there also. Then, for whatever reason, they were moved and dumped.'

Ulton resumes speaking the moment de Vries stops. 'Dr Kleinman found particulate in the lungs: this was dust from standard building concrete. In his report, he says that he suspects long-term absorption.'

Tiny steps, clicking in notches. De Vries realizes that he is wide awake again.

'Under the fingernails, there was also concrete

dust, from a similar source to that found in the lungs. This substance was also found on the underside of both boys' feet, and under their toenails. Again, he suggests a long-term build-up of particulate matter.'

De Vries stops him. 'A cell, or cells? Concrete floor, concrete walls, unplastered, unpainted?' He looks at Don, who frowns back at him, then at Ulton, who shrugs.

'Possibly, yes.'

'Anything else for us?'

'Yes.' He looks at de Vries. 'This could be nothing, but Dr Kleinman found on the right heel of this boy . . . ' he indicates Steven Lawson, pointing to the boy's heel with the tip of his pen ' . . . adhered here is a small trail of dairy product. He did very well to spot it. We've tested it, and it's cheese.'

De Vries ponders a moment. Says, 'I'm having trouble seeing how this helps us.'

Ulton is unperturbed. 'This matter got stuck on Steven Lawson's heel just before he was wrapped in polythene. This means that it occurred post-mortem. The cheese is made from goats' milk and contained one unusual ingredient: stinging nettle. As far as I know, there is only one cheese in the Cape which uses nettles, and that is Fineberg Roulade.'

Don asks, 'What is that?'

'It's a goats' cheese made at the Fineberg Wine Estate outside Stellenbosch. They make layers of cheese, cover them in wild nettle, and then roll the cheese to form a green spiral running through it.'

'I've never heard of it,' de Vries states.

43

'Not likely you would have. I only know because I visited the place about two months ago. As far as I know, they only sell it there.'

De Vries thinks out loud, questioning whether this could possibly mean anything. 'So, whoever wrapped those boys' bodies, or dragged them, bought this . . . '

'Fineberg Roulade.'

' . . . this roulade, at the estate.'

'Possibly, yes. It was certainly present at the site of the wrapping.'

'Which we can reasonably assume, for now,' de Vries adds, 'could have been where the boys were held.'

'And, if so, recently. The cheese doesn't keep, and the trace on Steven Lawson's heel isn't old. It's decayed because of the heat and the wrapping, but it isn't old.'

De Vries meditates on the information. He has something, however little, to feed du Toit. More importantly, there are slender leads he can now follow which might guide him to more concrete ones. He grimaces at the use of the term. He turns to Ulton.

'Thank you, Steve. It means a lot that you worked all night.'

Ulton holds up his hands. 'No problem. I just want to hear you catch this guy.'

He turns and walks briskly from the lab towards his office, holding open the door for a technician to return the bodies to refrigerated storage.

De Vries looks up at Don February.

'Right,' he starts, rubbing his hands. 'I'm going to brief Director du Toit, and you're going to find out where this Fineberg Estate is, and what time it opens. Then, you're going for a cheese-tasting.'

2007

The office of Superintendent du Toit is opposite the squad room. Even through the closed door, the group inside the office can hear the hubbub coming from outside: telephone calls, impromptu meetings, the desire of all to produce a break-through, a witness. Anything, to break open the case. Inside, the atmosphere is hushed, each man contemplative, yet wanting to contribute.

Du Toit sits behind his desk, four chairs arranged around it. He looks at Dr Johannes Dyk, consultant psychologist to the department. 'Assuming we hear nothing today, it will be seventy-two hours since Toby Henderson went missing. There has been no ransom demand; no communication. What can we take from this?'

Johannes Dyk replies blankly, 'In one respect, relief that there have been no further abductions. On the other hand, this is a highly unusual series of events. If the kidnappers of these children want to exert pressure on us for their own gain, then I would still expect to hear from them within the next twenty-four to forty-eight hours.'

Du Toit says: 'And if we don't?'

'Then . . . ' Dyk runs a small pink hand through his white hair. 'Then, I am afraid, you face a very serious situation. Unless you can identify some clue as to the identity of the abductor, or abductors, then you seem to have a cold trail.'

De Vries says: 'You think this is the work of a group?'

Dyk looks him in the eye. 'Possibly.' He turns back to du Toit. 'It is conceivable that this is a couple working together.'

'A couple?'

'There have been examples — very rare, I might add — of a married couple working in tandem to steal children. In those cases, it would be to form what they would regard as their family. It might be that they have lost a child, or children, through illness or accident, perhaps even by their own hand — and now seek some kind of surrogate replacement. But to abduct three children — it seems to me incredible.'

'So we assume a single perpetrator?'

'Based on precedent, yes, but there are concerns about organization. Is he keeping them or killing them? The longer we don't hear from this man, or men, the more inclined I am towards the unpalatable truth that these boys have been taken and killed.'

'A serial killer?'

'Well,' Johannes Dyk pronounces, 'that is a much misused term. It is not my area of expertise, but a classic serial-killer scenario would not begin with three murders in such quick succession. Such an extraordinary event would be the culmination and marked acceleration after many months, maybe years, of activity. So, unless you have child abduction and murder — white child murders — stacked up over years, then I am inclined to say no.'

De Vries says: 'No.'

46

Dyk bows at him.

'But,' du Toit says, turning to the rest of the group, 'I'm still unhappy about how they were taken so easily, in full daylight. Who do these boys trust enough to get into his car so easily?'

De Vries says: 'Parents of friends? Teachers, clergy?'

'A policeman?' Dean Russell says. There is a silence.

Du Toit is the first to speak.

'It would explain Toby Henderson,' he says quietly, 'but I don't know. Unless he was in a marked car, would a child get in? Even then . . . '

'If the officer were known to him, perhaps?' Russell says.

De Vries says: 'I've talked with the parents. They all say that their sons were intelligent, sensible young boys; that they would never go off with a stranger. I believe that's what they taught them.'

'We need to think about this more,' du Toit tells them. 'We know that whoever was targeting them wanted middle-class white boys, and we know that he took them in what appear, to us at least, to be public open spaces.' He drifts off, looks expectantly at his audience. No one speaks. Finally he turns to the one black officer in the room. 'Mikkie, nothing from the patrols at the abduction sites?'

Everyone turns to Sergeant Mikkie Ngolo. He has said nothing for the entire meeting; just listened and waited to be addressed.

'Nothing, sir. We have found no one who noticed the boys, saw a car pulled over at the kerb, saw anyone at the Family Day who seemed out of place.'

'Nothing?'

'Nothing. I think this is because these boys were walking on the streets, two of them after school when there were many children walking home; at the Family Day, there were also many children playing around the ground, they did not stick out. So what if a car stops, picks up a child? It is an everyday occurrence: cars and taxis stopping in the street. There is no reason for people to notice. Maybe whoever took them knew this — and he was right.'

2014

Don stays long enough to hear Director du Toit's eloquent and meaningless press conference descend into a tense stand-off as journalists return him to the original failed inquiry — which he led — seven years before. Don heard him admit that they had assumed Steven Lawson, Toby Henderson and Robert Eames to be dead, even though he denied that the case had ever been officially closed. He watched du Toit begin to sway slightly — a physical reaction to the blows landing, loaded question after loaded question.

There is a horrible moment, Don reflects, every time he is present at a SAPS press conference, when control shifts subtly, but completely, from police to pressmen. That is when Don steps outside for a moment, gets in his car, and drives towards Stellenbosch. He takes the N2 out of town, turns after Khayelitsha, the township in which he lived as a child, down the R310, turning onto the Annandale Road at the giant fibreglass strawberry

48

outside the petrol-station farm-stall. He weaves his way down an olive-lined driveway and parks to the right of the ultra-modern winery building — steel and stone, huge glass windows presenting a visual cacophony: the workings of the winery, and the reflection of a huge blue sky, lines of narrow poplar trees, goats in the pastures.

Already, there are other cars there. Through the double-height glass doors, Don can see the backs of white legs standing at a bar where the tastings are held. As he enters, he sees the white girls behind the counter look up and scrutinize him. Instinctively, he looks down at himself; his suit trousers are crumpled, but he is wearing a tie. He looks up at the girls again, all back to their business; he may not be accepted, but he is not deemed a threat.

'Warrant Officer February?'

Don turns to find a lanky man in khaki shorts, blue blazer and tie, proffering his hand.

'Yes, sir. I called earlier.'

'When did they change the ranks? What is a Warrant Officer?'

'A few years back, sir. I am an Inspector.'

'And I am Marc Steinhauer, the owner. I think you said you wanted to ask me about our cheese. Is our cheese a police matter?' The man laughs in staccato, choking bursts. He stops himself. 'Come on through. I've kept our Cheese Room closed until I'd spoken with you.'

He leads the way through a pair of oversized rustic wooden doors, into another brightly lit space. The room is unnaturally cool. A pure, fresh odour assaults Don's senses. It smells, Don thinks, of white man's piss.

'Not that we only sell cheese, as you can see.' Steinhauer gestures about the room, to limed wooden shelves, filled with bottles and glass jars. 'As well as our wine, we have olives, our own olive oil, and recently sundried tomatoes and artichokes.' He glides over to the low-profile, under-lit glass counter, pointing to the cheeses displayed within, his patter bland, over-rehearsed. 'We started off with one goat. My wife wanted a goat — I bought her a goat. Then she got us all onto goats' milk, then the cheese, and before I knew, I have a whole herd of them.' He laughs loudly again.

Don wonders at his accent: it is English, but he has Afrikaner intonation on some words.

Steinhauer starts up again: 'The story begins with plain goats' cheese. Then we added garlic, chives — which goes very well with our Chardonnay — then sundried tomato, and now, finally, the Fineberg Roulade.'

'That,' Don interjects firmly, 'is what I want to ask you about.'

Steinhauer shuts his mouth.

'Is it right that you sell it only here?'

'Yes. Though we are in talks — '

'This is a very serious matter, Mr Steinhauer,' Don interrupts. 'How many of these Roulades do you sell each week?'

'Maybe . . . twenty, thirty. Why?'

'And how long does it keep fresh?'

Steinhauer bridles at being ignored, then answers, 'In the fridge, ten days or so. We don't use preservatives.'

Don smiles at him. 'I do not expect the answer to be positive, but do you keep a record of who buys the cheese?'

A snort. 'No, Inspector. We have scores of visitors here every day. Mainly, they buy our wine, but many customers come here to our temperature-controlled Cheese Room. Some buy cheese also, some not.'

'Okay, sir. Who usually manages this section?'

'Any one of the girls. All my staff have tasted all the wine, our products, all the cheese . . . ' Steinhauer trails off, watches Don walk over to the display at the end of the counter, where he taps a basket containing business cards and completed forms.

'How many of your customers fill in your forms, or leave their business cards?'

'It's a way of building a database of customers. You see, we offer a case of wine each year — as a prize, but also an incentive — to whoever's card is randomly selected. I don't know what percentage of customers enter. Can you tell me what this is about?'

Don dismisses the database idea. Why should a kidnapper, murderer, enter his name for a case of wine? He turns back to Steinhauer.

'Your cheese turned up on a murder victim, sir. You tell me that it is sold in very small quantities, so naturally, we have to follow it up.'

Don watches Marc Steinhauer recoil, steady himself, concentrate on breathing normally.

'How terrible. I'm sorry. I don't know how I can help.' He runs a hand through his thinning hair, winces as he reaches the crown. Don

51

watches him; watches Steinhauer realize this.

'A bump. Our house is a converted barn. Low beams.'

'Okay.'

'Anything else I can do? A tasting?'

'No, sir. Nothing more now. But we might come back. Thank you for your time.'

Steinhauer unglues himself from his spot, legs heavy; ushers Don out into the main tasting room, and then into the entrance hall. They shake hands again; Steinhauer's hands are clammy and cold. Don walks through the huge glass doors, down the perfect stone steps towards a shining metal wall with water pouring down it in varying quantities. As he reaches it, the water flow hesitates just for a moment, and Don sees Marc Steinhauer reflected, standing stiffly at his glass doors, watching him go.

★   ★   ★

Don reaches his car and turns around. There is no one at the doors now. He strides to the furthest part of the car park and begins to walk around the winery. On two sides, it is bordered by vineyards. Don climbs stone steps up high behind the building, which has been partly recessed into the side of the hill. Above the winery building, the ground is planted with olive trees and lavender. Don realizes that the estate seems to have no roof; it is all planted up to blend perfectly into the hillside. On the fourth side, there is light woodland, a large grassy field containing the odd olive tree and several white goats, and a pathway leading down to a dam surrounded by eucalyptus trees. From his vantage-point, Don can see no fields of wheat or corn, no sign of a raw concrete building. He is disappointed; something had made him think that the most likely place for this cheese to turn up was at the estate itself. How sweet would that have been?

★ ★ ★

De Vries sees Don the moment he enters the squad room. Men are working the phones, compiling files, looking through records. There is a hum of industry. De Vries and Don February simultaneously open their mouths to speak; Don checks himself.

De Vries says: 'I think I know why the killer dumped the bodies at the farm-stall.'

'You do?'

'When we drove back to town, I noticed that the Somerset West Police had a random road-block operating both ways in the lead-up to the Gordon's Bay turning, before Sir Lowry's Pass. Looking for drink/drive, drug/drive customers. Fishing trip basically. I called the traffic controller over there, and he says he ran it the previous day and, listen to this, there was a second trapper unit four kilometres up the road on the other side of the farm-stall, an all-day operation, commencing seven a.m. If the driver got through one and heard about another, he might have panicked and decided to dump the bodies.'

Don says nothing.

De Vries insists, 'It's possible. The dumping indicates panic.'

Don still isn't sure.

De Vries sees it in him and temporizes. 'Anyway, I'm getting the names of everyone who was stopped that day. We'll run them and see if anything pops up. It's possible.'

Neither is convinced.

'It's the best we have right now,' he sighs. 'What happened at the cheese place?'

'Nothing good. Place sells maybe thirty of those cheeses each week. They last at least a week in the fridge. No cameras inside or out, half a dozen different staff, same number of other cheese products, olives, olive oil, estate souvenirs, same again of wine, and the place is busy. At ten o'clock the car park was half full.'

'Shit. You don't think it's worth canvassing?'

'If we had a picture, a sketch, then maybe. Even then, I doubt it.'

De Vries grits his teeth. 'It's running cold all over again.'

'One thing though. The guy who owns it seemed very jumpy about something. Talked way too much. And there is a strange connection I looked into. You are not going to like it.'

'What?'

'His name is Marc Steinhauer.'

De Vries' face is blank, then transforms instantly. 'Any relation to . . . ?'

'Nicholas Steinhauer? Yes, I checked online. Marc is his younger brother.'

De Vries shakes his head. 'Jesus. Can it get any worse?'

March 2007

As the camera pans across the small studio, pulls out to reveal both parties, there is a second when one of the studio lights catches the polished brass of the middle button of his dark blazer. The unexpected flash would mesmerize a viewer, force him or her to refocus their stare at the screen, blink a couple of times. When the studio lights rise, the camera is on the smooth black-clad anchorwoman, but the viewer scarcely hears what she says; he or she craves illumination of the other seated figure. They do not know this consciously.

'With the Western Cape Police stating that no ransom notice has been received, no communication with the abductor, the motive behind the abduction of the three Cape Town schoolboys on consecutive days at the end of last week remains a mystery. The South African Police Service, still acutely embarrassed by the disappearance of the third boy, Toby Henderson, son of SAPS Inspector Trevor Henderson, during an annual police function, stated bluntly again today that they have few leads.'

The camera angle changes; a flattering profile shot for her, the man appearing from silhouette.

'With me now, esteemed Cape Town criminologist and psychologist, Nicholas Steinhauer. Dr Steinhauer, the SAPS is drawing a blank in the search for Steven Lawson, Bobby Eames and Toby Henderson. Who should they be looking for?'

Steinhauer fills the screen, black hair slicked back against his head, dark tortoiseshell spectacles framing deep brown eyes. He nods in appreciation of his legend; his thin lips smile. He takes the anchorwoman into his confidence.

'Firstly, we only know what the police tell us.' His accent is a mixture of English, Afrikaans and German. It is a strangely soothing combination, accessible to many an ear. He enunciates clearly; his words are firmly spoken, his lip-movements precise. Everything about this man is precise. 'And they tell us little. If it is true that they have received no ransom demand, then my fear is that the missing boys have fallen prey to a team involved in child-trafficking which, in case your viewers do not know, is far more widespread in Southern Africa than might be assumed. This may bode well for the immediate physical health of the boys, but it presents the authorities with a massive task if they are to track and find them.'

'It would involve pan-African cooperation?'

'Yes — and more. The Arab states have shown themselves to be behind some of the more ambitious child-trafficking. Wealthy individuals order children, as if from a catalogue, and they are found and obtained for them. It is a grisly and inhuman business.'

'To what end?'

'It is a terrible lesson,' Steinhauer tells her, 'still not learnt by us. Back in the annals of history, men in Arabia have commanded great armies and been comforted by harems of beautiful women. Now, if such a man desires, he can buy himself young boys. These children, abused by their owners, will be used as his playthings, then sold into the lowest levels of the sex trade and finally discarded.'

'If this is their fate, do Toby, Steven and Bobby remain on South African soil?'

'You are asking me to speculate here, and that is not what I do. But if they have been taken by a highly professional team, there is every possibility that they have already left this country and even possibly the continent.'

The anchorwoman touches her earpiece: 'The SAPS imply that, at any minute, there will be a ransom demand and the inquiry will take on a radically different stance.'

Steinhauer smiles indulgently. 'To infer anything from the words of the SAPS is to take a substantial leap of faith. More than once, I have observed press conferences on major crimes and, without exception, I have felt that the media were being manipulated.'

'That is a serious accusation. In what way manipulated?'

'Let us be benign and suggest that the police are using the media to disseminate information which aims to promote public involvement in the case, to generate witnesses. More questionably, perhaps their actions are designed to suggest to a known suspect that he or she is not under suspicion and that they do not need to hide so carefully. More often, however, it is my contention that the SAPS use the media to disseminate flattering views of what are, in brutal terms, failed investigations. Nowadays, the budgets for the SAPS are spent profligately on public relations staff, spin doctors and training courses for officers on how to present bad news in a good light. The whole focus of the SAPS seems distorted and, frankly, in a country torn apart by crime, this is highly disappointing.'

'Is this a nationwide criticism?'

'To the extent that such policies are dictated by the higher echelons and that presumably their policy is nationwide, then yes. However, it is particularly relevant here in the Western Cape, where we seem to have a deeply fractured service — certain teams attending to certain crimes, older white senior officers being moved away from general duties to head up certain clique units. It is clearly unhealthy and, without question, deeply damaging to morale.'

'Are you directly criticizing the investigation into these abductions?'

'I'm observing that the SAPS seem utterly blind to their own shortcomings and apparently unable to make any headway whatsoever in this matter. The fate of these three boys is in their hands, and the question we must all ask is this: are they trying hard enough?'

* * *

Vaughn de Vries looks around the room of tired, expectant, unshaven faces and says, 'Thank you very fucking much.'

He looks back up at the screen, but the interview has ended. In the three seconds before he switches off the television monitor, he glimpses a bulky sports presenter wearing a small pink polo shirt, no sound coming from his fast-moving lips.

He turns to Dean Russell — sees that they are

the only two men in the squad room standing. Four officers are hunched over their desks half asleep; for the rest, the information drought has sent them to their beds, long overdue.

'Fuckhead. What the fuck does Steinhauer have to do with it?'

'There'll be more.'

'Am I so fucking out of touch, Dean? You tell me: am I?'

'We're white and old-school. It's 2007, no one trusts us. We're — what's that French phrase? Persona non grata.'

De Vries snorts, wonders whether Russell knows what he's said, savours a split second of release from the ever-increasing tension inside him.

'And it's the white fucking media doing this, that's what gets me. They didn't say this shit back then, in the good old, bad old days, when we were the front line.'

'Things were different then.'

De Vries stares at his Inspector, sighs and says, 'Go home, Dean.'

2014

'Steinhauer parlayed that one interview into a weekly column for the *Argus* and a television series. Shithead never got off our backs.' De Vries trails off, his mind overtaken with the image of Steinhauer that day on the television.

'My wife used to read that column first, every Friday,' Don mutters. 'She grabbed that *Weekend Ahead* section and got back to bed with it. Didn't like it when it ended.'

Everyone is thinking of something to say, to fill the void in information.

'It is a strange coincidence, anyway,' Don murmurs.

Vaughn feels the pressure in his gut tighten. He cannot let the case stagnate. He must push forward, somehow.

'Right, I can't see anything here on the polythene wrapping. How's that going?'

Don straightens up. 'Sally Frazer is on it. She has not found anything yet, but she is talking to a contact of mine right now. He has been a warehouse supervisor for twenty years; about that long again in factories. If he does not know anything, we will look further afield.'

De Vries nods.

'The crime-scene reports show that they cannot find any indications of a particular car tyre driving to the rear of the farm-stall,' Don goes on. 'I have got Joey Henkin to re-interview all the staff, asking about a nervous or panicking man, and whether or not any of them overheard conversations about roadblocks. He says not even a whisper from anyone.'

Vaughn feels his energy draining again.

'The lab guys are looking at the stuff on the boys again,' he says, 'trying to locate something which might give us an idea in what area this field might be. They say if they find certain pollens, that could rule in or out certain geographical areas . . . '

De Vries wearily lets his head laze back on his neck, then he snaps it back.

'Shit! You don't understand, Don. This is what happened before. No evidence, no information, nothing. He's going to get away with it again.'

★　★　★

John Marantz's house is high on the lush southern face of Table Mountain, where rains pour day and night for weeks on end, the sun's pale white winter rays absent behind the monolith. The trickling brooks swell to torrents and the mountain runs with foaming waterfalls. In the summer, the trees are lush and green, cool and dense, providing shade against the blasting sun; the same sentinels now protect the inhabitants from the South-Easter winds, and all is calm, the air scented and filled with fecund birdlife. He is high above the city here, his little house sitting at the end of a narrow cul-de-sac along from Kirstenbosch Botanical Gardens, as high on the mountain slopes as you can build. No one calls at his door, no neighbours bother him. He is just as he wishes to be: alone.

He lies floating on the surface of his dark rectangular lap pool, his body the shape of the crucified Jesus, his hands relaxed, fingertips breaking the surface tension of the water. All he hears is the low hum of the pool pump from below him, a heartbeat in his head. The tiny current drifts him slowly outwards until he is high over the mountain slope, his head inches from the infinity edge. At the other end, his dog — a glossy-coated Irish terrier — sits, front paws aligned, eyes blinking slowly in the afternoon sun. The dog cannot discern that John Marantz is crying, cannot imagine that he feels as if he is floating in a huge well of tears, dark and bottomless.

Marantz is home, but it is not his home. It is his chosen prison. Home would be back in London with his wife and daughter, but they have been taken from him and he has been forbidden ever to search for them. Now, he drifts alone, sometimes self-motivated to move, more often stirred by outside forces. He knows that he could break free from London, from his past career, be born again, yet something inside him hopes that there will be new instructions, even commands. It is as if ritual is all he has to keep him from crying all day long, forever.

★ ★ ★

De Vries sits unmoving in his dimmed office. He feels the weight of his responsibility bear down on him and wonders whether he can still shoulder it. There is no breakthrough; Don February's warehouseman knew about polythene, but had no ideas, no insights.

He meets with Director du Toit, an interview marked by long silences. He sits alone in his office, all through lunch and into the afternoon, smoking heavily, examining every angle he can think of — and still he has nothing.

His wife, transferred two years previously to Johannesburg, calls him. A weekly commute became fortnightly, then monthly — and now she returns only to retrieve more clothes, personal belongings. They say nothing to one another. De Vries wonders why he stays silent, wonders why he feels content that she is leaving.

Today she sounds happy, stimulated, feigning — Vaughn senses — concern for him and the reopening of the abduction case. She talks as if she is interviewing him. Seven years back, Suzanne de Vries had been a news reporter; she lived through the original investigation almost as much as he. Now, he suspects she only wants an inside opinion. He knows that she has bought an apartment in Jo'burg; his younger daughter has told him, but she has not. He knows he will not broach this subject now; knows that their marriage has ended, but she says nothing to him. When he tells her that he has no information about the case, she ends abruptly and hangs up. Intense, destructive frustration fills him. He has found acceptance; her cowardice disgusts him. In his dreams, he used to see her. Each night she appeared to him, smaller and smaller, further and further away. Now, in his dreams, she is not there. His daughters are present but out of sight; no one else in his extended family exists any more.

A knock, his door opening. Don February, clutching two sheets.

'I have run all the names Somerset West Police gave us for people stopped by the roadblock leading to Sir Lowry's.'

'Yes?'

Don arranges the two sheets on the desk in front of de Vries. He taps the first.

'Robert Ledham, fifty-seven, arrested and charged with kidnapping and sexual abuse of two

63

minors in Johannesburg in 1997 to 1998. The second kid got away after forty-eight hours, went straight to the police. Ledham served six years. He went to Port Elizabeth, stayed there until 2009 — but the journey is easy enough. Nothing since he arrived in Cape Town in 2009.'

'Ledham wasn't a name that came up in 07,' de Vries says, glancing back at the desk-high stack of files on the floor behind him. 'In any case, if he was living in PE, he wouldn't be abducting kids in Cape Town.'

'He is a convicted paedophile.'

'I'm halfway through reviewing everything we collected over seven years and there's nothing on a Robert Ledham.'

'So why is there no record of him on our database?'

De Vries opens his mouth, like a goldfish. 'I don't know.'

'Maybe if there had been, he would have been considered?'

'But he wasn't in town.'

'As far as we know.'

'As far as we know. This is stretching it, Don.'

'Okay,' Don goes on, charged with his news. 'This second guy, Deepak Tineer, forty-six, came to Cape Town from Durban in 2004, immediately got noticed by police because he was running what he called 'prayer and meditation' classes: everyone — and this was mainly young men — wore loincloths. A lot of laying on of hands. There were complaints to the council, accusations against Tineer for indecent behaviour with children.'

64

'Don. Our guy is white, not Asian.'

'Why? I thought that was just a theory because of who he took, where he operated. Tineer could be educated, integrated.'

De Vries leans back, then remembers that his chair has recently developed a dislike of such a manoeuvre.

'Look, this is good. Let's talk to both of these guys. I can't say I'm optimistic, but it's better than anything else.'

'Bring them in?'

'No. Find out where they are. We'll go to them. Gauge reactions — it might save us a lot of time.'

★   ★   ★

Main Road in Claremont used to be a little taste of Africa in the Southern Suburbs; street-stalls and hawkers, kiosks at the entrances to dark, hollow mini-malls, the incessant honking from taxis plying their trade, men stretched out of the side windows, screaming their route, importuning passengers.

Now, at the Newlands junction, sparkling office blocks, slick shop units and a gym for the beautiful slim have replaced dilapidated but characterful terraces of shops. The independent trader is out, and the big names have moved in. It's tidy, Don thinks, but dull, just the same as everywhere else. De Vries, who normally lets Don drive, screeches into a Waiting Zone, and applies the hand-brake heavily. They are right outside 'Kingdom of Beds'.

'It's a bed shop,' de Vries says, waiting for Don to close his door, looking up at the gaudy sign. 'Not a fucking kingdom.' He locks the car and turns towards the smoked-glass doors. 'You do it.'

★   ★   ★

Deepak Tineer stands very straight. He is wearing a narrow beige suit over his skinny frame, a striped tie in toning browns, tortoise-shell spectacles, and dusty light-brown plastic loafers. He speaks calmly, in a high-pitched voice; perfect, slightly accented English.

'Nothing was proved against me. No charges were laid. I was an innocent man. I have certificates proving my credentials: I am a listed practitioner of my craft.' He lowers his voice, his eyes scanning the shop-floor. 'Why are you asking me this now? That incident was many years ago. I am a hardworking man and a respectable citizen.'

Don February says: 'Do you remember, in 2007, the abductions of three children from around here, shortly after you moved to this area?'

'Of course. It is all over the papers — the bodies you found. It was you people who did not solve the crime in the first place.' Tineer curls his hands onto his chest.

'Why were you driving over Sir Lowry's Pass last Tuesday morning at ten forty-five a.m.?' Don asks him.

'I was visiting a client.'

66

'Where?'

'In Hermanus. He is a gentleman who moved from Claremont to Hermanus to retire. He and his wife have always bought their beds from us and he wished to do so again. He has two other bedrooms. For three beds, the manager sent me to his home personally. I considered it an honour. You can check if you like.'

'I will do that, sir. Did you drive directly from your home?'

'Yes. I took my own car.'

'You returned at . . . ?

'I was back here by three p.m.'

'Did you stop anywhere on either journey?'

'You know I did,' Tineer responds indignantly. 'You people stopped me at one of your pointless roadblocks.'

'Anywhere else? A garage, a café?'

'No.'

'You are sure, sir?'

'Yes, quite sure. What is this?' He points at de Vries. 'Who is he?'

De Vries raises his eyes upwards.

'What do you want?' Tineer persists.

Vaughn turns away.

'From you,' he says, loudly enough for Tineer to hear even with his back to him, even walking away. 'Nothing.'

*　*　*

'You honestly think,' de Vries asks Don once they are moving again, 'that the Somerset West traffic guys could stop a guy with two day-old bodies in

67

the boot, and miss it?'

Don says: 'Depends whether they are awake, or sick at being stuck out on a main road, pissing off the innocent general public.'

'Maybe.'

'Perhaps I would discount this altogether, but you know that trap before Sir Lowry's? You are in it before you see it.'

De Vries says nothing until they reach the M3 freeway down to Muizenberg and Kalk Bay.

Then: 'By the way, Don — tip for you. The general public: they're never innocent.'

He's pat; Don chuckles.

★ ★ ★

Robert Ledham lives in a gated community just outside the formerly grand seaside resort of Muizenberg. The estate is set well back from the beach, even from the inland lakes, next to some rough sandy ground and a busy local road. The complex is surrounded by a high wall, topped with razorwire. At the gate, de Vries shows his warrant card to the security guard.

'Robert Ledham, number sixteen.'

The guard looks at it, and says: 'Mr Ledham, yes?'

'Number sixteen,' de Vries repeats, reaching for his card, revving the engine. The guard turns away from the car and towards his wooden gatehouse. De Vries opens the car door.

'What are you doing?'

The guard turns back. Says: 'I have to call through. All visitors are announced.'

'What?'

'I am calling Mr Ledham, to check that he is at home.'

De Vries walks up to him and snatches his card from the man's hand. 'I don't want you to do that.'

The guard looks surprised to be challenged. 'Those are the rules, man.'

'Never mind, just don't call him. This is a surprise visit.'

The guard turns again.

'Hey!' De Vries shouts.

'I am calling my supervisor.'

'You — *wait*.' De Vries checks himself, so much frustration waiting to burst from him. 'Listen to me. I am the police. If I tell you to break the rules, you break the rules, okay? Do not call Mr Ledham. Do you understand?'

The guard looks blank.

'Do not call him, that is an order. In five minutes, you can call your supervisor if you want. I'll put him straight later. Now let me in.'

The guard looks past de Vries to Don February, sitting silently in the passenger seat of the car, staring straight ahead. The guard sneers and then he raises the gate. De Vries calls back, poking his finger out of the window: 'Don't make me make trouble for you.'

He accelerates up the short drive, takes a hard turn left and pulls up in the small car park of a large close of modern detached houses. The houses are modest, uniform in style, boasting a large garage with a pitched roof, and each with a little deck at the back and a tiny yard. Vaughn reckons that the view from the deck is probably the tall, solid, razorwire-clad wall.

'Like a fucking prison.'

Don looks at de Vries; for six months he has worked with this man. He has never seen him so disconsolate, so depressed.

'Come on, Don,' de Vries says. 'Let's meet another innocent member of the general public.'

He stomps over the pink brick pavement and up to the small frosted-glass porch. De Vries' knock is thunderous.

A shadow appears, casting more shadows in the mottled glass. The voice is whiny.

'There is a bell, you know.'

'Don't trust 'em.'

'What do you want?' The voice is just behind the flimsy front door.

'Police, Mr Ledham. We need to talk with you. Open your door.'

A chain and two locks are undone, and the door opens.

'I wondered if I'd get a little visit.' Ledham smiles unpleasantly and ushers them inside. The living room is airless and hot, stale cooking-fat lingering in the air.

De Vries recalls the little stoep. 'Maybe we can go outside?'

'And let my neighbours hear your questions? I don't think so.' Ledham sits in an old burgundy velvet winged armchair, at an angle to his sofa, where he points his visitors.

'How did you know we weren't a neighbour, when we knocked?'

'I don't choose to socialize with my neighbours.

That's the point of this estate; no disturbances.'

De Vries stands up and faces Ledham.

'You were crossing Sir Lowry's Pass last Tuesday morning. Where were you going?'

'I know you think that because of what I did, I'm public property, but I am a free man. I only have to notify you when I choose to move house.'

De Vries is studying him. Ledham is pasty and running to fat. His clothes are loose and faded; he is wearing elasticated trousers, his plaid shirt tucked in the waistband. Vaughn observes a gold crucifix flopping over his collar; long, thin fingers at the end of skinny wrists, Ledham's thumb and forefinger rubbing constantly.

He smiles patiently. 'It's a simple question, Mr Ledham. Just answer it.'

'You found the bodies of two boys, I know, at that farm-stall. And they were the boys abducted from here. Well, I was visiting an old friend in Knysna then — I was there for ten days in all. I remember reading about the abductions in the newspapers. On Tuesday I was driving to Greyton to visit that same old friend. He was staying at Greyton Lodge. I spent the night there and came back the next day, and I haven't been anywhere since.'

Ledham's speaking voice is precise and controlled, but his eyes don't match the words.

'Same friend both times?'

'Same friend.'

'You can give your Knysna friend's details to my colleague in a moment,' de Vries tells him. 'Did you stop on your way there?'

Ledham's tongue appears between his lips,

71

wetting them. 'I stopped at Tallons mini-mall, for some . . . snacks.'

'Anywhere else?' de Vries asks lightly.

'I also visited that farm-stall place.'

'MacNeil's farm-stall?'

Ledham's eyes stare straight ahead. 'Yes.'

'But you'd just bought snacks at the mini-mall?'

'That farm-stall makes their own pies. I was buying them to eat later on in the journey.'

'Where did you park?'

Ledham rolls his eyes. 'In the car park, obviously.'

'Where?'

'I don't know.' He purses his lips, squeezes his eyes shut. 'At the front, overlooking the road. It was busy.'

'Did you drive around the back of the building?'

'No.'

'What time did you arrive there?'

'I don't know,' he replies impatiently. 'I was stopped by the roadblock, spent ten minutes there, then drove straight up the pass and to MacNeil's. You obviously know I was stopped; that's why you're here. So, work it out yourself.'

Don reads the report. 'Stopped by Traffic Officer Jackson, at one thirty-five p.m.'

'So, two o'clock then. Something like that.' Ledham seems indignant. 'It's irrelevant anyway. I parked, went straight to the hot counter at the shop and bought two pies. There were . . . two people in front of me. I bought the pies, and then I got into my car and drove to Greyton.'

'What car do you drive?'

Ledham sighs heavily, pushes up gold-rimmed spectacles. Sweat droplets enlarge on his bare scalp, begin to move to the thin white strands of hair, clinging to the sides of his scalp.

'You know perfectly well what car I drive. It's in that report.' He points at Don.

De Vries keeps his voice low.

'Why do you find answering questions so difficult?'

'Because,' Ledham starts, rising from his chair and then sitting back down, brushing down his thighs, 'you know the answers to these questions. There is no point in asking them. It's a waste of time.'

De Vries holds his defiant stare until Ledham backs down.

'Shall we go and see it, sir?' Vaughn asks.

'Yes,' Ledham says. 'You look at it. Only car I've owned in the last six years. It's not very clean, I'm afraid — meaning I haven't had it cleaned — but you look at it.' He adds, pointedly: 'Put your minds at rest.'

He gets up, takes keys from a china saucer on a shelf and hurries to his front door. De Vries and Don February follow him. Ledham approaches his garage, presses a button on a remote and watches the large white door rise. Parked more or less in the middle of the double width space is a small white Toyota with fading paintwork. Don checks that the numberplates match those in the traffic report.

'Please open the boot of your car.'

Ledham walks around his car, finds the

73

correct key and opens the boot. It is lined with newspaper. De Vries lifts the paper and looks underneath. The blue carpet is faded, but otherwise clean.

'Why the papers?'

Ledham clucks. 'I went to the garden centre. The man who carried my plants laid it in there. They always do that.'

De Vries nods, opens the passenger side door and peers in. The back seat is clean apart from a scattering of dead leaves.

'All right,' he says. 'We'll come back inside again now.'

'Why?'

'I haven't finished my questions, Mr Ledham. You said you didn't want to talk outside. We can talk here if you prefer?'

'No,' Ledham replies. 'We'll go back to the lounge.' He locks the car, exits the garage and operates the electric door to close it. He re-opens the front door and walks in ahead of them, places his keys back in the saucer, and re-takes his seat as before.

De Vries sits down on the sofa, next to Don. There is silence, until Ledham twists around and faces them.

'What now? I've answered all your questions. You've seen my car. You know full well I have nothing to do with your inquiry.'

'Why do I know that?'

Ledham lowers his voice. 'If you have read my file, you would have seen that my . . . proclivities used,' he emphasizes the word, 'used . . . to lie elsewhere.'

'Where?' de Vries asks blankly.

'Girls, Colonel. I have always admired young girls. No doubt like half the male population of the country.'

'But they don't kidnap them and hold them against their will.'

Ledham narrows his eyes. 'You would be surprised at the will of the young. Some of them know exactly what they want, and society feels very challenged by that, I can tell you.'

'You have a computer?' de Vries asks.

'No.'

'No computer?'

'That's what I said.'

'Mind if we take a look around your house, Mr Ledham?'

'Yes, I do. I have certain rights of privacy. If you want to search my house, produce a warrant with good cause, otherwise no.'

'Fair enough. If you'd prefer we arrest you and take you into town for twenty-four hours, we can do it that way.'

'Arrest me? On what charge?'

De Vries leans into Ledham's face. 'Because you've lied, Mr Ledham. Some of what you've told me is true, and some of it isn't. When you tell me what I want to know, maybe we'll leave you in the peace you so obviously desire. Until then, here in your home or in my cellblock, I'm right in your face.'

Vaughn looks at Ledham's pale hands, liver-spotted and quivering. Ledham sees him watching, meshes them.

'About what, exactly, do you think I'm lying?'

Vaughn snorts. 'You want my party trick? It's not very impressive when I am so good at sniffing out a big fat lie, and you are such a total godawful amateur liar.'

Ledham recoils in his seat, colour in his bland cheeks. De Vries takes up his stance facing Ledham, his back to the window.

'When you drove to Greyton last Tuesday, where did you stop?'

'I told you — the mini-mall and MacNeil's. And at your roadblock. I told you.'

Vaughn studies him. 'What did you buy at the mini-mall?'

'Snacks.'

'What snacks?'

'I don't remember that.'

'A drink, sandwiches maybe?'

'Yes, I suppose so.'

'A hot pie?'

'Yes, a hot pie. A pepper steak pie . . . ' He trails off. 'No — at MacNeil's.' Ledham stops suddenly, realizes his mistake even before de Vries spells it out.

'You see, Mr Ledham, when you stopped near Tallons, it was for another reason, wasn't it?' De Vries stares him down. 'Where did you go in Somerset West? You stopped somewhere near Tallons, but why?'

He sees Ledham quiver, then let go, deciding to come clean.

'All right. I stopped at the mini-mall because I was thirsty and I wanted a cool drink, and . . . because there is an 'Adult Fantasy' shop there.'

76

'Oh, I see. I didn't know there was a branch there. Did you, Warrant Officer?'

Don thinks de Vries knows full well about an 'Adult Fantasy' store there. Don, however, doesn't.

'No.'

'What did you buy? Some magazines, DVDs . . . lingerie?'

'That's my business. I've told you I was there.'

'I think you'll find it's my business too. Now, go and show Warrant Officer February your stash. Don't worry, he's quite unshockable. And give him your friend's details too.'

Don gets up, but Ledham remains seated.

'I wish to call my lawyer. I want to know what he says about this illegal search.'

'Fine. You get one call before we lock you up.'

Ledham suddenly seems confused, disorientated. He looks at de Vries. 'All right, all right. You don't care how much you humiliate me, do you?'

'No.'

Ledham leads Don towards the bedroom, glancing back at de Vries as he goes.

The moment they are out of sight, Vaughn walks to the opposite end of the house, opens a door onto a guest room with a pink carpet and an old-fashioned exercise bike by the French door. He opens the cupboards, checks under the mattress and the bed. He walks up and down the carpet, feeling for a hollow space. When he finds nothing, he leaves the room and opens the next door. It is a large walk-in closet, containing cleaning equipment. He hunts for a light-switch, but can't find one. The third door he tries is locked. He trots back to the living room, opens every cupboard door he can find, searches an antique cabinet, containing only old half-finished bottles of spirits, and tracks back and forth over the carpeting. When he is satisfied that there is nothing obviously hidden, he goes to the window and stares out into the yard. There is a narrow deck, a short strip of grass, well-tended, and a narrow paved area. He can see where Ledham has planted some trees and climbers against the dominating wall.

He hears Ledham and Don returning. When they are back in the room, Ledham says: 'Everything legal. Maybe not to your taste, but legal. Isn't that right, Warrant Officer?'

Vaughn looks at Don, who nods, but looks disgusted.

'There's a locked room down there,' de Vries says. 'What's in that room?'

'You have no right — '

'What's in the room?'

'My work is in that room.'

'What work is that?'

Ledham straightens himself stiffly. 'I'm an illustrator. For books.'

'What kind of books?'

'Children's books. I create the illustrations for the *Davey and Pie* series.'

De Vries remembers the title. He wonders whether he has bought the books for his daughters.

'Just show us that room, please. Then we'll leave you.'

Ledham gets up and walks to the door. He

produces a key from his trouser pocket and unlocks it.

'If an intruder gets in, he can take everything but my work.' There is a little pride in his voice.

He enters the room, de Vries and Don February following. Two walls are covered, almost floor to ceiling, with beautiful, intricate drawings. Vaughn immediately recognizes the work; knows that his daughters have been enchanted by these pictures. He sees one wall covered with detailed pen-and-ink drawings, almost as atmospheric as William Blake etchings, each rendered much larger than he has seen in the books, the other wall showing coloured scenes of mysterious misty woodlands, medieval castles guarded by men in shining armour, and an underwater scene of huge colourful fish partying while the heroes are thrown around on a giant water-lily pad on the surface above them. He has read these stories out loud to his girls, admiring the artist. His daughters have gaped at the pictures, probably dreamt about the adventures.

'You write these too?' de Vries asks.

'No. I am sent the text. I have only met the author once.'

'The publisher knows about your past?'

Ledham spins around to him.

'No. I . . . I have no contact with anyone. I live here alone and mind my own business.'

De Vries thinks about it; there is something repulsive about the thought of Ledham enchanting his innocent children. He looks back at the man, drained and slumping now, his head lowered.

'That seems reasonable.'

Ledham takes a deep breath.

Above the long desk which runs down the entire side of the room, Vaughn sees giant versions of the lead characters: Davey, Pie, Salsa and Squash. On the desk itself, sketches and unfinished designs.

'There's a new one?'

'If I am allowed my peace, yes.'

'Doesn't everyone do this on computer nowadays? You don't use a computer?'

'No. All my pictures are hand-drawn, hand-coloured, as you can see.'

De Vries looks again at the pictures, and then at Ledham. He wonders how such a man's mind works: to create pictures that delight children; to defile and humiliate and abuse them.

'Thank you,' Vaughn tells him, 'for eventually cooperating. I hope that we won't disturb you again.'

Ledham opens his mouth, but shuts it again. He gestures them out of his studio, along the corridor to his front door. They leave and he closes it on them, standing silently, waiting to hear the car start up and drive away.

★ ★ ★

De Vries finds a new guard on duty at the entrance, but he is not a supervisor. He salutes de Vries and opens the gate.

When they are back on the main road, de Vries asks: 'What did he have in his collection?'

'Just teen stuff, hardcore, but seemed legal. He

80

had not unwrapped all of what he bought on Tuesday. It was still in a brown paper bag, with the receipt inside. Date and time shown. Fits.'

'Not nice.'

'I would not want my children looking at his pictures.'

'Mine already did. I always liked those books.'

'You would not like them so much if you saw what he really thinks about young girls, and what they should be doing to each other.'

'My kids love his work; they don't know the man.'

Don contemplates what he means. He says: 'I am sorry, sir, that those two leads were a waste of our time.'

'Had to be done. When Ledham started lying I wondered what we had. Problem for me was, the moment we entered his place, it didn't feel right. He didn't look right. Can you imagine him shooting anyone; lifting them into a skip?'

'What was bothering you then?'

'He lied to me. Twice. If he's lying, then he's hiding stuff, and I instinctively want to know what. I knew that he didn't stop for 'snacks' at that mini-mart. That was lame. You find out what it really was, and his evasion makes sense.'

'You said twice?'

'Oh yeah. When I asked him about a computer, each time he denied it, but the guy definitely has one, or uses one. Probably just Internet stuff, might be relatively innocent. I'll go back sometime and find out.'

'How do you do that?'

'What? Catch them at it? There are so many

clues: eyes, hands, saliva — a break in their voice.'

'So, when we get this guy, you will know.'

De Vries turns to Don. 'When I meet him? Instantly.'

* * *

Robert Ledham waits half an hour and passes through the walk-in closet to another door which leads into his garage. He takes the ladder from its place on the wall and leans it against a narrow beam on the ceiling. He climbs slowly, opens a trapdoor above him and clambers up into the roofspace. Stooping until he reaches the central part of the space, beneath the highest point in the roof, he moves to a trestle table supporting a laptop and a colour laser printer. He boots it up, enters multiple passwords and logs onto a forum. Then, he begins to type.

* * *

When Don February reaches his desk back at headquarters he sees four Post-it notes tacked to the side of his computer monitor. One is from his wife, three are from an Officer Morten manning the public response telephone lines. Don looks up at de Vries' office, but he is not there. He decides to see what information Morten has before calling him. As he strides towards the lifts, he is aware of his heart beating faster.

82

Ledham checks his work, and then posts his message. Soon, he knows that many hundreds of men throughout the Western Cape will read his words. They, in turn, will post them further afield. The news in Cape Town will keep them and many others absorbed, until the identity of this pioneer is revealed.

* ★ ★

Morten is the department's technophile; his office is shared with two assistants and what seem to Don to be twenty different types of computer, monitors on the wall and grey electrical devices with dials and needles.

'You have the recording here?'

'You'll hear,' Morten tells him. 'They tried to get her to give her name, but she refused. We can trace the cell number if I'm authorized.'

Don nods. 'Let me hear it, please.'

Morten taps his keyboard. 'I've set it up just to play what she has to say first.'

The woman sounds young, Capetonian, maybe in her early to mid-thirties. There are street sounds in the background. Don is not sure whether she is in her car or at the side of a road. She sounds nervous.

'Last night, I realized, when I was in the car park at MacNeil's farm-stall, I did see a car drive around the back. I remember thinking: That's a smart car for an employee, maybe it's the owner. I've never seen him. Is there a Mr MacNeil?'

Then, an officer's voice, calm, encouraging. 'What sort of a car was it?'

'I'm not good at cars. I think it was a BMW. That or a Mercedes. It was a metallic colour — grey, maybe . . . I've been thinking about a number plate, but I honestly can't remember.'

'What time were you there, madam?'

'Oh, of course, sorry. I don't know exactly, but I was on my way back from a friend in Hermanus. I left there at four p.m., so maybe five p.m. Not later.'

'Did you see who was in the car? The driver?'

'No. I — I think there was only one person. I'm not certain.'

'Did you see the car again? When you left?'

'No. I'm sorry, no. Look, I have to go now — '

'One more question — please?'

'Yes?'

'Did you notice anything about the car? Any damage, markings . . . ?'

'No — no, I don't think so. I must go.'

The clip ends, and Morten says, unnecessarily, 'That's where it ends.'

Don stands completely still for a moment, taking in the call.

'That is good,' he says, still in a reverie. 'You think it is straight?'

'Don't you?'

'Yes, I do.' Don says. He turns back to Morten. 'Let us pray this is something.'

He calls de Vries while he waits for the elevator back to his office. Before he can say hello, Vaughn tells him, 'I'm on my way down from the top. I'll be there in two minutes.'

Then he hangs up.

Don looks at his phone at arm's length, and smiles.

★ ★ ★

'Shut the door.'

Don does as de Vries tells him.

'I've just come from Director du Toit. He's getting heat from above. Politics, thick as shit. Tell me you have something.'

'I do.'

De Vries spins round to him. 'What?'

'Anonymous caller, sounds reliable, says she saw what she thinks was a BMW, or possibly Mercedes, metallic grey, probably the driver alone, pull around the back of the farm-stall at about five p.m.'

'Okay.'

'I have been checking. It does not belong to MacNeil, nor any of his staff. He says that it is not a car familiar to him. Unless it was just turning, there is no other reason for it to be there. Not stopped in either direction by the roadblocks. But, listening to her, it sounds like she has thought about it, and I think she saw a BMW — called it 'smart', so I am guessing it is quite new. It gives us something.'

'We need to talk to this caller.'

'She would not give her name, seemed nervous and hurried.'

'Can we trace the call?'

'If you give the official permission, the officer down there says so.'

De Vries stares at Don, who doesn't react.
De Vries says: 'Well, do it.'

March 2007
'A professional kidnap. This is what you think now?' du Toit says.

Johannes Dyk recoils.

'I have been speaking with my colleagues in the European agencies,' he says. 'They tell me that the Arab states are now the centre of child-trafficking, by order. A rich man, a group, seek Caucasian children. They want a certain type of boy, specific ages and cultural background. Middle-class, educated children from Europe, from America — these present problems, but now there is talk of Caucasian children being taken from Africa.' He arranges some notes. 'I have here a report on two children kidnapped from Kenya, discovered aboard a ship off Somalia. Investigators claim the ship was bound for Saudi. Everything taken into account, I begin to feel that this may be the more likely fate of our three victims.'

'Are they still alive?' de Vries asks, the words sounding perfunctory to him even as he says them. Three young children.

'My gut feeling?' Dyk says, tilting his head to the side. 'Abducted by an individual in this country — based on precedent, no, I think it is very unlikely that they are alive. One victim: perhaps he is being held captive, but three? No, I don't think so.'

'And your alternative theory?' de Vries says.

'If they have been taken abroad, I would say that they are definitely alive. That is the purpose of them being taken, the product for which a supplier will receive payment. But if that is the case, I don't know what to say. You must contact all your international colleagues immediately.'

'We will do that,' du Toit says.

De Vries says: 'If these boys have been taken by an abuser rather than a killer, how long would that abuser hold on to his victims?'

The group turn back to Dyk.

'I . . . I cannot say, generally. Obviously children can be abused and they continue with their lives, seemingly normally, until perhaps a later time. But, with kidnap, this is more . . . permanent. He, or they, has managed to abduct these children without being seen — without even, it seems, attracting attention. This leads me to believe that he would not risk identification by leaving his victims where they might easily be found. I suspect that he would have hidden those victims, and hopes that they will never be found.'

Dean Russell murmurs, 'Jesus . . . '

Dyk produces the handkerchief again, clears his throat into it.

'Furthermore, and I know that this is not what you want to hear, from the point of view of policing, the fact that he has now stopped is worrying. It may suggest that he has left the vicinity, and is now elsewhere, planning further attacks at a future time. It's an unpalatable truth, gentlemen, but I think whoever is responsible may have left Cape Town, taking with him all his secrets.'

2014

'This,' Sarah Robinson says, as she lets them in, 'is why I thought twice before calling you.'

De Vries and Don enter a grand hallway, a sweeping staircase with crystal balustrades, four marble pillars at its corners, leading through to an enormous living area and, beyond that, through wide French windows, a pool terrace and long garden. A typical, new-money Constantia mansion. She hurries ahead of them, back to her kitchen, where a boy and girl, about six or seven years old, are beginning to fight, their high voices rising, their energy causing them to bounce about on the spot.

'You two, enough! Just eat some dinner and then go in the garden.' The children pause, look at her, and then resume their chase, a little more quietly.

She turns to de Vries and Don. 'I thought the whole point is that those lines are anonymous.'

De Vries beams at her. 'Lovely house, Mrs Robinson. They *are* anonymous calls. We never trace callers unless it is a life-and-death situation. This is where we are now. We need your help. Will you take five or ten minutes to talk to me?'

Sarah Robinson glances at her children.

'My Warrant Officer, Don here, loves children,' de Vries says. 'Maybe he can supervise them for a few minutes in the garden?'

Agitated, Sarah Robinson looks at her watch yet again. Her head darts from de Vries to Don, to her children.

'All right. You two, go with this nice man. Show him your sandpit. And be polite.'

88

The children edge towards the door and Don leads them outside. The boy screams and runs off, the little girl holds out her hand for Don to take.

'They're quite a handful at that age.'

'Yes. You have children?' Sarah Robinson asks. 'How old are yours?'

'Older now: eighteen and twenty. Both girls. So many secrets, so much gossip.'

For the first time, Sarah smiles.

Vaughn says: 'Why don't you get yourself a cold drink, and then we can talk briefly.'

The concept of getting something for her own pleasure seems to stall Sarah.

'Yes.' She walks to the fridge. 'Would you like something?'

'Water's fine.'

'My husband prefers not to get involved in things like this. He won't be pleased. That's why I wanted to remain anonymous.'

'Your memory could be a major breakthrough for us. Even if it's nothing, we can eliminate that person from our enquiries.'

Sarah Robinson nods nervously, sips her drink. Vaughn sits on the edge of his seat and leans towards her.

'Think back to your journey, and tell me what you saw at MacNeil's farm-stall.'

She looks down from de Vries' insistent stare.

'I told you when I called your line.'

'I know,' Vaughn says soothingly, 'but I want you to cast your mind back again.' He looks up at her, meets her eyes. 'You need to trust me. Put everything else from your mind for a couple of minutes and we'll see what you remember.'

Sarah Robinson looks over her shoulder into the garden. De Vries' voice is gentle, but it brooks no argument.

'Imagine you are there; recall it as if you are seeing it for the first time. Don't let anything else intrude . . . ' She looks mildly suspicious. 'Try to think only of those few moments when you saw this car at the farm-stall. Sit back, just tell me what you see in your mind's eye.'

'All right. I arrived at MacNeil's, I think before five on Tuesday.' She is still sitting upright, her eyes open and fixed on her knees.

'Okay. Take it slow,' Vaughn tells her. 'I need you to trust me for this to work. Close your eyes; it helps. Visualize how you were sitting in the car, how you were feeling. Mention every detail, however unimportant.'

'Like what?'

'Why did you stop at MacNeil's? What was in your mind?'

She closes her eyes reluctantly; reopens them, closes them again.

'I wanted bread — dark rye bread. We were having guests that evening. My husband likes cheese to end the meal. I had bought cheese, and I wanted the bread he likes.'

'You have been to MacNeil's before?'

'Yes, many times. We have a house in the Wilderness. We would always pass MacNeil's. Sometimes my husband would go in, but usually it was me.'

'Take one deep breath; think only of your journey that day.'

She does so; allows her eyes to shut slowly. The house is silent.

'Are you on the road leading to the farm-stall?'

De Vries hears a clock ticking in another room. He hears five gentle pulses before Sarah Robinson says: 'Yes. The sun is going down. I'm thinking I may have to put my lights on at the end of the journey. My husband does not like me driving in the dark. I thought I must hurry . . . '

'You arrive at the farm-stall. You pull off the road.'

'Yes . . . '

'Where did you park?'

'I — I parked opposite the main entrance, but away from it, on the side nearest the road.' She opens her eyes, looks at him, then closes them once more, breathes. 'I get out, lock the door with the remote thingy, walk towards the stall, but . . . but, a car is coming towards me so I wait.'

'Is this the car you see driving around the back of the farm-stall?'

'Yes.'

'Good. Slowly now . . . Imagine first seeing the car. What do you notice?'

She squeezes her eyes and then relaxes them again. Vaughn hears nothing but distant birdsong, a light breeze in the trees.

'I don't know . . . It's moving quite quickly . . . It's very shiny. Grey, slate-coloured. I think the windows are slightly tinted.'

'And you watched it drive towards the back of the farm-stall?'

'Yes. I don't know why. I just waited a moment

91

or two. I think I thought it was moving too fast to be looking for a parking space.'

De Vries hears the timbre and speed of her delivery begin to mimic his and he knows that she is focused on what he needs now.

'Did you see anyone in the car?'

'No. No — I think there was only a driver. The windows were dark. Not black, but dark. I thought it was a man, I don't know why. Maybe because he seemed to be driving the car . . . assertively.'

De Vries continues, calm and focused. 'Did you try to look into the windows as it passed you?'

'No — yes . . . I suppose so.' She furrows her brows, eyes still pressed shut. 'There wasn't anybody in the back though.'

'Where did the car go after you saw it? What did you see?'

'It turned at the end.'

'How do you know that the car was driving behind the farm-stall?'

'I saw it. I saw it turn at the end of the car park. If you turn left, you can't get anywhere but round the back, can you? I mean, maybe he was going somewhere else?'

'No, you are correct, that turn leads to the back of the shop only. Did you see that car come back?'

'No. I went inside. I was late. I mustn't be late.'

'You never saw the car again?'

'No.'

'All right, we're nearly there. Think back again to when the car passed you. You watched it pass you. You looked at the back of the car before it turned left. Picture that now. What was on the back of the car?'

Her face is beginning to sag, her bottom lip moist with saliva.

'Blinds,' she says suddenly. 'There were blinds down the back window. Like you have for babies, but smart ones. Grey material — kind of folded . . . corrugated.'

'Anything else? Numbers, letters?'

Vaughn sees her eyes dart back and forth behind her eyelids. He knows that she is seeing what she saw all over again.

'Yes . . . Silver numbers . . . Five, three, zero, maybe. I think maybe that.'

'On the rear window?'

'There was a sticker in the right-hand corner,' she says positively. 'Oval, with gates on it, very pale.'

'Any more detail? Imagine you are seeing the sticker now . . . '

'It looked like a gate. Gold gates . . . ?'

Vaughn's voice is a whisper now. 'That's excellent. Look down now, to the boot of the car. What do you see in the middle of the boot?'

'A badge. I don't know. Circular, oval . . . '

A piercing scream from the garden, then laughter, but Sarah Robinson is straight up on her feet, disorientated, dizzy, turning to see outside. Her son is running circles around Don February.

Vaughn stands up.

'I'm sorry,' she says. 'Mothers' instinct. Run to your child.'

'That was excellent, Mrs Robinson. Thank you.'

'It was? What were we talking about?'

'You were telling me what you saw at MacNeil's farm-stall.'

She looks perplexed. 'Was I? Good.'

'It is standard technique. Relaxation, a meditative state. People can often recall great detail.'

'Did I?'

'You did very well. You remembered several small, but possibly vital details. I'll get my Warrant Officer and your children back now.' He walks through the doors and waves at Don, gesturing him to return. When he turns back, Sarah Robinson is looking at her watch anxiously. She sees him look.

'My husband will be home soon. Do I need to tell him about this?'

'That's up to you,' Vaughn tells her. 'But I doubt we'll need to bother you again. If we do, I'll make sure we are discreet.'

'Thank you.'

The children are bouncing around Don. She turns to them.

'You two!' she shrieks. 'Hey! Your father will be back just now. Remember what he warned you about?' The children fall silent, shoulders slumped, hands at their side.

'Thank you again,' de Vries says charmingly. 'And thank you for calling. It may lead to finding who took those three children years ago and who hurt them now.' De Vries offers his hand, and she shakes it gingerly. He pats the two children on the head.

'Goodbye.'

They both lower their heads shyly.

Don squats down and says goodbye to them also, but they do not meet his eye.

Vaughn and Don walk through the pristine entrance hall to the big double doors at the front of the house. When Don closes the front door, he says, 'Anything?'

'Yes,' Vaughn says quietly. 'More than I wanted.'

★ ★ ★

Once they've cleared the property's main gates, de Vries recounts his interview. The windows are open, air conditioning off. The car is filled with warm breeze, the engine sounds loud and strong. There is a feeling of movement in this car, right now.

'Write this down somewhere,' Vaughn tells Don. 'BMW 530, metallic grey, or — what do they call it — agate? Here's the really important bit. Rear window: blinds, maybe factory-fitted, pale round or oval sticker, bottom right-hand corner, perhaps with a gate or gates on it; maybe gold on white.'

Vaughn looks over at Don writing in his notebook. Tells him: 'Get that out to everyone you can, as soon as possible. Then we have to decide whether to advertise that description to the public. Let's get a print-out of all BMW 530 models licensed in the Western Cape. And, Don? Think about that badge. Maybe there's a website or something, where you can look up what a gate or gates might be?'

'We can try. Is this him? Is this our guy?'

De Vries tilts his head. 'It could be, couldn't it? Sarah Robinson may just be the first person in seven years to know that she's seen him.'

The car accelerates, the wind blows harder through the cabin. Don looks straight ahead, contemplating.

'What did you mean, back at the Robinson place, 'more than you wanted'?'

'Just an impression. She is afraid of her husband. That's why she didn't call until today; she doesn't think he'd approve. And those kids. Did you see what they did when she mentioned their father? I wonder what he said to them?'

★ ★ ★

De Vries wakes in his office, stiff and bleary. It is morning and, peering through his tightly closed blinds, still early. His desk phone is ringing. He snatches it up.

'De Vries.'

'Asleep on the job?'

'Who is this?'

'David Wertner, Colonel. You didn't do your job properly seven years ago, and now it looks like *déjà vu* all over again.'

'I'm busy.'

'So am I. Internal Investigation is looking at your failed investigation under the supervision of then Senior Superintendent Henrik du Toit. Let's hope we don't find any glaring errors, eh? Would be a shame to lose you and your Brigadier; whole department might have to

96

close. Courtesy call, Colonel. I'm on your case; I'm watching your every move, and the public is watching the man supposedly in charge, and none of us are remotely impressed.'

De Vries tries to stay calm, but his voice is hoarse.

'You find anything, you tell me. Unlike you, I have only one goal: find the boy, and the guy who did this.'

'Well, you find him, and make sure you tell me. Might save your career. And when this is all over, Colonel, when you're back to cherry-picking your cases and you have time on your hands, we'll have a little chat. Seems to be some missing time in your schedule a while back. An unannounced foreign trip, perhaps?'

'Whatever you think you have, Wertner, you haven't. Save your time investigating us and do some policework.'

'I am the police, and I represent the people. I know you hate the people, Colonel de Vries.'

Wertner chuckles and hangs up.

De Vries replaces the handset gently, aware of a mighty morning headache starting deep inside his brain. He wants coffee, but he doesn't want to move. He thinks about the Internal Investigations Chief's call, looks at his watch and realizes that Wertner must have come to work extra early, perhaps seen him asleep in his office; perhaps come into his office and watched him sleeping. The thought repulses him.

He struggles up, stretches, and raises the blinds. Cape Town is coming to work. Beneath him, the traffic is already beginning to become dense. De Vries studies the roofs of the cars eight floors below, searching for a grey BMW. When he can't see one, he leaves his office and walks the corridor to the squad room. Two officers are at work, hunched low in their booths; the coffee jug is empty. De Vries retrieves it and heads for the canteen, still half asleep.

★ ★ ★

'Come in, Vaughn,' du Toit tells him cordially.

Vaughn doesn't like this.

'Very good news about this car. For God's sake, let's find it, and the driver, and find out, one way or another. I'm with you on not publicizing it yet. You have my go-ahead on that. But make it happen, 'cos this thing is nearly dead in the water, and this department, and the whole damn SAPS with it.' Du Toit gestures to a corner of sofas. 'Let's sit over here. There's coffee and cake.'

De Vries has never before been invited to the sofas.

'I received a call from David Wertner this morning,' du Toit says casually.

'So did I.'

'He's been scrutinizing the docket and all the other files from the 07 abductions. I thought you had it all.'

'I guess unofficial copies have been made,' Vaughn tells him. 'I don't know, but the originals are in my office. I'm almost through them, but there's a lot there.'

'Well, keep your office locked, Vaughn. I'm

98

getting it from all sides. You know the new order would like nothing better than to be rid of us. I don't want to give them the excuse.'

'We haven't got time for politics.'

'Wertner's making some very unpleasant noises about you. Gone on record, calling for you to be replaced. 'Course, he probably doesn't know about yesterday's developments . . . Nasty, opportunist move, but par for the course. They're taking the fight public, Vaughn.'

Four years ago, Henrik du Toit got the nod to Director, officially the rank of Brigadier, though he encourages his men to use his old title, associated to Robbery and Murder, Western Cape Province, his own fiefdom. His rival, Simphiwe Thulani, riding the fading crest of positive discrimination, Assistant Provincial Commander, General now — a higher rank, but less freedom, more politics. Separate departments, but jealousy undimmed. Du Toit got de Vries where he wanted him: a free agent in Western Cape Province, leading tough investigations that needed a forceful approach. Thulani got David Wertner in to lead his brainchild: a new Internal Investigations Bureau. Since then, Wertner has been hunting for anything to hasten the downfall of de Vries and du Toit, leaving their places free for successors sympathetic to the new order, for the last of the old guard to be retired. As if the SAPS didn't face enough enemies. This is petty office politics, played hardball.

'You'd think the old school would stick together. I know there's a new generation of apartheid in the SAPS, but you'd think Wertner would realize that he's creating a glass ceiling for himself: the black guys won't promote Wertner again any more than they want us anywhere near the top.' Du Toit pours himself a cup of coffee, pushes the handle of the cafetière towards Vaughn. He picks up a biscuit. 'I had Thulani's lackey, Julius Mngomezulu, demanding updates for his boss.'

'I can't even pronounce the little fuck's name.'

'You're a dinosaur, Vaughn.'

'At least I don't have to practise it in the mirror every morning.'

Du Toit sticks his finger in de Vries' chest. 'You're damn lucky — I do.'

'I hope you told him where to stick his updates.'

'I told him that if Thulani wants in, he's in as the boss. His call. Doubt we'll hear anything more from him directly. He'd rather watch us crash and burn.'

'Men like Mngomezulu,' de Vries mispronounces it quite dramatically, 'whatever colour they are, I don't trust them. You wear a suit buttoned top to bottom, pointy little shoes, you're not planning on running anywhere, are you? Chasing down scum on a dirt track. You ever look at his collar? White as a fucking baby's bottom. I doubt that man has ever sweated in his life.'

'I'm surprised, Vaughn,' du Toit says, 'at your eye for the sartorial. To look at you sometimes, you wouldn't think it.'

'These are work clothes.'

'Forget Mngomezulu.' Du Toit pronounces his

name perfectly. 'It's Wertner and Thulani we have to watch.'

'They have to make a move sometime,' de Vries says. 'Kicking us when we're down must seem like the right thing for them to do.'

'Colonel Wertner hinted at information regarding actions of yours outside our jurisdiction. Do I know about this?'

'Nothing to know. Wertner's fishing. I may operate at the perimeters of the law, but always within it. You know that.'

Du Toit smiles. Neither man knows that, believes that, for a moment. The new South Africa sometimes needs the old South Africa's policing. Du Toit puts down his coffee mug, brushes crumbs from his dark, brass-buttoned jacket, sighs.

De Vries gets up slowly.

Du Toit says, 'Find that car, Vaughn. Find it today.'

2007
De Vries walks wet, damp-dog smelling, from an outdoor parking space in town, amidst rain thick and dark as fog, to SAPS city building, up in the elevators to the top-floor corridor, towards du Toit's office. He is dog-tired, and he knows what will be said: the official seal on his failure.

'I have sanctioned two officers to pursue the abductions,' du Toit tells him, without meeting his eye, 'until progress is made, or I deem it time to conclude the continuing inquiry. Trevor Henderson is off the radar. I can only imagine what the man is going through. I sent word for him to take indefinite leave, but I've heard nothing.'

'I was told his wife returned to the UK with their other child. No one has heard from him for weeks.'

'I take it,' du Toit says, 'that no new evidence — indeed, any evidence at all — has been discovered in the last forty-eight hours?' De Vries shakes his head. 'I understand how you feel, Vaughn. This is on my head too but, blunt as it is to say it, life goes on. And we must be available and responsive to police it.'

He looks across his desk to de Vries.

'Vaughn?' du Toit says, his voice almost imploring. De Vries looks up. 'There will always be cases like this. You must know that.'

'I am aware of that, yes, sir.'

'Nobody could have tried any harder. I reviewed all the files at the weekend and you covered every possible corner. Now, listen to me. There may be a media reaction to the announcement of the scaling down, but we'll just have to bear it. You look half dead. Take a week off, Vaughn. That's an order. I need you back fit and working well.'

De Vries nods silently. Then asks: 'Have you spoken with the parents yet?'

'No, but that is something *I* must do. You're off Lawson, Eames and Henderson as from this minute. Go home, go on holiday. Do something to get your body rested and your mind focused anew.'

'I'd sooner speak to the relatives, sir.'

'I've already made my decision. You, me, the department — we will all live through this experience. We will move on. We must move on.'

Vaughn sighs, begins to nod slowly; an acknowledgement that it is over for all but the families of Steven, Bobby and Toby. He wonders whether he can bear their sorrow.

2014

'The guys checked out all BMW 530 models, grey, silver, variations of the above, registered in the last five years. There are a lot of them. We have cross-checked with criminal records and nothing stands out.'

Don February jogs to keep up with de Vries. Finally, they reach his office.

'What is the matter, sir?'

De Vries curses. 'Too much traffic, too many people, too many BMWs, sanctimonious journalists and the public. I fucking hate the public. And you, Don, always telling me 'nothing'.'

'Sorry I asked.'

'I'm aware,' de Vries says, collapsing into his chair, 'that you are not personally responsible for 'nothing'. But once, just once . . . ' His hands make fists. 'I want one break on this. Seven fucking years it's been 'nothing'. Now, for Christ's sake: *something*!'

'I will extend the search. We will go to six years out, then seven. I can contact the main dealers if necessary. We both think this is a solid lead. I will work it.'

De Vries says: 'Good, Don. You try to solve

problems with work.'

'It is the only way.'

De Vries looks at his watch.

'Call me, anytime.' He sighs. 'I won't be sleeping.'

2009

For fourteen months he lived in isolation while his house was being built. Neighbours and acquaintances tried to lure him out, but he rejected them until, one by one, they gave up. Just before Christmas, his closest friend in town, a Capetonian he'd met at university, Simon Van Wyk, asked him to escort his new wife to a grand party, he being sick.

'You don't have to do much, man. These media types talk a lot but they don't say anything. Jane needs to network, but she can't arrive alone. The food will be good and the bar is free all night.'

John Marantz looked into his kitchen, saw staleness and, on a whim, agreed. He was sober enough to drive; the shaking had subsided sufficiently for him to be able to shave. For the first time, the thought of standing up in public, being seen, being spoken to, did not terrify him. He liked Jane Van Wyk — a prominent young architect; she and Simon had helped him with his house, and they never asked questions of him.

His car was valet parked, and they walked, arm in arm, to the main entrance of the grand Bishopscourt mansion. They stood in line to meet their hosts, and looked beyond them, through the huge triple-height chandeliered lounge to the vast terraces of the candlelit garden, full of South Africa's beautiful elite.

Perhaps she sensed his fear. She took his hand in hers and whispered, 'You don't have to stay, Johnnie.'

'I'll be in the garden.'

'If you want to go, that's fine. They'll have cars to take guests home. If you stay, I won't be long.'

He forced a smile, and they parted; partied.

★ ★ ★

On a far terrace, low down beneath tall Camphor trees, almost beyond earshot of the lively jazz band, a long wooden dining table boasts a single candelabra, candles dripping wax in the light summer breeze. Marantz sits alone with a bottle of fine Cabernet Sauvignon, sipping slowly, admiring the view of almost complete darkness, broken only by pinpoints of lights from houses across the valley, up where he would soon be living. He thinks that the darkness is like a cloak to him and for a moment he feels safe, unthreatened. Then he hears a wheezing, a stumble, and another guest appears from a smoky dimness, clutching his own bottle, talking, it seems, to himself and then, seeing Marantz, to him.

'Another man who travels with his own supply.'

Marantz looks up to see a tall, thin, middle-aged man, curly salt and pepper hair whitening at the temples, pockmarked skin, and a creased suit the wrong side of good taste. He looks tired and his eye seems jaundiced.

The man gestures to a chair at the head of the table. 'You mind?'

'Please.'

The man stares at him. 'English?'

Marantz looks up. 'From just one word? That's impressive.'

The man smiles, as if he knows it is, but he says, just too blankly; 'I'm a famous detective.'

Marantz holds out his hand. 'John Marantz.'

'Vaughn de Vries.'

Marantz echoes, 'A famous detective?'

De Vries tops up his glass, gestures at Marantz's, says disparagingly, 'An infamous policeman.'

Marantz frowns. 'I know the feeling.'

'What do you do?'

'Same sort of gig, in London, but I've been retired. Play a bit of poker . . . '

'Married?'

Marantz expected a shock; a moment when his breath might catch, but his reply came smoothly, almost nonchalantly.

'I don't think so.'

'Like that, eh?'

'No. Not like that. They're gone. Lost.'

'I'm sorry.'

'By-product of the job. You have a family?'

De Vries chuckles knowingly to himself. 'Two amazing daughters; dissatisfied, ambitious wife; no time, no energy, no motivation, no interest. You had kids?'

'I . . . had . . . ' Marantz shuts his eyes, feels such agony well up inside him, a band of pain

106

wrapped around his head, covering his eyes and ears. He waits maybe ninety seconds for it to become bearable. He looks up at de Vries, expecting confusion, perhaps revulsion. He sees a man waiting for him, accepting, but not asking.

Marantz mutters, 'Sorry.'

'Don't be. I interrupted your escape.'

'No.'

A waiter appears with a bottle on a silver tray. He bows at de Vries. 'Your wine, sir.'

De Vries scoops it off the tray, examines the label. 'If I'm still here in one hour, I want another.'

The waiter bows again and begins to climb the stone steps back to the big house.

'You have them well trained.'

De Vries tilts the bottle at Marantz's empty glass and then fills his own, almost to the brim.

'Escort's perks. She's only here for the career.'

'I'm with my best mate's wife. Same reason.'

De Vries gestures at the candelabra with his glass, then up at Marantz. 'Moths drawn to the flame . . . '

★ ★ ★

They meet to drink, to talk in stilted sentences and long silences. Marantz cries as he tells de Vries how he lost his wife and daughter, and he sees nothing in de Vries but compassion, devoid of judgement. That is the purest reaction he has witnessed.

★ ★ ★

107

One single day in 2008: the square grey concrete room, bare fluorescent tube, blatantly crude, a plain steel table, bounded on one side by a rudimentary iron chair, on the other by two plain steel armchairs. He is sitting next to a colleague, opposite a man with a Russian accent; three aliases in an anonymous room. The man is shackled to his chair, both his eyes purple, his nose broken. This is the third hour of the third day they have spoken to him. The man repeats his story, precise words. Marantz knows that it is a script, but nothing they do encourages him to depart from it.

The prisoner turns his head to his right, addresses Marantz's silent partner. 'You don't say much.'

Marantz waits; his colleague, by arrangement, mute.

'You have wife and children?'

The man turns back to face ahead, his stare dissecting them.

Marantz says: 'You may never see yours again, Mikael.'

A tiny smile appears at the corner of the man's mouth, his fat lip showing bright red.

'At least,' he starts slowly, facing Marantz and staring hard at him, 'I know where my wife and daughter are.'

Marantz thinks of Caroline and Rosie, wonders whether this man has merely guessed at the make-up of his family, glances to the fourth finger of his left hand, sees that his ring is, as he would expect, absent. The man catches the glance, smiles broadly now, splitting open the corner of his swollen bottom lip.

'You won't need it any more.'

A sharp tingle in his fingers: Marantz reads not stoic bravado, but a reflection of knowledge. He stands, his colleague matching him, and they leave the room.

There is no answer to phone calls; an empty house, a missing car. All the might of the British Intelligence Services find nothing. When he proposes travelling to Russia, searching the world of their suspect, they tag his passport, exile him to his empty home. And then, he exiles himself.

★ ★ ★

In Cape Town, Marantz drinks. When he is arrested over a fight following an illegal poker game; when he draws a gun and lets unfocused eyes aim at the other men, he questions whether he should call de Vries. When he does, de Vries is there, in person, and they walk away from the station together. Marantz will not forget that.

When he weans himself from the bottle, de Vries still comes, and Marantz smokes mild Cape Town dope, joint after joint. De Vries is pissed as ever but, in the morning, he begins to welcome the light. He speaks of his daughters and edits his wife from his history. One month there was Suzanne de Vries, then a wife, a woman, and now no one whose partner is Vaughn de Vries.

Marantz takes pleasure from a man who knows the world they both inhabit, knows to talk about the facts and never about the thoughts, the fears, the terror; knows never to ask how he is feeling, if he is seeing anybody, if he is killing himself with, first booze, then dope. These are the rules when you enter a relationship like theirs. Such men understand that life revolves around rules; the making of them, the following of them, the breaking of them.

★ ★ ★

'You know, Johnnie,' de Vries says, feet up on the arm of the chestnut-brown leather sofa, warming his socks by the fire, 'I've given up mourning my . . . proletarian marriage.' He takes a draught of the red wine, nodding appreciatively. 'My little girls are established. They have their network; they don't need their parents. Not as parents anyway, and they sure as hell don't need me. And, you know what? That's a fuck of a relief.'

Through a cloud of dope smoke, Marantz says: 'So, what else is there?'

'What I do. That's the point of me. That's always been the point. Believe it or not, I can have women, Johnnie. I can have them, but I don't want them to stay. I mean, there are women I want to fuck, and women I'll hang out with but, right now, I can't imagine a woman I want to do both with. Does that make sense?'

'To you, obviously.'

'I like knowing there's no one waiting, worrying, to make me feel guilty, no one making demands at home; like there aren't enough at work. I can get on with what I want to do, what I'm good at.'

'Then you've found your place.'

De Vries raises his glass shakily. 'I have.'

'The drink doesn't burn you? At work, I mean.'

'Never let it. Secret of successful hard drinking: know how many hours you have to recover, work backwards, stop at just the right moment. Can't say it's conscious, just happens.'

'You try so hard to be the cliché, but you just can't manage it, can you?'

'I try so hard to understand what the fuck you're saying.'

'You are a heavy-drinking, weather-beaten police detective with a broken marriage and anger-management issues — and somehow, you seem terribly pleased with your status. You're supposed to have a breakdown and go crazy.'

'Isn't going to happen. Work'll fuck me up, not the booze, not some stupid fucking woman. I've done the relationship and after twenty years, you know what? I like being single again. Like everything about it.'

John Marantz inhales deeply, keeping the laced smoke deep inside him, feeling the fire burn his throat and warm his lungs, feeling his fingertips tingle.

'Then you're a lucky man.'

De Vries snorts, smiles, lights his own cigarette and lies back on the sofa.

'Let me tell you, Johnnie-boy,' he says to the ceiling. 'Sometimes I'm not sure but, just now, I think you're right.'

2014

'One break. One. You ever have anything like this? Where there's nothing, and seven years later it comes back after you?'

'No.'

'Ever since that day, the time the first of them disappeared, nothing's run for me, nothing works. He's killed two of them, but one might still be alive. Bobby. Bobby Eames.'

'You need anything, if I can help . . . '

De Vries frowns, asks, 'You still have your contacts?'

'I am no longer employed by Her Majesty's Government.'

'Going to stay that way?'

'I received a call, the moment I landed in London. They're watching me, even now.'

'We're all being watched,' de Vries says. 'They want to shaft me and du Toit over this and get us out.'

'Don't let that happen.'

'Not within my gift.'

Marantz looks up at him. 'There is influence. It can be applied . . . clinically. You know I'll help you.'

De Vries nods slowly. 'It's good to see you, man.' He sighs, relaxing a little finally, the alcohol slowly working. 'Where's your dog?'

'Jogging with my neighbour's daughter. She says she feels safer with him there.'

'Good exercise for him. Probably enjoys it.'

'Guess so,' Marantz says. 'We've never talked about it.'

★ ★ ★

Into the city before dawn, already de Vries can feel the heat of a still, clear late-summer's day ahead. The squad room is deserted, the

112

telephone operators snoozy, resentful of a loud voice demanding if there are any messages, any calls for de Vries. There are none.

At 7.30 a.m., a knock, his door opening. Don. 'I have something.'

'Shoot.'

'I thought about Sarah Robinson's statement. She called the car 'smart'. I checked what cars her family own. They have a Honda 4×4, and an S-class Merc. Those are premium cars, so something that looked grand sounded bigger than a 5-Series BMW. I ran all the 7-Series BMWs sold in the Western Cape last year, found one name that is as weird as hell. Owner of a BMW 750iL — that is the long wheelbase version — Marc Steinhauer.'

De Vries, on his feet. 'The wine estate? The cheese?'

'There is more. I checked his website. The Fineberg estate logo is a gold portcullis — like a gate.'

'On the sticker Sarah Robinson saw?'

'Exactly.'

De Vries, his hands in his hair.

'Jesus. Fuck, Don. What does this mean? If Steinhauer's our guy; even if he's connected. His fucking brother ran me down day in, day out seven years ago, shat on all of us. It's too much of a coincidence.'

'Let us see, sir. We search his car, ask who he lent it to. Be a strange thing to do; it is brand new, sold four months ago.'

'Can we get a back-up unit from here? Are they in yet?'

113

'Already sorted. Four guys standing by, two unmarked vehicles. Thought we might go in very gentle: Steinhauer is jumpy. If there is any trouble, we have back-up.'

Vaughn nods. 'Agreed.'

'We need Scene of Crime there too. Thought you might express a preference.'

'Good.' Vaughn, adrenalin beginning to flow. 'Call Steve Ulton. Tell him to drive to Fineberg immediately. I'm sure they'll tow it back to the labs, but if there's anything, we want to know straight away.' He picks up the phone receiver, then slams it back down. 'No. We're going right now.' He gets up. 'Was going to call du Toit, but fuck it. You can call from the car. I want to wake this bastard up, no matter what.'

★   ★   ★

The unmarked cars wait at the entrance to the drive up to the estate. Don drives de Vries up the track to the gravel car park under old oaks. Theirs is the only car there. The winery and shop are dark and deserted. Don swings the car around towards the Cape Dutch manor house and stops outside the front door. Outside two garage doors is a white Range Rover, with vanity plates: WP FINEBERG. Vaughn exits, climbs the steps, ignores the bell-push and raps five times loudly with the heavy bunch-of-grapes brass knocker. The sound echoes around the court-yard, back again from the thick, dark trunks of the oaks. As Don reaches the door, it opens onto Marc Steinhauer, dressed but dishevelled.

114

De Vries says: 'Marc Steinhauer?'

'Yes.'

They show their warrant cards. Vaughn tries to push inside, but Steinhauer stands his ground.

'We need to speak to you inside, Mr Steinhauer.'

Steinhauer bustles out of the door and closes it.

'Whatever it is you want, we can discuss it out here. My children are getting ready for school.'

Don says, 'Sir, do you own a silver-grey BMW 750iL?'

'Why?'

Don, seeing de Vries clench his fists, calm: 'Just answer the question, please, sir.'

'Yes, I do.'

'We would like to see that car.'

'Why?'

Don does not break his calm rhythm.

'This is an official matter, sir. You must show us now.'

Steinhauer twitches minutely, but his composure is retained.

'I'll get the remote to the garage and my car keys.' He turns back to the house.

'Go with him, Don.'

Steinhauer says to de Vries, 'They are just in the hall. You can watch me. Please do not disturb my family.'

De Vries nods at Don, and Steinhauer lets himself back in, leaves the front door open and collects his keys from a basket on a heavy wooden chest. He comes back out.

'What is this about?'

'Have you lent your car to anyone recently?'

'No. I mean, my wife has driven it, but no one else. Is there something wrong? This man . . . Inspector . . . ?' He gestures at Don.

'Warrant Officer February.'

'Yes. You were here a few days back, asking about our cheese. You said that there had been a murder — those boys — and now you are asking about my car. Why?'

Don ushers him towards the garages. 'Let us look at your vehicle, sir. We just need to check certain things.'

Steinhauer operates the electric doors and the left-hand garage door opens onto his car.

'What things?'

He sees de Vries putting on gloves.

Flustered, repeats: 'What things?'

Vaughn takes the car keys from Steinhauer's hand, unlocks the car remotely. He opens the driver's door, reaches down and releases the boot-lid. He edges around the car and pushes the boot open wide. He peers inside. Says loudly: 'Have you had this car cleaned?'

Steinhauer leans into his own garage.

'Yes. I have it cleaned every week. It's my pride and joy.'

Vaughn sniffs the boot, examines the tyres, walks around the back of the car, checks the rear-windscreen for a sticker, and looks inside the back seat.

'I can bring the car out if you wish,' Steinhauer ventures.

'Do you ever visit MacNeil's farm-stall, up past Sir Lowry's?'

116

Steinhauer looks at de Vries, confused.

'I think we have. Yes, possibly.'

'Recently?'

Steinhauer thinks. His eyes roll up and to the right, then back at de Vries.

'Yes. I did go there. I quite forgot. A few days ago.' He looks around for de Vries. Finds him right behind him.

'Monday afternoon, was it, Mr Steinhauer?'

Steinhauer steps back from de Vries, brushes his shirt down.

'Yes, it may have been. Why?'

'Wait there for a moment.' Vaughn gestures to Don, walks him away, stops so that he is looking at Steinhauer over Don's shoulder. Vaughn speaks quietly.

'Call Ulton. Find out how far away he is. This guy has had the car cleaned — very thoroughly — but it would be easy to miss something. It's got the label at the back, and the built-in blinds. That's the car Sarah Robinson saw, and she said it drove around the back of the farm-stall. I want the car taken to the lab, so tell him he'll need a tow-truck. I want to bring Steinhauer back in voluntarily, unless he refuses to come or release his car. I get the feeling he might run for a lawyer straight away, but we might as well try to get him alone first.'

Don nods, asks, 'What do you think?'

'I don't know. He's very wary, but his reactions are off. I don't like it that he's admitted so readily to being at the farm-stall. He'll have a good excuse why he didn't answer our appeals, and then, if the car gives us nothing, we don't

117

have much.' He chews on some imaginary gum for a moment. 'All right, he won't have his car, so we'll drive him. I'm going to put him in the front, so he feels important. Small talk only in the car. Let's go.'

Vaughn, smiling now, almost warm.

'Your car was seen at MacNeil's farm-stall in the afternoon before the bodies of two murder victims were found on site. We need to take your car to be examined in our labs. I'd like you to accompany us, and make a statement. Are you prepared to do that?'

'Now? No, I couldn't.' The man runs his hand over his brow. 'I have a business to run. My wife has to take our children to school and I must open up.'

Low-voiced, compelling: 'I must insist, I'm afraid. You can let your family know that you are assisting us. Come with us now, or it will be necessary to arrest you.'

'Arrest me?'

'In front of your family. It's up to you.'

Steinhauer stares nowhere for a few seconds, makes up his mind, and turns back towards the house. Don follows him. Vaughn looks around the idyllic courtyard, hears nothing from the house, shifts his weight from foot to foot.

★ ★ ★

After an hour's silent journey, Steinhauer's lawyer is waiting for them at the headquarters building. He takes Steinhauer to a private room, away from de Vries.

118

De Vries gestures at their backs. Says, 'I thought so.'

Don says: 'He spoke to his wife out of my earshot. It is his right. We cannot stop him.'

'I know, Don.' Vaughn twists his left wrist, glances down. 'I'm calling du Toit. If they come back, put them in the suite. If he changes his mind, tell him to wait for me.' De Vries trots towards the escalators.

Don waits down the corridor from the consultation rooms. He has eaten no breakfast, slept uneasily. Minutes pass. No one ventures near the corridor. He can't hear any voices from the consultation room. His stomach rumbles.

De Vries returns.

'Du Toit wants to be the other side of the glass.' He tilts his head down the length of the corridor. 'Nothing?'

Don shakes his head. The door opens at the far end of the corridor, and he sees Ralph Hopkins walk slowly towards them. He is red-faced and silver-haired, lavishly attired in a dark blue suit, white shirt and silk tie: moneyed good taste. He speaks with a low, deep voice, little eyes behind circular gold frames and thick lenses.

'My client feels that he has been intimidated into this interview, against his will. I have advised him to decline your invitation. My client has, however, agreed to allow you to survey his car.'

De Vries says, equally conspiratorially, 'Your client will be arrested if he declines my invitation.'

'On what charge?'

'Suspect in a double murder, possible suspect in abduction, child abuse and false imprisonment.'

119

Hopkins smiles knowingly. 'I don't think so, Colonel de Vries. If he warrants arrest on those charges, you would have arrested him already.'

'If you want your client arrested, Mr Hopkins, I can arrange it. Tell him that and let me know his thoughts.'

Hopkins raises an eyebrow, turns and saunters back down the corridor.

'I've dealt with that asshole before,' de Vries tells Don, maintaining his *sotto voce*. 'He negotiated a plea bargain; got his client a minimum sentence. He goes out and rapes again six days later. The sick bastard was a wealthy white guy, separated from his wife, son at Bishops'. Hopkins is old-school; all his clients are rich — and guilty.'

Hopkins reappears, followed by Marc Steinhauer, who is walking very slowly:

'Marc has agreed to your interview, Colonel. Of course, I will be present. Then, he hopes that you will allow him to return to his business and family. Are you ready to proceed?'

De Vries looks at Steinhauer, nods.

Don encourages them down the corridor towards the interview suite. Vaughn waits until they are inside the room, and then calls Steve Ulton.

'We've run prelims,' Ulton tells him. 'The car's been very well cleaned. Professional steamclean too, underside also. I've run ultraviolet and show-up sprays and there's nothing, but we've only just started.'

'Take it apart,' Vaughn tells him. 'Call me with anything.'

'Vaughn. Can you get his DNA? Could be useful.'

De Vries ducks into an adjoining door; the room behind the mirror. Director du Toit is sitting on a high stool, sphinx-like eyes staring at Steinhauer. A technician supervises a video camera and recording machine.

He walks up to du Toit, stands next to him, examines Steinhauer through the window.

Du Toit says: 'He looks more angry than nervous.'

'Anger is usually a front.'

Vaughn stares at Steinhauer. He watches him tap his left foot on the thin carpet, his knee rocking up and down. He sees him glance at his watch, ask Hopkins if he can call his wife, Hopkins murmuring that he should wait, Steinhauer complying. He studies the man's face, which is tense, but no more so than he might expect in an interview room, in a police station. Steinhauer has a pudding-basin haircut, a weak nervous smile, soft pink hands. Vaughn sees him count the heartbeats he feels in his head. Something feels wrong.

Vaughn ducks back out, straightens himself, enters the interrogation room. Steinhauer looks up at him almost, de Vries thinks, hopefully.

'This interview will be recorded and a copy made available to you at the conclusion.' De Vries indicates the tape machine to Don, and he switches it on.

'Nineteenth March 2014, ten thirty-five a.m. SAPS headquarters, Suite One. Present are Mr Marc Steinhauer, his legal representative, Mr Ralph Hopkins, Colonel Vaughn de Vries, Warrant Officer Donald February.'

121

Vaughn sits next to Don, opposite Steinhauer. He relaxes in his seat, takes his time.

'To confirm for the tape: you are Marc Steinhauer, residing at Fineberg Estate, Fineberg Road, off Annandale Road, near Stellenbosch?'

Steinhauer leans towards the tape device.

'Yes.'

'Mr Steinhauer, you have agreed to make a voluntary statement to us regarding your visit to MacNeil's farm-stall on — '

'No.'

De Vries opens his mouth to continue, is taken aback by Steinhauer's negative.

'I was pressured into attending this interview, under threat of arrest in front of my family. I was left no choice.'

De Vries watches Steinhauer's little mouth moving, pink lips fluttering; finds him sanctimonious and annoying. He smiles, almost to himself, continues calmly, 'But you nevertheless consent to speaking with us on these matters?'

'Now that my client's objection is duly noted,' Hopkins interjects. 'Yes.'

'Very well. Can you confirm that you drive a silver-grey BMW 750iL, registration . . . ' He looks to Don.

'CA 785454.'

'Yes. That is my car.'

'Please describe how you came to be at MacNeil's farm-stall last Monday at approximately four forty-five p.m.?'

Hopkins leans forward again. 'I don't believe any specific time has been mentioned or agreed.'

De Vries nods at him, conceding the point. He

turns back to Steinhauer.

'At what time did you visit MacNeil's farm-stall on Monday this week?'

'I don't remember exactly. I intended to go there for a snack, so approaching tea-time, I suppose. I found the car park full and the place busy. I changed my mind, turned around and continued home.'

'From where had you been travelling?'

'I had been away for the night, visiting my aunt in Riebeek West. I left after lunch and was planning to drive to Betty's Bay, where my wife and I have a beach-house.'

Don asks, 'Why not take the coast road via Gordon's Bay? Is that not more direct?'

'I do sometimes. In fact, I usually do, but that day I . . . I don't know. I decided to drive the longer but faster route over Sir Lowry's Pass.'

Don follows on: 'What was the purpose of your visit to your beach-house?'

'It is our holiday home.'

'But you just told us that you had driven from the Riebeek Valley. You would have driven close to your main home. Why did you not call in there first?'

'Why should I?' He looks childlike and petulant.

'Did you, in fact, visit your house in Betty's Bay that day?'

'No. I changed my mind. I had been planning to collect some books I had left there and, as much as anything else, to drive my car, but I decided that perhaps I was tired and would go home after all.'

'So,' Don says, 'you decide to bypass your home to travel to your beach-house, but something makes you change your mind?'

'Yes — no. Not anything in particular. I realized I could collect my books another time and perhaps I was being selfish and should get home to my family more quickly.'

Steinhauer looks towards Hopkins and then back again at de Vries and Don February.

De Vries just watches, waits.

Don says: 'Just run us through what you did at the farm-stall, Mr Steinhauer?'

'What I did? I told you. I drove up the driveway, came into the car park, saw how busy it was, and decided not to bother.'

'So, what did you do?'

'I turned around and left.'

'Where?'

'Where?'

'Where did you turn around?'

'In the car park.'

'You did not drive around to the back of the farm-stall?'

Steinhauer frowns, thinks. Says, 'I may have turned at the back. I'm trying to picture it.' He closes his eyes; his lids flicker. 'I can't really remember.'

'You did not get out of your car?'

'No — no, I don't think so.'

'Well, surely you can remember that?' de Vries' voice echoes in the small room; Steinhauer jumps. 'Did you get out of your car or stay inside and just turn around?'

Steinhauer pauses; de Vries shifts in his chair,

his smile weak, his stare hard.

'No. I stayed in my car.'

'You stayed in your car?'

Steinhauer looks across the table at each of them.

'Yes.'

'At what time did you reach your home in Stellenbosch?'

'I don't remember. As I say, I had made lunch for my aunt, but not eaten myself. I was hungry when I got home.'

'What did you eat for your supper?'

Steinhauer is about to answer, but Hopkins interrupts him.

'Is this germane, Colonel? I appreciate your desire to have a casual discussion with my client, but surely his diet is irrelevant to your enquiries?'

De Vries shrugs; he asked the question to observe Steinhauer talking about something irrelevant compared to, perhaps, the disposal of the bodies of two dead teenage boys. He is frustrated to have been interrupted.

'Where do you have your car cleaned?'

'There's a hand-wash, valet service at the new shopping centre at the end of Annandale Road, on the main road into Stellenbosch. I take it there every week. It's a new car. A present to myself. I drive a great deal for my work: to markets, fairs. We are adding olive oil to our range. We own twelve hectares of olive groves; I am supervising the crop. I like my car clean: it presents a good impression of me and my business.'

'You have the full valet every time?'

'Up till now, yes. They steamclean the up-holstery, the underside of the vehicle, the tyres, everything. It's a very good service.'

'And when was it cleaned last?'

'Yesterday. I did the family shop while it was being done. As usual.'

'Your wife works?'

'She runs the business side of the estate. I am front-of-house. The face of Fineberg, you might say.' He manages a little smile; seems more relaxed.

'I need to take you back to the farm-stall, Mr Steinhauer. Where in the car park did you turn around? It was, as you said, crowded.'

Steinhauer sighs a little. 'I'm not sure. Is there a turning circle at the end of the car park?'

De Vries shakes his head.

'No, Mr Steinhauer. I want to hear what you remember.'

Steinhauer looks over to Hopkins, who says: 'Colonel, Marc has told you that he does not clearly recollect where he turned his car in this car park. It sounds to me as if you have a witness who recalls seeing Marc's car. Perhaps you could tell us what he, or she, thinks they saw, and we can discuss that with you?'

'You were seen turning your car left at the end of the car park, around the back of the farm-stall.'

Steinhauer blinks and shakes his head.

'I may have turned left — I didn't go behind the farm-stall. If I did, it was only to turn the car.'

'As opposed to what?'

Steinhauer freezes. 'I — I don't — What do you mean?'

'You said, if you did, it was only to turn your car. What else would you be doing in the back yard of the farm-stall?'

'If,' Hopkins interjects, 'you question every unassuming word in my client's replies, it'll be a long morning.'

Vaughn's eyes never leave Steinhauer. Ignoring Hopkins, he moves on smoothly.

'Did you read about, or see the reports on this murder investigation, currently under way?'

'I'm too busy to read the rubbish in the newspapers and we discourage our children from watching television. So, no.'

'You were not aware that we are actively seeking witnesses from MacNeil's farm-stall on that date?'

'No. I'm sorry, no. If I had, I would have contacted you.'

Snidely: '*If* you had remembered that you had been there.'

Steinhauer askance; Hopkins asking, 'What does that mean?'

'Merely that, when we were talking with Mr Steinhauer at his home, he claimed to have forgotten that he had been there.'

'I should have thought,' Hopkins pronounces, 'that if you went somewhere where you merely drive in and out of a car park, it is not something that will remain at the forefront of your mind.'

'Perhaps.'

'Do you have any further questions for my client?'

De Vries gets up. 'A few minutes more, gentlemen.'

He exits the suite, enters the observation room.

Du Toit says: 'What have you got forensically?'

De Vries, his cellphone at the ready. 'I'm checking now.'

Du Toit: 'I mistrust his manner.'

De Vries is listening to Steve Ulton. His phone snaps shut.

'Nothing. Ulton says he'll need all day to fully process it.'

'Damn. It's not him, is it?'

'It's his car. The colour, the make, the blinds at the back, the Fineberg label.'

'But Ulton has nothing. We can't prove it.'

'I don't know yet.'

'Get him out of here, Vaughn. Tell him we'll hold the car for twenty-four hours, offer to have it driven back for him. He's not going anywhere; he's got his wife and family there. If he's got nothing to do with this, you see how it'll look?'

'Look?'

'The case reopened. Nicholas Steinhauer publicly criticized you back then — both of us — all of us. Now you drag his brother into the station. The man's well known now, well respected. You know how Hopkins will work the press. They're supporting us for now, but you can imagine how this could play?'

De Vries takes a deep breath; he feels energy draining from him.

'Very well, sir. He's hiding something, though; he's a completely different man when he's with Hopkins. Whatever it is, he's afraid that his wife

128

and family will find out.'

'Unless you can tie that car to those two bodies, it's nothing. Probably cheating on his wife, that's all. And Vaughn — tell February that there is zero leak on this discussion. No one from the department is to mention a word about having him here. If it gets in the papers, we'll know who leaked it.'

De Vries nods, leaves the room, his shoulders down, prepares to let Steinhauer go.

★　★　★

Vaughn hands Don a DNA swab kit.

'DNA? Why?' Steinhauer released, then asked for one more cooperation.

De Vries: 'So that our lab can eliminate your DNA in comparison to any other traces found.'

Steinhauer glances at Hopkins, who nods once.

A huff. 'What do I do?'

Don takes an oral swab from Steinhauer's gums, places the cotton bud in the test-tube provided, seals it. Steinhauer makes a point of rubbing his tongue over his teeth, as if, somehow, a cotton bud had been displeasing to his system.

De Vries opens the door to the suite, ushers Steinhauer and Hopkins out ahead of him, offers Steinhauer a lift back to the Fineberg Estate.

'That won't be necessary,' Hopkins tells de Vries outside, standing between him and Steinhauer. 'I will drive Marc home myself. He's been under quite enough stress for one day. An early-morning raid, an interrogation . . . '

'That's not what happened.'

'I'm sure it won't be in your report. Make sure you call Mr Steinhauer this evening and let him know at what time his vehicle will be returned. He has cooperated fully. And, Colonel, if you wish to speak with him again, have the courtesy to permit him his legal right of an attorney — *before* you start your questioning.'

Hopkins turns away, leads Steinhauer towards the exit. Vaughn watches them go, his teeth gritted.

★　★　★

Don February, silent again, sitting in de Vries' office. Outside, scalding afternoon sun on the windows. He wants to be working; wants to be doing something. De Vries enters, slams the door.

'We wait. Steve Ulton says he's finding stuff. Nothing standout, but possibles.' He sits at his desk, struggles out of his jacket. 'What did you think?'

'Nervous, particularly when you spoke about MacNeil's; evasive. But he was jumpy anyway, when I first visited him. He had certain answers worked out but, other times, he stutters while he thinks of what to say. I think he is lying, or not telling all of the truth, but if we cannot link him to the bodies, I suppose we do not have anything.'

'That's what du Toit said.'

'You, sir?'

'I think that he worked out why we were questioning him; maybe Hopkins told him we

130

had to have a witness, and then he covered everything perfectly. Two key reactions: where he turned his car; he didn't know what the witness saw or didn't see, and that unnerved him. Second one, same thing: when I asked him if he got out of the car. It was such a simple question but he wasn't sure what he could say. If he's our man, then of course he did — unless there's an accomplice, but Sarah Robinson is pretty certain that the driver was alone. None of this fits his story, so he lied, knowing that he was risking contradicting the witness.'

'You think he is the man?'

Vaughn pauses.

'Yes, but with reservations. Something seems wrong . . . I don't know what. He didn't seem frightened by us.'

'He *looked* frightened.'

'But not of us . . . ' De Vries trails off.

'Two more little things I noticed, sir. His wife gets the Fineberg Estate number-plate; he drives around in a car with an anonymous registration. I looked up his registration history — his last car was a silver-grey 7-Series too.'

'He certainly wouldn't want a memorable plate if he's visiting those boys.'

'The other thing,' Don continues. 'I tell him that his cheese is found on the heel of a murder victim. He never asks about it — never, so he claims, reads up about it, or watches the television news?'

De Vries nods. 'That's what I mean. There's too much there for it to be nothing.'

'If I had the SAPS at my home saying I might

131

be involved in murder, or my product is involved, I would read the papers, look up on the Internet. It does not ring true.'

De Vries smiles to himself; he and Don are so different and yet now, when it matters, they are beginning to think alike.

'Get what you can on Marc Steinhauer. I want to know as much as possible about him. Even if we get a forensic break, I still think he and Hopkins will fight it like crazy.'

Don nods, starts to leave. 'I will find you if I hear anything.'

De Vries waits for his door to close, picks up his cellphone, presses a speed-dial.

'If I wanted to find out about someone's history, maybe his current circumstances, and I wanted to go beyond Google, or the usual channels, how would I do that?'

'Give me the name.'

He does. He disconnects the call, questions whether he has made a mistake involving John Marantz; dismisses it, sits up straight and thinks.

★   ★   ★

Just after 5 p.m., Steve Ulton summons them to his lab. Du Toit is already there, and Vaughn realizes that he probably has Ulton reporting everything to him first. Don is standing quietly behind the Director.

'It's only partially good news, I'm afraid,' Ulton says. He gestures to a large computer screen: an image, magnified greatly. 'Wheat chaff, pollen and seed have been recovered from

132

the interior filter of the air-conditioning unit. Not much, as you can see, but it is a new car. They are certainly similar to the wheat particles recovered from both inside and outside of the polythene covering which wrapped the two victims. This is obviously only coincidental, and I can't tell you at what point in time these deposits arrived in the car. They appear to be present regularly, but not continually. In other words, I hypothesize that this car is driven into the countryside routinely, where it picks up wheat detritus in its air-treatment unit.'

Ulton taps a button on the keyboard and a new image is displayed. 'A small blood smear on the interior of the boot-lid. We revealed it as blood, but it's almost negligible. It's been super-heated and diluted, obviously by a steamclean.' He looks up at the three policemen. 'Who has the underside of their boot-lid steamcleaned in a brand new car?'

No one answers.

'I can't even confirm that it's human,' Ulton continues. 'All I would say is that it's only sustained one cleaning — or it would have disappeared. So, if the owner can prove he has the car cleaned this way every week, you could say that the blood is recent.'

Image three: 'The best news. From inside the boot-lock: a small fragment of polythene of the same chemical type that wrapped the victims.' He turns to du Toit. 'You're going to ask me, can I be one hundred per cent certain that this is the same material used to wrap the bodies? I feel that it *is*, but my judgement is clouded by knowledge of other corroboratory factors. Objectively, to you I say, I am ninety-five per cent certain that this is the same material.'

Du Toit and de Vries both shake their heads in unison.

Ulton continues: 'We've already discussed that this type of plastic is no longer manufactured. I made enquiries and this seems to be the case globally. We can't say if some factory in China might still be using it, but it is very rare and, according to records, we haven't seen it before.' He stands back to judge their reactions.

'How big is it in reality?' du Toit asks, pointing at the image on the screen.

'Approximately one centimetre square, rhomboidal shape. I hoped that we could match it to part of the wrappings recovered but, as you may be able to see, the material has become milky and distorted. This is because it was trapped in the boot-locking mechanism, stretched and torn from the main sheet. I don't see any way of making a direct match from the source material. I can confirm a chemical match to the wrapping for the victims. It's the same material, likely to be from the same batch. But, for the purposes of evidence, it is disputable.'

Du Toit turns to de Vries. 'It's not enough. I don't think it's enough.'

De Vries says, 'Alone, no, but we've got him at the dump-site. We have his damn cheese on the heel of one of the victims. We have matching wheat on the bodies, in his car. We have blood on the boot-lid, and we have the same polythene material. That adds up to enough.'

'This is exceptionally good, Steve,' du Toit says. 'Is there anything more?'

'Not yet, sir.'

'You have further tests?'

'Particulate material in the carpets, the last places to search. Not much, I'm afraid.'

Du Toit hesitates, says: 'Wait there, Steve. We may need some clarification from you.'

He walks away from the bench, towards de Vries and Don February.

'I know what you're thinking, Vaughn,' he says. 'Don't think I don't feel it too.'

'I know the evidence is circumstantial. I know it's not enough for court, but it's too much to do nothing.'

'I agree,' du Toit tells him. 'But you have to be mindful of the position we're in. Once we arrest Steinhauer, the spotlight will be on us. If we don't have enough leverage, we could lose him, and get badly hurt in the process.'

'Your finger is on the political pulse, as ever.'

Don February steps back, away from loose shrapnel.

'You want a successful prosecution,' du Toit says. 'Don't think you'll sweat it out of him. Not with that bastard, Ralph Hopkins, you won't.' He draws Vaughn to one side, their backs to Don. Quietly, whispered hoarsely. 'For Christ's sake, Vaughn. We've waited seven years to find this bastard. If Steinhauer took those children, I want him — no escape.'

He turns Vaughn back around; glances at Don.

'You can rejoin us, Warrant.' He pats de Vries' back. 'Colonel de Vries and I have known each other for a long time. It's the difference in our approaches that has made us such a successful team.'

De Vries rolls his eyes.

'This is what I suggest,' du Toit continues. 'Very discreet, twenty-four-hour surveillance of Marc Steinhauer. Full research into the man's background and character. We press behind-the-scenes first, then, if we draw a blank, we make the decision whether or not to go in. On my order. Understood?'

De Vries nods.

Du Toit looks to Don. 'Any observations, Warrant? You are part of this.'

'One question, sir. For Steve.'

Ulton looks up, trots across his lab.

'The two eyebrow hairs retrieved from inside the wrapping. Have you cross-checked them for a match with Steinhauer's DNA?'

Ulton, suddenly realizing.

'No. I've spent all the time on the car.' He looks at de Vries and du Toit. 'I'll do it now.'

'Good question, Warrant,' du Toit says, turning to follow Ulton out of the lab. 'Keep me informed, and get that surveillance under way.'

'Yeah,' de Vries mimics. 'Good question.'

Don laughs.

'What else,' Vaughn asks him, 'do you think?'

'That I am not paid enough to think.'

Vaughn steps into the elevator. 'Very good, Warrant Officer.'

He jabs a button to their floor, suddenly more optimistic.

★ ★ ★

An hour later, two surveillance teams dis-
patched, de Vries is reading Don's report on
Marc Steinhauer. His cellphone rings.

'You want it now, on the phone?'

'Depends what you have.'

'Marc Erik Steinhauer . . . I'll leave out what
you can get yourself . . . Has a private income
from shares, previously his father's, some invest-
ments which he has established since getting
married. Possibly the wife or wife's family's money.
Mary Steinhauer was left three properties when
her uncle died twelve years ago. Together, they're
well off. Fineberg Estate is losing money. Can't
find anything Marc Steinhauer ever did that brought
in an income. He's just been a dilettante. Wife's a
religious type; donated over half a million Rand
to her church — mainstream Anglican. High
church, smells and bells . . . You getting this?'

De Vries is scrawling notes. 'Yes.'

'Marc Steinhauer withdraws fifteen hundred
Rand most weeks from the same ATM, in
Somerset West Mall. Pays for everything else
with credit cards. Bills always paid on time.
Perfect credit scores.'

'Fuck, Johnnie,' de Vries guffaws. 'Is there no
such thing as privacy?'

'Nope. You want more?'

'Yes, yes.'

'Diagnosed with epilepsy at the age of twenty,
was treated over a period of five years; now
appears cured. There's a Stellenbosch newspaper
item twenty something years back about 'Marc

137

Steinhauer, second-year student at UCT', trashing his room, and lashing out at fellow students. Police Medical Officer reported that Steinhauer was an epileptic, who had failed to follow prescribed medication. Released without charge. Suffers from depression. He's been on Seroxat — an anti-depressant — 30mg daily, for the last four years.'

'Where do you get this stuff?'

'Do you want to know?'

'Probably not. There's no trail?'

'Only to me. Can't do it again.'

'That's good. Thanks.'

'Anything happening?'

'Best not say.'

De Vries thinks he hears John Marantz start to reply, but he turns off his phone. He writes up the information, sweeps out of his office through the squad room to the Collator, has it added to the investigative files.

When he returns to his office, Don is there at the doorway, with Steve Ulton. Don sees him approach, starts walking towards him. De Vries senses a change of pace, senses acceleration.

Don says, 'We have got a match.'

De Vries to Ulton. 'Are you sure?'

'One hundred per cent. But listen: only one eyebrow hair. The other is not a match.'

'What does that mean?'

'It means your whole case rests on one tiny hair, a follicle of DNA.'

De Vries, controlling himself: 'Just tell me. Does it fly? Is it solid?'

Ulton. 'Yes.'

De Vries: 'Found on the inside of the

polythene wrapping?'

'Yes. Doc Kleinman noted that it was retrieved from 'inside the polythene wrapping, having been pressed up against the torso of Steven Lawson'.'

De Vries chops the air with parallel palms. 'Right. Let's be completely clear. There is no way this — hair — could be present on that wrapping unless either the wrapping or the victim came into contact with Marc Steinhauer?'

Ulton nods at de Vries, acknowledging the clarity of the question, knowing that this is all that matters.

'I'm not a lawyer. I guess you could argue that it could have reached the victim via a third party.'

Don says: 'The man who buys the cheese, gets one of Steinhauer's eyebrows on his clothes, in his hair, transfers it to Steven Lawson . . . '

'For fuck's sake!'

'We're only playing devil's advocate, Vaughn,' Ulton retorts. 'It could be argued that it is not, without reasonable doubt, conclusive proof of contact between Steinhauer and the victim. The chances against are astronomical but, if I was testifying, I would have to concede that it is possible, just possible, that the hair was delivered by a third party.'

De Vries is shaking, the blood vessels in his temples engorged.

'Jesus Christ. Why is nothing concrete? Nothing!' De Vries looks up, sweat on his forehead. 'Thanks, Steve. We're just so close. It's fucking unbearable.'

Ulton nods at him, leaves the office.

Silence.

Then Don says, 'Du Toit?'

Vaughn gurns, nods, reaches forward to his

desk phone. 'Brigadier du Toit? It's de Vries . . . '

From the corridor outside; his shoes squeaking, even on carpet.

'I'm here, Colonel.'

Don indicates the chair opposite de Vries. Vaughn stands.

'You've heard the news? We have a match.'

'I knew before you did, Vaughn — as you well know. Your reaction?'

'An urge to arrest Marc Steinhauer tonight. Question him at the end of a long day. I believe that we have a strong forensic case against him. He admits to travelling widely. He could easily visit wherever he held those boys. He was at the farm-stall dump-site. Circumstantial evidence is compelling. I think we have enough to pressure him under interrogation.'

Du Toit disagrees. 'Motive? He's a married man, two young daughters, successful business . . . '

'It's an unsuccessful business.'

'You know that?'

Vaughn clenches his eyes shut momentarily, his head angled away from du Toit. He turns back and nods. 'He was an epileptic with a temper. Took drugs to control it. Now suffers from depression. On prescription medication. Who knows what goes on in a man's mind?'

Du Toit frowns. 'How did you discover that information?'

'It's valuable information, from a reliable source.'

'My God, Vaughn. What the hell are you doing? You know you can't use that. You mention that outside this room and the whole case could collapse. And David Wertner will be down on you. He'll cut you to shreds. Don't you know he and Julius Mngomezulu are scrutinizing every move we make?'

De Vries baulks, but replies, 'It's background information. It helps us to judge what we have.'

'And you know General Thulani will also be watching from on high.'

'Why should we always work with our hands tied?'

Don sees du Toit about to retort, but instead he restrains himself.

'All right,' he says instead. 'I assume that Steinhauer is under surveillance now?'

Don, from behind him, says, 'Yes, sir.'

Du Toit speaks, looking at de Vries. 'Check on the current status, Warrant Officer. Go now and come back immediately.'

Don goes.

Du Toit, leaning forward, his hands entreating: 'For God's sake, man. Be careful. We're at what could be the pivotal moment in the case, and the deciding moment in both our careers.'

'I have only one interest, sir. One single goal.'

'To fulfil it, Vaughn, you have to make the case in court. It's no good to us knowing the truth, and Steinhauer walking away on a technicality. You think the guys in Pretoria are going to give a damn about that?'

'I don't care about the bosses.'

Du Toit thumps the desk.

'Well, I do, I do! And so should you. You want to leave the SAPS in the hands of people like Julius Mngomezulu and David Wertner? We're hanging in here. We've made a stand and kept open the chance of one department free of corruption, one entity which might, just might, get the job done. However much we both want this resolved, there is always the bigger picture.'

'The bigger picture,' de Vries scoffs.

'You're the policeman, Vaughn; I'm the politician. We have to have both.'

'I want to find Bobby Eames.'

'So do I. So do we all. Now, play it smart. Understood?'

'Understood.'

They pause to breathe.

'Steinhauer is under surveillance,' du Toit continues. 'Get some sleep. Spend time thinking. When you're ready tomorrow, we'll bring him back in. See where we get with him this time.'

'All right,' de Vries says gracelessly.

Du Toit stands; de Vries doesn't move. Don February knocks on the door, is called in.

'Officers are in position. Have made visual contact with Mrs Steinhauer, two daughters, and a maid. No visual of Marc Steinhauer yet.'

De Vries says: 'Shit.'

'I'll be in my office,' du Toit says. 'Tread carefully.'

When du Toit is gone, Vaughn comes around his desk to Don.

'Get the contact details from Steinhauer's interview. We owe him a call about his car. Call the house, ask for him. If he's not there, find out where he is. Casually. If he is there, tell him we'll deliver his car at noon tomorrow.'

Don turns to leave.

142

'Don. If it's the wife, listen to her carefully. I want to know if she knows.'

★ ★ ★

'He is in Betty's Bay. A beach-house. Their holiday home.' Don, back in de Vries' office. 'She is driving up tomorrow with her daughters, but the maid will receive their car.'

De Vries frowns. 'How did he get there then? We have one car, the wife presumably has the other?'

'I do not know. Perhaps there is a third . . . I will check licences.'

De Vries nods. 'Good. Verify the Betty's Bay address. It could be in her name; her family owned a lot of property. Then, switch the guys to there. Liaise with Betty's Bay — senior duty officer only. Utmost discretion, no fuss. No one in Betty's Bay can know we're there. Make sure they report immediately they see any sign he's leaving. And follow him.'

'Will do. And you?'

'Following orders: going home. I'll call you when I get there, check everyone's in place. Get some sleep, and I'll meet you here at six a.m. And, Don — tonight, go home to sleep.'

★ ★ ★

De Vries lies awake, windows and curtains open to gather the breeze. He's feverish. He hears his family talking in the house, yet knows they are 1,500 kilometres away. He hears wind in tall trees, yet the night is still; sees Bobby Eames in a tree-house, the little cut-out window barred. He sees Marc Steinhauer, with his pageboy haircut, huge cupped hands, his fingers around three young boys . . .

★ ★ ★

At 4 a.m., de Vries wakes, finds his bed wet with sweat, his limbs clammy. He stumbles to the bathroom, urinates, strips and towels himself down, climbs back into bed, rolling to his wife's side, cold and empty, but dry.

As dawn breaks, he finds himself in a jailyard scrum, jostled and beaten. Every man around him is crooked or crazy, greedy for violence, Machiavellian, deluded. Every man is ugly inside and out, and their stench is overwhelming him. He looks up at the overpoweringly dark monolith; in a tiny window at the top, he sees the faces of the top brass, the judges, the press, the public. They watch him falter in the seething mass. They do nothing.

★ ★ ★

By 6 a.m., de Vries knows that Steinhauer hasn't left his beach-house; knows that both du Toit and Don February have beaten him into headquarters. With his little sleep, intense dreams, he feels worse than he did before. As he drives into town, wired and dishevelled, the traffic snarls up at an accident on the Nelson Mandela Boulevard, leaving him to watch the sun come up over the harbour, seep between city skyscrapers, its soft rays already heating the thick air trapped beneath the glittering copper smog over town. To his left, the Mountain looms tall and dark, watching over the city.

★　★　★

'We're unanimous?'

Du Toit in his office, sealed in; four men in his sofa corner, coffee, biscuits: de Vries, Don February and Norman Classon, attorney-at-law.

De Vries says: 'The overriding factor must be Bobby Eames. Norman has told us that we have plenty to make the arrest, hold him. That gives us three days to get him talking, find out where he kept them.'

'But, I reiterate,' Classon pronounces nasally, 'that in my opinion, you will not sustain a prosecution based on the evidence you have. The bulk of your forensic evidence is circumstantial. That eyebrow is, in effect, uncorroborated. A decent attorney will blow that away, since we know that this Fineberg cheese was present at the crime scene. The hair is in the cheese. The cheese could have got there innocently. You have to find supporting links to the bodies. In effect, find the crime scene.'

'We have time,' de Vries tells them, charged. 'I want to interview the wife, his children, his friends. Find out about this so-called aunt in Riebeek West. We know if we do nothing, there's no way he'll visit wherever he's keeping Bobby

145

Eames. The boy will starve before he ever goes there again.'

He turns to Don, who says: 'We have an area to search for this site in. Steinhauer drives every week to Riebeek West. If we find that he usually travels with his family to their Betty's Bay house, then we can rule that out, and we will know he visited his captives somewhere between his Stellenbosch farm and Riebeek. Someone will have seen that big city car there.'

'In three days?' du Toit.

'We have no choice,' Vaughn insists. 'Steinhauer is unstable and we can bring it out of him. I think we have to use his family. He is most protective of them.'

Du Toit agrees. 'It's not going to be pretty, but you are right. Keep it simple, Norman: where are we if we don't get a confession?'

Classon balances his chin on the tips of his fingers, palms together.

'I am afraid I don't think I could recommend prosecution based on what you have. A powerful motive, or even history would carry weight. I agree that the circumstantial elements are strong; a judge could be swayed. But I think I have to say no. He would walk away.'

De Vries says: 'That's not going to happen.'

★ ★ ★

The squad room is busy, extra men drafted in, expectation electric. After seven years, a breakthrough.

Du Toit, de Vries at the board, Don a few steps

146

to one side. Director du Toit clears his throat; the room falls silent.

'Ladies and gentlemen. As you now know, we have a bulk of persuasive evidence, some forensic evidence, pointing to Marc Steinhauer as the murderer of Toby Henderson and Steven Lawson. This leads us to believe that he was their abductor back in 2007. Even those of you not with us then know how significant this crime was, and remains today. We must solve it, honestly, openly and fully.' He looks to Vaughn.

De Vries picks up his cue.

'Marc Steinhauer is under surveillance in Betty's Bay. I will make the arrest at nine a.m., bringing him here immediately by road. You are not to discuss this with anyone outside this room. That means no one. We have to keep this within a small group. We have seventy-two hours to produce a confession, or discover sufficient further evidence to assure a charge and conviction. If we do not get those, we do not have enough. I stress to each of you, if we don't get more, Steinhauer walks.'

He pauses, allowing the gravity of the comment to percolate.

'Steven and Toby were alive six days ago. We must now be optimistic that the third abducted boy, Bobby Eames, is still alive. We must find where Steinhauer imprisoned them, and rescue Bobby. Steinhauer will never return to that site. If Bobby is alive now, then he will starve to death if we don't find him.' He gestures to Don. 'Warrant Officer February will distribute your assignments. Ensure everything is done fully and by the book. Steinhauer's attorney has beady eyes. Everything will be checked. I will be interrogating Steinhauer myself. If we don't break him today, we'll try again tomorrow. You have that time to complete your enquiries and report. We have to make it happen.'

Don steps forward, begins to assign tasks to different officers. Du Toit leaves. Vaughn stands back, his brain numb, spinning with questions, for Steinhauer; for himself.

★   ★   ★

Don finds de Vries in the car park, smoking.

'All done.'

'Good,' de Vries replies. 'When do you leave?'

'Warrants ready in fifteen minutes, then we go.'

'Tell me again?'

'I will question Mrs Steinhauer at the farm. I have four guys with me. They will search the whole estate: focus on plastic wrapping materials, borehole water supply. Personal computers will be seized. Staff to give statements at the estate.'

'Good. I won't start with Steinhauer until I speak with you. I want to know whether they could both be involved. The longer he has to wait, the better. I want him to know we have his wife and children, his staff, everyone.'

Don studies his watch. 'He should be back here by ten forty-five for a meeting with Hopkins. Maybe one p.m.?'

'Whenever. I'm happy to keep him sweating. We need to know for how long Steinhauer went

148

away, how regularly. Was Riebeek West the only place he visited?'

'We have two teams heading there now,' Don says. 'They will go into every shop, every service station, with pictures of Steinhauer and his car. Two officers are visiting the aunt. She is old, but still living at home, with full-time nursing care.'

'Good.' Vaughn lights another cigarette from his glowing stompie.

A call comes from the rear exit of the building. 'Colonel? A Ralph Hopkins on the telephone for you.'

'What?'

'Ralph Hopkins.'

De Vries turns to Don, mutters under his breath, 'Shit.' He puts up two fingers, mouths, 'Two minutes,' watches the officer duck back inside and says, 'How the fuck . . . ?'

'It may be nothing.'

'It's seven a.m., Don. We've got a fucking leak.'

Vaughn can feel the pulse in his head, his heart pumping as if he has been running. He pushes his cigarette into the side of a black car, breathes, watches the bright sparks tumble over metal, flutter to the ground, the butt bounce on the tarmac, still smouldering.

'Get du Toit. Tell him. I'll take it in my office.'

⋆ ⋆ ⋆

He sits, breathes again, snaps the receiver to his ear. 'De Vries.'

Hopkins, wide-awake, calm: 'The truth, Colonel. Marc called me at midnight last night.

149

He claims there are police watching him at his house in Betty's Bay.'

'Marc Steinhauer is not under arrest, Mr Hopkins. I told you that you will be informed if that event occurs. You have my word.'

'You haven't answered my question. This a matter of harassment, intimidation.'

'Police operations are just that. Police matters. I would be very surprised if Marc Steinhauer can see any policemen in Betty's Bay.'

A pause.

'Is that all you have to say to me, de Vries?'

'You will be informed if and when.'

'Very well. Understand this: this is going above you, right to the top.'

Suddenly de Vries finds his voice. It is quiet.

'Anywhere you like.'

He hangs up, stands up. Du Toit appears at his door.

'I'm leaving now,' Vaughn tells him.

Du Toit blocks his way. 'What did he say?'

'Steinhauer called him apparently, last night, claiming he was being watched. He wanted to know whether that was what we were doing. I told him nothing but said that we would inform him when, and if, we arrest Steinhauer.'

'Damn. You better have watched what you said, Vaughn. He'll have taped that.'

'I stated the position. And he's going to pull rank on us, so you can expect a call from above.'

Du Toit swallows, pushes back his shoulders.

'Go get him. Make it textbook.'

★ ★ ★

At 8 a.m., a SAPS driver speeds de Vries across the arid, rocky plateau between the mountains guarding the seaside towns of Rooiels and Betty's Bay. Either side of them, the sun illuminates the tops of the rock-strewn mountainsides, nothing but scrubby fynbos on their lower slopes.

As they circle the guarding mountains, the outskirts of Betty's Bay begin: cluttered, poorly built little houses, architectural aberrations one and all. Behind them, two vast curves of mountain, barren and dark; to their front, the ocean pounding the rocky shore, sending up sprays to catch the first sunlight. The main road is deserted, the town still asleep. They find the mini-mall where the surveillance team is based, turn into the empty car park.

An officer meets them, presents the senior officer, leads them both through a small supermarket and up stairs to a storeroom above the shop. At the window: an officer looking through binoculars, three empty cans of Windhoek Light beer, a takeaway smell pervasive.

'He's there?'

The officer at the binoculars looks up.

'He is, sir. In his bedroom we believe from eleven p.m. last night. No movement noted after that time until five past six this morning. We can't see the kitchen from here, but he's been seen drinking from a mug and walking up and down in the garden to the rear of the property.'

De Vries gestures at the binoculars. 'Let me see.'

151

The officer stands, tilts the plastic chair towards de Vries.

'It's the house directly on the sea. Grey tin roof, open stoep at the back. You can just see the far left corner of the balcony at the front. We realized that we couldn't get anywhere near, so we found this place for height and angle.'

De Vries adjusts the focus on the glasses, then looks back up at the officer. 'Did he see you?'

'Unlikely from here, sir. No reaction. I've been on duty since two a.m.'

'He make any calls last night?'

'Not according to the log, and not while I've been on.'

'No marked cars at any time?'

'Ultra discreet. The shop-owner lives across the way there. We made it clear he was to contact no one, but he couldn't know who we might be looking at.'

De Vries puts the glasses back to his eyes, looks down to the main road to find his bearings, then raises them slowly past one house and garden to the house identified as Steinhauer's. He sees no one, but senses a flickering of light, as if Steinhauer is moving around. The building is modern, smart compared to most of the surrounding architecture. A track leads down from the main road, past a small single-storey property, and onto a wide plot, enjoying perhaps fifty metres of rocky beach. Beyond the narrow, rocky garden and patchy lawn, the plot extends onto the jagged rocks and down to a small horseshoe-shaped bay. De Vries sees a flash of white spray spewing into the air, the wind whipping it horizontally. He waits for Steinhauer, but he does not see him.

'Good. I will now arrest Marc Steinhauer. Continue your watch from above, should he resist. There are four officers at the perimeter. When we have him, we will be driven back, two more officers in a car to escort us back to Cape Town, stationed right at the end of the driveway there. We'll go in three minutes. Ja?'

The officer nods, heads to the back of the storeroom to tell his colleague. Calls are made, arrangements set.

De Vries addresses the Kleinmond officer.

'I'll make the arrest. I want you to keep him calm. If he wants to call his lawyer, inform him he can do so in the car. Agreed?'

They retrace their steps down the narrow wooden stairway, through the dark shop, and back out into blinding low sunlight. The South-Easter has risen and is blowing hard across the landscape.

There is no one in the side street; no one on the main road.

De Vries waits for the officers to disperse around the property. He hears a car powering up the main street, assumes it to be the back-up car, wills it quieter. His cellphone rings.

'Surveillance A reports unknown vehicle approaching, indicating right. Slowing, turning into . . . '

De Vries sees it. A dark blue S-Class Mercedes, one driver, a shock of white hair.

De Vries pockets the cellphone, shouts: 'It's his fucking lawyer. Go now. Go, go, go!'

He starts to run across the main road. Over his panting, the howling wind, de Vries can hear a tinny screaming. Still jogging, he fumbles for his cellphone, puts it to his ear, hears: 'Suspect and unidentified male are outside at rear; argument.'

They reach the house. De Vries shoulders a side gate, feeling the wood crack down the length of his right side. He and two other officers jog around the house to the garden. Vaughn can see two figures silhouetted against the blinding silver sea, Steinhauer stumbling. They run across the garden, around a dark narrow pool, and reach jagged rocks, pick their way gingerly across them. Vaughn shouts for Steinhauer and Hopkins to stop, but his cries are stolen from him by the driving wind.

He looks down for his footing, up again to see Steinhauer and Hopkins still moving away. Glances down, looks up; two officers sprinting from the perimeter, across the garden towards Steinhauer. Looks ahead, blinded by shimmering fireworks of light on the boiling sea.

Steinhauer has stopped at the edge of the horseshoe bay, steep vertical sides fall maybe five metres into chaotic, churning water. Ten metres out, Hopkins is shouting at him, gesticulating. De Vries stops five metres short of him.

'Step back, Hopkins!' he calls. 'Step back here.'

He hears Hopkins shout again.

De Vries runs up level with Hopkins, but maybe three or four metres away from him. Above the wind, he calls out: 'Marc. There's no problem. We've just come to talk. Your lawyer is here.'

Steinhauer turns his face to him, fearful and distraught, then looks away.

De Vries moves forward slowly. 'We just want to talk. We're delivering your car back to you this morning. We're speaking with your wife.'

Steinhauer looks down into the water, back at Hopkins, then at de Vries, holds up his palms, pushes them away.

De Vries stops, says: 'Can we talk in your house?'

Suddenly, Hopkins is shouting, 'Marc. For God's sake. Think of your family.'

De Vries snaps to him, 'Shut up and stay back.'

The two back-up officers reach the scene, stop well back from de Vries, hands on guns. They see de Vries step forward. They watch Steinhauer mime pushing him away. They hear what might be a cry. They see Steinhauer fall off the rocks, disappear. They all run forward.

De Vries steadies himself, away from the edge, but close enough to see down, without getting blown over. The wind howls, the sea is intense and unremitting, foamy, whisked by the jagged layers of interleaved rock. He is soaked by the sharp, stinging spray. He rubs fists in his eyes, tries to focus, finds Steinhauer, his head momentarily visible amidst the surf. An officer is slipping off his belt, preparing to go in.

De Vries stops him, barring his way. Shouts, 'Don't! It's suicide.'

De Vries sees flamingo pink in the foam,

155

Steinhauer's body limp, gashed, repeating soundless thumps against the curving, serrated rocks. Momentarily, it rises, and de Vries see the man's face slashed, spewing blood, his features blurred in the bloody foam on the water's surface. There is no struggle, no attempt to swim, no life in any limb. It is jerked away, underwater, dragged around the edge of the horseshoe, sucked into the next spiky inlet.

De Vries turns to the officers, his voice hard, demanding.

'His body must be retrieved. Call the Coast Guard. Do not enter the water, but do not lose sight of his body. Get him out of there and into a coroner's van. When he is secure, start writing up contemporaneous reports. Exactly what you saw. Everyone comes back to Cape Town.'

He turns to the Kleinmond officer.

'Get men here. Call whoever you need, tell them this is from me. I want this house sealed; the scene untouched and guarded until further notice. You understand?'

The officer looks very pale, unmoving.

Above the wind, de Vries bellows at him: 'Do it now.'

He turns to the other men. 'The moment back-up arrives, we go back to Cape Town in convoy. All of us. *Move.*'

The men run.

Ralph Hopkins comes up close, right in de Vries' face.

'You caused this, de Vries. I was getting through to him. He was going to come in. What the hell did you say to him?'

'You heard.'

Hopkins' face is red, windblown and lashed by salt spray. His eyes are bulging.

'You threatened him.'

'Fuck off, Hopkins. You heard.'

'You threatened him and he stepped back in fear.'

'That is not what happened — as you well know.' Their faces are almost touching now; neither man backing down. 'You have no right to interfere in a police operation. If you're not in Cape Town with the rest of us, I'll issue a warrant for your arrest.'

Quite deliberately, 'I'll be there.'

★ ★ ★

De Vries reaches the house, turns once more to the sea, closes his eyes, rubs them hard, screams into the wind. He feels a wave of blackness roll in towards him; more weight than he can bear. He pulls himself up, staggers back towards the driveway, and then across the main road to the side-street.

As he reaches his car, his cellphone rings. It is du Toit. He answers, listens, shouts above the wind: 'Imagine the very worst fucking scenario . . . Then double it.'

PART TWO

'Suspend de Vries,' General Simphiwe Thulani says.

'I have no power to stop you, sir.'

'Not me, Henrik. *You*. If you suspend him, if you are seen to suspend him, it will bolster your position. It will provide a chance for a new man.'

'That's what you want, isn't it?' Du Toit stares past Thulani and out to the tall grey buildings, reflecting the blinding sunlight; behind them, the tablecloth of bright white cloud peeping over Devil's Peak, seeping over the crest of Table Mountain. 'To have your own appointee take over this inquiry and sideline my department. I won't let that happen.'

'Henrik,' Thulani continues smoothly, calmly, 'you should consider your own position in all of this. De Vries is the de facto face of this entire business. If you want to remain where you are, it may be necessary to make clear your repentance . . . with a sacrifice.'

Du Toit, standing: 'Forget it. We have six witnesses who say de Vries was nowhere near Steinhauer when he jumped. The guy was unstable, and he was just about to be arrested for crimes stretching back seven years and all over the national headlines.'

'To be arrested and to be convicted are two different things. Now you have to find unequivocal proof. I have always felt that your loyalty to

161

de Vries is misplaced. He will take you down with him.'

Du Toit is scornful. 'I didn't know you cared, sir.'

'I advise once more, on the record: allow me to allocate a new department to this matter.'

'No. You have no authority. I have taken advice from above and they are clear that the investigation will be concluded by my teams.'

'From above,' Thulani echoes mockingly, raising his eyebrows. 'Then you have one chance: find the evidence, make it so clear even our blessed media can understand, tie it all up neatly and close down the case. Don't complicate it; don't go looking for hidden messages. If you can do that, the SAPS comes out of this well. Any other outcome and you, and your department, will struggle to survive.'

'That's what we intend to do.'

'If you've done your groundwork, Marc Steinhauer can be fully implicated, the case closed. No one will shed a tear over what might have happened to him.'

'He took his own life.'

'That remains to be seen.'

'That,' Du Toit snaps, 'is the fact of the matter.'

Thulani stands, brushes down his dark pin-striped suit, fastens a jacket button.

'So be it. Your department is responsible. Sort it out.'

'We will.'

'If you don't, we will all be making the trip to Pretoria — and some of us won't come back.'

Thulani's office door opens as Du Toit makes

for it. Julius Mngomezulu holds it for Du Toit.

'And Henrik,' Thulani says quietly, 'when I send Julius here for an update from you, I expect you to provide one. Do I make myself clear?'

Du Toit says nothing, sweeps past Mngomezulu, out of the brutally air-conditioned office, through the thickly carpeted anteroom, and into the tepid concrete corridor.

★ ★ ★

Five hours of interviews by the Police Incident Investigation team; efficient, unerringly inquisitive, but respectful. One saving grace: Steinhauer was not in police custody at the time of his accident. He had not been arrested. Four back-up officers, one surveillance officer, and Colonel Vaughn de Vries, all singing from the same songsheet, all recollecting corresponding facts, similar impressions. Ralph Hopkins, advocate, claiming threat and intimidation, but without conviction and, crucially, without corroboration. No witnesses have heard the dialogue between them. Hopkins cannot remember the exact words; indeed, no words he cares to repeat. The Warrant Officer from Kleinmond makes it clear he witnessed no intimidation and no vicinity to the victim: all were at least ten metres away from him. Two were unsighted; four believe he deliberately stepped over the edge. Hopkins is uncertain about this, but agrees that there was no physical contact between the SAPS and his client. His protestations become more vague; more quietly delivered. The investigators lose interest in Hopkins, hint at

163

a rapid conclusion to their enquiries. De Vries takes no comfort from this.

Don February, his questioning curtailed; Mary Steinhauer and her children to comfort, now protect and respect for their loss. His men still search their house, wrap what might be evidence in sterile plastic bags, label them with numbers and letters. Pathologist Harry Kleinman examines an unrecognizable, shredded human body, pickled in brine, rust-coloured scratches covering its surface like cross-hatching on a fading pen-and-ink drawing. De Vries, devoid of energy, still and despairing in his office, watching time pass, waiting for release from his procedural incarceration. Teams of officers work on, unsure whether all is in vain: there is no momentum, no direction.

★ ★ ★

Du Toit comes to de Vries' office at eight p.m.

'It's over, Vaughn. Incident Investigation have gone; signed off. No suspensions, no delays. They're independent for now so we'll get no undue influence. Thulani's been put in his place by the brass and we're still holding the reins. We have to tie this all in to Steinhauer as quickly as possible. I've told February that, whatever the circumstances, he proceeds with a full investigation into Steinhauer's activities. The beach-house remains under our control and all items confiscated from the main residence stay with us until we're satisfied. Whatever the tragic events of Betty's Bay, this man is still under suspicion on a number of counts. We'll take some stick in the press to begin with, but I think we can let it be known that he remains a very strong suspect for the dumping of the two bodies, and is therefore implicated in everything from their deaths to the previous abductions.'

'That all sounds very neat, sir.'

'That's the way it will be described by us; if the press want to mix it up, we can't stop them. I want you to review everything we have, and pray it all comes out as we think. The teams in Riebeek West, the surrounding areas, and approach roads are still active and will remain so. When we question Steinhauer's wife and staff, we may get a vital lead to the murder site, and with it, Bobby Eames' whereabouts.'

'Are you taking control?'

'No. I was merely . . . outlining future activities during your enforced absence from the inquiry. I will continue to oversee your conclusions and relay them to the press.'

'And what if my conclusions are not black and white? What will you do then, sir?'

'That is not an option. There are eyes everywhere, and they are not connected to very sophisticated brains. We need answers — simple answers.'

'The one thing I tell you, right now,' de Vries says miserably, 'is that this is not simple.'

Du Toit looks down at him. 'However bad you feel now, you have to keep it together. You have to lead this investigation, because if the pressure was on before, it's twice as heavy now — for both of us.'

De Vries stares ahead.

'Go home, Vaughn. I'll coordinate here, and get everyone away at a decent hour. I want you here at eight a.m. tomorrow morning and we'll convene before everyone is assigned new tasks at nine a.m.' Du Toit sighs. 'You're no use to anyone like this.'

'It keeps playing out, over and over again,' de Vries murmurs. 'I can't get it out of my head that he's gone. We wait seven years to catch him and he escapes.'

'Escapes?'

'Yes. Just that.'

'My God, man, he's dead. Don't go talking about 'escape' when every wall in this city has ears.'

'My mind has never left this case, sir, for seven years.'

'Get the evidence, tell the story. Find Bobby Eames: Steinhauer won't have escaped then.'

De Vries gets up, takes his jacket from the back of his chair.

'I need to think,' he says.

'You need to rest.'

'Can't.'

'You have to.'

'Not the way I'm made.' De Vries opens his office door, gestures du Toit out, locks the door, murmurs, 'Sorry.' Du Toit watches de Vries accelerate away from him down the corridor.

★ ★ ★

John Marantz drives his old Mercedes back home through tunnels of trees, the side streets of Newlands smelling damp and fresh after the evening

166

shower. It is dark around him; the streetlights have been stuttering to life in the mornings, fading away as night falls. He crosses the deserted freeway, turns up towards the mountain; changes to a low gear as he accelerates up the steep gradient leading to Vineyard Heights and his little mountain hideaway. As he reaches the end of the cul-de-sac, he opens his garage doors with the remote; he hears his dog barking. Under his neighbour's overgrown bougainvillaea, he sees a figure. He brakes, extra aware of threat, since he is holding stacks of 200-R and notes in his loose jacket pockets. He switches his headlights to full beam; the figure stirs, stumbles towards him. It is Vaughn de Vries.

'I couldn't drive, Johnnie.' He slaps his hand on the roof of Marantz's car, swaying slightly. 'I took a cab; it dropped me off here and drove away before I found you weren't in. I wasn't walking all the way down there, thought I'd wait. It's after midnight.'

'It's three a.m.'

'Must have slept. Where were you?'

'Poker game. You're lucky the security guys didn't pick you up.'

'They're probably in the next bush along.'

Marantz takes his arm.

De Vries says, 'I need to talk to you.'

'I thought you might.'

1985

At the age of nineteen, Vaughn de Vries served his two years in the South African Army. To

167

avoid active National Service, some of his friends studied subjects they couldn't begin to understand at universities both in the veldt and abroad. Others left the country for good; still more had family who rallied to exert influence to ensure home posting, desk jobs or the assurance of unsuitability. When Vaughn received his call-up papers, Piet de Vries was eating a big farm breakfast, swimming in oil. He watched his son opening the summons and just nodded.

'Best be over it, boy.'

★ ★ ★

Three months later, Vaughn finds himself out of training, buzz-cut and bruised, humiliated and dehumanized, with an acknowledged aptitude for logistics and planning, but to be used as a foot soldier. He refuses the chance to return home before being posted to the border — to fight, he knows, in Angola with the UNITA rebels against the Soviet-backed MPLA, who loathe the all-white South African army.

His troop-leader seeks to demean him, but always breaks their stare first. Vaughn silently questions every move, every tactic. He says nothing, but the other men know that he challenges the captain. He is allocated a scrawny, nervous buddy to supervise; a college dropout, bright but naive. Vaughn knows that his leader hopes that this man will drag him down, distract him for a moment, lead him to make a fatal mistake.

They climb down the koppie towards two

stone-built buildings perhaps fifty metres apart. They stop, crouch low in the crackling dry scrub, twigs scraping on coarse oiled fabric like chalk on blackboard. They are so close to one another that their arms in their thick fatigues are touching. He turns to meet Rikhardts' eye, oblivious to the sweaty painted mask of camouflage heaving and quivering. The man's eyes are bloodshot, encircled by burgundy not painted on. He takes out his water-bottle, unscrews the cap, offers it to Rikhardts. He watches the man take a first gulp, then restrain himself, still wary of squandering the ration; he sips three times, before passing it back to de Vries, his hand shaking.

'There's no time to rest,' de Vries whispers hoarsely. 'You okay to go on?'

Rikhardts nods, his eyes wide.

They scan the scrubby, sandy landscape. There is little cover between their position in the tiny valley at the edge of the koppie and the two buildings. The hot wind blows unrelentingly, deafening them on one side of their heads. De Vries gestures Rikhardts to take the right-hand building, indicates that he is to survey the building anticlockwise. He raises his weapon, proffering some cover.

'Go.'

Rikhardts scampers away across the barren rocky ground, sliding behind low windblown scrub level with the far wall of the building, looks back at de Vries, raises his gun. De Vries scans the perimeter quickly, checks his boots, scans from the other direction and then sprints to the corner of the left-hand building. As he runs, he catches a glimpse of four men running low, perhaps half a kilometre away. He recognizes their shapes, their gait, their attire. These are his men. He has his section to check, they have theirs. No one can fall behind.

He stands, back to the chalky stone wall, sees no windows on this far end, begins to edge around to the rear of the building, his back scraping against the crude bulging building blocks. He glances around the corner: nothing. He scans the ground behind the building, which drops down to a shallow river valley lined by skinny trees with a diagonal gait, before rising up into a large tor of heavy dark rocks. He is out of range should a sniper be hidden there.

He twitches around the corner again, neither sees nor hears any sign of life, and sharply twists his body around so that his back is now hard against the rear wall of the building, his gun pointing down the length of it. This wall contains a door almost at the far end, but no windows that he can see. He edges along the wall, suddenly crouches low. In the far distance, there is gunfire: the MPLA men are close. His heart starts to pump, his palms sweat. The wind propels harsh cries, another burst of fire. It is so hot that it is sucking the spit from his panting mouth, yet suddenly he freezes. To his right, he senses movement. He turns to see the wooden door of the building open outwards, the door shielding whoever might emerge. He raises his weapon.

The man steps out, the wind slams the door, and he suddenly twists, gun pointing. De Vries'

170

swollen, dehydrated fingers struggle to prime the weapon. He achieves it, faces the man, aware that they are mirroring each other: weapon under the right arm, left hand at his side, palm up, eyes bulging, breathing hard. Time stops. De Vries meets the eyes of the tall, thin, black man, sees the blood pumping in his exposed veins, his arm straining, shaking. The man's left leg collapses suddenly and he grimaces, eyes never leaving de Vries'. The MPLA fighter is topless, the left leg of his combat fatigue trousers ripped and shredded, a makeshift bandage over his left kneecap, a shining slick of dark oily blood running down his bare leg to his dusty boot.

They stare at each other. De Vries realizes that the man is downwind of him, must be able to smell his sweating fear. But the fighter is injured and his weapon begins to tilt towards the ground. De Vries finds that, almost subconsciously, he is allowing his weapon to fall too. The fighter nods at de Vries very slowly and de Vries echoes him. The fighter takes a wobbly step backwards; de Vries also, his mind racing, knowing that prisoners are not welcome, slows down the move forward, and he has neither will, nor heart, to kill this emaciated, wounded man. They both back off further, eyes locked, until the man reaches the end of the wall. He jerks his head upwards; de Vries sees only white discs flashing, and then he disappears around the corner of the building.

De Vries edges to cover at his corner and then he exhales; a breath that seems to last minutes. The utter futility of their action overwhelms him;

exhaustion hits his brain and he hunches up and dry-retches over the shifting dust of the ground beneath him. He draws himself up, shaking and dizzy, takes a swig of water, does not regret the stand-off, believes it to have been the logical stratagem, knows that he has no choice but to back his judgement, to store it away, never to reveal it to anyone.

He stows his flask, begins to edge back to the rear wall, prepares to push on to their goal. He surveys the territory once more, seeking the next point where they can find cover, remembers Rikhardts, turns around the corner once more and sees him, his back to the far building, moving towards the end of it. Rikhardts looks up, sees de Vries, tilts his weapon upwards and continues his move. De Vries takes a deep breath, then rounds the corner and begins to slide along the rear wall again. Rikhardts reaches the corner of his building and steps out to cross the twenty-metre space between the buildings. De Vries looks behind him and then, at the sound of two jarring, ear-piercing shots, sees Rikhardts fall, watches blood rise like a fish-pond fountain, be whipped low by the wind.

De Vries hears his heart thump three times, suddenly grits his teeth and charges along the back wall of the building, reaches the corner and runs straight out, weapon primed. He sees nothing, runs to the front corner, looks right, then left, sees the same MPLA fighter sprinting, bow-legged but agile, away across country towards the koppie they have climbed and then hard left towards the river and the giant rocky outcrop of the tor. He is already beyond range. De Vries contemplates giving chase, the anger in his stomach cramping him, leaving him breathless, but he knows that he wants Rikhardts to live more than he wants the fighters dead.

He sees breath in Rikhardts' body as he kneels over him, takes his head in his hands, tilts his upper body towards him gently, tenderly. He looks at Rikhardts' milky eyes, feels him convulse, watches his final breath and feels nothing but stillness and a hot, sticky damp as the blood oozes over his right arm.

De Vries lowers the body and crouches over him, eyes shut. He does not pray; does not meditate. He knows that this moment will never leave him, understands in a way he has never done before that every decision he makes will have a consequence, questions himself over and over as to whether what he perceived to be self-preserving logic was nothing more than selfish, unadorned cowardice.

2014

At 4.30 a.m., de Vries wakes, mind full of youthful memories, uncertainty, confusion. Marantz is smoking a joint, bare feet up on the coffee table; still running through hands played, pots surrendered, wondering how his luck can run so badly for so long, slowly accepting that whatever luck he has had has gone — that it is now a negative vacuum into which every moment of chance is sucked.

Outside, it is silent.

'What are you doing here?' de Vries mumbles. Marantz smiles at him. 'I live here.'

De Vries looks up at the tall ceiling, the empty minimalism.

'What do you want?'

'That's my line.'

De Vries struggles up, notices the wine, murmurs, 'I need to piss.'

He stumbles on the stone steps, turns on several lights before he finds the one to the guest bathroom. When he returns, he tops up his still-filled wine glass, takes a long sip, and then gets up. He gropes his way to the kitchen, spits out the wine in the sink.

'I need water.' He pours himself a full glass and downs it. Then he refills it and comes back to the fire, almost falling over as he sits back down.

'No home to go to, Vaughn?'

'You know,' de Vries says, stretching his legs and grimacing at his stiffness, 'that's the one thing I don't like. Not being alone in a house, not the absence of a woman in my bed, not even that I have to do everything myself — it's just that house. It's the family house, and that part of my life is in the past. I've done that, and now I have twenty years to do what I want to do.'

'And then retire?'

'Who wants to fucking retire? What the fuck will I do then? Twenty years before the cigarettes and booze get me.'

'You're not a normal man.'

De Vries chuckles. 'Not right now, anyway.'

'Your case — is that why you're pissed in my driveway?'

'Fucking suspect went and threw himself over a cliff right in front of me. That's two abused, tortured, teenage corpses and my number one suspect, jumping to his death. And there's one more boy — just maybe, please fucking God maybe, still alive — and the whole fucking thing is going dead again.'

'This the guy I researched for you?'

'Yeah.'

'What else do you want me to do?'

'Nothing, man.'

'So why come here, Vaughn?'

'I can't sleep in my office every night. Where the fuck else is there for me to go?'

★ ★ ★

The sun, still hidden on the far side of the Hottentots Holland Mountains, lights up the morning sky, bleaching out stars and extinguishing the freeway streetlights. They have been talking for two hours — mainly de Vries: everything he can think of. Marantz pushes him into the bathroom, finds him a towel, lends him his shaver, then calls him up to his car.

De Vries, bleary, says, 'I can call a cab.'

'No, man.'

'You've been up all night . . . '

'I can sleep all day.'

The old motor roars, silencing the dawn chorus, echoing back from the mountain face. Marantz backs out, watches his garage doors slide closed, the wasps following their moving nest precariously stuck there like honeycomb, before accelerating up the little hill to the apex of Vineyard Heights, then he freewheels down the long, steep street and turns hard left onto Rhodes Drive and left again at the traffic lights onto the freeway, past the University campus, towards the city bowl.

De Vries is silent, eyes half closed.

'Two observations,' Marantz starts. He glances over at de Vries, who nods without stirring. 'Abuse cases always lead back to family — father, uncles, grandparents maybe? Do you know anything about Steinhauer's family?'

'Not yet. What you gave me on Marc Steinhauer's private background — you gave me more in a couple of hours than we could ever have found. How did you get that?'

Marantz overtakes a smoking Toyota Corolla and swings around the uphill corner until the whole panorama of the docks, the Waterfront and beyond, the sparkling steel-grey water of Table Bay is laid out ahead of them.

'Favour from a mate of an old colleague. Can't make a habit of it, I'm afraid.'

'Shame. Hard information is what we never have here. Feels like I've been conducting this investigation with my hands tied behind my back. No breaks; no cooperation; no knowledge. What else do you think?'

'Just, it strikes me, three abductions, maintaining those kids all this time, never being noticed. Definitely sounds like work for more than one man, don't you think?'

★ ★ ★

Julius Mngomezulu still marvels at the audacity that has brought about the eighth floor of the SAPS Operations centre; the floor which houses Brigadier Director du Toit's department: four incident rooms for serious crimes within Cape Town and its environs: overarching, overreaching. Murder, kidnap and abduction, rape, robbery: all of it high-profile, all of it press sensitive for the reputation of the SAPS in general. Most of it, white crime.

He snorts to himself when he thinks that people might imagine the racial make-up of South Africa like a chessboard: black and white, black and white, each living next to the other. If it were like that, there would be sixty-three black squares and one white — on the edge, probably, he thinks, with a gap between it and the other squares. After 1994, it was never supposed to be like this any more: no innate privilege, no special treatment.

He closes Colonel de Vries' office door, locks it, and pockets the key. He checks that there is no one in the squad room and then walks confidently to the stairs and up two floors to the administration level. He has the materials to hand now; he has a boss who will act. Soon, there will be no special cases, no priority for the rich and newsworthy. He feels a long way from where he was born in Khayelitsha. His studio apartment which, from afar, overlooks the harbour, his education, clothes, even the branded watch on his wrist — all tell him that. But he knows that, until every crime against every person in South Africa is treated just the same, until every victim is equally important, he will never forget where he comes from.

★ ★ ★

'You look like shit, Vaughn.'

De Vries looks at du Toit's dress uniform.

'I don't have to look good on television,' he shrugs.

'So you haven't slept? Big deal. Neither have I and neither, I imagine, has Warrant Officer February.'

Du Toit looks out into his anteroom, sees Don standing by his secretary's desk, beckons him in, points at a chair in front of his desk.

'Firstly, this.' Du Toit gestures at the newspaper on his desk. 'Someone has gone to the papers. I don't know who it is, but this ramps up the pressure.'

De Vries murmurs, 'Probably Hopkins.'

'Whoever it was, it seems we have their support as of now. They could have gone down a very different route. Now, you two have to put everything together and prove that we were right.'

'I'm restructuring the investigation.'

Du Toit stares at Vaughn, says quietly, 'What?'

De Vries stands up.

'I'm sick and tired of guessing in the dark. I'm taking Don off what he was doing with Steinhauer's homes and Fineberg Farm. I want him to revisit the original case with objective eyes and see how Steinhauer — or known associates, whoever they may be — could fit in. I want to look into Steinhauer's background, his family in the past, and his family now.' He turns to his Warrant Officer. 'Who do you rate, Don? Who can you trust with what you've been working on?'

Don tries not to glance at du Toit, tries to stay focused on de Vries.

'Sergeant Thambo — Ben Thambo. He is an efficient officer, a good organizer and he is capable of collating all the information.'

Vaughn looks at du Toit, then back at Don.

'Thambo? Can he handle it?'

Don makes a point of turning in his chair, meeting de Vries' eye.

'Yes, sir.'

There is silence for a moment, before du Toit says, 'All right, Vaughn. If February here has faith in this officer, that's good enough for me. Get to the point.'

'The point,' de Vries tells him, 'is that once Don is fully up-to-date on the original case, we have a lot of people to interview — Steinhauer's brother, Dr Nicholas Steinhauer, for a start. I want to revisit the psychological profiling we were given at the time.'

'Nicholas Steinhauer?'

'He made a point of commenting at the time of the original abductions, as you'll remember, sir. Criticized our investigation on television, in print. He claimed to be an expert in child psychology. That strikes me as too much of a coincidence.'

Don clears his throat, receives a nod from du Toit.

'After we gave her the news about her husband, I asked Marc Steinhauer's wife about his family. She said that she would try to contact his older brother, but that he was abroad.'

'Where?' de Vries asks.

'She did not say. I can find that out.'

De Vries says: 'Where is she now?'

'With her father, in Rooiels.'

'Get her in.'

Du Toit announces, 'Be careful, Vaughn. We need people's cooperation. Leave Mary Steinhauer for a day or two. It's Sunday, for Christ's sake. Whatever Marc Steinhauer may have done, we must respect his family's right to grieve. This is an influential family, known to the media.'

'And what about Bobby Eames' family?' De Vries is loud. 'This isn't just a murder enquiry, this could be about finding that child and bringing him home.'

Du Toit opens his mouth, but stays mute.

'This is what I'm talking about,' de Vries says. 'We've been respectful for far too long. We have to get this moving now.'

Du Toit nods his head; Vaughn can see his thigh vibrate, his ankle twitching, tapping out some nervous rhythm.

'Twenty-four hours,' de Vries says. 'Out of respect.' He does not say the last word with reverence. He turns to Don, tosses him his keys. 'The case files are in my office, half on my desk, the remainder on the filing cabinet behind. Sit in there and read.'

Don gets up, leaves, shutting the office door quietly.

De Vries sits in silence, waiting for du Toit to speak.

'I trust you, Vaughn,' du Toit says finally, calmly, 'and I'll back you. But be mindful that everything we do will be put under the microscope.' He sees de Vries about to say something. 'And — be careful.'

Vaughn stands. 'I will be 'mindful', sir.'

'Good.'

'But I won't be careful.'

★ ★ ★

David Wertner works silently in a corner office. From time to time, he looks up and out to his adjoining squad room, where his officers sit at computer monitors, researching and reporting. Occasionally, he writes in a slim notebook to his left. He trusts none of his personal thoughts to the computers. He knows how information on computers can be found, can be studied, can even be altered or deleted. He does not even trust his superiors. Wertner likes the fact that his negotiated position grants him access to everyone's thoughts and deeds — no matter how trivial they may seem — no matter how important and influential they believe themselves to be. He sits back in his executive chair for a few moments. These reflections of power relax him; he has control.

★ ★ ★

La Perla is a long-established Italian restaurant on the Sea Point riviera. The old money of the seafront suburb lunch and dine here, either in the high-ceilinged main dining room, hung with

181

modern oils, or on the terrace under the gnarled branches of bottlebrush trees or the shady leaves of Carobs. The main road passes beneath, and then the promenade — and beyond, the Lido and the crashing Atlantic. It is the kind of restaurant that cultivates its regulars and greets them personally, with handshakes and hearty chatter.

Vaughn de Vries climbs the steps, is ignored by the staff, and walks briskly to a prime table at the front of the terrace in the shade. He sits down opposite Ralph Hopkins.

'This could have been merely a ploy, Colonel,' Hopkins greets him, 'to get me somewhere out of the way for a police questioning.' He chuckles, brays.

'This is two professionals behaving as such, helping one another to conclude a very difficult matter.'

Hopkins leans back in his chair. 'That sounds acceptable . . . if you're paying?'

★　★　★

David Wertner stops, turns back two pages in the file he is reading. He slips off his rimless glasses and stares out towards the main floor of the office. He looks down again, scrutinizes the pages; flips to the photographs he is studying. He releases the pages, pushes the file to one side and brings another next to it; flips pages until he finds the paragraph he seeks. He follows the passage with his thick finger, looks from where he stops to the adjacent file. Smiling grimly, he begins to write in his notebook. His writing is faster, the letters and symbols smaller. He feels his palms sweating, puts his pen down onto his desk blotter, wipes his hands on a handkerchief, and takes up his pen again. The tip of his tongue appears between his teeth.

★　★　★

Don February stops reading, but he stops physically, too; freezes. He studies the page, sits back down in de Vries' comfortable but delicate chair. He wonders what to do. As an individual, his loyalty lies with de Vries: the man is difficult, he is bigoted, but he is fair, has always treated him well. He could have been working nine to five in front of a radiation-oozing computer terminal in an office for David Wertner, but instead, he is here. De Vries intervened personally and took him in. As a policeman, as a husband, his loyalty is to the department, to the SAPS. He thinks some more, his heart beating out the seconds.

★　★　★

Ralph Hopkins eats fried calamari and a salad of prawns; de Vries orders a rare steak. This, Vaughn thinks, sums them up. He watches Hopkins peeling his prawns with his small pink fingers that look like prawn flesh themselves; feels mildly repulsed.

'Isn't it time,' the lawyer says, 'we cut to the chase? I mean, charming though your small talk is, Colonel, I am aware of the maxim about free lunches.'

183

De Vries lays down his fork.

'It's simple really,' he says. 'Your client is dead. We hope that you will cooperate with us in discovering the truth.'

Hopkins chews; looks up at de Vries.

'The truth is very important.'

Vaughn starts loudly, checks himself.

'If — and I know you think otherwise — if your client is guilty of these crimes, there is a chance that a young boy is still alive. That should be our priority now.'

Hopkins looks at him scornfully, looks at de Vries' plate: meat eaten, a bloody pool surrounded by untouched vegetables.

'My client's confidence is unaffected, Colonel, and you should know that I represent Marc's family also. I will be present when you interview Mary Steinhauer and, though I hope you will refrain from doing so, his two daughters.'

'I am aware of client confidentiality.'

'On that basis, ask your questions. You may not believe it, but my intention is not to disrupt your inquiry. We have all read about those children.'

De Vries reflects: no denial, no instant defence of his erstwhile client.

'Why were you at Steinhauer's holiday home yesterday morning?' he asks.

'I told you during our conversation that morning that Marc had called me late at night to tell me that he felt as if he was being watched. Your manner is revealing. When I asked you whether this was the case, you as good as told me that it was. That being so, I felt my place was with my client.'

184

'So early?'

'I wake early. What with the roadworks and the rush-hour traffic . . . you have to allow time.'

'Did you speak to Mr Steinhauer as you were driving?'

'I did not. I hoped that Marc would be sleeping. He was under pressure at work and your enquiries were disturbing, to say the least. Marc Steinhauer was a gentle man; he was emotionally exhausted and concerned for his family.'

'So why go to Betty's Bay? Why not stay with his family?'

'I can't answer that. I can't speak for Marc.'

'Were you concerned at his state of mind?'

'I considered his state of mind only so far as I have described it to you. I was aware that he was under a great deal of pressure. If you are asking me whether I thought he was suicidal, then of course not.'

'You accept now that his actions were entirely of his own doing?'

'As I have stated: I believe that if I had been left alone with him, I could have brought him back into his house. We might be in a very different position now. The approach of numerous men, some of them armed, probably tilted the balance to panic.'

'I don't accept that.'

'Then we will have to disagree.'

De Vries sits back, wondering what he can get from this man.

'Will you go to the press?' he asks.

'No. Why would I do that?'

'To manipulate them?'

Hopkins smiles, relaxed. 'Are you a conspiracy theorist? Why would I want publicity for a client I believed was innocent?'

De Vries nods slowly, making a show of accepting the logic of the answer.

'Did Marc Steinhauer describe what he saw in his house in Betty's Bay, that led him to believe that he was being watched?'

Hopkins opens his mouth, misses a beat.

'No — I don't recall. He said that he saw police cars, more than usual for the neighbourhood.' He picks up his fork, begins to turn over the leaves in his salad, hunting for avocado pear.

And you, thinks de Vries, your manner is also revealing.

'Did you believe him?'

'I didn't disbelieve him.'

De Vries snorts. 'That's what you get paid for, isn't it?'

Hopkins looks at him, his head cocked.

'Never to answer a question directly.'

Indignant: 'I did not disbelieve that you might have placed surveillance on my client; neither did I discount the possibility that Marc was paranoid. He feared that you would come for him without notifying me, and prevent me from representing him during questioning. Is that direct enough for you?'

'Did you assure him that I would do no such thing?'

Hopkins laughs sourly, sips his Sauvignon Blanc. 'Not in so many words.'

'Marc Steinhauer dumped the bodies of two teenage boys in a skip behind a farm-stall. We have a witness who places him there, behind the kitchens, DNA evidence that confirms he handled at least one of the boy's bodies.'

'I've seen no such evidence.'

'You will. If he dumped those boys, he knew who killed them, knew who abducted them and where they were kept. Did he tell you where they were kept?'

'Of course not. It would not be unethical for me to say that Marc revealed nothing privately to me that he did not discuss with you in interview. He maintained his complete innocence. I believed him then and, until you show me evidence to the contrary, I believe him now.'

'That is very professional of you.'

'This has nothing to do with professionalism. Marc admitted to driving into MacNeil's farm-stall. He was quite open about it. There is no evidence that he got out of his car — which he denies doing — and I have not been shown any evidence which links him, even remotely, to those two boys.'

The bill is laid at the centre of the table. Vaughn slides it towards himself, places a credit card in the small black folder, pushes it away.

'If I find that you have withheld any information which could lead us to where those boys were kept — where one boy is still imprisoned — for seven years, I will pursue you forever.'

Hopkins finishes his wine, smiles back at de Vries.

'Then I have nothing to worry about. Whoever took those boys, if one is still alive, I want to see the culprit caught and tried. Don't doubt me on that.' He places his napkin on the banquette. 'When do you intend to interview Mary Steinhauer?'

'When I'm ready.'

'In Cape Town?'

'Wherever I say. You will be informed.'

'I hope you will not separate her from her family. I hope this brittle exterior of yours conceals a man with some . . . compassion.'

De Vries repeats: 'You will be informed.'

★　★　★

Don meets de Vries in the SAPS building's main foyer, blocks his way to the elevators, ushers him onto the street, tells him to follow. They walk in silence to Long Street, then up to a small Mexican café. There is no one on the street but for some forlorn tourists. Don talks to the dreadlocked man behind the tatty wooden counter, and then leads de Vries through a door covered by a painted face of Che Guevara, and upstairs to a small private room: four threadbare sofas, a burned wooden coffee table, the smell of old cigar smoke, stale beer. Don gestures for de Vries to sit down. Don sits down opposite him, opens his briefcase, pulls out a file. He finds the page he is seeking, flattens it out and swivels the file to face de Vries.

'It's bad news.'

De Vries looks down at the file: a page to which a copy of a photograph has been stapled. Underneath the picture is typed: *Claremont, 9 March 2007?* The picture is a mug-shot of

188

Robert Ledham. The arrest date: 23 July 2005.

'Where did this come from?'

Don bows his head. 'The abductions docket. The original inquiry.'

De Vries shakes his head, frowns.

'There's no reference who submitted it, but it accompanies work reported by Constable Kohle Potgieter.' Don peels back a sheet and shows de Vries the previous entries in the same typeface.

De Vries stops shaking his head. 'It wasn't there,' he says. 'I have read these files repeatedly. It isn't even a contemporaneous entry: there is no page number.'

'It was in the pile you hadn't reached yet.'

'I've read all of it. Do you understand? All of it. Many times.'

'It looks like addenda material. Casual information, inserted as background. Easily missed.'

'No, Don. I would have remembered Ledham. When you came to me with his name, I didn't know it. I knew he had not been involved with the inquiry.' De Vries is completely certain. Almost completely certain.

'I've not reported this,' Don tells him.

De Vries dismisses that information. 'Du Toit has the authorized copy. I want to check that.' He falls silent, unmoving. 'You did the right thing, Don. Waiting to show me this first. It's not right.'

Now Don is quiet. Neither move, yet both are focused.

De Vries is the first; he stands up. 'This needs to be sorted out now.'

★　★　★

De Vries takes the authorized copy of the 2007 multiple abduction case from du Toit's office, his secretary shunned. He carries it down to his own office. Don February stands inside by the door, closes it after him, remains where he is.

De Vries spreads the file, rifles through the pages, pulls out the exact same page; a photocopy. He stares at it, doubt flooding him, his brain drenched and disorientated. He looks at the paper, compares it to the surrounding pages; the pages have the same hue, lightly faded and fingered with grease. He swallows. It is inconceivable to him that he has failed to process this page, this addition. He cannot believe it, yet it is there, in front of him. He looks up at Don.

'It — it's not right, Don. I trust myself.'

'So, what does that mean?'

'If I don't trust myself, I have nothing.'

Don stares at him, watching self-belief ebb. He says quietly, 'Talk to Kohle Potgieter. Ask him if he remembers submitting this material.'

De Vries sighs, rubs his face. 'I can't. He's dead.'

'What?'

'Shot four, five years back; interrupted an armed robbery in Kenilworth. Two officers murdered, one bastard killed, three more living at our expense somewhere, still with their lives.'

'Jesus.'

'This stinks, Don.' De Vries is still again, his hands bracing his desk.

'Do we bring in Ledham?'

De Vries turns to Don February, exasperated. 'No. Robert Ledham did not appear in the

190

original inquiry. I know I haven't seen this before
— *I know it.*'

He stands straight, points at Don. 'Find out
who has had access to the file in the last few
days. Ask his secretary, ask du Toit if necessary.
Tell him it's from me, because this . . . I don't
understand.' He gathers his jacket and starts to
move.

'Where will you be?' Don asks him.

'Talking with my Inspector.'

★ ★ ★

De Vries uses the snail's pace on the Eastern
Boulevard — or Nelson Mandela Boulevard as it
has been grandly renamed — to call Dean
Russell. First his cellphone, then his home. His
wife tells him that Dean will be home soon; he
has been playing golf. De Vries checks that he
has their new address, wonders how his old
colleague will look. He has not seen him for four
years.

The house in Rondebosch is a double-storeyed
Victorian on a large corner plot. De Vries walks
past the swimming pool, through a playground of
over-sized toys, follows Lizzie Russell to the stoep,
wide and airy, overlooking their tree-filled garden.
She gestures to one of the wicker sofas.

'We haven't seen you for ages,' she says as she
puts down a can of Windhoek lager in front of
him. 'Have you seen anything of Dean?'

'No,' Vaughn tells her. 'Too much work, too
much pressure. You know how it is.'

'Leaving the SAPS was the best move Dean

ever made. For himself. For all of us.'

De Vries gazes at the garden. 'Looks like it.'

She smiles out of the corner of her mouth. 'You still with them?'

'Just about.' He snaps open the ring-pull on the can, takes a sip, nods towards the garden. 'This is nice. When did you move here?'

'Two summers ago. It's close to the kids' schools; they have a garden to play in. Before, we could never have afforded anything like this.'

Vaughn murmurs, 'No.'

They hear a car drawing up, the gates to the short driveway opening, then the garage door rising, an engine idling, revving finally and dying. Dean Russell appears through the garden, almost jogging, cheerful. He sees de Vries, stops and frowns, walks forward and smiles uncertainly.

'Vaughn?' He looks up at his wife, who says: 'Your cell was off.'

Dean Russell pats his trouser pocket, leans forward to kiss her. He turns to Vaughn, offers his hand.

'Social call?'

'No. I need your brain for a few moments.'

Russell points at de Vries' can. 'Another?'

'No.'

'I'll get myself one and join you.'

He turns to his wife, smiles reassuringly, leads her back indoors. Vaughn hears hushed voices, and then Russell returns, sits at the other end of the sofa from him, swivels to face his old boss.

'What do you want, Vaughn?'

'Not pleased to see me?'

'Not if this is SAPS business, no. You could

192

have contacted my office tomorrow.'

'This is a personal favour.'

'Okay . . . '

De Vries leans back in his chair, focuses on Dean Russell.

'You look well. Security suiting you?'

'You know it is.'

'Girls okay?'

'They're eleven and thirteen, and they're women already. What is it, Vaughn?'

'Mine are good too,' de Vries continues blankly. 'In Jo'burg now, studying, but doing good.'

'So, everyone's good, man. Just tell me why you're here.'

De Vries puts down the can, sits up. 'Think back to Steven, Bobby and Toby.'

'Oh Jesus, I read about it. Those two boys . . . it's for real?'

'Oh ja. Very real and just like last time. Nothing concrete, nothing that links. But I need you to think back for me, Dean. I need you really focused. How many times did you reread the dockets?'

'This is six, seven years ago. I don't know. I got away from all that, put it out of my mind. Had to.'

'Well, I need you to think about it now. For me. Think of the suspects we questioned, those on the paedophile list. Was there a Robert Ledham?'

'How should I know?'

'We lived that case every single fucking day for months.'

'I don't know.'

'Think about it for me. Robert Ledham. Is

that a name you recognize?' He watches Russell thinking. 'Kohle Potgieter might have written an addenda notice on him.'

Russell shakes his head. 'No. I haven't heard that name before. I can't tell you that it didn't come up, but I don't remember it. Why?'

'Long story. You sure you've really thought, Dean? We've talked to him just now because he was in the vicinity of the dump-site for the two boys, but now a new page has appeared in the original murder book and the authorized copy. A page with his mug-shots from an earlier arrest, a note suggesting he might have been in Claremont on the date Bobby Eames was taken: ninth March, 2007.'

'That all? Why didn't we follow it up? We would have tied it up, for sure.'

'That's what I think.'

'What's going on?'

'I don't know. Either we missed this guy — God knows we had enough to work on — or maybe someone thought we'd spoken to him and didn't follow it through. But I don't remember that name and neither do you, so this is shit, and I have to work out what kind.'

'Is he a possible suspect?' Russell asks.

De Vries is in a trance.

'Vaughn?'

'No. That's the point. He's turned up now after we spoke to him. But if he was involved originally and we let him go, it's going to look bad, and I have Internal Investigations looking at me, scrutinizing everything we did, and they want to get me, Dean.'

194

'We would never have let a lead go like that.'

'I know.'

'Is someone messing with the docket?'

'It's possible. If they have, they've done a good job. The paper looks old; the copy feels right. I'm beginning to doubt myself.'

'For what it's worth, boss, I don't doubt you. Didn't then; don't now.' Russell lets himself relax into the wicker armchair, takes a draught of lager. 'This is why I left. Every day you deal with the scum of the earth. Not a fucking decent guy amongst them, and then your own colleagues, someone on the team, higher up, lower down, they come and stiff you.'

'Maybe you made the right decision, after all.'

'You ever doubted it, man? I lead trained men. They're mixed, and some of them are as thick as shit, but on the whole they're okay. I go to meetings, I organize and instruct. But, you know, things happen, work gets done, clients are happy — Jesus, I even get thank-you letters. There's even some respect. I don't have to work the front line, no stress. My migraines are gone. I have a happy wife, happy kids. All I worry about is paying the mortgage each month, and wondering if I'm going to get laid ever again.'

De Vries raises his beer can. 'Welcome to a long and happy marriage.'

Russell laughs, but he is still serious. 'In truth, I couldn't take it. I had to leave to survive.'

De Vries gets up. 'I'll leave you to your braai.'

Russell stands, shakes Vaughn's hand, meets his eye.

De Vries says, slowly: 'Robert Ledham?'

Russell pauses, but Vaughn knows it is only for show.

'Nothing. It means nothing.' He puts his hand on Vaughn's shoulder. 'If we didn't follow it up and run it down, it wasn't there.'

De Vries, almost completely certain now, says: 'No.'

★ ★ ★

Don February reads: 'Robert Ledham was arrested on twenty-third July 2005. Pinelands division were called to a playground where Ledham was taking photographs in the kiddies' park. Two mothers called them in, suspicious of a middle-aged man with a bag of sweets in his lap, photographing their children. According to the report, he became abusive when officers tried to move him on. They arrested him. He was questioned and then released; no charge.'

'Despite his conviction?'

'For whatever reason, they did not find his conviction in Pretoria.'

'Why didn't we know this before, when Ledham's name first came up?'

'It is the same story as usual: one piece of information is lost, then the whole chain of data becomes contaminated. Even the divisional computers do not talk to each other. There was not a charge. They did not know about Pretoria. It probably was not even entered.'

Don February is sitting up in his chair, facing de Vries across his desk.

De Vries mutters: 'Fucking circus.'

Don looks back at the print-out on his lap.

'He was required to check in with police in PE when he moved there a couple of months later. That is where he lived until 2009, when he came back to Cape Town, to Muizenberg, where he still lives.'

'The entry is only a question: was Robert Ledham in Claremont the day Bobby Eames was taken? And, even if he was, did he take him? Why would he, eight hundred ks from home? And he's into little girls, isn't that right?'

'It does not say here, but that is what he told us.'

De Vries scowls. 'This is bullshit, Don. Someone is messing with us. Who had that authorized copy?'

'I spoke to the Director himself. He said that Colonel Wertner requested it yesterday.'

'Wertner?'

'Kept it until twelve noon today, then had it delivered back to the Director's office.'

'Anyone can get into my office,' de Vries muses. 'Wertner probably has a key to every fucking office in the building.'

'Why would Colonel Wertner try to mislead the inquiry? Why would he take that risk?'

'Wertner has his own agenda.' De Vries starts tidying the files on his desk, locking certain ones into a filing cabinet behind him, slamming each door.

'What now?'

'We ignore it. You're going to have to trust me, Don. If I screwed up back then, I'd tell you, and I know that I didn't. Whatever the reason for this shit, whoever is responsible, it is designed to delay us — and that is not going to happen.' He looks at his Warrant Officer. 'You satisfied with that?'

Don hesitates only for a second. 'Ja. If I change my mind, I'll tell you first.'

'All right.' Vaughn stands up, starts to count items off on his fingers. 'Tomorrow, we go to Rooiels to interview the Widow Steinhauer. I want two local cops there with us. Call Ralph Hopkins — he's the family's lawyer too — tell him we'll be there at ten a.m. Next, find out where the psychologist is, the guy who profiled our abductor. His name was Dyk. Tell him what we want to talk to him about and set up a time in the afternoon, say three p.m.'

Don nods.

'Did you find out about the brother?' De Vries asks.

'I have someone on it. He left South Africa five weeks ago, flying to Buenos Aires, Argentina. We called his office in Johannesburg, but there is just a recorded message saying it is closed for two months from five weeks back. I requested that local officers visit it to find a contact number, but I have not heard back.'

De Vries pats his Warrant Officer's shoulder. 'Good, Don. That's good.'

* * *

David Wertner has worked with the now General Simphiwe Thulani for eighteen years. Where Thulani has gone, Wertner has followed: loyal, dependable, predictable. He is under no illusion

198

as to why Thulani has kept him so close. An honourable black man keeps a grifting coloured man at his side for one reason only: it is his dream ticket. Thulani will ride it all the way to the top. He has his Zulu supporters and Wertner will keep the embittered, disenfranchised coloured men and women officers quiet with veiled promises of happier times to come. And David Wertner knows that if Thulani can rise under Mandela and Mbeki, it is certain that under a Zulu like Zuma, he will move further and faster.

When Thulani got the nod for his promotion this time, Wertner knew he had to move then — to diverge from his leader's path. The deal was simple: his continued patronage, but his own department. A new Internal Investigation Bureau, structured to his strengths, with promises to realign the old guard so that men like Henrik du Toit and Vaughn de Vries would never rise again. Let them believe that there is no glass ceiling and then entomb them. And Thulani, so pleased to be ahead, at last, of Henrik du Toit, agreed. Now, Wertner has control. He could even break Thulani if he pleased. This independence gives him such confidence.

'Who watches the watcher?' He often meditates on this theme, rubbing his wide buzz-cut scalp, smiling to himself that the new South Africa is not entirely new.

★ ★ ★

Don February drives de Vries along the same twisting coastal road that leads to Betty's Bay.

199

They draw up in the preceding cove, down at the edge of the beach where, in a sprawling Tuscan villa, Tony Hansall waits with his mourning daughter and his confused granddaughters. He meets the officers as they get out of their car, leads them inside to the kitchen through the side entrance, and offers them coffee. They take their mugs, but Hansall stands between them and the internal door.

'My daughter, Mary . . . she is still coming to terms with what has happened.' He bows his head, breathes deeply. 'I haven't shown her the newspapers.' He stands over them. 'You have to understand. Marc wasn't a clever man — he wasn't particularly talented. I have been lucky, so the family have money. But he was a good husband, a good father. What they are writing in the press — it isn't true. I would have known. Mary would have known, and she would have come to me.'

De Vries says gently, 'Nothing is proven. That is why we needed to speak to your son-in-law. Now, regrettably, we must speak to his wife. I give you my word that we will do our best to be sympathetic. But we must discover the truth. I hope you understand, sir.'

'What made him do that?'

That, de Vries thinks. Take his own life.

'I don't know. He may have been involved and feared for his family — what such revelations might do to them. Perhaps he couldn't face it.'

'I don't understand,' Hansall replies grimly. 'I don't understand where you, or the press, could get these ideas.' He opens his mouth, searching, but nothing comes out of it except the sound of the waves on the shore over his shoulder. He snaps to.

'I accept that it is your duty.' He stands aside from the doorway, puts his hand on the handle. 'Mary is in the sitting room through there, with the lawyer.'

Vaughn nods and turns, but Don asks, 'Ralph Hopkins: is he your lawyer also, sir?'

Hansall shakes his head. 'No. I don't care for the man.' He looks at de Vries. 'I will be with my grandchildren. Call out if you need me.'

★　★　★

Mary Steinhauer and Ralph Hopkins rise as the two men walk the length of the sitting room to join them by the wide French windows which overlook the rocky beach and the waves coldly crashing onto it. Hopkins handles the introductions and gestures for them to sit. He sits on the edge of the sofa close to Mary; de Vries and Don on the soft, low sofa opposite them.

'I want to start,' Hopkins announces, 'by thanking you both for coming here. This is a gesture that is appreciated at this time.'

'And we,' Vaughn responds, meeting Mary Steinhauer's gaze properly for the first time, 'commiserate with you, and apologize for disturbing you. As I hope Mr Hopkins has told you, we need to ask you some questions about your husband. I know that they will not be easy for you to answer, but I ask you to be candid with us, so that the truth in all these matters

— whatever it is — can be discovered.'

Everyone looks at Mary Steinhauer, perched primly on the edge of her sofa, back straight. She speaks in a brittle tone, impatient, without a trace of hesitation.

'Let's get on with it, shall we?'

Don physically recoils; de Vries sits back and looks at her.

She is wearing a dark fitted suit, businesslike, her hair tied back from her face.

'Don't misunderstand me,' she says. 'I loved Marc. But when it is the middle of the night and you are all alone, and it is so black, so hopeless, that there is nowhere lower to fall, it allows you — allowed *me* — to think clearly. So I will tell you what I know, and you will go away, and one day, I hope you will tell me the truth, because not knowing . . . I can't bear not knowing.' She turns to Hopkins. 'Let them ask anything. What does it matter now?'

Hopkins smiles kindly at her, says: 'I am here to support you, Mary, my dear.'

Mary Steinhauer looks at Don.

'You visited the winery, didn't you? When you left, Marc would not look at me; would not talk to me. Then you came back,' she turns to de Vries, 'with him — and took Marc away. When Ralph brought him home, I had never seen him like that before, not in fifteen years. It was as if he could not focus his thoughts. He was burning up, couldn't sit down, couldn't think. I begged him to stay at the house, but he would not. He could not talk to me; could not even interact with our daughters. I knew then that he was in

202

serious trouble, that he had done something which he could not face discussing even with me.'

'Mary,' Hopkins intervenes. 'We do not know that.'

'But I knew Marc,' she tells him firmly. 'We always spoke about every problem, every decision that presented itself to us. We worked through every dilemma. So, forgive me, but I know what his behaviour meant.'

'I have to assume,' de Vries says, 'that Mr Hopkins has explained to you, or you have seen reports in the media, the reasons for us deciding to arrest your husband?'

'I think the implication is quite clear: that he was involved in the deaths of those two boys. What evidence did you have to support that theory?'

De Vries hesitates. The interview is so different from how he had imagined, how it had played out in his mind, as he sat alone but for the triangle of dark bottles, late into the early hours in his big empty house.

'I don't think that it is helpful to tell you only part of our investigation. I want to tell you the full story, once we have it.'

Hopkins says, 'The police were arresting Marc on suspicion of involvement, merely suspicion.'

'Can you tell us,' de Vries asks quietly, 'did your husband make any comment to you, either after he was first visited by Warrant Officer February, or latterly, following his interview in Cape Town?'

'He was upset that his cheese had been found near those dead boys. He said that he couldn't understand it, how it was impossible. We sell more and more products now — they must get everywhere — so I thought it an overreaction, but Marc seemed to take it very badly.'

'Did he make any further mention of it?'

'No. But he looked unhappy all day long, very pale.'

'And after his interview?'

'As I said, he was distraught. Ralph told him, in front of me, that there was no evidence suggesting that he was involved, but that did not reassure him. He told me that he was going to Betty's Bay to be alone, to think. I begged him to stay; to share his anguish with me, to be with his family, but he was resolute. We agreed we would join him the next day at lunchtime, once I had arranged everything at the winery.'

De Vries continues smoothly, 'Did you speak to him after that?'

'Marc called me just after he passed this house, to tell me that he was almost home.'

'But not from your home in Betty's Bay?'

'No. We don't have a landline there, and the signal on the cell is intermittent because of the mountains. Often we get no signal at all.'

'Did he make any other comment?'

'No. He wished me goodnight; told me not to worry.'

'And the next morning?'

'No. That was the last time I spoke with Marc.'

They pause for a moment, then de Vries says, 'How often did your husband travel away from the winery and your home?'

'Most weeks. He took it in turns with his brother to visit their aunt in Riebeek West. We also own an olive farm, about thirty kilometres past Riebeek-Kasteel. He would combine both duties.'

'Would he stay away overnight?'

'Very rarely.'

'And would he travel to the Betty's Bay house on his own?'

'On occasion. He would go there to read, or just to get the house ready for when I and the children arrived.'

'Any other travel?'

'No.'

De Vries smiles reassuringly at her; she seems to look through him.

'How close was Marc to his brother? Nicholas, isn't it?'

She looks at de Vries scornfully. 'Don't patronize me, Inspector.'

Hopkins corrects her. 'Colonel.'

'Colonel, then. Ralph has already told me that you were the officer who ran the inquiry into those boys disappearing all those years ago. I know that my brother-in-law made much of the failure of the police, made himself quite the celebrity. It embarrassed Marc. What do you want me to say about Nicholas? That he is a conceited, arrogant man professionally, cold and unsupportive personally? He might have charmed the cameras, but it did not work on me. We never saw Nicholas socially: I met him only a handful of times, but I know Marc saw him at their aunt's.'

'Did you ever visit your husband's aunt?'

Mary Steinhauer is about to answer, but she checks herself.

'I — once. I had insisted on seeing how the olive farm had progressed. We called in on her briefly. She was very deaf, very crippled. I never had cause to go to our land again; Marc told me that there was no need for me to visit her. Perhaps I should have done.'

'Did your husband make any comment to you about his brother?' de Vries asks.

'He was afraid of Nicholas — afraid and, I think, in awe of him. He rarely said anything about him. I don't believe theirs was a close family.'

'Your husband just had one brother?'

'No. There was a sister. She came to our wedding, but I haven't seen her since, and Marc never spoke about her. She lives in the country, in the Karoo, I think. If Marc did see her, he didn't tell me about it. But, as I said, his was not a close family. There were never any family occasions, not even Christmas.'

De Vries leans forward, speaks quietly.

'You mentioned that you remembered the initial incident, seven years ago now, when the three boys were abducted from Cape Town?'

'The moment I read about the boys' bodies being discovered, I remembered that time.'

'Do you recall whether your husband was in Cape Town at the time of the abductions?'

'I do.' She answers quickly, precisely. 'And he was not. He was at our farm on all those three days. He did not travel anywhere.'

'You remember that clearly,' de Vries says, 'seven years back?'

Again, scorn, irritation.

'No, Colonel, I did not remember that. I keep a diary. I have done so since I was a child. Last night, while I was thinking about everything that has happened, I looked at the diary from 2007. I did remember that I wrote in it about those events, because we organized a prayer meeting for those children at my church, prayed for them every week, for many months. But there is no mention of Marc leaving, and I would have noted that. I would prefer not to show you my diary but, if you deem it necessary, I will fetch it for you.'

De Vries says, 'Why did you check your diary?'

'I just told you that.'

'But why? Why check at all?'

She stares at him steadily. Very slowly she replies, 'For the reasons you are thinking.'

'What are they?'

'That a wife knows when something is wrong. I had never doubted Marc before. But . . . ' She stops, her mouth open.

'Mrs Steinhauer?'

In the hush, they hear the waves breaking over rocks, one swell after another. De Vries counts the ebb over and over again, wonders how anyone could live with the incessancy. Mary Steinhauer is frozen.

'Perhaps a break?' Ralph Hopkins murmurs.

De Vries holds up his hand; repeats her words.

'You never doubted your husband, but . . . ?'

She starts calmly. 'I should have insisted he stayed with us. I should never have let him drive off alone.'

'You couldn't have known.'

'I did know.' She throws her head back, closes

her eyes, the first sign of an emotional rather than a factual response. The first time, perhaps, that she has departed from what she had planned to say. 'I did know. I knew when I asked him whether he had anything to do with those boys. I knew when he told me no. I knew when he looked at me and tried to make me believe. I knew when he told me on the telephone not to worry.'

'You felt that your husband might take his own life?'

Hush falls again.

'I knew,' she begins, 'that you had discovered something in my husband's life, so shameful, so awful, that he could not tell me.' She grimaces, seems far away. Suddenly, she looks up at de Vries. 'Do not question my daughters. Do not put them through that. Children do not need to see every facet of their parents. Mine saw love and care, and compassion, and happiness. Do not destroy everything I have worked for.'

'I don't need to talk to your daughters.'

She exhales deeply, as if her breath had been held all this time.

'Thank you.'

De Vries looks to Don, still writing on a pad on his lap. Don bows his head respectfully at Mary Steinhauer.

'You said your husband rarely stayed away from home overnight. Did he stay away last Sunday night?'

She answers him very quietly. 'He did. He told me that his aunt had asked him to stay. I suppose he was lying then, just as I now realize that he lied to me throughout our marriage.' She echoes

Don's bowing, her whole body quivering. She does not look up.

'We are nearly done.' De Vries turns to Hopkins, then asks Mrs Steinhauer: 'I need permission to visit and search your olive farm. Do you have any objections?'

She swallows, drawing herself up. Tells him, 'You have searched my homes already. What do I care if you search there? Ralph will give you the address, and directions.'

'Good.'

'I may be with my children now?'

'Yes, of course, and thank you.'

She stands and the men follow suit. She indicates Don.

'Ralph, please take this officer into the hallway and provide him with the details of my olive farm.'

Hopkins looks taken aback, eventually nods uncertainly, gestures to Don, and they walk away. She watches them leave, waits until the door to the sitting room is closed, the brass handle stops moving.

'I have a terrible fear,' she tells de Vries, 'that I have been blind. I do not know why I think Marc was involved with those boys, but when I thought back over the years, tiny things came to me, and I realized that I had been nursing a feeling of unease all this time — a tiny doubt, deeply repressed.'

De Vries thinks of his own inner questioning of his wife: her reports to him of her day; her returns home late at night; strange scents outside his expectation; her mood unmatched to her description of her acts.

'We never really know anybody,' he says.

'I remember one more thing, Colonel. I couldn't say it in front of everyone else. It came to me just before I was about to fall asleep late this morning. When I thought about it, I sat bolt upright. One day, many years ago, when we were alone together, he said to me: 'Thank God we had girls'; that we have two beautiful young daughters. I hadn't thought of those words in all this time and, suddenly, I knew they had meaning.'

She stands back from him, blinking, refocusing. 'Perhaps you think I am a terrible wife. Perhaps you think that a wife should stand by her husband, come what may. I would, if he was here. I would have laid down my life for him, for my children. But now . . . There is one boy unaccounted for, isn't there?'

'Yes. Robert Eames.'

'He is why I have said what I have said. Perhaps some good will come of it. But you must find him, bring him home to his family.'

'That is what we want to do.'

'Then do it.'

De Vries nods, begins to turn away.

Mary Steinhauer says: 'When you know what Marc did, tell me first. I need to know, and I need to prepare my daughters. Do you promise me?'

'I will tell you as soon as I can.'

She holds out her hand, delicate but steady. 'Don't forget me, Colonel.'

'I will not,' Vaughn says.

★   ★   ★

'That was not what I expected,' Don says when they rejoin the main road, heading back along the coastline towards Gordon's Bay and then Cape Town. 'Not at all.'

'No.'

'What did she want to say to you when she sent us out?'

De Vries seems lost in thought, murmurs, 'Marc Steinhauer told his wife that he thanked God they had had daughters. Meaning, I suppose, not sons.'

They sit in silence as Don steers around the sharp bends and up onto the raised road, curling its way along the wild coast. It is a beautiful road, unnoticed by the occupants of this car.

De Vries says, 'You were very quiet.'

'I was amazed, and I was writing, trying to understand her. So was Mr Hopkins. I think she silenced everyone.'

'And what did you learn?'

'I want to reread my notes, but the matter of the phones stood out. She said that he called her from Rooiels, because there was no landline at their house, and the cellphone reception was bad, sometimes non-existent.'

'So?'

'Ralph Hopkins said that Steinhauer called him at midnight from his Betty's Bay house. That does not sound right now, does it? Perhaps we should check Marc Steinhauer's cellphone and see if that call was made?'

De Vries nods thoughtfully. 'Yes.'

'Mrs Steinhauer said that she read all about Steven and Toby's bodies being found; had

211

watched the television reports. When we asked Marc Steinhauer why he did not react to appeals for information, he said that they never read newspapers or watched television.'

'Indeed.'

'But,' Don says sadly, 'maybe it is nothing. Maybe she reads the papers and watches the television and he did not. I think it is only more of what we have already.'

De Vries turns towards the driver's seat and states: 'Marc Steinhauer knew about the murders; maybe he was responsible. Either way, he dumped their bodies. He was probably involved from the start, and I think his wife suddenly realized it, too. That must have been a terrible moment.'

'But to tell us all of that, so calmly, so factually.'

'I think,' de Vries says, 'that she felt betrayed. And ashamed, that she had not noticed anything before. That's why she spoke out.'

De Vries lets Don concentrate on pulling out from the Gordon's Bay turning onto the N2 freeway.

Then he says: 'I believe her when she said that Marc Steinhauer was not in Cape Town when Steven, Toby and Bobby were taken. Why lie about that? That means there are others involved. We have to speak to Nicholas Steinhauer, because I think he is implicated in this. I think he played us all for fools seven years back, spouting that crap on television. I remember what he said very clearly: child-trafficking; 'the children will be out of the country'. That's what he said, and I think he said it for my benefit, to throw us off.'

'We have not located him.'

'Johannes Dyk said that whoever was responsible was trying to make a point; to prove his psychological superiority. Maybe that's what Nicholas Steinhauer was doing.'

'According to the reports, Dyk also said that the children had been trafficked and were no longer in the country. Maybe he too tried to put brakes on your investigation?'

De Vries turns to Don. 'You're right. Does that implicate him? You see what I am saying? Everything and everyone seemed to be working against us then.'

'I set up a meeting for us with Dyk at two-thirty. But I spoke to a nurse who looks after him. He is very ill. Cancer, Alzheimer's Disease. She says that he is not always able to speak, that he is not . . . '

'Compos mentis?'

'I do not know what that is. She said 'lucid'.'

'We'll deal with that. Jesus. Where does this thing begin?'

'What do you mean?'

'How many people were involved? Look at what we have: Nicholas Steinhauer and Johannes Dyk — two experts — and they both give us opinions which were diametrically wrong. Were they deliberately misleading us? Could one have been pressurizing the other? Whatever it was, it served to distract from a trail that led to those boys.' He shakes his head. 'All right, whatever state he's in, we find out what Dyk has to say, and before that, I want to locate the sister too. I want to hear what she knows.'

'I will find her.'

'This is messy, Don. Marc Steinhauer is dead; Nicholas may be in the wind. We may never learn what really happened.'

'Surely we only want to find Bobby. If he is alive, he tells us everything.'

'That's why I'm worried they won't have left him alive.'

'What about the Fineberg olive farm?'

'The moment we get back, find it on a map and get teams out there straight away. Tell them to take dogs, to look for a cellar, some completely secret or underground building. Tell them to take armed officers. We don't know if someone was guarding them. If those brothers visited the boys, that would be the obvious place.'

'You do not sound excited?'

'I'm not. The logic seems faulty. What was Marc doing with the bodies in his car at Sir Lowry's Pass if they were kept out at Riebeek? And to find Bobby there, to find him alive . . . It seems too simple and, so far, nothing about this business has been simple. Nothing at all.'

★　★　★

'She thinks he's guilty?'

De Vries looks at Director du Toit's disbelieving expression.

'Incredible, isn't it? But after twenty years doing this job, I know that you can never tell with the public. Never predict anything.'

'All the same . . .'

De Vries briefs him on the meat of the

214

interview, his plans for a full search of the farm, his concerns about Nicholas Steinhauer.

'Somehow,' du Toit says, 'that doesn't surprise me so much.'

'Abuse cases, paedophilia — it all goes back to the family. That's what I was telling you before. I'm going after them. There's a sister too. We have to find her. I want the teams that were canvassing everyone in the Riebeeks to take a photograph of Nicholas Steinhauer, re-question everyone. See if he was there regularly.'

'Be careful with Nicholas Steinhauer. Your run-in with him back then plays just too well for the press to ignore. They'll root it out and broadcast it to everybody. We cannot let it look like revenge.'

'He's either involved, in which case I don't care what the press say, or he's not, and maybe we'll find out what the hell is going on.'

'All right, this is good, Vaughn. But don't forget. Whatever we know, we have to prove it to the media, or this thing isn't over.'

'We have to find Bobby Eames. To hell with the media.'

★ ★ ★

As they reach the house of Johannes Dyk, Don takes the call that tells him that teams have arrived at the Fineberg olive farm, thirty kilometres north of the country town of Riebeek-Kasteel.

'Ben Thambo suggested contacting the architect of the olive farm, to see if the plans included cellars.'

215

'Good idea.'

'He is doing it now. He will relay any information to the search teams.'

They ring the bell on the wall guarding the tall Victorian house in Kenilworth. There is a sharp buzz, and they push open the heavy gate, enter a lush garden. On the open stoep, sitting in the shade with a blanket over his knees, they see an old man with straggly white hair, seemingly asleep. Vaughn realizes that this is Dyk.

They are met by a rotund white woman, and a young black woman in a dark blue nurse's uniform.

Vaughn proffers a hand. 'Colonel de Vries, SAPS. Mrs Dyk?'

The white woman's voice is clipped and precise.

'I am Nancy Maitland. I look after Dr Dyk.' She turns to the black nurse. 'This is Beyonce, one of Dr Dyk's carers.'

Beyonce smiles grimly, remains several paces back.

'I think,' Nancy Maitland says, 'you should come with me.'

They follow her around the house to a side room, its doors opening onto a small parterre garden. They take seats under the pergola.

'Dr Dyk is a very sick man,' she says. 'He has lung cancer, which we hope radiotherapy may have caught in time. However, he is very weak, and the treatment seemed to bring on what the doctors call Alzheimer's. To me, it is senility, but it leaves him very confused.'

'But he still lives here, at home?'

216

'Dr Dyk is wealthy enough to be able to have care at home. If the cancer comes back, he will only have a few months.'

'And you?'

'I have looked after Johannes since he moved to Cape Town over thirty years ago. I ran his home for him. He is a very brilliant man, a fine man to work for. I was not going to abandon him in his time of need.'

'That is good to hear,' de Vries says.

She shifts in her chair.

'Why do you want to speak to Johannes? Am I permitted to know that?'

'Dr Dyk helped the police with some psychological profiles a few years back. We want to ask him about the case — if he remembers — to see if he has thought any further about it.'

'I doubt he will be able to help you. I am afraid that the treatment has affected him very badly.' She brushes her lap, sits up straight. 'When you talk to him, be patient. Sometimes he seems lost and then, suddenly, he will remember everything.' She rises, gestures at the nurse. 'Beyonce will take you.'

* * *

They sit alone with him. From one moment to another, he does not seem to remember they are there. It is almost as if he is dropping into a momentary deep sleep, waking anew, unaware of reality only seconds before. First Vaughn, then Don, try speaking with him, but each time he looks up he sees them with surprise, asks them

217

their names, over and over again. De Vries just stares at his bleached pink face, the sagging skin, tiny claw-like hands.

Don asks: 'Do you remember the boys who were taken? Steven Lawson, Bobby Eames and Toby Henderson?'

Dyk's expression changes; his eyes open more fully.

'Yes,' he says. 'Those boys were taken, but nobody ever found them. The police never found them.'

'We think we know who was involved now,' Don tells him.

'Oh, good. That's nice.' Dyk seems unconcerned, his attention waning.

'Two of them were found dead, shot only a day before, last week. Do you want to know?'

'Those boys?' Dyk says. 'Did you ever find who took them?'

Don glances at de Vries, turns to Dyk, enunciates slowly.

'We think Marc Steinhauer. Nicholas Steinhauer is his brother. He is a psychologist, like you. Did you ever meet him?'

Dyk looks blank.

'Steinhauer,' de Vries repeats.

'I am a doctor,' Dyk tell them proudly. 'Not in general practice. I work with the human mind. That is what I do.'

Don's voice is calm, and soothing. 'Did you ever work with a Nicholas Steinhauer, sir?'

'No,' Dyk tells them positively. 'I came from Kenya in 1979, and I have been here ever since.'

De Vries closes his eyes, stands up, begins to wander away down the stoep.

Don leans forward in his chair, touches Johannes Dyk on the back of his hand. The little man jumps.

'Hello,' he says.

'Marc Steinhauer?' Don repeats.

'No.'

'Did you know his brother, sir? Dr Nicholas Steinhauer?'

'Oh yes,' Dyk says, quite brightly. 'I like Marc. He is a gentle man. Not very strong, mentally or emotionally, but kind.'

'Marc?'

'Yes, Marc.'

'You met him?'

'Yes.'

'When?'

Dyk shifts uncomfortably. 'I lived in Kenya. Then I moved to South Africa, but Kenya is in my blood. I knew I would come back.'

'Where did you meet Marc, sir?'

'Marc?'

'Marc Steinhauer.'

Dyk thinks deeply for a moment, says: 'No.'

Don smiles at him, nods. 'I go now, sir. You rest.'

Don walks the three steps down to the garden, pauses and looks back at Dyk. Dyk waves at him, almost smiles.

'I like Marc,' he calls out weakly. 'A kind man. Not like the other two.'

Don turns back to him, hops up the steps. 'What other two?'

'There were three boys . . . three boys. Then there were only two. Three then two? Three or

219

two? I know that I liked one and I didn't like the other.'

'When was this?'

'Oh, a long time ago. When we were all young.'

'You knew the Steinhauer family a long time ago?'

'Oh yes. I knew the boys' father. Herbert, Hubert? He was a doctor, like me, and we worked together with children . . . Hubert?'

'The father's name?'

'The father? Never trusted him.'

'Sir? You worked with Marc and Nicholas's father?'

Dyk tilts his head. 'Is that what I said?'

'Did you, sir?'

'Steinhauer — the old man. Didn't like him.'

'Which man?'

Dyk blinks, frowns, his eyes blank once more. 'How did you find me?'

★ ★ ★

As Don walks around the house, he peers through the ground-floor windows into the darkened room at the corner. He assumes it to be Dyk's bedroom. He sees that there is an oxygen tank next to his bed, a mask hanging from a hook on the stained metal pillar, and a high table with bottles of pills. He squints, cupping his hand around his eyes to block the reflection of the afternoon sun, sees a long counter at the other end of the room, facing the bed. On it, there are maybe fifty model aeroplanes of varying sizes and eras. Beneath the counter are books, piled roughly in stacks. There is something about them which intrigues him. He walks back around the house, past Dyk, who seems now to be sleeping, up to the front door. He turns the solid brass handle and the heavy door swings open onto a wide, cool hallway, the floor and ceiling clad in dark yellowwood. He walks in, almost on tiptoe to stop the floor creaking, turns to his right and finds Dyk's door open. In the distance, he can hear Nancy Maitland's imperious voice talking to de Vries about Dyk's medication. Don walks over to the counter, glances at the aeroplanes, and then squats down by the books, lifting five large-format volumes from the top of the pile.

When Don retraces his steps, de Vries is shaking hands with Nancy Maitland. Don holds up the books.

'Ms Maitland. These books. I think that they were in Dr Dyk's room.'

She looks suspiciously at him. 'Yes?'

'Does Dr Dyk have grandchildren?'

'No. Johannes has no family. I bought them. He asked me to. Very specifically by title. Why are they of interest to you?'

'They are children's books.'

Nancy Maitland smiles. 'Yes, indeed they are. Life's great circle. Johannes has reverted to childhood.'

★   ★   ★

When they reach their car, they get in silently.

'I know what you're going to say,' de Vries

221

announces. 'Those books.'

'She said he asked for them very specifically,' Don replies. 'Books illustrated by one Robert Ledham.'

'It's a nasty coincidence.'

'And there is more,' Don says. 'After you left, Dyk said some things. I do not know how reliable they are, but they are interesting.'

'What did he say?'

'That he knew the Steinhauer family a long time ago. That he knew Marc Steinhauer. Why would he know him? His brother perhaps, but why Marc? Then he said that Marc was a kind, gentle man, not like the other two.'

'So?'

'We were only talking about the Steinhauers. He said 'man' quite deliberately. If Marc Steinhauer is one, then who does he mean when he says the 'other two'?'

De Vries suggests, 'There's a sister?'

'I do not think he was referring to her. He was talking about the Steinhauer boys.'

'I think you're reading too much into his words. He wasn't with it, Don.'

'But just for a moment, he was. In and out, like the nurse said, but coherent for a minute.'

'Unreliable testimony.'

'Maybe, but he talked about three boys, and then only two. What does that mean? And then he said something about an old man — Hubert or Herbert — said that he did not like him.'

'Jesus,' Vaughn says. 'Two days ago, we have no one, and now there are two Steinhauer brothers, this man Dyk, and 'another'. This is sounding like a group of men. A paedophile ring working together.'

'With Robert Ledham somewhere there as well.'

'I don't know.'

'Maybe it is beginning to break. Maybe Marc Steinhauer did something and now it is all going to unravel.'

De Vries says: 'Speak to du Toit, find out if the department has anyone else who can help us on this.' He sucks in air. 'Or better still, don't. Call the University, or one of the private hospitals. Find me someone who can tell us about these people.'

Don nods. 'Nothing from the search teams?'

'Nothing.'

★   ★   ★

Sergeant Ben Thambo shows them photographs of the olive farm, describes his search. The farm building is a huge barn conversion. The roof, once thatch or tiles, is now a curved corrugated-steel structure. One half of the barn contains equipment for curing the olives, the other a small production line for bottling the products.

'There are four permanent staff who live in a pair of workers' cottages, around the back here.' Thambo indicates on the laptop screen where these are located. 'They're locals. Say they see Marc Steinhauer about once a fortnight. Sometimes he speaks to them, sometimes not.'

'Anyone else?' Don asks.

'They see other cars, but they don't know who and what they are. They said that people drive in thinking there is a shop, and when they find out that it is just a quiet working farm, they turn around and leave again.' He looks up at de Vries. 'In any case, sir, I think they are asleep most of the time. They don't seem to do very much. The farm is very busy in April and May when the crops are harvested and the olive oil is pressed, and the farm buildings are busy for a couple of months after that, with local women coming in to bottle and pack the products. Most of the time, they seem to be there just to keep an eye on the place.'

'Did you contact the architect?' Don says.

'Yes, sir. He found the plans for me, said that there was no cellar specified or designed or, as far as he knows, built. The workers certainly didn't know of one. Scene of Crime took samples, but they say there's nothing to suggest that it is anything more than a farm.'

De Vries says: 'Did you search the whole property, all the land?'

'It's rolling countryside. We took both teams out to a peak, and we couldn't see any sign of a dwelling. We asked the workers and they told us about a place in one corner: it's where the workers change, shelter if there is rain. One team took the dogs, but there was nothing suspicious.'

'How big is the property?'

'According to the deeds, about a hundred hectares.'

'All olives?'

'No. I would say, maybe twenty hectares. The rest is just wild. There are some areas of gum trees, a couple of small dams.'

'Ben?' Don says. 'Around the farm, is it crops? Wheat, mealies?'

'I don't know what,' Thambo says. 'But, yes, crops growing.'

Don nods.

'The teams are still there?' de Vries wants to know.

'I left one there to show the new photographs you want, but I brought the other back to town with me.'

De Vries says nothing.

'Did I do the right thing, sir?'

'Yes,' de Vries says absentmindedly. 'You did.'

★ ★ ★

At 7 p.m., de Vries sits with Don February in his office. The squad room is quiet, and Vaughn drinks whisky out of a plastic beaker.

'You need to get home after this, Don. You've been working hard.'

'We all have.'

'But you especially. Thambo was a good choice. He seems okay . . . How long will it take me to reach Steinhauer's sister tomorrow?'

'Her name is Caroline Montague. She lives outside Shelton village, just beyond Nieuwoudtville. I think it will take you three and a half hours, maybe four. That is why I told her eleven a.m.'

'What does she sound like?'

'Nervous, I think. She kept asking what it was about. I did not tell her.'

'She'll find out soon enough,' de Vries says,

225

lighting a cigarette by the open window, blowing the smoke out into the breezy evening. 'What else?'

'We are still working on any other Steinhauer relations. The family only moved to South Africa in 1976. The records are not complete, of course.' Don looks down at his trusty pad. 'There is no sign of Marc Steinhauer's cellphone. He could have had it on him when he jumped into the water. If it fell out, it is gone. We will check tomorrow with the network, but we have had problems with them before.'

'What kind of problems?'

'They lose records sometimes; claim they do not exist.'

'What a fucking country. Does nothing work?'

'I found a psychologist from Vincent Pallotti Hospital. Leader in the field. I explained about Steinhauer, and she says that she has read somewhere about the Steinhauer name, but going back years. It could be the father.'

'She?'

'Yes.'

'Can you trust her?'

'She has worked with the SAPS before, sir.' Don tries to remain patient. 'But only since 2009, so she cannot be connected to before. I stressed our time constraints. She promised to report as fully as possible in forty-eight hours. We can contact her if we need any questions answered before then.'

'And she's heard of a Steinhauer senior?'

'She said she had read about a man called Steinhauer during research. She could no remember where.'

'Something is moving now, Don. I don't like that we're no closer to Bobby Eames. I was thinking earlier, if this *is* a group, someone could be wherever they kept them, shutting it all down, killing Bobby Eames — if he's not dead already.'

'Perhaps the sister knows something about family properties?'

'Maybe. What about Nicholas Steinhauer?'

'Still nothing. Two officers in Pretoria traced a number for his secretary and spoke to her. He is in South America for two months. He is giving a lecture and promoting a book. She said she had not heard from him, and would not expect to. He is due back in three weeks.'

'I wonder whether he'll be on that plane?'

★   ★   ★

De Vries sleeps well for the first time in weeks. He wakes early; relishes the extra time it affords him. The South-Easter has dropped, clouds roll in slowly off the mountains, making the morning air cool and refreshing. He eats breakfast at the table in his big kitchen, enjoying the solitude, the peace. He feels quietly charged: breakthroughs after seven years of drought. He dismisses his calculation of the distance to the end, focuses on what must be done to take each step. Before this case, he has always reached the end.

He piles days of dirty crockery into the dishwasher, finds the tablets, sets the machine going. He collects his dirty clothes, stuffs them in a black plastic rubbish sack and throws it into the boot of his car. He checks the tank for petrol, spreads open a map on the passenger seat. He then drives to the parade of shops at the bottom of his road, cracks a smile at the elderly woman who takes his washing. Then he heads towards the tangle of roads which lead to the freeway, and out into the countryside.

★　★　★

After an hour, he stops at a garage, buys a pepper-steak pie and a can of cold Coke, and stands under a tree by a little dam next to the forecourt. In the surrounding trees, weaver birds dart in and out of their dangling basket-nests. He wonders whether they are feeding their chicks; wonders if, once they fledge, they give their offspring another thought. He calls Don February.

'Get onto the Land Registry for the Riebeek Valley. Find out what land was for sale, what was bought in the last, say, ten years. Find out if the Steinhauer family, or the wife's family, bought other land.'

'Okay.'

'And one more thing: any underground, or isolated structures which could be used as a hideaway. It's a long shot, but try everything. We're down to the wire.' He snaps the cellphone shut, throws the foil pie tray in the refuse bin and gets back into his car, brushing the pastry crumbs off his suit trousers before swinging his legs inside. He checks the map, then his rearview mirror, sees his lips caked with pastry crumbs, wipes them off with the back of his arm, puts the car into reverse and sets off once more.

★ ★ ★

Once he has climbed to the top of the plateau, he turns off the freeway. Before him, the land opens up into a huge expanse of low rolling hills, sprawling fields animated by the shadows of the drifting clouds, massive, some white and bright, others dark and threatening. Like cities on the horizon, the hills loom up ahead of him, maybe 200 kilometres away. So much space, de Vries thinks; so much beauty. So much room for everybody in South Africa. He thinks of the squatter camps along the N2 freeway, one rusty corrugated-tin shack on top of the next; the heat, the wet, the cold, the noise . . . the crime.

Finally, he approaches Nieuwoudtville, the nearest country town to Caroline Montague's address. He idles at a four-way stop at its centre and checks his route. Ten kilometres out of town, he turns down a narrow dirt track, rutted and meandering, skirting fields, until eventually he reaches a wooden gate. It is hotter here; he notices the cool of his air-conditioning as he re-enters the car after opening the gate. He starts slowly down the uneven track, taking care not to graze the underside of his car on the raised grassy centre. Finally, within a horseshoe of tall, distorted eucalyptus trees, he sees the homestead which he hopes is his destination.

★ ★ ★

229

John Marantz uses his cellphone to call a local number which links and encrypts a call to a hidden London number.

A voice says: 'Please wait.'

Marantz continues walking up Kirstenbosch Botanical Gardens. At the top of the steep site, he comes to the Protea Gardens, which few visitors ever reach. He sits on a favourite bench down a narrow path lined with low flowering trees. In the branches, there are Sunbirds and White-eyes, hovering and chirping, dancing from bough to bough, the incessant hum of insect industry.

'I didn't expect a call so soon.'

'It's not what you think.'

'What then?'

'I want to help a friend,' Marantz says. 'A policeman, pertaining to a long inquiry here.'

'What will you need?'

'Nothing sensitive.'

'Will it expose us?'

'No.'

'I'll email you a contact — to be used sparingly. But if you continue like this, I might be tempted to think that you are, in some form, operating again. That would not be appropriate.'

'It wouldn't.'

Marantz hears a long, hollow silence.

'You're sure you won't come home?'

Marantz says: 'I'm not sure of anything.'

★   ★   ★

Caroline Montague stands in her doorway, timid in her greeting, suspicious of this man in his city car.

'Let's walk,' she says.

'Fine.'

She looks down at de Vries' shoes. 'Are you wearing those?'

Vaughn glances at his black leather shoes, already caked in dust, the bottom of his suit trousers orange.

'I have boots in my car.'

De Vries struggles into a pair of denim jeans in the driver's seat, lays his jacket on the back seat of his car, and puts on his boots. He keeps these items in his boot for crime scenes out of doors. Now he is pleased he has brought his own car.

'This is official,' he explains. 'It's not a day out for me.'

'We can make it an official walk in the country then.'

Caroline Montague smiles at him, swings a small backpack over her shoulders and begins to lead him away from the house, out across the fields, towards a rocky outcrop in the distance. De Vries reflects that her backpack had been packed and ready; he wonders whether she has planned this walk, had never intended to invite him inside her house. He looks around, breathing deeply, sees sheep standing in line, seeking shade, each one with its head under the other's tail. He wonders what the one at the front does.

'They take it in turns,' Caroline Montague says.

'What?'

'The sheep. The one in front will walk down the line and tuck in at the back. They take it in turns: all very democratic.'

De Vries laughs; she has read his thoughts.

'You live here alone?'

'No. I have a husband. He is a writer. He's in Jo'burg just now, talking to publishers.'

'Do you know why I'm here?'

'Because history is catching up on me?'

'What do you mean?'

'After your officer called yesterday, I drove to the village. The café there has the Internet. I saw the press reports.'

'Had no one informed you about your brother?'

She pauses. 'I really meant about the boys being found dead. I looked you up, and that was the first article — how it harked back seven years. I did see about Marc, and it was a shock, but . . . I'm sorry for his family.'

'Not for you?'

'That's what I mean about history.' She picks up speed momentarily, crosses a stile and begins to walk across a field of grasses.

Vaughn catches her up again. She waits for him.

'What do you know of my family's history?' she asks. 'I'm sorry, I don't know what to call you.'

'My name is Vaughn, Vaughn de Vries. And we don't know anything, I'm afraid.'

She offers her hand, and Vaughn shakes it.

'Then I will tell you.' She looks at him

232

stumbling on the grassy mounds in the field. 'Are you all right, Vaughn?'

De Vries looks up at her. She is trying not to smile. He thinks that she is rather beautiful; troubled perhaps, but elegant and physically fit. Her hair is dark blond, tied in a simple ponytail. She wears heavy, well-worn boots, slim jeans and a thick wide-check shirt. He discerns no make-up; just carved wooden beads around her neck. He feels infatuated, like a child.

'You can tell I'm an urban animal?'

'A day in the country will do you good. I have something to drink in here,' she twists her thumb over her shoulder, 'and some food; just sandwiches and biscuits. We can have them at the gorge. It's about two kilometres over there.' She points into the distance. Vaughn wonders how far two kilometres is; how far it will feel on foot. He is thankful that he has not smoked an entire pack this morning.

'That's nice, thank you.'

She starts to stroll forward, checking that he is following.

'My father was called Hubert Steinhauer. As you can probably tell from the name, he was German, and Jewish. His family left Germany in 1938 and, I think because there was a family connection, they travelled to Kenya, where they made a home. My father became a doctor, and he met my mother, not Jewish, not anything; just a middle-class English girl, brought up on the outskirts of Happy Valley, and all that decadence. She bore him four children.'

'Four?'

'My brother Michael died when he was a teenager. And now Marc is dead, there is only Nicholas and me.'

'I'm sorry.'

'Thank you, but it's not necessary. I think you will understand.'

'I'm sorry that I interrupted you.'

'No, you must. I am only telling you this because I think it's what you want to know.' She leaps a wide dry ditch, holds out her hand for de Vries. Vaughn takes it, and struggles over.

'I was the youngest of the four, and I don't remember much about growing up in Kenya. I was six when we moved to the Cape. My father bought a huge house in Constantia, with lots of land. This is before they sub-divided every plot to hell and built those horrible gated communities. It was a big old estate house, under ancient English oak trees, and the garden seemed to go on for ever. We had a roof tiled in slate, and that was very rare, very luxurious in those days. Stables with ponies, and stable boys to do all the hard work. It should have been an idyllic childhood.'

'Why wasn't it?'

'My mother was very unhappy. I don't think I knew it then, but in retrospect, it was obvious. He never took her out; they never seemed to entertain friends. She played bridge once a week, the same four women for years and years, but other than that I think she hardly met anyone. We children never socialized with other people at our home, or theirs. We would go to school, and the driver would be waiting at the gates to drive

234

us straight home. My father worked in various hospitals and clinics in Cape Town, and I suppose the work was very demanding, but he was always in a filthy mood, always angry with my brothers. Most evenings, my mother and I would be in the parlour and we would hear him bawling at them. They became afraid of him. Sometimes, Michael would take Marc and they would hide in the garden. Nick was sent to find them, and then there would be even more trouble.'

'Why was he so angry?'

'I never really found out. Perhaps he was less angry and more just a very strict father, at least with the boys. I think he had a reputation for perfectionism at work. I know that he wasn't very popular. I remember waiting in the car once when we were picking him up, and hearing two young doctors complaining about him, calling him a bully and a sadist. I had to look up the word in the dictionary, and I was shocked.'

She takes a deep breath, angles her face to the sun.

'I suppose he was a Victorian father. He would take the boys out onto the mountain and walk them until they were dropping. They would come back complaining of aches and pains; their arms and legs would be scratched and bruised. But he never took me, even though I would have liked to go. And he was rarely angry with me.'

She stops, and de Vries trots up next to her, puts his hands on his knees and breathes deeply.

'You are very unfit,' she tells him. 'Do you want water?'

'Yes, please.'

She unhooks the rucksack, pulls out a plastic bottle, unscrews the cap and passes it to him. He gulps down about a quarter of it, hands it back to her, wipes his mouth with the back of his hand.

'Thank you.'

She takes one quick swig, and reseals the cap.

'It's hotter than I expected,' de Vries says.

'Are you happy to go on? We are halfway there now.'

'Yes,' de Vries tells her, clearing his throat of phlegm. 'No problem.'

They set off again, and she continues speaking.

'One day in the school holidays, when all the boys were teenagers, he took them to the Orange River. You can traverse a long section, canoeing and wading, camping on the banks. It was an eight-day trip. None of my brothers wanted to go; they pleaded with my mother to talk to their father. But he took them anyway. When they returned, they were black and blue: bitten all over their bodies, bruised and scratched. They couldn't stand up straight, they couldn't sit down. I tried to ask them about it, but they wouldn't speak to me. I think they were in shock. They didn't want to talk to my mother either. I knew something was very wrong, but I was only about eleven or twelve: I didn't know what it could be.'

'But later?'

'I think my father was a very cruel man. He turned Nicholas — he is the oldest — into his lieutenant. He would bully Marc and Michael. He went through all the motions of being a good father, but he seemed to hate his sons.'

'But he never threatened you?'

'Never. But I think he drove my mother to an early grave. She went into hospital — we thought for exhaustion and depression more than anything else — and she never came home. The doctors said she just faded away before them. I think maybe she wanted to die.'

'What happened to your brother?'

She turns to him. 'It was in the winter. I think I was about fourteen or fifteen, so Nicholas would have been in his early twenties. I think Michael was just nineteen. I know that they had been arguing for days; Michael looked drained by it. The two of them went for a hike across the mountains, up onto Silvermine. It's pretty bleak up there — like a rocky moonscape. What trees there are, are crippled, blown on their sides, but still struggling to survive. It's rough hiking at the best of times, but in midwinter it must have been treacherous. I can't imagine that Michael would have wanted to go but, for whatever reason, he did.'

Caroline Montague looks far into the distance. 'I must have been at school when they left, but by the time I returned, it had happened. Nick was back at home, in tears, screaming at Marc, trying to find his father. They had been climbing one of the tors at the apex and Michael had fallen. Nick had scrambled down after him, but he said that Michael's body was crumpled in a heap, that his neck was broken. He was sure that he was dead. By the time my father returned home, it was dark, and it wasn't until dawn the next morning that they went back up with a search-party. They said Michael must have died straight away, but we'll never know. He may have been out there all night, alone, terribly injured.'

She walks on in silence, de Vries almost trotting to keep up, panting. She stops a little further on, realizing that she has lost him again. When he makes up the ground, she continues.

'After that, there was a disturbing atmosphere at home, quite different from the way it should have been. Marc and I were grieving for Michael, but it did not seem that the other two were. My father spent more and more time with Nicholas, comforting him, supporting him, telling us angrily that it wasn't his fault. Then, one day, there was a fire in the garage. It was a wooden building with a thatched roof and it went up so quickly and burnt to the ground. I remember that Nicholas and my father blamed Marc, but he told me he had done nothing. They seemed to ostracize him after that. Marc then left for university, and didn't come home during the holidays. I learnt to enjoy my own company, and started taking extra courses, going on school trips — anything to avoid being at home.'

'Did you think that the fire was not an accident?'

'After the fire, I watched Nicholas very carefully. I became convinced he had set it, then tried to blame Marc, but I couldn't for the life of me think why. As for Michael . . . I don't know if, then, I ever consciously thought that his death

238

was not an accident. I probably did without distilling it down to that simple thought, but later, I wondered. More from the reaction afterwards.'

'Did you ever discuss it with Nicholas or Marc?'

'Nicholas, no. He ignored me. With Marc, I tried, but he would never engage with me. Maybe he was afraid that his own fears were so bizarre, I would take against him. Little by little, Marc broke off contact with his father and with me. I think that Nicholas made a point of visiting him, helped him avoid the Army afterwards. As soon as I left school, I enrolled at university in Durban. My father didn't seem to care, and I made a new life there.'

'And did you see anything of your family after that?'

'Almost nothing. Nicholas tried calling me a few times but he always sounded strange. Frankly, I didn't want him in my life. I didn't trust him, and the more I considered the thoughts I harboured about him, the less I wanted to face him. Besides, I had made friends for the first time, had learned that life needn't consist of round after round of fear and apprehension. I enjoyed myself, became an adult, and realized that it suited me. There was no way I wanted to go back. When our father died, just over seven years ago, I saw Nicholas and Marc at the funeral. I attended the service at the graveside, and then I got back in my car and came home.'

'When did you move here?'

'When I met Franz. He lived in the village. When we got married, he built this house for us, and we've been here ever since. Nearly thirteen years now.'

'That's fantastic. He treat you well?'

She stops, turns to him, curious. 'Yes. Why?'

He shrugs, embarrassed. 'You are all alone here — kilometres from anywhere.'

She smiles. 'I can look after myself.'

'I'm sure you can. You haven't children?'

'No — no. I told Franz that I didn't want children. He didn't seem to mind. He is very supportive, very loving, but he is an independent thinker. He spends all his time in his study writing, or walking with me.'

'You're not lonely?'

'Not at all. We have friends in the village who visit. I love cooking. I help out on the farm. We lease the land to local farmers, and I enjoy the harvests, sheep-shearing, helping with the lambing. I have been teaching myself to paint too, just watercolours. The light here is so amazing; trying to catch it is a lifetime's work.' She points ahead. 'Look, you'll be able to see the view soon.'

They push on until they start walking on flat rock, laid on the ground like giant paving-stones, tiny mossy plants struggling up through the cracks. When they climb some natural steps in the rock, they suddenly see the landscape opening out in front of them, an almost 360-degree vista. Ahead, sunken into the landscape, is a vast canyon, its sides steep, sprouting outcrops of shrubby green. To Vaughn's left, he sees a waterfall, a thin sliver of water trickling down maybe 200 metres, turning to glitter before it disappears in shadow and the dark pool at its base.

'In the winter and spring, the falls are amazing, but now, they are nothing,' Caroline tells him. She stops, unhooks the rucksack and sits on a cube of rock; gestures Vaughn to sit across from her on a similar outcrop.

He stands in awe at the magnitude of the view, letting the breeze cool his forehead and under his arms. She takes out some fruit juice, the water, and a bottle of beer.

'I didn't know whether you would be drinking on duty?'

Vaughn eyes the bottle. 'You know?' he says. 'I think I will.'

She cracks off the top against the side of the rock and hands it to him. She then pulls out a foil-wrapped bundle of sandwiches, squashed and battered.

'They don't look much, but they are ewes' cheese — from the sheep you saw — and homemade pickle. I imagine you've worked up an appetite?'

'I have.'

They each take one and munch silently, Vaughn listening to the breeze whispering hoarsely in the shrubs, still taking in the enormity of the gorge, which curls lazily away into the distance, narrowing until he cannot see where it ends. As they eat a second sandwich, they hear a deep series of barking staccato roars which echo down the sunken valley. Caroline jumps up, peers down the canyon sides.

'What is it?' Vaughn asks, following her, standing just a pace behind her.

'Baboon,' she replies, not turning around. 'Probably the dominant male calling all his women to him. There was fighting in the spring, and the outcast males are at the other end, probably plotting his downfall.'

'It's a remarkable sound.'

'It's wonderful,' Caroline agrees. She turns round. 'I can't see him, but he's down there somewhere. You can get down to the bottom; sometimes I swim there, and I am always afraid that when I get out, he'll be waiting for me.'

'That's a worrying thought.'

'Well, not really. He has enough women.' She chuckles. 'In any case, when you're in the water, you're quite safe.' She gazes down into the canyon again. 'I'm sorry. There's probably more you want to know.'

'I don't know. I came to find out about your family, your brothers. If Marc was involved, then I wondered whether Nicholas might be also.'

'You must ask them.'

'I was enjoying the moment,' Vaughn replies. 'Whatever happened in your childhood, you seem to have made a good life for yourself. Living here must make you appreciate all that nature has to offer.'

'It does. I wouldn't want to be anywhere else now.'

They share the water bottle again, finish a last sandwich each.

'And what about you, Vaughn? You have a wife and family?'

'Me? Two daughters — both at university now. My wife and I are . . . well, I think our marriage ended some time ago. We both have our careers, and they are demanding, time-consuming jobs. They tend to exclude relationships, and we've kind of . . . I guess we've let it happen.'

She takes his hand, squeezes it. Says quietly, 'You never know what will happen next.'

He feels embarrassed at first, but he smiles back at her. He does not want to talk about Suzanne de Vries, would prefer not to ask about her family, questions which will bring the frown back to her clear, tanned face; her inquisitive eyes. He would happily stay where he is all afternoon and just converse with Caroline Montague.

'Have you the energy to walk back now?'

'Yes,' Vaughn tells her. 'Thank you for lunch. This certainly makes a change from my desk and the corridors. My building is all corridors.'

He hands her his empty beer bottle, and she packs it away in her backpack.

'On the Internet, it says that Marc took his own life,' she says. 'Are you sure about that?'

'I am,' Vaughn tells her. 'I was there.'

She looks up, surprised.

'I was the officer who went to arrest him. His lawyer was there too, and colleagues of mine. We couldn't stop him. He jumped into the sea, a deep inlet of jagged rocks. It was blowing a gale and there was no way anyone could rescue him.' He turns to look at her, but her face is blank, her gaze straight ahead.

'If Marc was involved with those children,' she says, 'it wouldn't have been his idea. It would

243

have been Nicholas. I think he could influence Marc to do anything he wanted. Marc was frightened of him back then, and I'm sure he was still afraid. Have you spoken to Nicholas?'

'He's abroad. I have no idea if he will come back.' De Vries stops her. 'I need to ask you something.' She looks back at him. 'You said that your father bullied and manipulated his sons.'

'Yes.'

'Do you think he abused them, sexually?'

He expects her to recoil, to be shocked at such a question, but she merely pauses to consider her answer.

'I wouldn't have said so. I think he bullied them, perhaps abused them physically, but I had never considered . . . But then, I don't know. Maybe that's why they were how they were when they came back from the Orange River. There were things they could not face, could not discuss. I guess I was very young and naïve when I was at home. Perhaps he did.'

'And when you talked about your brother Michael's death, do you suspect now that it was not an accident?'

'Now? Thinking back . . . I couldn't be sure at the time, but there was something strange about the way my father and Nicholas became so bound up together afterwards. Somehow, it was as if they had, if not planned it, then . . . expected it. I thought about it again after my father passed away. He had seemed relieved that Michael was gone. I can't tell you any one thing that led me to believe that. He never said so, but I got an impression, and I remember I was shocked

244

at myself when I thought it.'

She sighs sharply.

'You see now why I needed to get out of there; to leave as soon as I could. All my life, I have tried to forget my name: Steinhauer. So much . . . evil. I don't think that's too strong a word. Even saying that name brings back so much hurt, so much unhappiness. I am not a Steinhauer, that I can tell you.'

'Your brother, Nicholas. He never married?'

'Not that I know about. He always struck me as asexual, somehow. I couldn't imagine him with a woman. He was so immature about that part of life. The boys I met at school would boast and brag, but I never heard him even mention girls, let alone talk about a girlfriend. He seemed above all that; considered himself superior.'

'I'm sorry I have brought back all those memories.'

'Do you believe that those three boys were taken by my brothers all that time ago?'

De Vries glances at her, thinks that she is gritting her teeth; sees her fingers and thumbs flicking off each other nervously.

'I think it is a possibility. If there was a pattern of abuse at home, that might explain why they would do such a thing.'

She turns to him. 'I have fought all my life to escape from my childhood, to drown those memories out with happiness in my adult life; to look ahead, and not back. Maybe Nicholas did the opposite; he evolved from his childhood, and became like his father, only with other people's children?'

'It's possible.'

'Were those two boys locked away, mistreated? Abused?'

'I'm afraid so.'

'Was Marc involved?'

'It looks like he was. We know he dumped their bodies. We don't know if he killed them, whether he was involved earlier.'

'Whatever he did, it would have been because of Nicholas.'

'You said that before.'

'I know Nicholas. Or rather, I knew him. I don't know him at all now.'

'You think he had that much influence?'

'Oh yes,' she says, very certain. 'It frightened me when I read that he had become a psychiatrist. Did he — does he — ever work with children?'

'I don't know. I have people researching his work.'

'And the third missing boy?'

'That's one of the reasons why I am here. I need to ask you. Your family: did they own any property in the Western Cape? A farm, a country house?'

'Not that I ever heard about. My father left me nothing in his will. He left what he had to Nicholas, maybe something to Marc, I don't know, and that was it. I don't think there was any property apart from the house in Constantia, although that must have been worth a lot of money seven years ago — ' She stops. 'Seven years. That's when those boys were taken, wasn't it?'

'Yes.'

'My father died at the end of 2006. When did those boys disappear?'

'March 2007.'

'Four months later. Oh my God . . . You know what I'm thinking now? It's too awful. He could have made himself a father by proxy, by force. Is that possible?'

'For seven years, all I have had is theories and speculation. Even now, the facts are sparse, and I have to keep guessing.'

'But perhaps it fits? I hated that part of my life. I thought of it like a Grimm's fairy tale: all big dark rooms and booming men and frightening things happening. But now, it feels different. As if there was evil in that house.'

They walk on, Vaughn beginning to tire. Eventually, he can see Caroline Montague's homestead, and he feels new energy in his legs.

When he reaches his car, she says: 'If you need to contact me again, please call me personally. I would rather speak to you, now that I have met you.'

'I'll make a point of it,' Vaughn tells her. 'And if you were to hear from your brother, I hope you could call me? And tell me anything else you think might be helpful?'

'I haven't seen or heard from Nicholas for seven years; haven't spoken to him for half my life. I doubt he even remembers that he has a sister but, as I say, I don't care. I have a completely new life now. I had to escape. I had to get away to survive. I don't know how I will sleep tonight, thinking about those children.' She turns

247

to face him, meets his eye. 'Should I have known? What could I have done?'

Vaughn puts his hand on the side of her shoulder.

'Nothing. You couldn't have told anyone what you suspected. There was — is — no proof. What you've told me now — it may help.'

'I hope so. I'm glad we don't have television here. There is so much ugliness. I can't take it any more. I have to hide away. I feel happier that way.'

He says to her, gently and slowly: 'Don't tell yourself differently. You were not — are not — responsible.'

She steps closer, hugs him. 'You are a kind man.'

'It's only the country air. It won't last.'

She smiles. 'Are you sure I can't offer you some Rooibos tea . . . or another beer?'

De Vries smiles back at her. 'I would like that very much, but I must get back to the office. I have a lonely, terrified teenager to find.'

'Of course.'

'But another time, if I'm passing this way . . . '

She leans forward, kisses him on the right cheek.

'Thank you for the walk,' Vaughn says. 'It was beautiful.'

'You'll be stiff tomorrow,' she says. 'And remember, if you ever need to round up your women, you must just roar down the valley.'

'I'll remember that.'

He gets into his car, lowers the window.

'Goodbye. And thank you, Caroline.'

She purses her lips, nods at him. As he drives away slowly, she calls out: 'Go well.'

★ ★ ★

Don February listens to de Vries recount his meeting with Caroline Montague. This time, it is Ben Thambo who stands at his door, listening from afar.

When he has finished, Don comments, 'That fits. Ben's teams canvassed all over Riebeek West and Riebeek-Kasteel, and the surrounding villages. There was positive identification of Nicholas Steinhauer from people in Riebeek West — where you expect, since he visits his aunt there. But two workers at the olive farm say they saw him too. That places him somewhere he has no reason to be.'

'So why can't we find where he kept those boys?'

'I've arranged for a helicopter to fly there and then over the whole area of the farm, as well as surrounding fields. I had to appeal to Director du Toit, but when I explained, he agreed pretty quickly. It will not be until late, maybe tomorrow.'

'That's good work, Don.' De Vries looks over at Thambo. 'And you, Sergeant.'

Don continues: 'Dr Matimba called me about an hour ago. She says she will meet us tomorrow morning. She plans to work late tonight, and give us what she has.'

'Matimba?'

'Dr Matimba, yes?'

Vaughn trances for a second, then smiles at Don.

249

'Good. Anything more on Nicholas Steinhauer?'

'Unless the SAPS has a contact in Argentina, or we can get in touch with the police there, I cannot imagine how we will find him.'

Vaughn frowns. 'I think he's the man behind this,' he says. 'I think he got his brother doing deeds for him and I think he got other people to take those children. We have to find out how far this thing goes.'

'If we find Bobby . . . '

'Yes, I know. If we find Bobby Eames, maybe we'll know everything. You are a lot more optimistic than me, Don.' He addresses Thambo. 'That's not for public consumption, by the way. None of it is. Unless it contributes to this investigation, it doesn't leave this room. Yes?'

'Yes, sir.'

De Vries turns back to Don. 'Have any of the teams in Marc Steinhauer's wine estate, or at his house in Betty's Bay, found anything at all?'

'Not anything to interest us. Steve Ulton was looking for you, but he told me there is nothing to suggest that the boys were ever there. Director du Toit asked me to close the scenes at both properties and let the family back in. I did not think you would object?'

'No. Fair enough. Marc Steinhauer's phone?'

'Still no sign. I asked the network to look in his account, but without a warrant, they refused. I am working on obtaining a 205, and expect to hear first thing tomorrow.'

'What have you told Director du Toit?'

'Just kept him up to date. He left the office early: an official meeting with General Thulani.'

'All right. It's time we all went home. Things are accelerating. We need to rest. Early morning for us, Don.'

★ ★ ★

Ben Thambo follows Don out. He collects a backpack and Don a briefcase. Vaughn watches them trudge down the corridor to the elevators. He sits back in his chair, reflects on his day; the revelations which slowly open up a case begin, agonizingly slowly, to cast light on what has been dark and featureless for so long. He thinks about Nicholas Steinhauer on television at the time of the abductions, and judges that if he is the ringmaster, then he has no shame, no remorse. A taxi honks repeatedly in the street below. He looks down but sees nothing, glances up at the sliver of sea visible between the skyscrapers. He watches as a gas-container ship passes between them, its three silver domes each catching the sun. He closes his eyes, tries to imagine the warm smell of Rooibos, the magnificent canyon, and the echoing bark of the baboon. He thinks about Caroline Montague and realizes that this is the first time he can remember — the thought strikes him: probably for seven years — that he has appreciated beauty. His life has been to bludgeon his way through the ugliness; stare ahead to the end . . .

He wonders whether he should pour himself a small drink. There is no one in the squad room now, so he pulls out his pale blue beaker, pours some Irish whiskey in it, up to the halfway point.

251

He raises it to his lips but, almost subconsciously, senses a change in the light in his field of vision. He looks up to the corridor ahead of him, sees a figure he does not recognize. He puts the beaker down, squints. The silhouette is short and squat, shaved head domed. Then, he realizes: David Wertner. He opens his desk drawer, drops in the bottle and the beaker, shuts the drawer hard, hears the beaker fall, smells the whiskey aroma seep up from his desk.

Wertner knocks on his door; opens it before de Vries has answered.

'You have a minute, Colonel?'

'I suppose so. What do you want?'

Wertner sits down, flips a thin file onto de Vries' desk, says tersely: 'You recognize this man?'

De Vries glances at the picture.

'It's Robert Ledham, convicted child abductor. We've spoken to him.'

'I know you have. But you seem to be ignoring him. Why is that?'

'He has no direct involvement in either the original abductions, or in the murders of Steven Lawson and Toby Henderson.'

'Despite the fact that the original inquiry files suggest that he was in Claremont at the time of the second kidnapping?'

'That item was never in the files, Wertner. That has been added later. Someone is fucking around with my inquiry.'

'Is that so? It's in both the original and the authorized copy. Looks to me like it's always been there.'

'Well, you're wrong. It was never there until

252

those boys' bodies were found last week and we reopened those files. Anyone could have added those pages.'

'Added them?' Wertner chuckles. 'Sabotaging your inquiry?'

'For whatever reason. What business is it of yours?'

'It's precisely my business. You are under scrutiny, de Vries. No one thinks that you and Brigadier du Toit did a good job seven years ago, and no one is impressed now. There will be questions to answer. Why are you so focused on this man, Steinhauer, when Robert Ledham fits the profile so perfectly?'

De Vries snorts. 'You are so far behind the arc, it's unreal. Read my report when this is over, then you can investigate me as much as you like.'

David Wertner sniffs the air; the aroma of whiskey fills the room. 'Sundowner?'

'Fuck off out of my office.' De Vries stands up, comes around his desk to Wertner, who also rises, stands, bulldog-like, head low.

'Don't lose your cool, Colonel,' Wertner sneers.

'When you wake up and remember what it is to be a policeman, I'll talk to you, Wertner. Right now, you're just in the way; another fucking politician. You want to fuck around with your little schemes, do it in your own time, and don't waste mine.' De Vries opens his door, stands by it expectantly. Wertner moves slowly towards it.

'And who do you think is planting evidence in your old cases, de Vries? Me?' He smiles. 'I don't need to do that. You make it too easy for me as it is.'

'Goodnight,' Vaughn says forcefully.
Wertner pauses at the doorway.
'Enjoy your last case, Colonel.'

★ ★ ★

At 7 a.m., de Vries is sitting up in bed, feeling behind him for a glass of water. His chest is heavy, head throbbing. His cellphone trills and he snatches it up, puts it to his ear.

'Good morning, sir.'

'Don.'

'Dr Matimba called me. She's ready to meet us this morning — 9 a.m.'

De Vries tries to shake his head free of the vice, grimaces as a flash of pain shoots through his sinuses.

'Where does she want to meet?'

'A café, near her hospital.'

'A café?'

'I thought it was odd too, but then she told me that it was at Oude Molen Lifestyle Village.'

'Where's that?'

'Just opposite Pinelands station.'

De Vries can hear drums; their low pulsations reverberate through him.

'What's Oude Molen?'

'It is a cooperative venture: farming and crafts, next to Vincent Pallotti Hospital where Yvonne Matimba works. What's interesting is what it used to be. Until the mid-90s, it was a hospital too: a mental asylum.'

De Vries feels sick, physically sick.

'Eight-thirty, Don. Have to go.'

He throws his phone on the bed, runs for the bathroom, vomits into the sink.

★ ★ ★

Oude Molen is very quiet at 8.45 a.m. They drive through the main gates, past a long, seemingly derelict building billed as a backpackers' hostel, and around towards the café. Don has to brake and swerve to avoid the tail of a snoozing blond dog in the road and, when they reach the car park by the horse paddocks, there are more sleeping dogs on the scuffed grassy verges, in the parking spaces, catching the first rays of the morning sun. As they exit the car, a group of small hens hurry up to them, and Vaughn has to watch his step.

He grumbles, 'You've brought me to a fucking menagerie.'

In front of them, under a long green corrugated-iron stoep, a young black man is playing a guitar, a cigarette in his mouth, his eyes closed. At the other end, a slim, fit, young black woman is standing against an old cart. Her hair is tied up in a bun, encrusted with beadwork. She is watching them get out of their car and approach her. She has a smile in the corners of her mouth and dimples in her cheeks. She gets up and holds out her hand to de Vries.

'I am Yvonne Matimba.'

'This,' Don says, stepping forward, 'is my boss, Colonel de Vries.'

She shakes his hand firmly, steps forward and kisses Don on the cheek.

255

'You know each other?' Vaughn says, looking sideways at Don.

'Yes,' Don says blankly.

She gestures them through to the little garden at the side of the building, which looks onto market gardens, beyond to the Black River and Devil's Peak.

'They've only just opened. I ordered coffee and muffins. Is that okay?'

The men nod, take their seats. Yvonne Matimba focuses on de Vries.

'Don said that you don't have much time, so I prepared what I found. Some is fact, and some is stories, but I will tell you it all.'

They watch in silence as the coffee and cakes arrive. An exceptionally fat pink pig waddles over the lawn and sits itself down under their table in the sun. Don leans down to stroke it, and it rolls over onto its back in slow motion, batting its long eyelashes, resting its weight on Don's right foot. De Vries shakes his head gently, grabs a muffin and then remembers to offer the plate to Yvonne Matimba. She takes one, but sets it aside.

'Back in the nineteenth century, they sent psychiatric patients to Robben Island . . . '

De Vries opens his mouth to object to the history lesson, but his mouth is full of muffin.

'Don told me about this with you,' she says, 'but, like I say, you get it all.'

De Vries swallows; nods.

'Even you, Colonel, must appreciate that the history of Robben Island — and the effect on the human mind of being incarcerated there

256

— might be of interest to a wide number of South Africans.' Her tone is scolding, but friendly. 'After a short time, it was found that the patients' condition deteriorated rapidly, and many took their own lives. The government belatedly bought this estate and set up an asylum here. Then, later, they built a huge psychiatric hospital either side of the river. The other side they closed long ago, but Valkenberg East — this side — they kept open until 1992.' She pauses, checks her notes. 'When I was studying for my PhD, because I am really doctor, Dr Matimba,' she winks at Don, 'my thesis concerned psychiatric provision in Cape Town — and that was when I read about Hubert Steinhauer.'

'That's the father,' de Vries tells Don. He smiles at Matimba, nods. 'Sorry.'

She continues in her low, clipped voice, the words racing from her mouth.

'Hubert Steinhauer joined Valkenberg East in 1978 and stayed there until September 1984. He specialized in paediatric care: child cases of serious mental illness. Steinhauer's work, which seems to be a proactive intervention, combining strong anti-psychotic medication and psychiatric role-play, did not seem either in keeping with the palliative style of Valkenberg East, nor did it meet favour with the authorities. More significantly, a number of complaints were lodged against Steinhauer — I assume by relatives of his patients — and, in this report, there are additional complaints indicated by fellow members of medical staff. I looked at the staff records and there are several requests from staff to be

257

transferred from Steinhauer's department.' She looks up at de Vries. 'You can infer that his work was considered controversial. Not necessarily improper in itself, but certainly unwelcome to the hospital authorities.' She looks down again at her notes, her pace still not slowing.

'Early 1984, there is a record of the suspension of Steinhauer, pending a full inquiry by senior hospital authorities. Steinhauer resigned in September, a few weeks before the report was made public.'

'What did it say?'

Matimba smiles bitterly.

'Guess what? No report. I'm sure one was filed, but it has been lost, or more likely, removed.'

'So we don't know what he was accused of, or whether the authorities found him guilty?'

'As I said, we can't know. But later, there is mention of the 'damning report into the work of Dr Hubert Steinhauer'. This was written in an internal report regarding the likely closure of the hospital.' She looks up at both men.

'I think it's clear: this man Steinhauer behaved inappropriately with his child patients, was about to be found guilty of malpractice and was warned by someone who knew the contents of the report. So, he resigns in advance and the report is hushed up to protect the reputation of the hospital in the light of a threat against its future.'

'Is there any mention of Hubert Steinhauer's son, Nicholas Steinhauer?'

Matimba smiles. 'I thought you might ask me that.'

De Vries looks at her curiously.

'Nicholas Steinhauer was not registered as working here, but it is possible that he visited the hospital with his father.'

De Vries nods absentmindedly; focuses, asks: 'Would a family life with a dominating, possibly abusive father, and a passive, maybe bullied mother — would that be a breeding ground for further abusive tendencies amongst the children?'

Matimba puts down her coffee mug.

'That is a quite different matter,' she tells him. 'I am not an expert in that field.'

'But what do you know, Doctor?'

She contemplates a moment and then says: 'It is well established that abused children carry a higher likelihood of becoming abusers themselves than those who come from a stable background. Abuse is about power, and a child who is abused is disempowered until he himself abuses.'

'And what about,' de Vries asks, 'children who have been kept in very controlled conditions, who do not get to socialize? Is this a factor that would lead to a desire for them to control children themselves?'

Matimba replies: 'Many abusers are sociopaths. I think I know why you are asking, because those boys were kidnapped and then held — at least, that is what we read in the newspapers — but I cannot tell you whether what you ask is true. I do not know.'

'I'm sorry,' de Vries says. 'I know what I want to ask, but it is difficult.'

Don February's phone vibrates and then rings stridently. De Vries shoots him a stare.

'I have to take this.' He walks away from the

table, starts wandering towards the field of horses. Suddenly he turns back.

'We need to go.'

Don looks up at Yvonne Matimba, smiles at her. 'Sorry.'

She smiles back: 'Go on, then.' She watches them trot off towards their car.

'What is it?' de Vries asks, panting.

'We began a detailed search of the land surrounding the Steinhauer olive farm. Joleen Knox went through the Riebeek Valley Registry and she has found something; it could be the hideout.'

'What? What is it? Where is it?'

'I have the grid reference, but she says it is on land adjoining the Steinhauer olive farm.'

De Vries starts the car, while Don switches on the SatNav.

'What is it?' de Vries asks again. 'What has she found?'

'You will not believe it. What do you suppose is built deep in the Swartland countryside, thirty kilometres from Riebeek West?'

'Just fucking tell me, Don.'

'A nuclear bunker. Government building: Emergency Control Centre. Decommissioned. It is underground, a few hundred metres off the land owned by Marc Steinhauer, next to a farm owned by a family called Caldwell. Must be a leftover from the nineteen fifties, sixties.'

'We're going now.' De Vries accelerates out of the complex and onto the side road leading to the freeway. 'I am heading for Riebeek, yes.'

'Go for Malmesbury, and I'll plot a route from there. Cross the freeway to the M5, then onto the N1 and then onto the N7. You want me to call back-up?'

'Ja. Give me a minute to think.' He glances at Don, and then back to the road. 'This is it, Don. I can feel it. This is the beginning of the end.'

'If the information is good. If the place is still there.'

'Why wouldn't it be? Those things were built to protect the great and the good in the event of a nuclear explosion. It'll still be standing after fifty, sixty years.'

'Underground. No wonder no one saw or heard them.'

De Vries pulls out his cellphone, speed-dials his own department, listens to the phone ring and ring.

'Has Knox told anyone else?'

'I told her only to report to me and no one else.'

'Good.'

Still the phone rings: 'Will someone fucking answer!'

⋆ ⋆ ⋆

After negotiating the roadworks on the M5 link road, de Vries accelerates onto the N1 freeway and prepares to stay left at the Century City road division. Once he has found the N7, he settles down to a steady 140kph.

'How do you know the industrious Doctor Yvonne?' he asks Don.

'We went out together for a while; became friends.'

'That doesn't sound good.'

'She was out of my league — we both knew it. At least now, my wife, it is only she who thinks she is out of my league.'

Vaughn chuckles, glances at the speedometer, presses his foot down hard to build up speed as the road dips before rising ahead of him. De Vries focuses on the furthest point he can see and imagines that soon he will be driving over it, wills the time to pass.

They reach the Fineberg olive farm and drive straight to the barns, but no one is there.

Don says, 'We have to find the perimeter road. Thambo says we follow that to the far left corner, take the right turn and we are only a kilometre or so from the building.'

'He's been there?'

'No. He has just cross-checked with his detailed map back in Riebeek-Kasteel.'

Vaughn circles the large gravelled courtyard by the processing buildings, then spots a track leading off into the distance, heads for the gate that guards it. Don is out of the car even before it has stopped, opens the gate, runs after the creeping car with de Vries urging him in. As soon as Don is seated and before he shuts his door, Vaughn puts his foot down.

'I left it open for the others,' Don says. 'Do you think that is safe?'

'I don't care.'

The track is a rutted dirt road, bumpy, but perfectly passable for any vehicle. In the wing mirror, de Vries sees the car send plumes of orange dust into the air, blown across the fields.

At the far point of the farm, they find a small barn, the shelter for the workers. Then they turn ninety degrees, tracing the perimeter of the Steinhauer property. De Vries' cellphone rings; a voice tells him that the back-up squads are twenty minutes away. He tells them to hurry, snaps shut the phone, stares up at the SatNav GPS in the windscreen, tries to calculate the distance from his current point to the detailed grid reference. Ahead of him, there is only the orange track, wheatfields stretching into the distance, and to his left, a low wooden fence, beyond which there is a wide band of overgrown, rocky land. Other than a small copse of low trees further ahead, the entire vista is featureless.

A few moments later, de Vries sees the end of the track. As they reach it, there is a left turn just before the corner, and a new track laid through a break in the fence, towards a steeply rolling field. They edge onto the track and begin to drive down into a little valley. De Vries studies the GPS and his own reference.

'We're here.'

He stops the car and they get out. Immediately around them there are only fields of natural shrubby fynbos. De Vries stands on the running board of his door. Ahead and to his right he sees just the tops of eucalyptus trees. The image is illogical, and then he realizes: the land dips still further. He begins to run down the track. Don gets back into the car, follows him until he reaches the end of the track, where he can see that there is space for a car excavated under some fallen trees, covered with smaller branches to conceal the position. Don switches off the engine, hurries to catch up with de Vries, whom he finds staring at a small rectangular area of scrubby land, fenced by a low electric wire. Something about it is wrong. De Vries walks the low fence until, suddenly, he stops, bends down and studies the ground, before picking up various small branches, throwing them aside. He stays bent over with his finger pointing at the ground as he moves sideways, scuffing away leaves and twigs with his right shoe. Without warning, he gets down on his knees and begins sweeping away branches with his hands. He pulls up what looks like a trapdoor. Don sprints over. De Vries looks up at him.

'Jesus. This whole thing is camouflage. Look down here. The entire roof is man-made.'

Don peers through the door and sees a huge, dimly lit concrete basin, cast into the ground like a high-sided rectangular swimming pool.

'There is a padlock on the metal gate down here,' Don says.

He looks up at de Vries, who is holding his revolver.

'I know.'

Don stands up, but does not move from the trapdoor.

'Wait for back-up,' he says.

'Why?' de Vries asks angrily.

'Because it is possible there is someone there, guarding him.'

'I don't think so. I'm going in. If you want to stay here and guide in the teams when they come, that's fine by me.'

'No.'

'Stand back.' He pushes gently but firmly past Don, begins to climb down the metal ladder. He is about to shoot at the lock, but he looks back up at his warrant officer.

'It's been seven years, Don.'

'So, what difference does twenty minutes make?'

'Because it's twenty minutes longer. You don't understand. Now, stand clear.'

He aims his gun, turns away from the lock, and pulls the trigger. The shot reverberates around the concrete container, but Vaughn still hears the clink of metal as the lock hits the ground. He looks back to see the gate swinging open.

He calls up: 'It's open.'

He jumps down to the concrete floor, waits for Don to follow. When he reaches the floor, Don draws his revolver, keeps it in his palm. They walk quickly across the wide space, looking up at the chickenwire mesh ceiling, on top of which are logs, branches and fynbos to hide the entrance. Through the occasional gap they see sunlight, and there are sufficient beams to light their way. Ahead of them, set into an otherwise blank grey concrete wall, is a pair of metal double doors, painted dark green. As they approach them, de Vries stops, points down at the ground.

'Blood — and drag-marks. Look, heading towards the doors.' He moves around the area, looks out from the dark patch, then steps at a diagonal. 'And down here. More blood. Much more.' He squats by the patch, picks up a small twig, pokes it into the pool: thick shavings gather at its point. 'This isn't old.' He looks up at Don. 'This could be where Steven and Toby were killed.'

He rises, steps around the blood and moves towards the door, following the second trail, the parallel indentations as feet on a dead body might make. This second trail is bloodied. He takes out a handkerchief, and is about to pull at the door handle when he stops. To the left of the door, lying on its side, is a long roll of thick grey polythene, about two metres in height.

De Vries says: 'That's the wrapping. This is it. We've found the murder scene.'

Don moves to the wrapping, examines it without touching it. 'It looks the same. And there is blood all around here.' He jumps back when he realizes that his shoes are caked with a mixture of sticky dark red glue, fallen leaves and twigs. He looks for de Vries, but he is already reaching for the doors.

'We should wait.'

'No.'

The left-hand door is heavy, and even with both of them pulling, it opens stiffly. Ahead Vaughn sees only a long wide passageway, concrete-lined, slowly descending.

'Find something to jam this door open,' de Vries says. 'We'll need the light.' Don collects short fallen branches thick enough to jam under the door, pinning it back against itself. De Vries steps inside, stops; indicates to Don. It is a rifle, thrown down behind the door.

'Murder weapon. Let's hope to God it's

covered with Marc Steinhauer's prints.'

He waits for Don to study it, then begins to walk. Don follows him down the damp, cold walkway, out of the sunlight into almost complete darkness. Their footsteps echo and are then swallowed; Don believes that their breathing sounds louder.

As the passageway levels out, so the gift of daylight evaporates. Don reaches for his key-ring, switches on a tiny key-finder bulb. It lights only a few metres ahead of them, but it is enough for them to be able to keep on. Don takes each step gingerly, but de Vries strides on into the dark, and Don finds himself scampering to keep up. They reach another door, half open, darkness beyond. Don searches the area around the door with his flimsy light. It seems to be the only access to and from the corridor.

The door itself is incredibly heavy. When de Vries tries to shift it, it scarcely moves. He turns sideways and squeezes through the gap, stands in the pitch-black, his hands searching for a side wall, for a switch. He feels only cold rough concrete. Don pushes his hand through, lighting his way, squeezes through. Now, a corridor, this time painted in grey-white, stretches at right angles to the entrance walkway. To de Vries' left, there is a pair of double doors, the word *Decontamination* stencilled on it, black on dark green. He shivers, turns back and faces right. He gestures Don to keep up with him and begins to walk down the corridor.

The first iron door to his left is locked. There is no title on the door. The second is open wide.

Don takes the lead into a room which resembles a boardroom, wood panelling lining three walls, maps and diagrams displayed on the fourth side; a long dusty table with chairs either side of it. The smell of damp and decay is pervasive, bitter in the nostrils, tickling in the throat. Don walks the perimeter quickly; finds no other exits. He runs his hand over the back of an upholstered chair at the head of the table and recoils. His fingertips itch from the icy velvet sensation of mould. He wipes his hand on his trousers, rejoins de Vries and they move back into the corridor, shadowed by flickering silhouettes of men both cowed and charged. At the far end, de Vries can see a low green light.

'Look — there. Ignore the other doors.'

They shuffle quickly down the corridor, De Vries stumbling and regaining his balance, until they reach a pair of doors on their left leading onto yet more passageway, and a single extra-wide door, above which a small green light glows. On the door, stencilled in black, is the single word: *Gevangenis* — prison.

Don pushes on the door and it slowly opens inwards. De Vries puts his shoulder against it, heaves until it is wide enough to allow them entry. His hand automatically feels the wall adjoining the doorframe, finally hits a switch, presses it. Four glowing grey lights illuminate the room in which they stand. Don switches off his key-fob light and pockets it. De Vries realizes that they are in an anteroom. To his left is a counter with kitchen equipment, including a microwave and a pair of camping gas rings. To

268

his right, old-fashioned tape machines stand in a line on a trestle table. Above them, incongruously, a line of hooks holding handcuffs and rigid arm-restraints. At the far end, three pale grey garments. De Vries baulks: they are straitjackets. The smell in here is different; staleness, but somehow fresher than the previous rooms. Ahead of them is a second door containing a very small square observation window, glazed with wire-hatched safety glass. The door is ajar, and through it de Vries can see steel prison cells — three in a curving line.

De Vries turns to Don. 'Touch nothing.'

Don nods. De Vries pushes the door, and it swings open easily. The cell-block is concrete-lined, without paint; only three dim white lights illuminate the room. There are no windows, no natural light. Ahead, three cells, divided only by iron bars. The smell is faint, but pervasive: sweat and urine. De Vries looks around, realizes that he is holding his breath; consciously breathes, the smell infecting his nostrils. He looks up again.

On the walls nearest the cells, he sees A4 digital prints on thin, mottled paper: the three abducted boys, frightened and humiliated, naked in their cells. Pictures indicating growth; their heights and weights marked in felt-tip next to years at the bottom of the shots. On the floor, there are toys: old boxes of board games, lids stained and dirty, puzzles, colouring books, even some soft toys. He looks up, away from them, away from what he sees as totems of his failure, and surveys the cells. The outer two cell-doors are open, but the middle cell is locked shut.

269

There is no one inside any of them.

De Vries stands at the threshold of the far-left cell, looks inside at piles of clothes, a narrow mattress atop a concrete base, a toilet, basin and shower head above a drain in the floor. There are no possessions to be seen.

'He is not here,' Don states.

De Vries just stares at him, his eyes wide with shock, shoulders slumping.

Don looks at his cellphone.

'There is no reception. They do not know where we are. We should go back to the surface, at least the entrance. Let them know we are here. Let them know we have found it. The Crime Scene guys will need to search this. We should back out.'

He sees that de Vries is frozen.

Don walks over to de Vries, holds out his hand at de Vries' shoulder. Before he touches him, de Vries jumps, announces, 'Bobby Eames could have escaped; he could be somewhere else on site.'

'Why not discuss that when we have back-up?'

De Vries suddenly walks away, out of the room.

'No. You go up. I'm searching the rest of this place.' He brushes past Don roughly, hurries through the anteroom, then comes back and opens the door to the microwave; swings it shut again.

'You have not got gloves . . . sir,' Don insists.

De Vries ignores him, turns sharply then exits the door to the prison and turns to his right, pushes through the double doors leading onto yet another passage. He stops, looks back at Don, who has followed.

'Give me your key-torch. You go back up.'

Don hands him his key-ring reluctantly. Then makes up his mind.

'Okay. Be careful — and if you see us coming, call out so that we know it is you.'

De Vries nods grimly, watches Don begin to edge his way back along to the corridor, knows that once he reaches the corner, daylight will leak into the area and guide him.

He switches on the light. There is complete silence; a stillness to the cold air which chills him deeply. He shivers in his summer suit-jacket, feels the sweat on his torso, begins to swing the light from one side of the passage to the other. Most of these doors are open, leading to dormitories on one side, lines of metal beds topped by thin, mouldy mattresses. On the other, spartan offices, a desk and a single metal-framed chair. Each room untouched, waiting to be woken.

The corridor runs deeper and deeper away from the entrance, downhill, and de Vries' breath shortens as his adrenalin kicks in. The key-light flickers. He shakes it, and it begins to fade. He switches it off, stands stock-still, waits for his eyes to adjust, realizing that when the interference on his eyeballs slows, he has a vague awareness of his surroundings. He moves forward, letting the blurred grey-scale pictures in his head change slowly, refocus. He enters one of the side rooms, hunting for a light switch, but finds nothing. He backs out, squints, sees nothing, moves on. Then he hears a sound which stops him. He halts, listens, but hears nothing. He draws a breath; holds it.

'Bobby?' His voice is tinny, strained. He listens as the sound-waves move out from him and evaporate. He steadies himself in the dark.

'Bobby Eames? This is the police. You are safe.'

He hears the words vibrate again in the concrete walls, feels a wave of motion roll ahead of him. He perceives no reply. He shivers, suddenly disorientated. He makes himself step forward, his arms extended, knows that he must move. Ahead of him, he senses a change, and when his hands touch icy, sticky metal, he recoils. He has reached the end of another corridor. The only exit from it is through more double doors. He leans against them, but this time they are unmoving, locked. De Vries wonders what he can do now.

He turns back and sees nothing but ephemeral floating ghosts on his retina, the kaleidoscope of pictures he used to see when, as a child, he rubbed his eyes and then closed them. He has reached the end . . . It takes him several seconds to understand this.

He stands on the spot, begins to turn slowly, hunting for any speck of light. The cold closes around him and he begins to shiver uncontrollably. He tries to steady himself, to think clearly, but his mind seems numb. He holds his breath. In the background, he hears a low hum. He tilts his head in the darkness, all his focus on identifying the sound and from where it emanates. He walks back up the pitch-black

272

corridor, hugging the right-hand wall, sensing more than knowing that he is getting closer to the sound.

He finds a door, grasps the cold metal handle and pushes down, gently shouldering it open. He stands in the doorway, sees no end to the darkness, hears nothing louder than a hum; he no longer knows if this is real or just a memory deep in his head. He backs out and continues along the corridor, finding the next handle, nudging the door open. This time, the noise increases markedly, and he can see a faint green light glowing just above floor level. He walks gingerly towards it, feels the top of a counter or cupboard. He impatiently pulls out the key-light from his pocket and fumbles with the switch with frozen fingers. The pale light illuminates a grey-white chest freezer. He reaches to open the lid, but sees the tainted gold metal of a padlock. The key-light begins to fade and he switches it off once more. He knows that whatever is in this freezer is considered worth preserving. There is very limited power in this place, yet this machine consumes, presumably every day, all day. If it is perishable food, its source may provide a crucial clue; could even lead to identifying the purchaser.

De Vries waits for his eyes to adjust again, and then he leaves the room, hands extended in front of him. He negotiates the door, turns right and walks as fast as he dares to the cell area at the far end. In the small kitchenette he finds a tin-opener and a can of baked beans. He retraces his steps to where he thinks the open door to the freezer room is located, his own heavy intermittent breathing blocking out the humming. He runs his hands along the wall, feeling the chalky, damp paint on the concrete cover his hands. Finally, the noise is discernible and he almost falls through the open door, stumbles to the far side and places the key-light on the lid. He switches on the light once more, long enough to insert one handle of the tin-opener between the lock and the front edge of the freezer. Then he takes the tin can and, using it as a hammer, he tries to lever the lock either from the front of the cabinet or from its lid. The light flickers and de Vries knows he has little time.

He takes one last swing at the tin-opener. The lock comes away from the lid, the key-light jumps and lands on the floor — extinguishes — and de Vries hears the metal of the lock jangle against the side of the freezer. He catches his breath, struggles to find the fallen key-light, locates it, and returns to the cabinet. His fingers fail to find purchase on the front of the lid and, when he locates a small groove, the lid still will not open. He sweeps his right foot around the floor until it hits the tin-opener. He bends and picks it up, finds the groove beneath the lid once more and inserts the handle. Now, with leverage, he hears the seals break and a pronounced hiss as the lid opens.

He pushes the lid up and back until it hits the wall. He retrieves the key-light and wills it to produce a few moments of light. He shakes it and switches it on. The beam is brighter for a moment and de Vries points it inside the freezer, and sees nothing but a long white-wrapped

274

parcel. His brain tries to process what he is seeing, tries to form a coherent guess as to what it might be. As he leans inside, it produces an answer: it is a small body, legs bent slightly upwards. De Vries feels his heart begin to pump. He sees that the form is covered in a white sheet, frosted and stiff. He takes hold of an iced flap and pulls gently. It does not budge. The key-light falters once more. He pulls harder and there is a high-pitched cracking squeak as it comes loose in his hand. Beneath, de Vries sees a waxy, frostbitten face, brittle stalks of hair, an indentation in the boy's cheek where skin has come away with the sheet — skin that de Vries has pulled from him. The key-light dims and dies, and de Vries fights the icy bile in his throat, his eyes bulging.

He throws the key-light to the floor, hears the plastic click echo and hiss between the walls. He knows he has seen Bobby Eames. Cannot know from the flickering glimpse, but knows all the same. He begins to hyperventilate, his mind racing through seven years of yearning to find this place, seven years to dream that he could tear down the walls of hell and rescue his lost boys.

He stands in the absolute darkness, listening to his own straining breathing, feeling the huge weight of concrete, of earth, on top of him. At that moment, he hears himself speak, but does not understand the words; hears himself cry out, registering only a screeching like an animal in pain, an animal to whom you cannot explain what it is feeling. Now he feels only a determination, an iron sense of self-will, that the walls will

275

close in on him, collapse over him; seal him in with seven long years of wretched failure and hopeless misery.

He stumbles towards the door, but he does not pass through it. He finds it and slams it, lets the deafening echo run through his entire body. He crouches down, falls forward, his palms grazing the cold rough floor. Then he struggles to his knees, wraps his arms about himself, staring straight ahead, overcome with the finality of his failure, enveloped by the darkness. He tries to hear something, anything. Not even the unending hum from the freezer breaks the silence he endures. He cannot even hear his own sobbing.

★   ★   ★

Vaughn de Vries searches empty corridors, opens one door after another. Each room is like the next: cold and dark but for a single dim green light. Each time he sees it, it fades to nothing. In the blackness, he sees children's faces; each baring a grim smile — a rictus. He slams the doors, listens to the shattering noise echo and reverberate down the never-ending corridor, until it joins the patter, chatter, of distant echoes. He opens a door to a freezer that takes up an entire room, and from it tumble score after score of rigid, frosted childlike bodies. As they fall before him, they disintegrate, one after another — until nothing exists but piles of bones that seem nothing so much as an avalanche of jagged snow. He turns to the room behind him and sees three frozen corpses on metal tables. He sees the children struggle to open their eyes, desperate to breathe. Their lips part and then their faces begin to crack and shatter . . .

He wakes up. He is at home. It is a dream. His daughters stand either side of his bed. They do not smile. He looks down at himself and he is frozen rigid. He lifts his arm to hold out a hand and it cracks at the shoulder and drops to the bed and then to the ground . . .

He wakes up. Sits up quickly, doubles over, a thick cough grabbing his chest and shaking him. It was a dream . . . He retches. Then he remembers: it is only partly a dream; it is also a memory.

★ ★ ★

He cannot stay awake, cannot move to get out of bed, cry out for attention. It is not a hospital; he thinks a guest-house. A man claiming to be a doctor visits his bedside, speaks soothingly. He does not remember more. Then he wakes to find evening has come and it is almost dark behind his thin curtains. Don February looks around his door. He comes to his bedside; Vaughn cannot wake up, but Don tells him: the body is being driven to Cape Town, to Harry Kleinman, to be identified. Nothing, and no one else, has been found. The building is almost untouched, but two bedrooms have been used at some point. An air-conditioning system was in operation — generators deep underground, with settings to change the air in the middle of the night. The Crime Scene team have taken hundreds of samples and will be reporting in due course.

De Vries cannot focus; cannot think.

His warrant officer says, 'Go back to sleep. Tomorrow morning, we walk through the crime scene.'

De Vries tries to speak; nothing happens. His eyes close.

★ ★ ★

He sees that it is now 5.23 a.m. His head drags him back down to his pillow. His legs ache, his head throbs — perhaps, he thinks, from lack of alcohol. Eventually, he pulls himself up to sit on the edge of the bed, his head in his hands, and tries to focus, tries to string logical thoughts together — and fails.

At 6.30 a.m., de Vries is dressed and washed. He leaves his room, pads down a creaky wooden corridor, and finds the Crime Scene leader, Steve Ulton, sitting at a dining table, eating a cooked breakfast and drinking coffee. When he sees Vaughn, he stands up.

'Vaughn. Are you okay, man?'

'Yes. Think the bastards doped me. Can't wake up.'

Ulton glances around, pulls out a chair and gestures to de Vries. Vaughn sits, and Ulton pours him coffee. He leans into de Vries, his voice hushed.

'They couldn't find you, man. They got to the end of the second corridor and the doors are padlocked and you aren't anywhere. It was like, there's nowhere to go, but you're gone. When they found you, they nearly shot you. They said you were . . . ' He searches for words. 'In shock. They carried you out. Do you remember any of this?'

'No.'

'Don't think it's a problem; Warrant February handled it. That place is a dungeon.'

'I don't care.'

'Eight of us are billeted here for the night, in Riebeek-Kasteel,' Ulton continues. 'Some more of the team are up the road. The press arrived after about an hour — the boys from the city — and they're probably in every spare room between here and Malmesbury. How the fuck do they find out so fast?'

He sees de Vries' blank, blurred expression, takes a long sip of coffee and stays silent.

A coloured waitress comes into the room and looks at de Vries, who has his head on his chest.

Ulton says: 'More coffee, and bring him a cooked breakfast like mine.'

'Brown or white toast?' she asks, oblivious to the scene.

Ulton smiles. 'He looks like a white man to me.'

She ducks back out of the room.

Ulton says, 'Your boss is due here at nine a.m.'

Vaughn pulls himself up. 'Du Toit?'

'Ja, and General Thulani. Wants a full briefing, like always.'

'So he can deny he knew anything.'

Ulton chuckles.

'Shit,' de Vries croaks. 'And then the press. He'll love that.'

'Doc Kleinman told February that he would try to have a positive ID by eight a.m.; would phone it through to him from town.'

De Vries nods. 'Where is Don?'

'I think he's here, but we were working very late last night. We couldn't decide how to deal with the body. We couldn't get it out, as it was frozen in. We had four guys carry the entire freezer out. It took eight of them to get it up out of that tank area, up to ground level. Shit, man. That was after midnight.'

De Vries hunts for more coffee, but Ulton's pot is empty.

'She'll be here just now,' Ulton tells him. 'I know it's the worst possible scenario, but at least it's over. It's all over.'

'No, it isn't,' De Vries tells him, his bloodshot eyes still blinking in the light, sounding like he is ending a long day. 'Whatever we know now, it's nothing. It's only just beginning, I'm telling you.'

★ ★ ★

'It is Robert Eames,' Kleinman tells de Vries by telephone at precisely 8 a.m. 'Several strong indicators — long and short of it, it *is* the boy. I can't place time of death accurately, but combining the information derived from the remains directly, comparing skeletal growth with his last known measurements, and the development of the other boys, I would say that he died between two and three years ago.'

'How?'

'I know you want something, but I can't give it

280

you. He was placed in the freezer immediately after death and his remains are well preserved, but there are no immediate physical signs. So I can discount some obvious causes: he wasn't shot or stabbed. I don't think he fell and there is no sign of blunt trauma. In fact, so far, I can't find any physical evidence on his remains. Toxicology will take longer.'

'Any thoughts?'

'Not really.'

'Thanks, Harry.'

'Vaughn? I'm around if you want me. If you want to talk . . . '

'Okay,' de Vries says tonelessly, and hangs up.

★ ★ ★

De Vries ends up with over an hour to survey the outside of the bunker. Officers have moved several areas of camouflage from on top of the rectangular basin. Inside, there is bright daylight to illuminate the scene. Steve Ulton, Don February and a police photographer trail de Vries. Together, they try to recreate the scene of the shootings of Steven Lawson and Toby Henderson.

At 9.20 a.m., General Simphiwe Thulani and Director Henrik du Toit arrive for their tour. De Vries accepts no congratulations for finding the site; he stays blearily focused and stutteringly abrupt.

'Based on what we know so far,' he tells them, 'we are certain that Steven Lawson was shot here . . . ' He indicates the bloodied area further from the entry doors to the bunker. 'And Toby

281

Henderson was shot here.' He points to the messier scene closer to the entrance.

'Putting together this information with the coroner's reports suggests that the boys were walking or running towards the entrance of the bunker, and were then shot by Marc Steinhauer. We have Steinhauer's fingerprints and DNA all over the rifle — that was the first comparison the Crime Lab made — also on the unique polythene wrap, and the entry doors.'

The senior officers glance at one another.

'We have speculated that Steinhauer either released the boys from their cells or they escaped by force. They may have attacked and overpowered Marc Steinhauer, on whom we witnessed a head wound, and then attempted to flee. They located the main exit but, once in this tank area, they were unable to escape. The exit gate may have been padlocked, or they may simply not have seen how they could escape. Steinhauer may have recovered, collected the rifle and gone after them. When they ran towards him, he shot them.'

'And after the shooting?' du Toit says.

'In the eighteen hours following their deaths, Marc Steinhauer wrapped the bodies in this distinctive material and subsequently transported them to his car boot.' De Vries moves the party back towards the trapdoor into the concrete tank. 'There are drag-marks here, and also here, leading up to the trapdoor. Getting the bodies up the ladder must have been very difficult, but you have to remember that both children were very light.'

'But why move them?' du Toit asks.

'We don't know,' de Vries tells him. 'That doesn't make sense. One boy was already dead inside the building. Why not leave the bodies here, seal up the building, and leave the site? It hasn't been discovered in seven years — why should it be located now?'

'He worked alone?'

'There is no evidence that Steve Ulton and his team can find to show that there was more than one person involved in either the shooting or the removal of the bodies from the site. However, as you can see, the scene is messy, and could easily have been compromised.'

'What have you found inside?' du Toit says.

'Only what is in the Crime Scene report. We can't begin to put together a picture of what might have happened to those boys, but we know that they were confined within that cell-block for the last years of their lives; seven in the case of Steven and Toby, and at least three or four for Bobby Eames.' He lowers his voice. 'Background research has revealed a family history of abuse, both physical and sexual, going back at least to Marc Steinhauer's father, who worked as a doctor at the Valkenberg Mental Hospital. There were complaints made against him concerning the mistreatment of his child patients. I have spoken with his sister; she recounts a frightening home-life.'

'And what about Nicholas Steinhauer?' du Toit says. 'The media darling?'

'Abroad, apparently in Argentina. We have made no contact with him.'

'You think he's involved?'

'Based on circumstantial and historical evidence: definitely. However, until we hear from the Crime Scene guys, we won't know if we can place him here.'

Du Toit turns to Thulani. 'My God, sir. If it turns out that he is behind this, the media will go crazy.'

Thulani nods, very grave.

'What else?' du Toit says.

De Vries straightens his hands outwards.

'Nothing I can tell you for certain, but everything fits. Ulton's team found that damn cheese in the entrance, along with what looked like a basket of packed lunch, and there's masses of stuff which may, in time, be traceable. In terms of what we know right now, that's what we have. We don't know whether it was just one, or both Steinhauer brothers. We don't know if others were involved. That'll come when we start getting test results. We've tied up the shootings of Steven and Toby, but we don't know how Bobby Eames died. Dr Kleinman says we might know in due course, but there are no obvious signs as to cause of death.'

'All right,' du Toit says. 'We have something to give the press. What are you doing next?'

'I'm going back to Cape Town. There is information coming in all the time, and we'll put it together. This isn't over yet.'

'What do you mean?' du Toit asks.

De Vries regrets saying that, regrets revealing anything; puts it down to sedatives and too much coffee. He knows that this is where their paths diverge. Thulani and du Toit want closure — his hated phrase — neat and packaged and closed to challenge. He wants the truth, the explanation, however complicated, however messy. He knows that he will have to fight for it.

He says, casually, 'Either Nicholas Steinhauer was involved, or there will be others. This wasn't organized by Marc Steinhauer alone.'

'Based on what?'

De Vries turns to du Toit, annoyed that he seems to be allied with Thulani and against him but, mostly, frustrated that he has trapped himself.

'I met him. I spoke to him. I'm telling you: he is *not* the brains behind this. Besides, think about it: this is a substantial operation and it would have taken more than one man to sustain it. It wouldn't surprise me if he came to rescue those boys while his brother was away, and it all went wrong. He was a puppet.'

Du Toit nods. 'We'll keep that to ourselves for the moment, I think.' He looks over at Thulani, but he gets no reaction.

'So,' Vaughn says, 'if you don't need me, I'll get back to Cape Town.' He looks first at du Toit, and then at Thulani.

His voice low and calm, General Simphiwe Thulani says, 'We don't need you, Colonel.'

★   ★   ★

De Vries wakes in the middle of the night; finds himself slumped over his kitchen table. His day is blurred, already, in his memory. The drive back: Don February at the wheel, braking suddenly on the fast narrow highway, jolting him awake. Pathologist Harry Kleinman, in his office, telling him he has nothing more on the means or date of Bobby Eames' death; urging him to go home. He cannot recall the journey to his house, wonders if he has his car, or whether he was driven. He looks at his watch, sees that it is 2 a.m. He fights to stay awake, unsteadily walking through to his bedroom; considers brushing his teeth, but instead sits on the edge of his bed. He takes off his shirt, fumbles with his socks, struggles out of his trousers, and gingerly swings his legs up and lies down. He groans loudly, is asleep within moments, yet in his head, he feels awake, afraid.

★　★　★

'Tell me about the aunt.'

Ben Thambo looks around the table, at Director du Toit, de Vries and Don February. He says, 'Herself, she is no help, but her carer said that Marc Steinhauer did not stay there on March the fourth.'

'So,' de Vries says, 'we assume he stayed at the olive farm after he killed the boys. Marc Steinhauer was there perhaps once a fortnight. That doesn't sound enough to sustain three boys. So, who else was visiting it? Assuming that the reason these boys were taken and held was for some kind of sexual abuse, there must have been others.'

Ben Thambo looks at his notes.

'The evidence from the workers at the olive farm is not clear. When we showed them the pictures of Nicholas Steinhauer, two of them claimed to have seen him, but neither could tell me when, only that it was some time before. They did say that other cars sometimes parked briefly at the barn and processing area, but they couldn't specify any makes of cars, or whether or not they had seen the occupants.'

Don February says: 'In any case, if people were visiting the bunker, they would not park there. They would drive around the property on the perimeter road as we did.'

'Did these workers say they had seen cars driving there?' de Vries asks.

'I didn't ask them that specifically, sir, but I did ask if they had seen cars or people on the property generally, and they said that there were always a few people around.'

'Are we certain,' du Toit asks, 'that the road on which we approached this bunker is the only access to it?'

Don says: 'There is no road access from the other farm. An off-road vehicle could probably reach it, but the team found no tracks to suggest that option was taken, certainly not recently. It looks like the only access was from the Fineberg olive farm, along the track we took.'

De Vries asks: 'Have the owners of this other farm, where the site actually lies, been questioned?'

'Two members of the team visited the farmhouse,' Don February replies. 'The owners are away, but there are farmworkers. They told us that they were employed by an Ernest Caldwell, who bought the farm eleven years ago. They had never been to that area of the farm, since the cultivated fields end almost a kilometre from the site. Because of the sloping nature of the land, it seems to have been left untouched.'

'We need to talk to the owner,' de Vries says.

'He is due back tomorrow.'

'I don't like this,' du Toit announces. 'Any number of people could have visited that site without drawing attention. Without suspects, it's going to be almost impossible to identify them.'

De Vries says, 'We have a possible interest in Dr Johannes Dyk. He was the consulting psychologist on the original abductions.'

'In what regard?' du Toit asks.

'He is sick and old now, but we believe that he knew the two Steinhauer brothers professionally, even socially. There are coincidental links to a known paedophile, and . . . ' de Vries tries to frame the sentence ' . . . in the light of what we now suspect about the abductions, the information he provided to the investigation now looks misleading.'

'Deliberately so?'

'I stress,' de Vries says, 'he is a person of interest, and we will be talking to him again.'

'That would be bad, Vaughn.'

De Vries looks at du Toit, thinks: that would be complicated. He does not care how du Toit feels. He will have these men now, every one of them.

Du Toit turns to Don February.

'What has Steve Ulton come up with regarding prints and DNA?'

'Nothing yet, sir. He says there is a mountain of potential evidence. His team focused first on the weapon recovered and, as you know, matched the prints found on the butt to Marc Steinhauer, similarly with the plastic wrapping. Marc Steinhauer's prints have been found inside the building, in the anteroom and in the cell area.'

'So,' du Toit continues, 'if we find other prints, they are meaningless to us unless the owners are in the system.'

De Vries says, 'This evidence is always the same: if we apprehend a suspect, it will confirm his, or her presence, but it won't help us to identify that suspect. We're working backwards again.'

'Nonetheless,' du Toit says, 'we are working, and we have discovered answers.' He stands up. 'Your team has done well, but we need this wrapped up. The moment CSL Steve Ulton finds a match to someone we have in the system, let me know. We find one, maybe we'll find all the others too.' He nods at each man in turn, leaves the room.

De Vries shakes his head. 'He just doesn't get it,' he mutters.

Ben Thambo and Don February catch each other's eye, then both stare straight ahead.

* * *

Don February reviews the notes he took of their informal interview with Robert Ledham. He confirms that Ledham had told them that he had been away during that week, in Knysna. He

289

checks the address and contact number of Max Dearman, the friend with whom Ledham said he stayed. He calls a former colleague of his at Knysna SAPS, arranges that he interview Max Dearman as soon as possible; to report back to him personally. He is disobeying de Vries, but he is also fulfilling his brief: the truth, however messy.

★ ★ ★

De Vries walks from the labs back up the staircase to his office, worrying. The squad room is almost dark, empty, officers exhausted from the enormous workload on top of their unending schedule of investigating death. He sits back in his office chair, steadies himself, and considers what he will have to do. After a few moments, he gets up, locks his desk drawer and reaches to switch off the desk lamp. His telephone rings. He answers and listens:

'Send him up, then.'

De Vries adjusts his tie, puts on his suit jacket, brushes down the lapels. He opens the door to his office, and sits back down. He hears the faint 'ting' of the elevator and sees Ralph Hopkins enter the corridor. De Vries frowns. Behind him is another man. He sees him only as a dark male form but, as they approach, the figures turn from silhouettes to three-dimensional beings. As the stranger's face appears, albeit older, more tanned and more lined, even the beginnings of loose skin at his neck, de Vries suddenly recognizes him. He stands, walks to his door.

290

Ralph Hopkins says, 'Colonel. I am here to represent Dr Nicholas Steinhauer.'

Steinhauer looks down at de Vries.

'I am here,' he says, 'to bury my brother.'

PART THREE

'I still do not understand,' Don February says, without looking away from the road, 'why Steinhauer gets forty-eight hours when he could hold the key to this?'

'Politics. We're not seen as victimizing him. Nicholas Steinhauer attends his brother's funeral, is seen mourning, then we take our chance with him.'

De Vries unwraps a chocolate bar, bites into it. He has eaten one for breakfast also; not shopped in over a week.

'Besides,' he continues, 'this gives us time to work up everything else.'

They pull up outside the big house in Rondebosch, push the bell, and are let in. As they walk through the garden, de Vries looks towards the stoep, but there is no sign of Johannes Dyk.

Nancy Maitland meets them, shakes their hands formally.

'I'm sorry to tell you,' she announces, 'but Dr Dyk isn't well enough to speak with you today.'

'Why not?' de Vries says.

'Johannes is extremely ill. I explained to you last time the nature of his condition. This morning, he told me that he could not speak with anyone, that he was too confused.'

'I see,' de Vries says, 'but not too confused to tell you that.'

She bridles. 'For you to bully a very sick,

295

elderly man would be immoral.'

'Who suggested bullying?'

'You know precisely what I mean. He is not well. That's all there is to it.'

De Vries says: 'Did you tell Dr Dyk that we were coming this morning?'

'Of course. I told him yesterday afternoon after you called. And then I told him again this morning.'

'And is this when he decided he was too ill to speak to us?'

Nancy Maitland folds her arms.

'Colonel de Vries, you talk to any doctor, any expert in the field of dementia, and he will tell you that Dr Dyk does not know what he is saying. If he didn't want to speak with you, perhaps it is because he is afraid that he will mis-speak and you will then misinterpret him.'

'Mrs Maitland,' de Vries says, 'even if Dr Dyk 'mis-speaks', and incriminates himself — '

'Incriminates?'

'Even if he were to incriminate himself — which is, I think, what you fear — the SAPS have no time to pursue a man who is, as you say, very sick and elderly.'

'I do not fear that. I am afraid that you will upset him. That you will frighten him to death.'

They stand facing each other, intransigent.

'Perhaps,' Don February suggests, 'I could see him. I spoke to him last time and Dr Dyk was quite calm.'

'I've made my position clear,' Nancy Maitland says.

Don exchanges a glance with de Vries. Then

he says, 'Well, madam, you must hold your position here, with Colonel de Vries, but I am going to see Dr Dyk. He does not have to say anything.'

He begins to walk towards the front door. De Vries watches Nancy Maitland watch him go, smiles to himself.

Don pushes open the heavy door, retraces his route to Johannes Dyk's room. His door is closed, so Don gently turns the large brass handle and goes inside. Dyk is lying on his bed, eyes closed. Don sees them flicker for a second as he turns to look at him, knows that he is actually awake.

He moves to the bedside, speaks quietly. 'Dr Dyk?' Dyk does not move; does not alter his breathing.

'Dr Dyk, this is Don — Don February. We spoke a few days ago. Do you remember?'

Don sighs, looks down at the inert figure, the shrunken form under the white sheet, rising and falling, almost imperceptibly. He turns but, as he reaches the door, he says: 'You are acting like a child. I know you can hear me, Doctor.'

★ ★ ★

De Vries sees a thick copper smog hang over the city, two thirds of the way up the ABSA building. He glances at Advocate Norman Classon, resplendent in a broad chalk-stripe black suit and blood-red bow-tie; watches du Toit pouring tea from the pot. Thinks, This is all the man does now.

Du Toit says: 'Ten a.m. Monday. Steinhaue agrees to be interviewed.'

'Good.'

'Be careful, Vaughn,' Classon booms. 'He' already contacted the media, and his plan i clear: parlay this into a big drama, with him a the centre, seemingly in control. He's going to dig up the failed investigation seven years ago and try to put the blame for everything onto the SAPS. Be aware that what is said will not remair secret.'

'I don't care.'

'Well, you should,' Classon says. 'You have no firm, criminal evidence against this man Everything is hearsay or coincidence. If he see you have nothing, it will look very bad to the public, and it will serve to strengthen hi position.'

Du Toit says: 'What has the Crime Lat determined?'

'Nothing. No prints from Nicholas Steinhaue found, so far, at the bunker site.'

'No direct link to Nicholas Steinhauer, Classon says. 'He has alibis for the times o abduction and killing. No link to the property o to the victims. This is why we have to be careful.

'Careful.' De Vries takes a deep breath, check himself, aware of the other people in the room.

He says, with forced calmness, 'For sever years, anyone connected to this case has mislec us, delayed us, diverted us. Steinhauer has the family background. His father was an abuser anc he groomed his eldest son to follow him. Ther are textbook indicators: bullying, arson, worl with children, superiority complex. Anyone discussing him says that he is a controller: his younger brother was in awe of him. Everything he said on television turns out to be wrong. He said the boys were certainly abroad and, if not, they were dead. Both possibilities were designed to discourage us to hope that they were still alive. We have to wrest control from him, put him under pressure.'

Du Toit looks to Classon, who nods, saying, 'Clearly, there is circumstantial evidence to warrant deeper investigation.'

'Don't ever forget,' du Toit says, 'I led the abduction investigation. We've got Marc Stein-hauer for the murders of Steven and Toby, and we'll catch who took them, held them and killed Robert Eames. But, be completely clear: it doesn't matter what we think, even what we know. If we can't prove it, if we can't explain it so that the correct information is disseminated to the media, then it is useless.'

'I am resigned to that,' de Vries says, trying to seem casual. 'But sometimes you have to push to find those answers. It feels like we are being straitjacketed.'

'That's because the world has changed,' du Toit says. 'We are being scrutinized every centimetre of the way: by the media, by public opinion online, by our own people — David Wertner's bureau is reviewing the original inquiry and our actions now. It makes no difference what I say to Thulani; he and Wertner are tight.'

'Ironic, isn't it? Just when you want racial

299

tension, there is none.'

'That isn't helpful. Wertner and Thulani know what's good for them. And I know what I have to produce.'

'The truth.'

'This is what you have to learn, Vaughn. Sometimes that is not a quantifiable concept.'

'The more I learn,' de Vries says sadly, 'the more helpless I feel.'

★ ★ ★

Don February sits typing, cellphone jammed between shoulder and ear.

'Robert Ledham had warned him to expect a visit from us. Admitted it straight away. Max Dearman is a very self-confident man. Ran off all the facts. According to him, Ledham didn't leave Knysna for ten days; gave me a list of witnesses who saw him in restaurants and at socials at Dearman's house, but it's seven years ago and even if I could find these people, I don't think it will help.'

'Did you believe him?'

'I didn't like him, Don. Everything he said he'd rehearsed. I don't know though, I got the feeling he was basically telling the truth.'

'And, what about the ninth of March 2007 specifically?'

'He wasn't expecting that. He said he didn't remember, but Ledham couldn't have been in town because he never left Knysna. It was his holiday.'

'Is Max Dearman married?'

'I wouldn't think so. I got the feeling that he and Ledham hung out with the boys . . . ' He stutters. 'I — I didn't mean like young boys, kids. Just that they were part of the Knysna old-homosexual network.'

'What, both of them?'

'I don't know. All the friends he talked about were male. I just assumed.'

Don thanks him, opens a new file on his desktop, taps in the information he has received. He has covered what he wanted, yet it is not resolved.

★ ★ ★

De Vries changes gear roughly as the road banks sideways and up. He has been here often enough to know the road, but each time, he almost stalls. He pulls up at the end of the cul-de-sac.

'Stop looking at my beautiful face and open the fucking gate, boykie.'

The voice on the video intercom says: 'Boykie?' The gate buzzes and de Vries pushes his way through.

At the bottom of his stairs, as de Vries opens the front door above him, John Marantz says, 'Good evening, Vaughn.'

De Vries clomps down the stairs, pushes past Marantz, stands in the middle of his living room.

'How old are you?' he demands.

'I told you,' Marantz tells him. 'I'm forty-two.'

'I have four years on you; therefore you are, officially, a boykie.'

Marantz stares at him.

'The information you got for me,' de Vries says, 'on Steinhauer: can you do it again?'

'Possibly.'

'What does that mean?'

'That I would have to consider it.'

'Why?'

'Why? Because every time I do that, I compromise myself.'

'Quid Pro Quo.'

Marantz frowns. 'I didn't know we were keeping score.'

De Vries goes into the kitchen, opens Marantz's fridge and extracts a beer.

'You need to realize something. This case is fucking me up and I either give in and go under or I fight. I will do anything to get these men. They've pissed on me for the last seven years and it's stopping now. So, you owe me — you just want to help me — you want me in your debt? Whatever it takes.'

Marantz nods. Says, 'I've already established a contact.'

'Who?'

Marantz laughs. 'You know I can't tell you that. I'll help you, Vaughn, but you have to protect me. Nothing comes from me. You understand?'

They sit down facing each other across the wide coffee table.

'You already established a contact?' de Vries says.

'Yes.'

'Why?'

'To help you, if I can.'

'Why?'

Marantz recoils. 'Because you are my friend, Vaughn. Because I *want* to help you.'

'This doesn't have anything to do with your former employers?'

'I told you. I am no longer employed by Her Majesty's Government.'

De Vries studies Marantz, feels uneasy.

'Don't think you can recruit me, John.'

Marantz shakes his head.

'Why would you think that?'

'Because a confidence trickster doesn't just take you into his confidence . . . ' He returns the stare. 'He gives you his confidence. Didn't you teach me that, Johnnie?'

Marantz turns away.

'No good deed goes unpunished.'

De Vries stares at him until he turns back to face him.

'What I do,' Vaughn says, 'trust doesn't come easily.'

Marantz meets his eye. Says, 'Vaughn, I'm not playing you. If I were, you wouldn't know it.'

★   ★   ★

De Vries sees all three men facing him yawn simultaneously.

'The funeral,' de Vries says, raising his voice, 'is this morning at ten.'

'That's quick.'

'I want someone who can handle a camera outside the crematorium. Pick a white officer, Don. He won't stand out. Tell him: if he's

303

challenged, he's press. I want a record of everyone who attends that Steinhauer service; from the media, the family and friends. Brief him carefully. I don't want the Steinhauers, or Hopkins, knowing we're there.'

'You think someone might show up?'

'It's possible. But maybe we'll see who doesn't turn up.'

Don frowns. 'Why?'

'Think about it. Your friend, colleague, relative, is accused of double murder, with links to abduction and paedophilia. Would you go to the funeral?'

Don smiles.

'Samples from Johannes Dyk?' de Vries asks.

'That is my next call.'

'Good. Don't go yourself. I want new information for Steinhauer, stuff he's not expecting. Did Dyk ever work with Steinhauer, Nicholas or Hubert?'

'I will check just now.'

'Because, Don . . . all of you. Make no mistake. We need more.'

★　★　★

Perplexed, de Vries meets her at the elevators, leads her past the squad room to his office, offers her tea.

Mary Steinhauer says, 'You told me that you would not forget me, Colonel.'

'I did.'

'You seem to have done so already. My father hid the newspapers from my daughters, but I saw the headlines. You promised that you would warn me.'

'You're right, Mrs Steinhauer. I did just that. What can I say to you? Everything has moved so quickly; I am not in charge of what is said to the press. The fact is: I forgot to contact you. I apologize.'

'At least,' she concedes, 'you seem a straightforward man. Tell me this: did Marc . . . hurt those children?'

De Vries opens his hands. 'We don't know. There's nothing to say that he did but, on the other hand, he knew where the boys were held and he visited them regularly.'

Mary Steinhauer shuts her eyes.

'It's not just a lost husband, an absent father. It's everything we've worked for. The Fineberg Estate . . . ' She looks up at him. 'How can devotion turn to resentment so quickly? May God forgive me, but I hate him. I hate him for betraying everything he knew I believed in, for destroying my daughters' lives. He could have spoken to me. He could have sought help.'

De Vries sits silently.

She says: 'Have you spoken to Nicholas yet?'

'No.'

'Well, you should. Marc was in thrall to that man. If he met him so often at their aunt's house, surely Nicholas would have known about those boys?'

'We are due to speak to him shortly.'

'Good.'

De Vries clears his throat. Says, 'The funeral for your husband. It . . . ' He trails off, feels that asking if it went well perhaps sounds wrong.

Mary Steinhauer sits up in her chair.

'It was for public appearances only. At least for my daughters. And then we are staying in Cape Town tonight. Tomorrow, I am consulting my lawyers. I want them to sell that olive farm to sell the Fineberg Estate. I want nothing more to do with any of it.'

'You're not represented by Ralph Hopkins?'

'My family use another firm. I think Hopkin was retained by the Steinhauer family.'

'Your father commented that he didn't like him. Is that your view too?'

'I have no view on Ralph Hopkins, except perhaps that he should have protected Marc.'

'Protected him? In what way?'

'He was at our house the morning Marc ... the morning he died. What did he say to him?'

'I don't know. I asked him but he maintained that it was client–attorney privilege.'

'How ridiculous.'

'Yes. Did you ask him?'

She looks down. 'No.'

'The farm outside Riebeek-Kasteel — it's in your name?'

'It would be. I dealt with financial matters Marc and I had discussed the possibility of cultivating olives, adding bottled preserves and so forth to our range. About a year later he told me he had found some land already planted with olives, ideal for a small farm unit, outside Riebeek-Kasteel. He said that he'd seen it when he was visiting his aunt.'

306

'You didn't see the land before you bought it?'

'I should have done, but I was pregnant with Sarah, my younger daughter, and I wanted Marc to make the decision. He was always a follower, never a leader. I wanted to show him that I trusted him. I think about it now and I realize that everything I did controlled him, yet that was never my intention. I tried to make him independent, answerable for his own decisions.' She shakes her head mournfully. 'Perhaps some people cannot cope. Perhaps I should have been less trusting and more diligent.' She looks back up at de Vries. 'I arranged the bank transfer; he did everything else. When the farm buildings had been restored, I visited it then. I thought that he'd done a good job. I was proud of him.' She freezes. 'You think he knew that underground building was there?'

'I don't know. If he didn't abduct those children — and you assure me that he didn't leave your estate on those days — then we know that there are others, possibly many others, involved.'

'That's horrifying.'

De Vries nods. Then he asks, 'Did you know that your husband could shoot?'

'I would have said no, but then I thought about what Marc had told me when we were first married: how his father had ensured that his sons did not go into the Army. Instead, he took them into the countryside and taught them how to hunt; how to survive. I think Marc hated it. The only reason he allowed me to keep goats and hens was because we never had to slaughter them.'

'Did you ever meet his father?'

307

'No. Marc told me he had died before we met. Both his parents. I think his mother died when Marc was only quite young. That is why Nicholas has such an influence over him.'

De Vries hesitates, confused. Asks: 'Did he ever talk about Michael?'

'Michael who?'

'His brother, Michael.'

'No.' Her expression changes slowly as she realizes what this question means. She asks warily, 'His brother?'

'You were not aware that Marc had two brothers?'

'No.'

'This is what I understand from your sister-in-law, Caroline Montague.'

Mary Steinhauer tilts her head. She seems afraid to ask.

'What happened to Michael?'

'We understand he fell during a mountain hike with Nicholas. He was killed.'

She opens her mouth; closes it again. Struggles to comprehend.

'Who else was with them?'

'Only his brother, Nicholas.'

Her expression is one of shock. De Vries says, 'I'm afraid it sounds as if there are more secrets. We confirmed that your father-in-law, Hubert Steinhauer, died in December 2006, not eight years ago. We think it is possible that this was a trigger for what followed.'

He looks up at her, sees her cheeks drain of colour. She slumps back in the chair, empty.

'I'm sorry,' de Vries repeats.

★　★　★

'The problem,' Steve Ulton tells Don, 'is that our computers don't work like they do on TV. There's none of that flashing through a database, the screen freezing with a match. It kind of crawls through what we have. And the beeping! Have you ever heard a real-life computer make those noises?

Don interrupts him, quietly, firmly. 'Please tell me that you have Dyk's fingerprints at the site?'

'We have repeating partials, not recent. Collectively, they add up to a match. So far, only in the anteroom.'

'But we have him there, at the bunker?'

'Yes.'

'Indisputable in court?'

'I thought you said Dyk was dying?'

'I ask you what I know de Vries — Colonel de Vries — will ask. Is it indisputable in court?'

Ulton looks up. 'Yes.'

Don thanks him, then walks out of the darkened lab and over to the elevators. Back in the squad room, he checks what his officers have discovered about connections between Nicholas Steinhauer and Johannes Dyk. De Vries calls him to his office and sits him down.

'Well done. I called Ulton and heard he'd spoken with you. Have we managed to connect him with Steinhauer?'

'Yes and no. They worked in the same hospital in the late 1990s. It was about then that Dyk started acting as a consultant to the SAPS and, professionally at least, we have not managed to

309

find any other links.'

'How old do you think he is?'

'I know,' Don says. 'He was born in 1935. S‹ he is seventy-nine.'

'How do you know that?'

'Because I know things.' Don smiles and d‹ Vries laughs. 'Why?'

'Is there any chance Dyk knew Huber‹ Steinhauer, the father?'

'I do not know that. I can ask them to check but it is getting late.'

De Vries sits forward. 'We need everything w‹ can get before tomorrow.'

'All right. Where am I with this interview?'

'Next to me, Don. Next to me.'

'Thank you, sir.'

'This is our case. Anyway, these guys at th‹ top, they wouldn't touch him right now. Did yor see this article he wrote in the *Argus*?' He hold‹ up a half-page spread on Steinhauer. 'He says h‹ knows nothing — how shocking it is profession ally, how it will . . . What does it say?' H‹ scrabbles for the paper, flips it around and trie‹ to find the passage. 'Yes — here: 'It will forc‹ me to look back at my family history and drav some hard conclusions.' This guy is full o‹ bullshit, Don, because I know he knows.'

'How do we prove it?'

'We catch him in the lie.'

'If we can.'

'I met with Classon and our esteemed Director, and you can guess what they said‹ Watch what we say, what might get back to th‹ media; treat the suspect like delicate glass, fo‹

fuck's sake. We have to get him off-balance and we have to keep pressing. We'll talk more in the morning, but I want you on Hopkins. Every time he interrupts, I want you to get him to back down. I want to focus on Steinhauer. You think you can manage that?'

'I am not experienced on the law, but I will try.'

'Good.'

Don stands up. 'I will look now for any connection to Hubert Steinhauer. I have to be home by six thirty. I told you.'

De Vries nods, smiles. 'Go when you have to, Don. Keep the wife happy. In the long run, it's for the best.'

★   ★   ★

As he lies awake in the early hours, de Vries thinks about his wife. He does not imagine her naked, nor bearing his children, not even all together on family holidays. In half-sleep, he sees her approach him with her microphone, a huge microphone, camera crew in tow.

'I want,' she tells him, 'to speak to you about your failure.'

★   ★   ★

Don February says, 'He is still down there, sir. Looks like he is conducting a press conference. There is at least one television crew and about thirty reporters.'

Director du Toit looks again at his watch. He already knows that it is 10.30 a.m.

'He is,' he says to de Vries, 'acting like a man above the whole business.'

'Exactly,' de Vries says. 'What did he do at the time of the abductions? Got himself in a position to pronounce on them — above suspicion. This is exactly where he's positioning himself now.'

'Is Sergeant Thambo still waiting to bring them up?'

'He is, sir,' Don tells him.

De Vries thinks: a big, tall, black African officer — very telegenic.

'Since this is supposedly a voluntary interview, I suggest we wait,' du Toit says.

De Vries leans against the wall between the two elevator doors.

'I have all day . . . '

⋆ ⋆ ⋆

'We may have a copy of your recordings?' Hopkins asks.

'It is a private meeting, sir,' Don replies. 'I would not be advisable to relay details to the public.'

'I think we'll decide on that.'

'It may be background material for my book,' Steinhauer muses.

De Vries turns to him, stares at him, says nothing.

'Shall we begin?' Hopkins says.

'We have been waiting to begin for over an hour,' de Vries says calmly. 'Is your client ready to answer some questions now?'

Hopkins looks at Steinhauer, who shakes his

head and looks bemused. 'It seems so, Colonel.'

Vaughn nods, leans down to a briefcase and produces several thick files, places them on the table in front of him, but leaves them closed. Steinhauer watches him curiously.

'A book?' de Vries says, meeting Steinhauer's gaze for the first time.

'Yes,' Steinhauer says, smiling, nonchalant.

'A novel?'

'An investigation into the human psyche. Why should a man, seemingly happily married, with a supportive family, become involved in kidnapping and murder?'

'And you'll reveal everything?'

'What I uncover; what I deduce, yes.'

'Well, I'll certainly want to read that.'

'You'll be in it.'

'I'm sure I will,' de Vries says. 'What about you, Dr Steinhauer? How will you feature?'

Ralph Hopkins says: 'Is this getting us anywhere?'

'This is an informal interview,' Don tells him. 'And your client first mentioned his book.'

'I do not appear. I know it would suit your agenda that I feature front and centre, but sadly for you, I play no part. However, clearly I have questions to answer myself. How I could have failed to detect this trait in my brother? As a professional, I should have seen warning signs.'

'What would they have been?'

Steinhauer tilts his head. 'I think perhaps the cause of my brother's depression. Of course, we scarcely discussed it, since this was a matter for Marc and his therapist — not that he was keen on psychoanalysis. He probably ignored me and

313

did not even employ one. I think, for him, he believed that it was a chemical imbalance.'

'What kind of depression did your brother suffer from?'

'It would be termed chronic depression. He was not bipolar, but his depressive episodes were, I believe, quite serious.'

'Had he attempted to commit suicide before?'

'He had not, I am sure, before been driven to the point of contemplating it.'

'What do you suppose drove him there this time?'

Steinhauer smirks.

'You, of course. Harassing him until he felt there was no escape.'

De Vries glances at Hopkins, lowers his voice.

'That is not the case, as your lawyer should have told you.'

'Well,' Steinhauer says, 'I will form my own judgement on that.' He sits back and folds his arms. Even reclining, he is taller than de Vries. He looks down at him, eyes seemingly half closed.

'You were not involved in your brother's treatment?'

'Naturally not.'

'Why, naturally?'

'Because it is not appropriate for a member of the same family to be involved in such a way. It is unlikely that Marc would have felt able to confide in me.'

'That is a shame.'

'It is usual.'

'And you never discussed it, even privately, on occasion?'

314

'As I told you: I rarely saw him. We did not socialize per se.'

'You never spoke about it when you saw him at your aunt's house in Riebeek West?'

'We were there to visit her.'

'And you visited your brother's olive farm, I suppose?'

'I went to see it, yes. I have no interest in such things, but Marc seemed pleased with it. I was happy that he had arranged the project himself.'

'He told you that, did he?'

Steinhauer frowns. 'Did he not?'

'That's not my question, sir,' de Vries says very calm, very even. 'I asked you whether he particularly told you that it was his project?'

Steinhauer blinks. 'Well, I assume so. I know that he bought the land and worked on the buildings.'

'You knew that he bought the land? Did he tell you that?'

Steinhauer sits up, looks at de Vries.

'I was aware of that so, yes — he must have told me. Perhaps he mentioned it at my aunt's, that he had bought some land nearby.'

'But you don't recall him doing that?'

Steinhauer flicks his right wrist, loosening his metal watch-strap so that it falls beneath his cuff. 'I do not recall Marc telling me that specifically, no. It would not be a particularly memorable comment.'

'Did you know the area in which your brother bought the land?'

'No.'

'But you visited it?'

'I told you, yes.'

'You didn't help him to pick it?'

'No. I had nothing to do with Marc's business.'

'You didn't assist him whatsoever in the purchase of that farmland?'

'No.'

'That's interesting,' de Vries says, pulling out a pen, opening the top file. He flicks through a few pages until he comes to the deeds of the Fineberg olive farm. Then, in silence, he writes a note in the margin. He rereads what he has written, and then replaces the pen in his pocket, closes the file and restacks it. In his peripheral vision, he is aware that Steinhauer is watching him.

Steinhauer asks casually: 'Have you heard otherwise?'

De Vries says, 'I am noting inconsistencies and contradictions between statements made.'

'I see.'

'Did you ever visit your father at the Valkenberg Mental Hospital?'

Steinhauer shifts a little: 'My father had retired from there before I began practising. I never had reason to visit him at work.'

'Have you visited it since, perhaps to read over case-notes?'

Steinhauer narrows his eyes. 'Why would I do that?'

'I don't know,' de Vries says. 'I just need to confirm or deny with you certain information, and statements made.'

'What statements?' Hopkins says.

Don February says, 'Your client is not under

316

arrest, sir. When he is, all relevant information will be released to you.'

Hopkins and Steinhauer both recoil minutely, and de Vries marvels at the effect of one tiny word in a sentence — 'when' as opposed to 'if' — and how well, in his precise, slightly stilted manner, Don has delivered it, all innocence.

'When my client is arrested?' Hopkins repeats.

'At such a time that he may be arrested, sir. At this time, this is merely a voluntary, informal interview.'

'I may have visited the Valkenberg Hospital,' Steinhauer announces. 'But I would not be looking at another doctor's notes. I never practised there.'

'So you *did* visit that hospital?'

'In my professional capacity, I may have visited it.'

'But you do not remember?'

'I have said that I probably, at some point, have visited it.'

'Perhaps you were seeking reports on a disciplinary proceeding?' de Vries says.

Now Steinhauer's smirk reappears. He says, 'I see.' He folds his arms. 'No, Colonel, I have never seen any report into the unfounded allegations about my father's patient relationships.'

'They are unfounded?'

'Of course.'

'Of course simply because he was your father, or because you had actual, factual knowledge?'

'My father was highly regarded and universally respected.'

De Vries shakes his head. 'I don't think so.'

Steinhauer looks at Hopkins, but says nothing.

'How did you know that there was an investigation?' de Vries presses.

'I think that it was mentioned at the time.'

'By whom?'

'I don't know.'

'Your father?'

'Perhaps. But there are always such risks where pioneering research is carried out. To gain ground one must risk much.'

'But you knew that there was an investigation? You weren't interested to find out the result of such an investigation?'

'I was still at medical school. I had other matters on my mind.'

'You were not concerned that, true or not, such a report might reflect on your own career?'

Steinhauer says: 'Was such a report even written?'

'You've checked?'

'No.'

'So, how do you know that there is no report?'

'Is there one?'

'Doctor,' de Vries says slowly, 'if you were my shrink, would you let me answer every question you posed with a question?'

'I don't understand the meaning of your questions.'

'The meaning,' de Vries says, 'is perfectly clear. Your answers are deliberately obtuse. Why are you doing that?'

'It is not intentional.'

'I think people in your profession would call it diversionary, perhaps even — what's that word you like? Transference — is that it?'

'If you persist,' Steinhauer replies, leaning forward, speaking directly to him at last, 'in asking me obscure questions relating to the minutiae of a conversation long ago, or whether I have ever in my life visited certain sites, my answers are unlikely to be very revealing. Who remembers that kind of thing?'

'You're doing it again.'

'Colonel . . . ' Again, Hopkins tries to interrupt.

'You see,' de Vries persists, his hands on the table between them, his face moving closer to Steinhauer's, 'the more you try to elude my questions, the more suspicious I become.' They stare at each other for a while until, eventually, Steinhauer sits back, breaks his gaze from de Vries. He looks to Hopkins.

'I am being obtuse?'

Hopkins shakes his head.

'Let's try again,' de Vries says. 'Have you checked if there was a report into your father's behaviour at the Valkenberg Mental Hospital?'

'No.'

'You've not checked if your father was officially found guilty of abusing children in his care? I'm surprised that a man in the media spotlight would not want to know what the press might be able to find.'

'Of course he was not guilty of any such thing! I knew my father. He was a complete professional. He would never have mistreated a patient in his care.'

'Did he mistreat you or your brothers when

319

you were growing up?'

Steinhauer displays a look of boredom, perhaps even mild annoyance, but he answers in the same tone.

'My father was a very loving man. He had to deal with many tragedies in his lifetime: the premature death of his wife, my mother, and his second son. He was a strict father, but I could not have wished for a better childhood. It was very happy.'

'Your sister does not think so.'

Steinhauer snorts. 'Well, my sister was very much attached to her mother. I think that when she died, it was a very grave blow to Caroline. My father was devoted to his sons. He taught us everything. Then, both Marc and I went to UCT, and Caroline left for Durban. We rarely saw her.'

'So you discount her account of an unhappy home.'

'When did she tell you this? I cannot discount what I have not heard. If she claims not to have had a happy childhood, that is her interpretation.'

'As is your version,' de Vries says.

'It is not a version, Colonel. It is my memory of the facts.'

'Happy, despite the death of your younger brother, Michael?'

'My brother,' Steinhauer says, 'was a daredevil, a tearaway. When we went walking, he would climb sheer mountain faces without ropes, clamber up tors, jump great distances. We had climbed together, and I believe that he tripped and fell. It was a terrible and profound shock to us all.'

'But it was not your fault?'

Steinhauer looks askance.

'My fault? Certainly not. I had the misfortune to be with my brother when the accident happened. I was nowhere near him when he fell. I tried to rescue him, but it was too late. I think that his neck was broken from the impact of the fall.'

'You said a misfortune. Why was it a misfortune that you were with him?'

'Have you ever seen a close relative fall to his death?'

'I thought you said that you were not sure how he died?'

'I said I was not sure of the cause.'

'But you saw him fall?'

Steinhauer rolls his eyes, clearly irritated by the questions.

'Perhaps you have misunderstood my words. I had the misfortune to be out with my brother at the time he died. To discover him and have to return home to break the news was a harrowing experience. You can empathize with that, surely?'

'Wasn't it also your misfortune to be suspected of involvement in his death?'

Steinhauer's mouth opens; he looks astonished.

'I have never been suspected of any involvement.'

'Oh,' de Vries says, not breaking his stare. 'I think you have.'

'This is ridiculous, Colonel.' Hopkins stands up.

'Please sit down, sir,' Don tells him.

'If you wish to make allegations against my

client, then do so formally, and backed up by evidence.'

'Sit down,' Don repeats. 'Your client agreed to answer all questions.'

'It's nonsense,' Steinhauer says.

'Your sister claims that Michael was a reluctant participant in these outdoor activities, that he did not wish to take part. This would also be wrong?'

'If that is how she remembers it, then I am surprised, but I can assure you that he was the keenest of any of us when it came to walking and hiking.'

'But when he died, there was only you there. So that is just your memory of the facts?'

Hopkins says, 'All witness evidence is merely a matter of recollection.'

De Vries ignores him. 'Dr Steinhauer?'

'That is what happened.'

'But you would agree, like your sister's testimony, I should remain open-minded about these matters?'

'That is a stupid question.'

De Vries looks down at his file, continues smoothly, 'There was a fire at your family home in Constantia. A shed or small barn was burned down. Do you remember that?'

Steinhauer continues to stare at de Vries.

'It is an incident I only remember vaguely.'

'It was considered arson. Did you set that fire?'

'I?' He sniffs. 'Why should I?'

De Vries waits. Steinhauer shifts again.

'No.'

'No?'

'A simple yes or no answer.'

'Did you form an opinion as to who might have done so?'

'It was an accident. Perhaps one of the staff had left a cigarette there. None of us took any notice.'

'You were in Port Elizabeth from March the eighth to March the thirteenth 2007, I believe? That's when the three boys, Steven Lawson, Robert Eames and Toby Henderson, were kidnapped.'

'I think so.'

'You flew from Cape Town on flight 734 to Port Elizabeth on the eighth at one forty p.m., and then you landed back in Cape Town on the thirteenth at five thirty-five p.m. on flight 739.'

'If you say so.'

'I don't say so, sir. The airline keeps records. That was, apparently, your schedule.'

Steinhauer shrugs.

'The reason for your visit to Port Elizabeth?'

'I was asked to consult on a very troubled patient by a colleague of mine. I have already provided Dr van Neuren's contact details. I assume that you have seen them?'

'When was that invitation issued?'

'I don't remember. I suspect that it was quite last-minute.'

'You had your own practice in Cape Town?'

'Yes.'

'Quite busy, I should imagine?'

'I had established a certain reputation.'

'So, you are asked by this colleague to consult

on a patient in Port Elizabeth and, despite having a busy practice of your own in Cape Town, at short notice you presumably cancel all your own patients for five days and fly off to Port Elizabeth. Is that right?'

De Vries' stare never leaves Steinhauer's face. He sees a tiny catch as Steinhauer breathes in to answer. Steinhauer gestures with his long narrow fingers, his wrists not leaving the table. De Vries watches his fingers fly; his perfectly manicured nails reflect the grey fluorescent light. De Vries cannot imagine a man having a manicure. It revolts him.

'I imagine I was not that busy, and I felt that this was an important case with which to be involved. As I have said to you, these are minor matters in my life. I would not remember specific cause or reason.'

'This wasn't a minor matter though, was it, sir? You've told us that it was an important case. Surely you remember what that was about?'

Steinhauer smiles smugly. 'That is patient confidentiality. I could never discuss that.'

'But you remember the case?'

'As I say, I cannot discuss it.'

'But you remember it yourself. What it was about?'

'Yes.'

Steinhauer smiles. De Vries sees a man affecting relaxation, but he knows that something he has said has disturbed the surface of the veneer.

'Had you travelled to consult on other such cases before that one?'

'I probably did. I don't recall.'

'You don't recall,' de Vries echoes. 'And subsequently, how many times have you travelled across the country for such consultations?'

'I really don't know. I travel regularly.'

'But for such a reason — to consult on a private case.'

'A serious case.'

'How often, Doctor?'

Steinhauer shakes his head, flutters his right hand. 'I don't know.'

'Once or twice? Ten times? Thirty times?'

Steinhauer says nothing. De Vries looks sideways without moving his head, watches Hopkins, sees him frown. He lets the silence beat away in the little interview room.

'I can check my diaries if such information is important to you.'

This time de Vries stays silent. Then he asks: 'You were on a tour in South America when your brother took his life. Argentina, was it?'

'Yes. I am promoting my book. The Argentinian Association of Psychiatrists invited me to present a paper at their conference and to launch my book at their institute. It is very highly regarded and I decided to accept the invitation.'

'And you left your brother in charge?'

Steinhauer shakes his head. 'What are you asking?'

'What instructions did you give to your brother, Marc?'

'Instructions? I think you misunderstand our relationship. Marc was his own man. He had his own life, his family, his business. I had no

325

influence over him whatsoever.'

'Influence?'

'Interest . . . Involvement, in his business affairs.'

'But you saw him regularly at your aunt's house?'

'I saw him on occasion.'

'How often is that?'

'Perhaps once a month, while I was in Cape Town. Less often when I moved to Johannesburg.'

'So when did you contact him to let him know that you would be away for six weeks and therefore would not be visiting your aunt as usual?'

'I . . . I did not contact Marc.'

'No?'

'I only visited my aunt occasionally since being based in Johannesburg. I did not need to let my brother know about my trip.'

'But you would normally communicate with your brother about visiting your aunt?'

Steinhauer's shoulder twitches.

'I have, on occasion, discussed these visits with him, yes.'

'But not when you will be away for six weeks?'

'I have told you, no. I did not contact Marc regarding my trip.'

'So he was not aware that you were abroad?'

'I don't know that. He may have known.'

'Because you told him?'

Steinhauer shrugs. 'Yes. Perhaps.'

'So, just for the record, when did you last see your brother, Marc?'

'I — let me think . . . I don't know. Not

recently, certainly . . . I am not sure.'

De Vries waits. 'Any idea at all, sir?'

'I suppose maybe three months ago. Our paths rarely crossed. I would visit our aunt at one time, he another.'

'What did you talk about when you last saw him?'

Now Steinhauer sits up, laughs. 'I have absolutely no idea. Why would I remember such a thing? My aunt's wellbeing, I should imagine. Marc rarely stayed the night there. He would drive back home sooner than stay over. We might confirm when we would next visit, but other than that . . . '

'And when did you say you would next visit?'

'Excuse me?'

'When you confirmed with Marc when you would both next visit?'

'I don't know.'

'You said you would discuss when you would both next visit. I just wondered what you had agreed.'

Hopkins taps the table hard.

'Enough now, Colonel. Dr Steinhauer has stated that he does not remember the details of conversations long ago. This is going nowhere.'

De Vries ignores him, immediately continues.

'So, you say you were involved in no business matters with your brother whatsoever?'

'I cannot think of any occasion where I was involved in my brother's personal or commercial business, no.'

'You ever discuss business with him at your aunt's?'

'I think,' Hopkins says, more assertively, 'that we have exhausted that line. My client has made it quite clear that he had no business relationship with his brother. Can we move on?'

'We have a long way to go, sir,' Don tells him. 'I think it is best to let the Colonel continue in order to make this as quick as possible for you and your client.'

De Vries says, 'You worked with Dr Johannes Dyk at St Magdelene's Hospital in the late 1990s. Is that correct?'

'I worked within the same field as Dr Dyk, yes. We were never colleagues as such.'

'But you remember him?'

'Obviously.'

'Why obviously? Before, you told me that you forgot unimportant matters.'

'I remember him. He was considered an authority in his field.'

'You worked with him professionally?'

'I said to you, no.'

'You socialized with him?'

'No.'

'So why would you remember him so clearly?'

'I just do. Dr Johannes Dyk was at St Magdelene's Hospital, and I remember him.'

De Vries just looks at him; face blank. Neither man speaks. After maybe thirty seconds, Steinhauer says, 'I do not recall ever socializing with Dr Dyk.'

'So, when would he have met your family? He told us that he knew both you and Marc.'

'Dr Dyk is very ill — Alzheimer's Disease, I believe.'

De Vries smiles. 'So you have kept up with him.'

'No. I haven't seen Johannes in . . . I don't know, many years.'

'Johannes?'

'Dr Dyk then.'

'So how did you know that he had Alzheimer's?'

Steinhauer hesitates momentarily. 'One hears news about colleagues.'

'But you said he was not your colleague.'

'He was . . . a man who worked in the same field as I. We are a small community of professionals.'

'A small community, but you scarcely knew him? You never socialized with him; he had been retired for several years. From whom did you hear this information?'

'Is it not correct?'

'You're doing it again, Doctor.' De Vries waves his pen, tone scolding. 'In this interview, I ask the questions, and you try to think of answers. From whom did you hear that Dr Dyk was suffering with Alzheimer's?'

'I have no idea. I was aware that he was ill, that is all.'

'I understand that the diagnosis was made only recently. Surely you must recall who told you about it?'

'I do not. I am sorry.'

'Do you suppose that he knew your father, perhaps from the Valkenberg Hospital?'

'Valkenberg? No. No, I don't know that. I suppose it is possible, but he never spoke of knowing my father.'

'You conversed with Dr Dyk?'

'Yes, on occasion.'

'And your father never came up in conversation?'

'No. I spoke rarely with Dr Dyk and, had he known my father, I am sure that it would have been one of the first things he mentioned.'

'And your brother never spoke of him with you? Dr Dyk speaks about your family as if he knew all of you quite well.'

De Vries watches Steinhauer gently breathe in and release a long, silent sigh. He gathers himself again, says, 'I met Dr Dyk only at St Magdelene's Hospital. I do not recall him at the family house, and certainly not at my own home.'

'Whose interpretation should I believe then, sir? Yours or Dr Dyk's?'

'That,' snaps Steinhauer, 'is not my business.'

'Will you be mentioning Dr Dyk in your book?'

'My work is not up for discussion.'

'It was, a few minutes ago. You deliberately brought it up.'

'I mentioned my book. I will not divulge its contents.'

'But if Dr Dyk was an old family friend . . . '

'Which, as I stated, he was not . . . '

' . . . a colleague who predicted, quite incorrectly, that the abducted children were the likely victims of child-trafficking, *exactly as you proposed*. You would not mention him as a fellow expert who gave the same false advice — '

'The advice was not false.'

'The advice was wrong; the opposite of correct.'

'The advice was offered in good faith. I can only speak for myself. Dr Dyk concluded much as I did, based on the information available to us. I am sure that others in our position would have done the same.'

'Did you discuss the case with Dr Dyk before he advised the SAPS?'

'No.'

'Not at the time of the original kidnapping, nor later?'

'No.'

'You didn't try to contact him for your television programme?'

'No.'

'Why was that? You asked *me* to appear on your programme.'

'You refused.'

'Why did you not approach Dr Dyk? As a friend and close colleague, he might have been more inclined to accept.'

Steinhauer narrows his eyes. 'You continue to insert words I have not used into your quotations of me. It is a pointless activity for you. I remember very well what I said, and the tapes will back me up. So, I repeat, solely for your benefit: Dr Dyk and I were never professional colleagues, nor would I regard him as a friend. As far as my television programme was concerned, it was my producers who made such decisions on who should appear as a guest.'

'You never made suggestions?'

Steinhauer bridles. 'Naturally, I had influence.

I certainly suggested subject matter and those who might contribute to it.'

'Did you suggest inviting me?'

'No — I don't recall. Probably not.'

'Why not?'

'I don't have much faith in policemen.'

De Vries smiles. He looks over to Don, smiles at him too.

'Not much faith . . . ' he muses. 'I'm sorry to hear that. Is that based on personal experience?'

'It was you specifically, and the SAPS generally, who failed to uncover the kidnappers of those three boys.'

'You and Dr Dyk didn't find them in some Arabian harem, did you?'

'The actions of three kidnappings in three days is audacious: it is likely that it was planned by a very experienced, highly intelligent mind or group of minds.'

'You told everyone that you were convinced that the boys were out of the country.'

'That they were being held must be considered most unlikely. The fact is that you and your people failed.'

'It was your brother who killed two of them.'

'That's enough.' Hopkins bangs the table ineffectually with his fist. 'This is not an interview to establish facts. This is a hounding of my client, who is being especially patient and indulgent. But I am not prepared to accept it. Either ask factual questions, or we will conclude proceedings.'

Vaughn sits back; continues to stare at Steinhauer.

'Your client,' Don says to Hopkins, 'has not refused to answer these questions. If he were under caution, you could warn him to stay silent if you were concerned that he might incriminate himself, but this is a voluntary interview.'

Hopkins shakes his head at Don, jabs his thumb at him as he turns to de Vries. 'Is he talking for you today, de Vries?'

'Mr Hopkins . . . '

Hopkins turns to Don. 'No. If you wish to address me, I expect the lead detective to communicate with me.'

De Vries smiles, but does not alter his gaze.

Steinhauer taps Hopkins' wrist, nods at him.

'It is fine, Ralph. Colonel de Vries has many years of resentment to work through. Perhaps this is a kind of therapy for him? He believes that I was not helpful to him in 2007, and now, because poor Marc got himself involved in something terrible, he thinks that I must be involved too. It is something of a conspiracy theory, but it really will be easier if we let it run its course.' He turns back to de Vries, settles himself on the small chair, affects relaxation. 'Please, ask your questions. I have a lunch appointment.'

'Dr Steinhauer, for your information, you had no influence over the course of the inquiry. However, Dr Dyk was the consultant psychologist on the case, and he *did* influence our direction. What was your professional opinion of Dr Dyk when you worked near him in the 1990s?'

'I had no opinion.'

'We have been told by several witnesses that you had a strong influence over your brother, Marc. How did that manifest itself?'

'I disagree. I have already stated: Marc was his own man.'

'Marc's own wife felt that you were a strong influence over him.'

Steinhauer snorts. 'Then that says more about her than me.'

'You didn't feel protective towards him?'

'From whom would he need protecting? No. Marc made his own way.'

'Even when you were younger?'

'I was his older brother; the oldest child of four. I hope that I had some influence on, perhaps even respect from, my younger siblings.'

'But no undue influence?'

'I do not understand the use of the word 'undue', but no.'

'You've never married yourself?'

'No.'

'May I ask your sexual orientation?'

Hopkins takes a breath but Steinhauer says, 'I have had several relationships with women. I have not found the woman with whom I would wish to share my life. My work has always proved demanding. I imagine I will come to regret such a situation.'

'With hindsight,' de Vries continues, 'is there anyone who you think might have been able to influence your brother in such a powerful way?'

'You talk of influence. All I know now is that the evidence seems to point to my brother being responsible for the death of two teenage boys who had been previously held captive. As I have always believed, if the motive was kidnapping and abuse, the course of events suggest a single perpetrator and, loath as I am to believe it, my brother appears to be that man.'

De Vries grins sourly at him, speaks very quietly.

'You were wrong then, and you are wrong now. This was not the work of one man working alone. We already know the identity of others involved in these crimes and, even as we speak, we are working on further identifications. Now that we have found where they were kept, the site is yielding many indicators.'

'I will be interested to learn about these others — '

'Just for the record,' de Vries interrupts, 'I want to be clear on this. You state that you never visited the former government bunker located at the far north-eastern corner of your brother Marc's land outside Riebeek-Kasteel?'

'Never.'

'So if we were to find forensic evidence linking you to that site, you would be surprised?'

'No, Colonel, I would be astonished, and indeed afraid. Since I have never visited this place, it is impossible for any evidence of my being there ever to appear. If it were to do so, I would know that something was amiss.'

'In what way, amiss?'

'Since I was never there, there could be no forensic evidence to find. Therefore, if it were to be found . . . Even you can draw a conclusion from that.' Steinhauer then turns to Hopkins and back to de Vries. 'Am I permitted to make a statement myself?'

'Go on.'

'Whatever you think of me, Colonel, let me confirm what I believe you already know. I was not in Cape Town when these three boys were taken. I have never had any knowledge of their whereabouts, and I have certainly never visited the site. I was over ten thousand kilometres from South Africa when you say my brother shot two boys. No matter that I commented on the original case, and it turns out that my brother was, horrifically, involved, I myself have no involvement whatsoever, and you will never find any evidence to the contrary. So, I suggest that we 'bury the hatchet' and consider working together.'

De Vries waits to see if Steinhauer has any more to say. Then he places the files in his briefcase and stands up.

'That's all, Doctor. I formally request that you inform us if you intend to leave Cape Town.'

Steinhauer stands up and offers his hand to de Vries, who keeps his hands at his sides. Steinhauer shakes his head.

'I will be in my Cape Town office for a week or so. After which, I should imagine I will return to Johannesburg. Ralph will inform you.'

'Mr Hopkins,' de Vries says, 'I require you to inform me *before* the event. If we wish to question your client further, we will do so here. Are you clear?'

'On the law. Yes, thank you. I will fulfil my duty as set down therein.'

336

Don looks to de Vries and then opens the door to the interview room. He leads Steinhauer and Hopkins away, towards the elevators. De Vries leaves the room. As he passes the door to the observation suite, du Toit opens it, says: 'Vaughn. My office, ten minutes.'

As the door slowly swings shut, de Vries hears du Toit murmur to Norman Classon, 'Jesus Christ.'

★ ★ ★

Du Toit swivels his chair to his desk, faces de Vries.

'I hope you are going to tell me what was gained by that.'

'You were observing.'

'I tell you what I observed: a man against whom there is not one jot of evidence to suggest that he had any personal involvement in these matters.'

'I agree.'

'You do?'

'Steinhauer has gone out of his way to ensure that there is no physical evidence to link him to these crimes. Even the dates of his absence from Cape Town: he leaves the morning of the first abduction; he returns one day afterwards.'

'But you've confirmed he was there?'

'We've spoken to the doctor he says he was with, and he confirms that Steinhauer was there. He won't provide any details.'

'So, he was there. What he said was true?'

'It's too perfect, because he has it all worked

out. Every question I asked him confirmed that.'

'So, we move on?'

'No, sir. We don't move on.' De Vries is impatient. 'You have to be alert to the undercurrents; the movement beneath the surface. Every question I asked him about evidentiary links he answered fluently: that is because he had prepared those answers. Every question relating to connections he finds less . . . shall we say, stable . . . like what Dr Johannes Dyk may or may not have told us, his reaction is quite different. He does not reply; he parries. He answers questions with questions. He does this for a reason: he knows that it is not safe to answer.'

'I think that is open to interpretation.'

'When I ask him about his brother, he tells us that he knows Marc bought the land. Do you see the significance of that?'

'No.'

'If Marc Steinhauer is 'his own man' as Nicholas claims, why would Marc mention this fact to him? Why would Nicholas Steinhauer go out of his way to emphasize it?'

Du Toit shrugs.

'I'll tell you why: because it is a significant area of questioning. It contradicts what we know about Marc Steinhauer — that this was an exceptional action by him, that he was more happy following instructions than issuing them. Nicholas Steinhauer knows this, and he is trying to control the scope of questioning. Suspects do that subconsciously, although in this case, I think he knows exactly what he is doing.'

'It's an interesting theory, Vaughn. It sounds like something from a handbook, but I don't see what it proves.'

'Did you observe his concern when I told him that I was noting inconsistencies between his statements and others received? It was palpable. This is because he can control events and his involvement in them, but he can't control what other people may say. He's afraid of that.'

'I think we all appreciate your instincts, but this proves nothing.'

De Vries stands up, shouts in a hushed voice, 'For fuck's sake, Henrik, when will you understand? This man is too clever to leave physical evidence. He is not a physical man; he is a mind man. He knows we will find nothing — that's why he is so confident. Probably he never set foot on that farm, but there are microphones in that cell area. For what? For who? *For him*. He is controlling this nightmare, but he is detached. It is unattributable. But there are uncontrollable elements — human elements. That is what frightens him, and those are what will, eventually, capture him.'

'Sit down, Colonel.'

'Don't do that,' Vaughn tells him, pacing around the chair but not sitting in it. 'You have my respect. But we have both been at this too long to piss about. I appreciate the pressure you have to bear from above. I understand that your position is at stake here, and the longer you back me, the more you risk. But I am telling you: *I know that Nicholas Steinhauer is behind this.* You may not be able to see it, but I can. I know.

339

And I will catch him in the lie.'

Du Toit looks uncomprehending. Sighs. Says, 'What do I tell the press?'

'Nothing. Confirm that we interviewed Nicholas Steinhauer, and tell them nothing.'

'That is not a commodity in which they deal.'

De Vries snorts. 'That's exactly what they deal in. They just take it and blow it up. Give them nothing and let them print whatever they want. Better they do. Let Steinhauer think he's got the better of us.'

'Did he not?'

De Vries looks away and shakes his head despairingly.

'Just because lots of people can't see something doesn't mean it isn't there.'

'By lots you mean me?'

'I mean anyone who sees one and one and won't make two.'

'Vaughn. Enough. It doesn't matter one jot that you can see it. You have to prove it to the court — and that requires evidence or a confession. So, just concentrate on that.'

'I will do that, sir.'

'And you wish the press told what?'

'I've told you, tell them anything. Tell them that he is assisting us with our enquiries or whatever you usually say when we are knee-deep in shit.'

'That won't play well.'

'For God's sake! Who cares what plays well? I want these men caught, and whatever it takes — within the law — I will do it. You're a policeman, Henrik, remember that. Sometimes

340

you can't play it straight. You have to come at your suspect from an angle they are not expecting. And that requires confidence. The press can wait.'

'Classon agrees with me,' du Toit says unhappily. 'If you go after Steinhauer with nothing, you will turn opinion against us. You know that there are forces upstairs who would rather see this experiment, and all of us, disappear. You are playing with the fate of this entire department.'

De Vries grits his teeth. He feels an unutterable frustration build, and he knows that he must contain it.

'Cut me loose. Don't support me — I don't care. I'm tired of playing politics. I'm sick of having to impress the media. I just want to do my job. I want every last man who knew about Steven and Bobby and Toby and, for God's sake, Henrik, so should you.' De Vries sits down opposite du Toit. Du Toit says nothing. They sit, not looking at one another. Minutes pass.

★   ★   ★

'Come in. Sit down, and listen.' Don February sits in front of de Vries. 'Time is running out. Du Toit is losing it. He cares more about his damn department than about finding the truth. We have to keep the pressure on and resolve this. What did you make of Steinhauer?'

'Before that, I have to tell you: Marc Steinhauer did *not* call Ralph Hopkins on the night before his suicide.'

341

'What?'

'I finally got an answer from the network. He made no call after eight thirty-four p.m. when he called his wife from Rooiels. I checked with Telkom; there is no landline connected to the Betty's Bay house. I have rechecked the surveillance report, and spoken to the officer on duty. Steinhauer did not leave the property after he arrived.'

De Vries scratches his head. 'Why would Hopkins lie?'

'I do not know.'

'Can we trace received calls on his cellphone?'

'If we obtain a warrant, yes.'

De Vries thinks. 'He would know?'

'If we applied for a warrant, yes. The Constitution does not permit a secret application.'

'The Constitution . . . ?'

'As I understand it.'

'What is Hopkins' role in this?' de Vries muses. 'Before Marc Steinhauer jumped, Hopkins had spoken to him, maybe for a minute or two before we arrived . . . ' He closes his eyes. 'I'm trying to think what he did when he was following Steinhauer with me . . . ' He says nothing. Then he snaps open his eyes. 'Don, I want you to push on with any link between Dyk and any member of the Steinhauer family. Get your men to call hospitals throughout Cape Town if necessary. And call that doctor friend of yours: Matambo.'

'Matimba. Yvonne Matimba.'

'Yes. Find out if you can look at her sources. Ask her if she can help. Nicholas Steinhauer didn't like talking about Dyk. We know there is a

342

link because both Marc Steinhauer and Dyk visited that bunker. We have to find out what that link is.'

'You think it is worth keeping an eye on Steinhauer?'

'No. I told du Toit — he isn't a physical guy. He's not going to call anyone, meet anyone. He's thought every step through; it's in his head. That's where it will stay.'

'So, what do we do?'

'If he's the brains, and we know neither Dyk nor Marc Steinhauer is the physical presence, then there's at least one more to find. That's the weak link. If we find that person, or persons, it all comes crashing down. That's what I'm counting on.'

'Okay.'

'Don. From now on, whatever else happens, we're on our own. Du Toit is going to bow to pressure, and Thulani is going to try to close this down, tie it all to Marc Steinhauer and make the SAPS look good. They need a success too badly. We can't let that happen. We need to get lucky. After seven fucking years, we need one thing — anything — to go our way.'

★ ★ ★

Don February hands out puff-pastry canapés, smiles at his guests, hears nothing they say. In the kitchen, he lays down the empty platter and walks to the bathroom. He locks the door, puts down the cover to the toilet seat, sits on it, his head in his hands.

He faces a decision; it haunts him every week of his life. He has to align his loyalty; he has to be confident that he is correct, certain of himself.

He recognizes in de Vries a blind passion which, though admirable, is dangerous to the case, to Don himself, even to the SAPS. He wonders, as he has done so many times, whether he should cut himself free of this man. He is a poor leader, a bigot and misogynist, probably a drunk, who has alienated colleagues, friends, even his family. Yet, despite this, there is something significant in de Vries that Don rates most highly of all. Amidst the jargon and paperwork, the bureaucracy and office politics, he stands for something which has always meant a great deal to Don, has defined his decisions for fifteen years: the pursuit of justice. Don thinks about his peers, reflects that amongst the university-educated black officers — the first batch of these black South Africans to reach the workplace in the new country — all their conversation, all their ambition, is their own. Whatever it takes to rise, inexorably higher; higher, especially, than the white man.

Don pulls off a length of lavatory paper, wipes his eyes and blows his nose, flushes the cistern. He unlocks the door and walks out to the party, so long-anticipated by his wife. She is standing there.

'Donald,' she says. 'What are you doing?'

He smiles back at her, kisses her on the cheek, whispers, 'You don't need a policeman to tell you that.'

De Vries hesitates at his door. As he drove up the side of the mountain, he was so certain, but now he wonders whether he is compromising too much to achieve his aim. He is still frustrated by the knowledge that Johannes Dyk will reveal nothing; will almost certainly never break, never divulge his secrets. Suddenly, he knows his mind. He has weighed the consequences and he understands that no one can hurt him. He will not allow the top floor to capitulate; he will not allow Nicholas Steinhauer to walk away, to recover his precious reputation and to scorn the SAPS and de Vries himself in some gaudy fiction passing as fact. Everywhere around him, exploitation thrives unpunished because the law binds him and serves only to protect them. He has made his decision.

★　★　★

'This is a bigger decision for me than for you.'

'I haven't heard the favour yet.'

De Vries looks at Marantz, wonders to whom this man's loyalty truly lies. He takes a breath.

'I need a list of patients' names from a private medical practice.'

'Names?'

'Just names. I don't need patient records, anything more confidential.'

'Those of Dr Nicholas Steinhauer, perhaps?'

'Ja.'

'He was just on television, you know? I had it

on while I changed.'

'Doesn't surprise me.'

'What is it? You think he's involved?'

'I don't think it, I know it. I just can't prove it.'

'Why his patients?'

'Because he kept himself out of the actual kidnappings. He probably never visited the boys, but I know that he knew about them. I'm certain of it. That's why I know he used somebody else and I was thinking: Who would he use? Who is weak and easily influenced? Who trusts this man and will do anything he asks?'

'A vulnerable patient?'

'Could be, couldn't it?'

'It could. Why not a simple warrant?'

'I need to work independently.'

'Off the record?'

'For the moment.'

'And you know it's him?'

'I've told you before, Johnnie: I meet them, I know they are guilty. This guy: he thinks he can run me, control my investigation. He did it seven years ago and he's trying to do it now. He's got the media lapping up every word he says; he's going to write a fucking book, for Christ's sake. The difference is, this time the SAPS guys on the top floor want him to be right. They want to pin this on Marc Steinhauer. For them, that reads well. They want to close down the case and make it go away, and I made my decision. That isn't going to happen.'

John Marantz sticks out his bottom lip, nods slowly.

'Who knows about me in your department?' he asks.

'I don't know. No one.'

'What about your warrant officer? February?'

'He knows we know each other. He's a sound officer. I think he knows what to ask and what to tell.'

'You have to understand, Vaughn,' Marantz says, meeting de Vries' eyes. 'I have nowhere else to go. This is my home now.'

'No one will know.'

'You talk about trust. When we met I liked you; when we talked I admired you. And then, when you got me out of custody, made serious charges disappear, you came down yourself to the station, drove me home. That bothered me. Made me wonder what was going on.'

'Why?'

'It was too much. You could have instructed them to let me out, but you came down, made yourself known, allied yourself to me. It made me wonder why.'

'You're as paranoid as I am.'

'I hope so.'

'It's the glue in our friendship.'

Marantz smiles. 'You have to promise me one thing, Vaughn. I have to know that I am protected.'

'How protected?'

'I'm an ordinary citizen — not even that. I'm not even a permanent resident yet.' He shakes his head, sighs. 'To hell with it. Tell me where I have to go.'

Vaughn de Vries raises a glass to himself, lets his eyes shut with relief.

'Tomorrow morning. Perhaps you should make an appointment?'

★ ★ ★

He drives home slowly. It is only three kilometres. He keeps smoking, his elbow out of the open driver's window. Dusk is falling over Newlands' leafy side streets, and a fresh breeze is just beginning to shift the hot, smoggy air. De Vries has a feeling building inside him, which he gets only when he thinks he is on the verge of a breakthrough. Occasionally, he wonders who Marantz really is, whether involving him may be his last mistake as a senior officer in the SAPS but, equally, he knows that what this man does releases him to do what he is good at: to hunt down the guilty, to corner them, to make them submit. And there is another thing too. Whoever Marantz is, he is like him. They are both men who have lost everything else in their lives; who are free to act. He realizes, almost for the first time, that this man not only wants him as a friend, but needs him; that in each other they recognize men who seek goals unequivocally.

He pulls up at the traffic lights on the corner of Rondebosch Common. Ahead of him, he can see silhouettes of runners from the club that uses the Common for circuit training. Next to him, a motorbike pulls up, its motor raucous. De Vries turns and, suddenly, the flash explodes in his face. He ducks, closes his eyes, sees bright fireworks burnt into his retina. Looks up, but away from the window, and accelerates fast, left

348

and away. He looks in his mirror and sees the motorbike still idling at the lights. He pulls up sharply, his breathing fast and short, considers whether to turn and chase the photographer; wonders how he has been followed, and whether the journalist saw him at John Marantz's house. His heart pounds, hands sweating.

'Fuck,' he shouts, the short, sharp word reverberating like a gunshot around his car, leaking out of the window into the night air. He looks behind him. The bike is gone. He lets out a quivering breath, starts his car, soberly drives the last few hundred metres to his house, his eyes darting around him, fingers tingling.

★   ★   ★

When the doors to the elevator part on the top floor, de Vries finds himself facing Ralph Hopkins, who is waiting there.

Hopkins beams at him. 'Good morning, Colonel.' He tries to slip past de Vries and into the lift, but de Vries blocks him. They wait until the doors close.

'What is this?' Hopkins says.

'Marc Steinhauer didn't phone you at midnight, the day before he died.'

'Of course he did,' Hopkins says soothingly.

'No. We know he didn't call you. We've checked his cellphone records.'

'Well, you must be mistaken, because I definitely spoke with Marc that evening.'

'He didn't call your number on his cellphone. He didn't stop anywhere, and there is no landline at his Betty's Bay house.'

Hopkins watches the lift doors closing behind de Vries.

'I have to go,' he says. He reaches to press the call button for the elevator, but de Vries stops him, slapping down his arm.

'Perhaps,' Hopkins says, making a show of rubbing his arm, 'we'll speak with your superiors.'

'Fine,' de Vries says. 'You can tell them what I want to know.'

Hopkins looks at de Vries disdainfully. 'Why would I lie?'

'I don't know. But I know you are. Someone else called you — perhaps from here?'

'No.'

'So you would have no objection to retrieving the call records for that day from your cellphone, and showing them to me? It's barely a week ago, so I'm sure they'll still be there.'

'Definitely not. There could be confidential information contained within those records.'

'What? From some dates and times and numbers?'

'Indeed.'

'So, to be clear,' de Vries says calmly, 'you refuse to confirm the source of the telephone call you claim to have received at midnight on the ninth of March?'

'On the contrary, I have just confirmed it to you.'

'You have repeated your challenged testimony. You're a great stickler for proof. Simply extract the call received from your telephone records, via your service provider if necessary, and the matter is closed.'

'I will consider that request, Colonel. Now I have another appointment to attend.'

'What did you tell Marc Steinhauer when you raced into his house? We don't know that, do we?'

'I made a full statement after the event. If you'd bothered to read — '

'And what you shouted to Marc Steinhauer, just as I was making contact with him — what was it? 'Remember your family?' What did *that* mean?'

Hopkins steps backwards, flushed. 'What do you think? I wanted him to focus on his wife and daughters.'

De Vries steps up to him, his face right in front of Hopkins', his voice rising.

'Not his family of boys then? Not his prisoners, or the plans he had hatched that could never be talked about?'

Hopkins' rosy complexion is bright red now, sweat beads forming on his high forehead.

'Of course not. Don't be ridiculous.' He stares at de Vries' intense expression, sputters, 'You — you don't think I . . . ? I have nothing whatsoever to do with this. I am a happily married man.'

'So, according to you, was Marc Steinhauer.'

'My God! My God, when I called you a conspiracy theorist, I realize now that is exactly what you are. Is that it? You find one desperately confused man is embroiled with paedophiles and abusers, and suddenly everyone you meet is

351

under suspicion. Is that what happens?' He pulls himself up, begins to strut back and forth, murmuring to himself.

'This isn't just about one man though,' de Vries tells him. 'It's a conspiracy of powerful, influential, probably rich men, all working together in their evil ring. I will find every last member of this group and I will bring them down, no matter who they think they are.'

Hopkins is recoiling from de Vries' fervour.

'Good luck, Colonel.'

'You still haven't answered my question,' de Vries says, keeping him within striking distance. 'Why did you lie about being called by Marc Steinhauer?'

'I did not.'

'Was it someone from here, in this building? Is that what it was? They called you to warn you that we were about to arrest Marc Steinhauer, that we had conclusive forensic proof against him?'

'No.'

'Did they want you to warn him?'

'Absolutely not.'

De Vries is about to speak again but, at the end of the corridor, a tall figure can be seen, a booming voice heard.

'Colonel de Vries. Come here.'

De Vries knows the voice. It is General Thulani, Assistant Provincial Commissioner.

Hopkins brushes past him and punches the call button on the lift. De Vries slowly walks towards Thulani. As he goes, he hears the familiar 'ting' of the elevator, and imagines

Hopkins stepping into the car, descending to street level, walking away to his wood-panelled office, or his club, or a smart restaurant for a rich lunch.

Thulani is wearing his full dress uniform: a uniform for funerals and press conferences.

'Come in to my office,' the man says.

Vaughn follows him through his anteroom, past his white secretary, and into his cold office.

'Sit down, Colonel.'

De Vries sits, says nothing; wills himself to calm down, to regain control of his emotions, his frustration.

'What was the cause of that altercation?' Thulani seems to loom over him from his raised, throne-like chair.

'I was asking Mr Hopkins some questions, sir.'

'Controversial questions, it seems. I don't think that a public corridor is the right place to hold an interview.'

'Mr Hopkins has provided crucial evidence which is not backed up by any facts or records. He is lying. I need to know why.'

'Then you must undertake that enquiry officially.'

De Vries nods, keeps his head down. After a few moments of silence, he looks up. Thulani is still looking at him. Finally, Thulani says: 'Aren't you going to ask me?'

'Sir?'

'What Ralph Hopkins was doing on the top floor? Surely that interests you.'

'I try not to think about what happens on this floor.'

Thulani laughs tightly. 'He requested a meeting with me, to discuss what he perceived to be harassment, on your part, of his clients.'

De Vries shrugs.

'I told him that I did not agree and that this investigation demanded cooperation from everybody, regardless of who they are.' He looks at de Vries, but sees nothing which suggests approval or gratitude. 'He also wanted to inform me that Dr Steinhauer wishes to return to his main home in Johannesburg.'

De Vries sits up. 'What did you say?'

Thulani smiles. 'I told him that as long as he undertook not to leave the country without notifying me, I was content that he should do that.'

De Vries shouts. '*What?*'

'Colonel . . . '

He clenches his fists under Thulani's desk, pushes his tongue hard up against the top of his mouth, ungrits his teeth, says calmly, 'I think that's a mistake, sir. Nicholas Steinhauer remains a serious suspect in the imprisonment and abuse of Steven, Bobby and Toby. We should be seeking warrants to search his homes, his office . . . buildings he has used, not letting him travel freely around the country.'

'I disagree. There's no evidence whatsoever. I've read the transcripts of your interview, been reviewing your reports regularly. Coincidence, yes, but that is not sufficient to restrict this man's freedom of movement.'

De Vries tightens his fists.

'Furthermore,' Thulani says, 'there is no question of further interfering with this man's freedom. There are no grounds for seeking warrants in relation to Nicholas Steinhauer since there is no evidence. You are out of line, Colonel.'

'This man,' de Vries says, 'has played all of us — I suspect me especially — since this whole thing began, and he thinks he's going to get away with it again.'

'Be careful, Colonel,' Thulani says. 'You are beginning to sound paranoid. The SAPS cannot be seen to support a vendetta. I was not here seven years ago, but I know that Steinhauer gave you and Brigadier du Toit a rough time in the media. You may think that this is a good opportunity to regain a little pride — '

'That's not what this is about. He may want you to think that, but it isn't. If you give this man a chance to escape, he will.'

'Well,' Thulani says, leaning back, 'I've made my decision. It was taken, as always, as a matter of law. If you need to speak to Dr Steinhauer again, he has told us that he will be moving to his Johannesburg address in a few days' time. We have no reason to doubt him. If he had not been prepared to face questions, why would he have returned from South America? He is not a flight risk.'

'I hope you're right,' de Vries mutters.

'I think,' Thulani says slowly, seeming to mull over his words, 'that if nothing more can be uncovered in this matter — and I read that we have nothing but a dying old man refusing to speak, and half a dozen unidentified fingerprints and DNA samples — you will wrap this investigation up. You, of all people, should know just how busy we all are.'

De Vries closes his eyes, takes a deep breath.

'Those 'half a dozen fingerprints' probably belong to half a dozen men who are guilty of illegal imprisonment and sex offences against minors, and who are complicit in murder. Does that mean nothing?'

'It means a great deal. But how many more murderers and rapists are still free because we do not have the resources to track them down? Do you know how many cases most officers have on their books? You live a charmed life here, Colonel. While you spend considerable time and resources on the death of these three white children, there are ten times as many every single day on the mortuary tables of the Western Cape: poor and black and coloured and just as mourned by their families as your three victims.' He takes a breath. 'There will be no end to this list, and getting stuck on one case for however many years it is, does no one, least of all yourself, any favours whatsoever.'

De Vries stays sitting upright, his jaw clenched. He can feel the pulse in his neck throbbing and he is sure that Thulani is observing it now, knowing how easy it is to rile him. A steely calm comes over de Vries' brain, if not his body.

'I will,' he starts, 'begin to conclude my inquiry, sir. Perhaps by the end of the week?'

'Forty-eight hours.'

'That's not possible.'
'Then I will find a man who thinks that it *is* possible. That is what will happen.'

★ ★ ★

Don February finds de Vries leaving the building at noon. De Vries opens his mouth to speak but instead the Noon Day Gun sounds on Signal Hill, echoes around the City Bowl and back from the sheer flat face of Table Mountain.

'Where's that hamburger place you took me to?'

'Top of Long Street.'

'I'm going there.' De Vries waits to cross the street.

'Dr Matimba says that she will look for us,' Don tells him, 'for references to Johannes Dyk and also Nicholas Steinhauer. We are lucky. She says that she will make this a chapter in her paper.'

'That and Steinhauer's new book. No cloud without a silver lining.'

'I am sure she does not mean — '

'Forget it. If she finds what we need, I don't care.' He strides into the road, stops midway to wait for a speeding Mercedes, hears his cellphone ring and runs to the other side. 'Ja?'

'It's John. I have the information you want.'

De Vries turns his back on the SAPS building. 'What's there?'

'I'm driving home. I don't know.'

'How do I see it?'

'I'll sort it out; email it to you.'

357

'Good. How long will that take?'

'Maybe an hour. I'll try to send you what you want and not the rest of the rubbish.'

De Vries gives him a private email address and hangs up. He looks back across the road and sees that Don is still standing there, watching him. He waves, and strides up the hill and across town.

★ ★ ★

Yvonne Matimba says, 'In relation to Valkenberg and St Magdelene's Hospital, I can't find any references to Nicholas Steinhauer whatsoever. Johannes Dyk, yes. He was at Valkenberg at the time Hubert Steinhauer was running whatever experiments he was involved in when he was suspended.'

'They worked together?'

'It seems so. Most of the records, as I told you, are incomplete. It looks like someone has deliberately removed files.'

'When did Dyk stop working at Valkenberg?'

'Only a few months after Steinhauer had resigned. The news item I found was that Johannes Dyk had retired after thirty-five years, the last fifteen spent at Valkenberg East.'

'What did he do?'

'From what I can see, Dyk specialized in brain formation in young children. He wrote several academic papers concerning the influence on children of their parents, their peer-group — perhaps at school — and external forces, such as deprivation, family strife, or abuse. He was one of the first experts to suggest that children were far less influenced by their parents and far more vulnerable to influence from their peer-groups and siblings.'

Don shudders. 'Maybe this is what he witnessed Nicholas Steinhauer doing; helped him to do it.'

'We can only guess as to the workings of the human mind.'

Don shakes his head slowly. 'My guesses are still way out.'

★   ★   ★

De Vries stares at the names of some 370 private patients and former patients of Dr Nicholas Steinhauer. He has burning indigestion from the burger he has wolfed down at lunchtime, no antacid pills in his desk drawers; a feeling of deterioration and humiliation about his physical state.

Getting up from the café table, surrounded by students, walking downhill, feeling the flesh on his chest jog up and down like breasts and, above all, seeing the look on the faces of the people in the streets, he has realized that, despite his height and weight, he has no presence. As a young officer, he would walk the streets of the city and people would part to let him through. Now, it is he who dodges and dribbles his way around the populace. It makes him feel weak.

He has scoured the list for any name he might recognize, but there is nothing. Now, he is checking each name against those with a criminal record in the SAPS system. He is certain that there would be an easy way to check all the names simultaneously, but he neither knows how to enter them into the system en masse, nor how to begin such a protocol. There are a few hits for minor offences, as well as two for rape, but both of these crimes were for men against women.

De Vries notices two intriguing factors: firstly, that there are the names of Steinhauer's patients seen in his Johannesburg office, as well as those here in Cape Town; that the profile of Steinhauer's patients consists almost exclusively of teenagers and young men under the age of thirty-five. There are no women and no older people.

Don February knocks at his closed door, and Vaughn calls him in.

'We have a definite link between Johannes Dyk and Hubert Steinhauer at Valkenberg,' Don says. 'They worked together on the same research investigating the brain formation of children. It looks like Dyk tried to support Steinhauer at the time of his suspension.'

De Vries says, 'So when Dyk talked about Steinhauer's sons, he was telling the truth?'

'They worked together for several years, so it is quite possible that Dyk was a friend of the family.'

'Nicholas Steinhauer lied then, when he said he scarcely knew him.'

'I think so.'

★ ★ ★

'Hold the door.'

Before the identity of the voice registers, Don has already depressed the button which reopens the doors of the elevator. Colonel David Wertner steps in, nods at him and stands by the buttons. As the doors close, he presses the red Stop button. Then he reaches into his trouser pocket and produces a set of keys, selects a small gold one, inserts it into the elevator control panel and twists it. The light for Don's floor goes out. Wertner presses the button for the basement, the doors close and the lift begins to descend. They ride in silence and, when the cubicle jolts to a stop, Don remains in the corner until Wertner tells him to follow him.

'Take ten minutes,' Wertner tells the female officer at the reception desk to the archive files. 'Go for a walk in the sun and buy yourself a nice cup of coffee.'

Don stares at Wertner, sees teeth in his smile.

She walks towards the lift without a word. Wertner moves around the desk and sits in her chair.

'I've brought you here, Warrant Officer, so that we can talk without interruption.'

Something, Don reflects, easily achievable in Wertner's own office, without the need to bring him to the windowless, echoing hallways of steel shelving and brutal fluorescent lights; the key that overrides the elevator settings, the demonstration of rank and control of those he watches.

'Stand here.' Wertner gestures in front of the desk. 'There is only one chair.' He leans back in it. 'You find yourself in a difficult situation. To be

361

promoted and to work for a senior officer on a high-profile case such as this may have seemed a gift, but it can also be a curse. You are observed more carefully and your decisions will be analysed. Because I am not alone in recognizing your talents, I am going to take you into my confidence. I expect you to respect this. Colonel de Vries has made few friends because of his working methods, but he suffers from paranoia that he is persecuted by his peers. The facts are simple in this matter. The SAPS has changed, clearly for the better, and Colonel de Vries' style of policing is now outdated and, frankly, ineffective. My department was ordered to scrutinize his failed investigation seven years ago into the disappearance of those boys and, concurrently, for incidents between then and now, leading up to his handling of this current murder investigation. Do you understand me?'

Don hesitates. Then he says: 'I understand what you have just told me. Yes, sir.'

'As his Warrant Officer, you will be judged alongside him. It would be . . . unfortunate if your career were to suffer because of the misjudgements of your superiors. A modern SAPS seeks officers who are ardent in their duty, but alert to the demands of the modern age. There are political considerations, there are media responsibilities and there is adherence to, and public support for, the changes so successfully introduced. I would hate to see you branded as out of touch, or in some way inappropriate for future promotion. Colonel de Vries will be found wanting in his execution of duty. In this current investigation, there are already many matters that trouble, not only my department, but those at the very top of the SAPS nationally. Notwithstanding the alleged suicide of a suspect, there are allegations of bullying other possible witnesses and, in so doing, bringing the SAPS into disrepute. You understand that, with the problems we face, we cannot accept behaviour that discredits all of us.'

He stares at Don. 'Warrant Officer?'

'I understand what you are saying, sir.'

'Then understand this: you must be prepared to distance yourself from Colonel de Vries if you judge him to be erring from the prescribed path. Since this current case is drawing to a conclusion, you have an opportunity now, during the final report stage, to reflect on this investigation and your working relationship. Let me leave it at this: if you feel that to continue working for him would compromise your own integrity, then you can be assured of a favourable hearing from my department. I urge you to come to me if you feel at all uneasy. If you were to officially register your concern at an early opportunity, it would serve you well in the long run. Are we clear?'

Don meets his eye and nods.

'You don't say much, do you, Warrant Officer?'

Don shakes his head.

★ ★ ★

'Vaughn?'

'What is it, John?'

'Why aren't you answering?'

'Getting a lot of calls just now.'

'You could see it was me.'

'Questioning my faith.'

'In me?'

'I don't trust anyone, boykie. Don't take it personally.'

'You know what they say about that phrase 'Don't take it personally'?'

'I don't care.'

'It's *always* personal.'

'Well?'

'Well, get someone you *do* trust to cross-check payments the SAPS made to a business called 'Tokai First Practice'.'

'What's that?'

'It was a private psychology clinic in Tokai, which the SAPS used from 2004 to 2009 when they decided to outsource psychological support for officers from in-house.'

'What is this place?'

'Your men probably called it the funny farm or something like that. Stress counselling, psychological assessments, therapy — you should try it.'

'Fuck off.'

'This could be important.'

'How did you find this?'

'It was on the secretary's computer in an archive file. It struck me: you aren't looking for current patients — you're looking for patients in 2007. I only searched those subsidiary files afterwards. Went back years. Accounts received, corporate clients and so forth. They show payments received from the SAPS.'

'Why do I need to know about this clinic?'

'Why? For fuck's sake, Vaughn! Because SAPS officers from Cape Town went there between 2004 and 2009. And one of the specialists in rotation was Nicholas Steinhauer.'

★ ★ ★

Du Toit watches him as he speaks, knows that the pressure inside him must be growing, distorting its container.

It blows: 'Jesus Christ, Henrik!'

Du Toit checks the door to his office.

'What the fuck are you doing to me?'

Du Toit stares him down, keeps his voice controlled and even, treats him like a dog needing calming.

'You're up to your neck in anti-anxiety treatment, Vaughn. If not, I'd suspend you for drunkenness. You look like shit and I don't trust your judgement.' De Vries splutters, but du Toit speaks over him, slowly.

'I have been appointed. We know what went down and it needs to be completed, explained and closed. That's what I will do, and then we can all move on with our lives and careers. That's the deal here now.'

'The deal?'

'Those are my orders.'

'It's indoctrination, Henrik. Ask yourself why they don't want the answers.'

'We have the answers.'

De Vries snorts.

'What, Colonel?'

De Vries shifts in his chair, steadies himself as he feels the structure give.

'You know nothing about this case,' he says. 'Vaughn . . .'

De Vries stands up now.

'We know Dyk worked with Hubert Steinhauer. We know he knew Marc Steinhauer, and I spoke to Caroline Montague, née Steinhauer, and I can prove that Nicholas Steinhauer lied to us.'

'We've been through this, Vaughn. If the only witness to contradict Nicholas Steinhauer is his sister, then you have nothing.'

'I have a lot more than that. I am about to check information which links Nicholas Steinhauer to the SAPS from 2004 to 2009. Right before the abductions, all through the first investigations.'

'What information?'

'Steinhauer was part of a team responsible for psychological support and counselling for Cape Town SAPS arranged through a private service called Tokai First Practice.'

'So what?'

'So what? Steinhauer had a direct inside link to officers within the SAPS. He may even have had access to information about our inquiry. He has never mentioned his connection. He knew and worked with Johannes Dyk — the man who we consulted for psychological background into the likely perpetrator. These two men fed us useless or misleading information from day one. I want permission to release the names of the officers who came into contact with him.'

'You'll never get it. Patient confidentiality.'

'We sent them, so someone within this building

will have the files. You could have signed the papers yourself, Henrik. And we don't need to know what they said or what they were told. We need to know who went to which doctor and we need to look at anyone who met with Steinhauer, and check his connection or even involvement.'

Du Toit stands up, exhales. 'All right,' he says, 'that might be possible.' He narrows his eyes. 'And who found this information?'

'Information received.'

'That won't do, Vaughn.'

'It will do. It's a logical progression of the inquiry. I'm betting that someone was giving Steinhauer information and, since I know that he's involved, that gives him a huge advantage in controlling and directing our inquiry.'

Du Toit holds up the palms of his hands.

'Stop, Vaughn! Just stop! I will find a way to request this information. I don't want you involved. I know how you are just now, and it won't work any more, not with the scrutiny we have to endure. If we need warrants or permissions, I will arrange for them to be obtained. The information will come to me and then we will look at it together, but privately. I don't want this registered as part of the inquiry.'

'Why not?'

'Because it is better not.'

'Better, for what reason? For who?'

'Vaughn, you don't do politics and that's fine. But this case is going to destroy the department and take both of us with it unless someone controls what is happening. I have the brass on one side, the media on the other, and David

Wertner everywhere else. Steinhauer is politically connected and we have to be careful.'

'Connected, how?'

'It seems that he was contacted by the provincial Justice Department back in 2007. He was their backroom consultant on the case.'

'Jesus.'

'Vaughn . . . I have had calls from the Mayor's office. The word is that, publicly, this case is to be concluded. They know that the first rule of politics is don't tell the public any more than you have to.' Du Toit breaks off, spins around at speed to see who has entered the office. It is Don February. 'What do you want, Warrant Officer?'

February glances at de Vries, straightens up to face du Toit.

'Durbanville SAPS, sir. Major Kuzwayo has just communicated an abduction. A child — an eight-year-old boy — was abducted from the roadside almost two days ago. Major Kuzwayo's men have followed up all the usual reasons for a disappearance, but everything checks out. Then, this morning, a female witness comes to the station and reports that she has seen a child matching this boy's description, being dragged into a car off the R430.'

'White?' De Vries.

'Ja.' Don looks down at the paper in his hands. 'Joe Pienaar. His father is estate manager of a wine farm there.'

'What kind of a description?'

'The witness says she saw a young boy being bundled into a car, seemingly against his will. Her description of his rugby shirt matched what

Joe Pienaar was wearing.'

'And the abductor?' du Toit says.

'She thinks a white guy, possibly coloured, tall, perhaps 1.6 to 1.8 metres. She thinks the car was a hatchback, perhaps navy blue or black.'

'I want to go there. I want to talk to the witness and the boy's parents.'

'Vaughn,' du Toit says, holding his arm up as if to block de Vries' exit. 'This has nothing to do with us. This is something else.'

'No,' de Vries argues. 'Same-age boy, same race, same style. Picture it, sir. This takes place between the Riebeek Valley and Cape Town. This fits perfectly. It's their next victim.'

'I think you're reading too much into everything. I heard about you and Hopkins — '

'Listen. Just listen to me,' he remembers they are not alone, 'sir. These people — they have kept three boys for seven years and now they have none. Can't you see this fits? Imagine what they might be thinking now that we are getting closer. You or I might go underground, but these people are not normal. They have no one to control, so they take another boy.'

'Just wait,' du Toit says. He turns to Don February. 'Let the incident room know that this is a possible — stress *possible* — connection. I want to speak with Major Kuzwayo in ten minutes. Ensure that he is available. I will call him directly from my office. Then come back here and take your orders from Colonel de Vries. Go now.'

Don leaves and du Toit walks up to de Vries.

'Sit down, Vaughn.'

'I can get more out of that witness than those guys ever can.'

'Whatever this is, we have to tread carefully. If we link our investigation with this event and it turns out to be unconnected, we cannot defend ourselves. I am required to scale down the inquiry, not ramp it up further.' He lowers his voice. 'If the two converge, then the nightmare has begun again, and I am not prepared to accept that, based on what we have.'

'And by waiting you'll let the trail go cold. For God's sake, if this is the same man who took those children seven years ago, then this is the best chance we've had to follow him.'

'Follow him? Vaughn, the witness statement is two days old.'

'Listen to me!' Vaughn realizes that he is shouting and checks himself. 'Sir, this man didn't take Bobby, Steven and Toby and then drop out of the picture. He visited them, fed them, probably abused them. That means that he was in the Riebeek Valley week after week, month after month, and if that is the case, then he is there now, with Joe Pienaar.'

'He could be anywhere.'

'There are repeating fingerprints all over that scene. Ulton can't match them because they're not on record, but he's already identified six independent sets. One belongs to Marc Steinhauer, another we now know is Johannes Dyk. One of those sets will match this man, and the others correspond to those boys' abusers. With Marc Steinhauer dead, his brother lawyered up, controlling the media, Johannes Dyk off his head, we

370

have one last chance to find them.'

'Let the Durbanville boys deal with it.'

'Look at the pattern, for God's sake.' De Vries bangs the heels of his hands against his forehead in frustration. 'Nicholas Steinhauer makes a point of saying he's leaving Cape Town. He announces it to us. Then, another young white boy disappears.'

'Vaughn . . . ' Du Toit stares at de Vries' pale cheeks beneath the dirty stubble, grimaces. 'General Thulani has made it clear. You are answerable to me, and I have the responsibility. Follow your leads here. I will ensure that I know everything that happens there. I'll talk to this Major Kuzwayo and then we'll find out whether what you were asking me about: officer referral to this clinic . . . ?'

'Tokai First Practice.' He spells it out.

'Yes. Whether we have the information here in this building or whether we need a court order. If we do, I want that warrant application delivered to my office as soon as you can. Classon is here somewhere. I'll run it past him and we'll see where we go.'

'Henrik — sir — if this *is* the same man, we'll catch him from this crime, not from those seven years ago.'

'And we may yet. But you aren't going anywhere, Vaughn. Stay in the building and don't leave it without checking with me first. That's an order.'

★　★　★

371

John Marantz drives his dog to Muizenberg Beach, negotiating the roadworks and the chaotic traffic-flows, until he reaches Sunrise Beach. He is dragged on the end of a taut lead through the dunes and onto the broad swathe of pale yellow sand, turning left, away from the busy town and towards the horizon. If it was safe, you could walk all the way to Gordon's Bay here, thirty kilometres of near-perfect beach in the distance. He lets Flynn off the lead and watches the fit red-haired terrier bound towards the water. The dog runs into the waves and sprints beside the seemingly unending parallel lines of breaking surf. Marantz follows him down to the water's edge, angling his face towards the sun, letting the autumn heat burn into him. He takes off his sandals and walks ankle-deep in the surf. The water is cold, but it is warmer than elsewhere around Cape Town, warmed by the Agulhas Current.

He closes his eyes, enveloped in a long-distant memory — a recollection of happiness and domestic contentment which seemed at the time nothing but a trivial entitlement, yet now unattainable: a husband with his wife; a father with his daughter. Here, there are couples walking hand in hand towards him, children chasing dogs and running away from incoming waves. He remembers brushing damp cold English sand off the warm, soft soles of his daughter's feet, kneeling in front of her legs dangling from the floor of the hatchback. He can picture her foot in his hand, so small that his fingers can encompass it. It is only the memory of a dream, but it makes him so sad that he feels his breathing quicken, his heart strain and ache. He feels the deep well of guilt inside his stomach. He should never have given them up; he should never have believed them lost. He should still be searching now, without respite.

He recalls friends in London, and realizes that all have fallen away. He analyses the tone of Vaughn de Vries' voice as he might assess the significance of a bet at the poker table and understands that somehow there is a distance between them, stoked by mistrust, not in each other — but in the world; in things good. He swallows, opens his eyes again, and begins to stride down the beach into the shimmering heat-haze.

★   ★   ★

'I made a mistake,' de Vries says.

'What was that?'

'I showed my hand, Don. Thulani has cornered du Toit and he is going to go along with the politicians and the press and the brass all trying to protect their fucking reputations. He's got ten years yet and he's a frightened man.'

Don says nothing, looks down at the floor.

'What, Don?'

'Maybe he is not the only one.'

'What? What do you mean?'

'I am required to report to Director du Toit, sir. But you have this investigation in your head.'

'I've added everything to the crime book.'

'You receive information from a source you will not reveal.'

'Don . . . ?'

'I do not know you well, sir. I respect you, but I do not know you. But you expect me to trust you, while you do not trust me. I have a wife and family members to support. I cannot afford to lose my job, or ruin my career.'

De Vries hears the anxiety in Don's voice, notices his right hand, thumb and forefinger rubbing back and forth.

'Sit down, Don.'

Don sits. 'I am not questioning — '

'Don. You are a good officer. Your motives are sound. You have to understand: this is no ordinary case. This has haunted me for seven years, day after day, and when those bodies were found, I vowed that I would not stop until I found those responsible. That is how I work, how I function. It is what gets me up in the morning. Because while everybody else is watching their backs and building their careers and being politically . . . expedient, I have only one thought in my head. I will bring these men to justice. I will avenge Bobby and Steven and Toby.'

'Yes, sir.'

'So I am going to tell you. I am going to tell you — but it is for your ears only, and not for Director du Toit. Is that fair?'

'I do not know. I am confused.'

'Well, you have to know,' de Vries snaps. 'You have to agree or I won't tell you. I have to know I can trust you, Don. After this is over, request a transfer, report me, whatever, but I have to know

374

that, right now, I can trust you. You can say no, but if you do, that's it. I'll just carry on alone.'

Don February shakes his head sadly, wordless.

De Vries struggles up from his chair.

'Be a man; decide what is important to you. You can live an easy life and play the game and smile at the right people and arselick your way up the ladder. The way things are now, you have a following wind. Be a black SAPS officer who goes all the way to the top. But is there any point to that, if you leave the rapists and paedophiles and murderers out there? Sit in a big leather chair in your dress uniform and take your money back to your wife in your comfortable home, but what have you actually done?'

'It is not so black and white. There are ways of operating . . .'

' . . . within the rules.' De Vries snorts. 'You're right. Follow the fucking rule book. That is what they want: that is what your wife wants, the brass want and, most importantly, it's what the gangsters and drug-dealers and child-abusers want. They'd pay you off to do the job like that. And you know what? If that's what they want, then I want to do the exact opposite.'

De Vries sits on his desk and looks down on Don. His Warrant Officer does not move. 'I'm not sitting here much longer, Don, so you have to decide. You can talk to Wertner or even Thulani. Go to du Toit, tell him that I'm leaving the building and going to Durbanville and then back to the Riebeek Valley. Tell him and he'll suspend me and probably lock me in a cell, and

I guarantee you, no one will find this young boy, and whoever took Bobby and Steven and Toby is going into hiding — and he won't make the same mistake again. Or I'll trust you and tell you what I know.'

Don February shuts his eyes and breathes deeply, but silently, through his nose. His head throbs. He draws in his breath and hears himself say:

'Tell me.'

★ ★ ★

De Vries leaves the building through a fire exit on the side which opens onto a dark alley, usually only the preserve of confused hobos and furtive police smokers, and knows that an alarm will sound in a control room somewhere. At the corner, he sees the edge of the throng of media assembling at the front doors, turns away from them and, his body aching, trots unevenly down the street towards Don's SAPS-issue vehicle. He snorts at the thought that he must hide from the media as he goes about his job; that he must disobey his seniors to keep moving forward. It disgusts him that they want to curtail the investigation — *his* investigation — because it would be neater that way; because it would play well. He has been taught a simple rule by which he lives: get from A to B and never allow yourself to be distracted because, in those moments, the thief will run, the murderer vanish, or the pistol turn on you.

He reaches the white Toyota Corolla, kicks its

rear tyre in frustration and climbs in. He knows his route. He realizes now that he has known it all along.

★　★　★

Julius Mngomezulu raps lightly on General Thulani's office door and lets himself in even before there is a reply. He waits until Thulani's head rises from his desk.

'I thought you would want to know, sir. De Vries has just been informed of the changes you commanded. He has not taken them well. It looked to me as if he was planning on leaving the building.'

Thulani shakes his head.

'For fuck's sake.' He grabs his telephone and punches three buttons. He waits for a few moments before slamming it back in its cradle. 'Go and get Brigadier du Toit. Bring him here to my office. That is my direct order to him.'

Mngomezulu turns on one shiny leather sole of his black boots, emitting one perfectly toned squeak on the dark linoleum, and pulls the door to after him.

★　★　★

De Vries endures the slow-moving traffic on the M5 link road, completed after so long a time and now, unbelievably, dug up anew. Finally, he swerves onto the flyover which takes him towards the N1 — the road which bisects the entire country, as far as Johannesburg and Pretoria. He

377

accelerates past Century City, cursing the traffic, jockeying for position and, in Cape Town-style, undertaking and overtaking to gain a little advantage. He almost misses the dividing road which takes him towards the N7 and Durbanville. His shoulder aches and his head throbs. He fumbles for the painkillers in his top shirt-pocket, tips what he hopes are two into his mouth and swallows them dry. The bitterness lingers in his throat as he feels them descend slowly through his oesophagus.

★ ★ ★

Don February sees Julius Mngomezulu whisper in Director du Toit's ear; witnesses the draining of colour from his boss' face, the petulant turn and, when Mngomezulu holds the door open for him, the Director's hand on the black officer's chest, holding him back.

Don goes to the desk he is using and picks up the phone. Then he replaces it, walks out of the squad room and down the corridors towards the stairs. These scarcely used walkways enjoy the best views of the city, a narrow gash of Waterfront vista. The sun casts hot white panels of light against the textured concrete walls. He steps out of one into the shade, takes out his cellphone and speed-dials de Vries.

When he hears his voice, he says, 'Director du Toit has just been summoned by that snake, Mngomezulu. Maybe they know about the abduction; maybe he saw you leave.' He hears de Vries curse. 'Perhaps they will warn Durbanville.

Maybe do not stop and carry on.'
He hears the line disconnect.

★ ★ ★

'Do you understand, Henrik? Do you?'
Thulani and du Toit stand by the floor-to-ceiling window that overlooks the Central Business District. Thulani is standing too close to him and du Toit would like to take a step back, but the General has him cornered.
'The Commissioner wants de Vries out of sight, out of reach of the media; ideally out of this building. When we have concluded this matter, that is what will happen. You told me that he would accept your assumption of command. Where is he?'
'In his office, working some last leads.'
'Leads? At this stage? Anyway, I hold you responsible.' Thulani jabs the air. 'Keep him away from me. I fucking hate the sight of him.'
'With respect, sir — '
'No, not with respect. With nothing. That is the end of the matter. De Vries is off the case. You have it. You finish it and we move on. As for you, God knows where you'll go now, because this is not the end; it will taint all of us here in the Western Cape.'
Du Toit wants to agree and bow out of the office. He wants to stand smiling in front of the press and announce that the investigation is concluded. He takes a deep breath.
'De Vries has new information. I have instructed him to work it from within this

379

building. No one knows more about this investigation. It would be illogical, immoral . . . to prevent him.'

'Immoral! How, immoral? To say 'after seven years, you've had your chance and now we put an end to it'. Is that what you're telling me?'

'Let me be clear then, sir,' du Toit tells him. 'My department has this inquiry and I take responsibility. But I will not compromise justice for the expediency of a neat ending and a dazzling headline. If you order me to relinquish control, then I assume you have another senior officer in mind who can bring it to its conclusion?'

Thulani's face darkens; the prospect of responsibility in any form disagreeable.

'Let me remind you. This has been your case for seven years. You were chief investigator in 07 and now you are the director of the unit — the unit for which you canvassed so hard — which has control of the case at this time. You want to end it now, or are you not content until all faith in the SAPS is destroyed in the public eye?'

Du Toit hesitates, but only momentarily. He knows that he has travelled too far in just a few emotional seconds to step back, realizes that he does not want to retreat any more.

'Another child has been abducted. Are you, sir, aware of that? He is a white boy, aged eight, name of Joe Pienaar. He was taken close to Durbanville from a side road off the N7. A witness reported seeing him taken by a white man forty-eight hours ago.' He sees Thulani freeze for a second. 'You want to close down this inquiry? Imagine how it will look if this is connected and you tell the press it's over and it starts all over again? *That* is why I have not concluded my report, and *that* is why — until I hear otherwise — I remain in command of this until it is resolved. For the sake of the reputation of the SAPS.'

Thulani takes a step back, turns away towards his desk. He turns round. 'When was this reported to you?'

'Moments before your insolent attaché took me away from the Incident Room.'

'Control yourself.'

'I was attempting to contact the chief at Durbanville. You would have been informed the moment I had confirmation.'

'I want a report in one hour. I want to know what evidence connects this alleged crime to your investigation, and I want to know that de Vries is contained within this building and that he is allowed nowhere near the press. Do you understand?'

⋆ ⋆ ⋆

De Vries sees the Durbanville Hills on his right as he speeds up the N7 freeway towards Malmesbury and the Riebeek Valley. He has drunk his share of wine from those vines. He reaches the top of the long rise where the road narrows and becomes a single lane in each direction. He wishes he had a blue light, a siren, but he knows that the puny engine in the car would not propel him past the speeding BMWs and Mercedes, that the insulated drivers, cocooned in their leather cockpits, would neither see nor hear him, euro-pop blaring from their umpteen speakers. He changes down a gear, tries to pass an articulated lorry before it is too late, struggles to make up the ground and swerves ahead of it just in time. Before him, the long, straight road stretches like a tarmac scar across the endless brittle landscape. He grits his teeth and repositions his hands on the wheel.

★ ★ ★

Don February hides out in the cleaners' storeroom on the ground floor of the stairwell. He reasons that if du Toit cannot find de Vries, it is better that he cannot find him either, assumes perhaps, that they are at work together elsewhere in the building. He calls Ben Thambo. The officer answers as usual on the second ring.

'Where are you?'

'Riebeek-Kasteel.'

'Where?'

'On the main street.'

'You know the news?'

'What news?'

'Another child has been taken, the day before yesterday, from Durbanville. Colonel de Vries thinks it could be the same people. I have emailed you the picture of the boy, the witness description too, but it is only that it is a white man — probably — tall, of average build. What have you seen? Anything at all?'

'Nothing. I speak to the same people again.

382

That is all. Why would he return to this town? Why would he come back here?'

'We are told that it is possible. Go to the guest-house where you stay. Colonel de Vries will meet you outside just now. Have all your files, all the statements ready for him.'

'De Vries? But I thought he — '

'He is on the warpath, man. Just do as he says and keep notes of his orders. We have ourselves to protect, too. You understand what I am saying?'

'Yes, I believe so. He thinks they have brought the boy back to the Valley?'

'That is what he thinks, yes.'

'We will need more men. Will you coordinate with the locals or bring in people from town?'

'Ben — listen. De Vries is coming alone. He is on a mission, man. Nothing will stop him. Give him what he wants, but stay out of it. If anyone from HQ calls you, anyone at all, do not tell them anything. You have not spoken to me and you have not seen de Vries.'

'I do not understand.'

'He is . . . Just do as he says, that is all. He will either find this boy or get us all sacked and himself killed. One or the other.'

★　★　★

Once he has negotiated Malmesbury, cut through the narrow side streets to the main country road, de Vries guns the car out of town and up towards the bulge of mountain which stands between him and the Riebeek Valley. He strains up the short pass through the mountains, and sees the vista open over rolling vines and olive plantations which encircle the towns of Riebeek West and Riebeek-Kasteel. He crests the apex and changes gear to free-wheel fast down the other side, the centrifugal force of the bend pushing him out against the driver's door. He brakes, crudely changes gear to take the left turn onto the road to Riebeek-Kasteel. He slows and turns onto the main street, down towards the landmark steeple of the Dutch Reformed church. The guest-house they stayed in is past the church, but he sees Ben Thambo standing in the shade on the opposite side. He pulls across the road, winds down the passenger window.

'Get in the car.'

Thambo hesitates.

'Bring those files with you, but get in the car.'

Thambo pulls open the door, ducks inside.

'You have talked to everyone around here, in the town, in Riebeek West?'

'Yes, sir. There are only three of us, but teams have worked through both towns twice. We have no new information.'

'Around the bunker, there are farms, yes?'

'Yes.'

'I want you to tell me who is there and who you have talked to.'

'It's all in the report.'

'We don't have time for reports. Whoever held those boys lived within the vicinity, must be known to people. This man has spent seven years living this life and he may not have anywhere else to go. If he took Joe Pienaar, he could bring him

384

back here, because no one knows who he is. Take me to the farm or farms which back onto the Fineberg olive farm.'

'Yes, I can show you.'

'You were sent the picture of this new boy who has been taken? Joe Pienaar?'

Thambo produces the crudely printed emailed photograph of a smiling young boy.

'Show me.' De Vries grabs the picture from Thambo's hand and flattens it against the centre of the steering wheel.

'No one will have seen this boy except for those involved, but you study that, because we are going to be meeting him again, Thambo. I'm not leaving till we do.'

★ ★ ★

They drive for twenty-five kilometres, deeper into farming country, only tin-roofed workers' shacks and the occasional derelict farmstead blighting the near-perfect view of pastoral life. Thambo indicates the first of the two farms adjoining the Fineberg olive farm, and de Vries takes the turn too quickly; he skids on the dusty red gravel and accelerates down the dirt-path, its surface rutted with tiny waves, like the hard sand by the water's edge on the beach. The Toyota jiggles and weaves; a plastic fitting from a maplight above his head falls into Thambo's lap.

'How far is this place?'

Thambo looks up. 'About four kilometres down this track. Thuissen's farm adjoins the Fineberg farm on the western side.'

'Was this the guy we couldn't get hold of originally?'

'Ja. He says he had trouble with his bakkie; spent three days in Riebeek West with a friend while it was being repaired. I spoke with him last week and he said he hadn't seen anything at the Fineberg farm. Had never had any dealings with them there, didn't even know who owned it.'

'You search his farm buildings?'

Thambo looks across to de Vries.

'No, sir. You had found the bunker. I just talked to the guy, that's all.'

De Vries jerks the steering wheel sideways to avoid a deep rut, throws both of them to the right and then jolts them back again. It does not occur to him to slow down.

'What about his workers? You get a list of them?'

'Ja. It's in the file.'

'Any of them white?'

'No. They are either black workers from the camp down there, or his managers are coloured guys.'

'They live on site?'

Thambo looks at the vibrating notes in his lap.

'Two couples. Farm manager, his deputy and their wives. One of them is a domestic worker at the farmhouse, the other helps with the farm shop.'

'This Thuissen . . . he married?'

'His wife left, he says. He is a bad-tempered man.'

'Been married myself,' de Vries grunts. 'Can't blame him.'

Thuissen snaps open the farmhouse door, steps out and stands right up to Thambo and de Vries.

'I've already spoken with this guy,' he tells them, pointing his chin at Thambo.

'I know. We want to talk to you again,' de Vries tells him.

'Why?'

'*I* want to talk to you, Mr Thuissen.'

Thuissen examines de Vries, head to toe.

'All right. Come in then.'

He looks back at Thambo, but de Vries says, 'Just take a look around, Sergeant.'

Thuissen frowns.

'Look around? Why?'

De Vries gestures for Thuissen to enter his own front door, follows him in.

De Vries says, 'There's been another abduction. We have to check everywhere for a fugitive.'

De Vries looks around at the big kitchen, taken aback by the mess: filthy dishes in and by the sink, blackened pans around the stove, one upturned on the quarry-tiled floor, plates and boards on the worktops. The smell is of sweating old cheese. The kitchen table is covered in papers, half a dozen odd-coloured mugs, pieces of bread and the remains of a leg of lamb. Everywhere is the low, insistent hysteria of flies feeding, fighting for the finest detritus. De Vries recoils.

Thuissen notices his reaction.

'My maid is sick,' he says. 'I don't have time. Come through.' He leads de Vries into a similarly untidy, but relatively fly-free lounge. Two

387

Labradors wag their tails wanly as they enter, but do not move from their beds in the corner.

Thuissen sits down and de Vries chooses the frayed arm of a chair to face him; he watches Thuissen in silence, watches him murmuring to himself, looking from side to side, refusing to meet de Vries' eye.

Finally, the man looks up, licks his lips, says, 'What do you want?'

'I told you, Mr Thuissen. Another child has been abducted and, since the others were held here in the Riebeek Valley, just off your land, we have to check everywhere again.'

Thuissen nods slowly.

'You've seen anyone or anything unusual in the last forty-eight hours?'

'No.'

'A tall white guy and a boy, aged about eight?'

'I've been here — around the farm. I don't have a vehicle, except for that little car. My bakkie is still in the garage.'

'Did you know about that government building, that bunker? You know it was over there, just off your land?'

Thuissen shakes his head.

'You have any white workers on your farm?'

'No.'

'See any white guys on Fineberg farm up there?'

'No. I'm up by that boundary maybe two or three days a year, checking the fences, nothing else. Never seen anyone there.'

De Vries stares at him.

'What?' Thuissen asks him.

'You okay?' de Vries says blankly.

Thuissen smiles sourly.

De Vries waits, saying nothing, feeling that Thuissen is contemplating, meditating on something, wondering whether it is something he might tell him. After another minute, Thuissen has said nothing.

De Vries says, 'What's the matter?'

'I'm okay. You?'

'You have something to tell me?'

'No.'

'You sure?'

'Are you finished now, with your questions? I have to work.'

Thuissen doesn't move and de Vries stays where he is, aware of the silence, but for the breathing of the sleeping dogs.

'My wife,' Thuissen starts. 'My wife fucked off six months ago, emptied our bank account, took all our savings — not that there was much. I have no money to pay the guys, the harvest won't even pay my debts and the guy at the garage won't give me back my bakkie, so no, man, I'm not all right. I feel like shit.'

He keeps his head down, but de Vries rises. The pressure has been released, and de Vries believes him, but he will not be distracted.

'I'm sorry.'

De Vries walks back through the rancid kitchen, out into the muddy courtyard. Thambo is waiting for him.

'Come see this, sir.'

'What?'

'Look at this barn.'

De Vries follows Thambo around the back of

the farmstead towards a long, low modern shed with a corrugated-iron roof. He pulls open the door and ushers de Vries inside.

The room is dimly lit by a string of low-voltage bulbs in tin pendants in a row down the length of the room, and at first de Vries discerns only a storeroom of old furniture. As his eyes adjust, he observes order: a selection of old white goods — fridges, stoves, freezers — some with their doors open, against the walls, a line of trestle tables covered in blankets and six narrow iron beds in a row at the far side. Every other bed has a large knitted soft toy on it: a giraffe, a zebra and an elephant.

De Vries walks in further, considers the scene. Through an internal door to the left is a scruffy tack room with saddles and horse blankets hanging from a horizontal beam, horse-feed, brushes and reins arranged reasonably neatly on shelves. He turns back into the main body of the barn. It makes no sense. He exits the building, finding Thuissen at the corner of the courtyard.

'I thought you were leaving,' Thuissen says quietly.

De Vries gestures him towards them with the tips of his fingers. As Thuissen approaches, he points at the door to the barn.

'What do you use this room for, Mr Thuissen?'

Thuissen looks up glumly and studies the open door of his own barn. 'War games.'

'What?'

'They come the last weekend of every month. Fifteen, sixteen of them. Bring their computers, wire them up, plug 'em in, sit there all night

390

Friday through to Sunday afternoon. Sleep in shifts, eat in shifts. Some of them don't see daylight all weekend. Then they get in their cars and go home. All I know is, they pay me, and right now, I need every cent I can get.'

'Who is this?'

'Men. All men. From Bellville. It's a club. Men in their twenties, some in their sixties. Pale as ghosts, some of them, never take their coats off. Looked in once, but they don't look up. All they want is power for their computers and a couple of heaters in the winter. My wife offered to make them a braai once, but they said they couldn't stop, couldn't leave the war.'

De Vries trances for a moment.

'They stay there all the time?'

'Ja.'

'They don't go out, wander around?'

'No. They just sit and play and sleep in shifts.'

De Vries ponders.

'All right, we're leaving. Goodbye, Mr Thuissen.'

Thuissen follows de Vries across the yard, blurts out, 'I heard shots.'

De Vries spins around. 'What? When?'

'Fortnight ago, Sunday. Could have come from that bunker place. Wasn't sure. The bakkie had broken down. I was walking home. Thought they were shots.'

'The officer who came here to talk to you — you tell him this?'

'No.'

'Why not?'

Thuissen looks at Ben Thambo, back at de

391

Vries. Mumbles, 'I don't know.'

'You didn't report it?'

'Could have been hunting.'

De Vries stares at Thuissen's face. 'But you knew it wasn't. What else did you hear?'

'I don't know,' Thuissen says firmly.

De Vries shakes his head.

'I think you heard the murder of two young boys.' He moves towards the car, and then turns back again. 'And you did nothing, said nothing.'

De Vries gestures to Thambo, marches away from the man, gets into the driver's seat of the car. Slams the door.

Thuissen raises a hand, leaves it there unmoving, staring at them.

'These people,' de Vries sighs. He says to Thambo, 'The other farm: get us there as quick as you can.' He sets off at a pace back onto the dirt track.

Thambo says: 'You think he would not speak to me because of my colour?'

De Vries thinks exactly that.

'I think he has no one and nothing in his head but himself.'

'I'm sorry.'

'Why be sorry? What's the name of this other place?'

'It's owned by an Ernest Caldwell. He came from England twenty years ago. He was away when the teams first came, but I spoke to him later. We have to drive around Thuissen's place and rejoin the Riebeek West road.'

★ ★ ★

They approach the Caldwell farm down a narrow track lined with gnarled bottlebrush trees. To his right, de Vries can see grain fields, blackened by fire where the stubble has been burnt to the ground after harvesting. He powers down the track, ignoring the sound of the underside of the car being caught on the raised grassy centre of the lane. His stomach rumbles from having eaten almost nothing all day, but he disregards it, presses on, stopping the car in front of the farmhouse. A middle-aged woman opens the front door while they are still getting out of the car. She has her arms open, smiling warmly. She registers them and the smile evaporates.

'This is a private farm,' she tells them. 'Private land.'

De Vries shows her a badge. 'We're police.'

'Oh. I was expecting a friend. How can I help you?'

'Who are you?' de Vries asks.

'Who am I? I live here.'

De Vries opens his mouth and closes it again, takes a breath.

'It's not an accusation. I just need to know your identity.'

The woman laughs. 'Sorry. I'm . . . what would you call me? I guess I'm Ernest's girlfriend.'

'Do you live here?'

'Yes,' she replies firmly. 'For the last two years.'

'Mr Caldwell did not mention you when I spoke to him last week,' Thambo says.

She stands at the front door, nonplussed.

'I'm sorry,' de Vries says. 'We're in the middle of a very important investigation. We thought we

393

knew everybody who was living in the vicinity. What is your name?'

'Deirdre. Deirdre Trott.'

'Miss Trott, I need to speak to Mr Caldwell. Is he inside?'

'No. I mean . . . no. He'll be out by the perimeter barns. He'll be checking the feed harvest is safely away for the winter. You want me to show you?'

De Vries hesitates. 'No, thank you. Just tell me where to go, then speak to my Sergeant here.'

'All right.'

He looks at his watch. 'Hang on a moment.' He turns Thambo away from her and walks him towards the car.

'Sergeant, call your guys in Riebeek-Kasteel and get one of them to pick you up. Speak to Miss . . . Trott here, and just check she doesn't know anything. Maybe take a look inside. Make copies of the picture you've been emailed, get out and about and see if, by some freak chance, anyone has seen this child and a tall white guy. I'll meet you back at the guest-house later.' He has an afterthought. 'And Thambo — tell no one I am here, except for Don February, and even then make sure it's on his cellphone and not on landlines. Do it for your own sake as well as mine. You haven't seen me, okay?'

Thambo nods, calls his team while de Vries gets instructions to the barns from Deirdre Trott. When he has the route, he takes the Toyota and finds the track which leads around the farm. He opens his cellphone and checks reception. It seems good enough. He calls Don February.

'Can you talk?'

'Ja.'

'I'm at the Caldwell farm. Nothing yet. What about your end?'

'I'm in trouble, sir. I stayed out of sight until after three, then I had all hell let loose on me when they could not find you. I told them you felt sick and had gone to find a chemist. I do not know if they believed me, but now they are worried that you will talk to the press and the media.'

'I don't care, Don. If I don't find this boy Joe, I don't think I want a job any more. You just keep your head down and nothing will stick.'

'You have visited the bunker?'

'No. Can't see the point.'

'Why not?'

'We still have guys there, don't we? It's still sealed off.'

'Not since Monday. It is sealed, but there's no one there as far as I know. You could ask Thambo.'

'I didn't know that. I'll go after I've spoken with Caldwell. Thambo may call you. Ask him then. Call me if anything comes up — but Don? Watch yourself.'

He hangs up, negotiates a right-angled turn, continues up the hill towards a copse of gum trees.

★   ★   ★

395

He takes almost fifteen minutes to wind his way gingerly over the deeply rutted track past fallow fields and then up a long stretch towards the summit of a broad rolling hill. As he crests the summit, the low evening sun hits the windshield and blinds him. He pulls down the sun-visor, squints at the road ahead, makes the turn and sees two huge barns some 300 metres ahead of him. Apart from their dark forms, the whole scene is bleached white by the low autumn sun, and de Vries keeps his left hand raised over his left eye to block out the intense light.

He finds Ernest Caldwell smoking by his car outside the entrance to the first of the two barns. Caldwell waves at de Vries and starts to trudge towards him the moment the Toyota's engine is switched off.

'De Vries? Deirdre called me on my cell. If she'd thought, I could have come back to the house.' He grips Vaughn's hand firmly, shakes it. 'We're all in shock here. We can't believe it. Those poor children only a few kilometres from our house, just off our land. We can't get our heads around it.'

'I was searching for them for seven years. I knew they, or their bodies, were somewhere.'

They stand silently for a moment. There are swallows on the wing; their plaintive cries drift on the strong breeze.

Caldwell nods. 'What can I do for you?'

De Vries studies him for a moment, shuffling around until his back is to the sun. Caldwell is the first person he has met today who has seemed relaxed and content, his face and body-posture open, his eyes met with his own. Everyone is hiding something, but Caldwell just smiles affably, awaiting instruction. It almost throws him.

'We have an ongoing situation, sir,' de Vries tells him, leaning in to speak above the persistent breeze. 'I need to review some information. Is that all right?'

Caldwell offers him a cigarette. De Vries declines, pulls his own pack from his pocket and they both stick one in their mouths. Caldwell passes him a heavy, industrial-looking lighter.

'Wind-proofed. Vital here. Deirdre gave it to me.' De Vries nods, fires it up, and passes it back to him. 'Ask whatever you like.'

'You told my men you had no idea about the government building, the bunker, just off your land?'

'Yes — I mean, no.' He laughs. 'I was amazed to discover it was there. I would have expected the Land Searches to have thrown it up, but I guess it was secret. There are all sorts of rumours going ar — '

'What about the rest of your workers?' de Vries interrupts. 'Did they ever speak to you about it?'

'No, Colonel. You can see for yourself if you want to drive around the farm. It's at the furthest corner from us. We don't even cultivate those distant fields at the moment, so there's no need for any of us ever to go there. And as you'll see, it's in a dip. I went up there after everything had happened. I couldn't get a bakkie anywhere near, it's too rough.'

'So, none of your workers would ever have been there?'

'No. I suppose Terry might have ridden out that far, but I doubt it.'

'Who's Terry?'

'Terry Hardiman. He's our groom. We have stables here and he oversees the team. Spends most of his time in the saddle, training my kids, or taking visitors for rides.'

De Vries feels his fingers tingle. 'Your groom. A white guy?'

'Yes.'

'How long has he worked for you here?'

Caldwell looks taken aback. 'I don't know. Maybe six or seven years. Why?'

'South African guy?'

'Yes. Well, English originally, I believe. I think of myself as a Bokkie now . . . ' He chuckles, but checks himself when he sees de Vries' frozen expression. 'We don't spend a lot of time together. He knew my last girlfriend better — and my kids, of course. He has his own cottage with its own stables, just along from the cottages and the main stable-block. I think he said he came from Port Elizabeth, spent some time in the UK. I'm from Derbyshire originally. Got divorced, wanted a new start. Why?'

De Vries considers for a moment. Then: 'Got a picture of him?'

Caldwell splutters. 'Not on me.' He laughs. 'Is there a problem?'

'Probably not. You have any other white employees?'

'A couple of girls who work in the shop. They come in from Riebeek West three days a week. Otherwise, no.' Caldwell clicks his fingers.

'Actually, I *do* have a picture of Terry. Come inside.'

He leads de Vries into the first of the two barns and then through an interior door into a small office with a chipboard desk and an old iron filing-cabinet. On the wall is a distorted piece of paper, printed with a photographic image. The first thing de Vries notices is the broad band of deep blue sky that runs across the top. As he approaches it, he sees that it is a group shot of people in front of the two barns.

'We took this when we built and opened these two barns. It was a big thing for us. February before last. It was a kind of barn-raising, like in that film . . . ' Caldwell reaches up and pulls the sheet off the corkboard. '*Witness*, that was it.' He hands the sheet to de Vries. 'Terry is right here.' He points to a tall figure at the back of the group of about forty people.

De Vries squints at it. Says, 'I need to take this outside.'

He trots back into the sunshine, stares at the picture. The inkjet printing has begun to fade and, close up, it is pixilated and fuzzy. De Vries holds it away from himself, tries to focus on the partially obscured face. He is experiencing the same sensations he felt when he studied the picture of Toby Henderson in the mortuary. He swallows hard, aware that his hands are shaking and that he cannot keep the picture still enough to stare at it any longer. He is almost certain.

He looks up to see Ernest Caldwell lighting another cigarette. He takes a breath and steadies himself.

'I ought to speak to this Terry myself. Where will he be?'

Caldwell looks down at his watch.

'It's coming up to five now. He'll either be at his place or out riding. He often takes his horse for a run at dusk. I'll drive you down and we'll see. You need to go right away?'

'Yes.'

Caldwell points a remote-control key fob at the barn and the huge door begins to descend.

'Follow me down.'

He ducks into his Subaru. De Vries gets into the Toyota, struggles to push the key into the ignition, finally fires up the engine and pulls out after Caldwell. He is thinking about the face in the picture. The face with a beard and sideburns; not complete but, he thinks, complete enough. He wonders whether he has seen correctly and wishes he had taken the picture with him.

★   ★   ★

When they pull up outside the cottage, de Vries can see how isolated it is. Further down the gentle hill, perhaps a kilometre away, is a group of plainer workers' cottages in a semicircle of gum trees, some with lights in the windows, but this house is bigger, completely dark.

Caldwell gets out of his car and walks over to Vaughn.

'Looks like he's out just now. He has his own stables around the back. We can check and see if Derby is missing.'

'Derby?'

400

'His horse.'

They walk briskly behind the house to a small courtyard bordered by three stables. Caldwell peers into each box. From the second one a white horse's head appears but, from the others, there is no sign of life.

'Yes. He's out riding. He'll have taken his dog, William, with him too. Do you want to wait?'

De Vries wonders. He affects nonchalance.

'No. I'll catch him tomorrow. Will you see him this evening?'

'Probably not. I can call him later. He never takes his cell out with him — the reception isn't great around here.'

'That's fine. I'll call by tomorrow morning.'

Caldwell looks at him. 'Are you sure? You seemed concerned back there up at the barns.'

'No. It's been a long day, that's all, and I could do with a break. Tomorrow is fine.'

Caldwell waits a moment longer, then turns towards his car. He stops and looks back at de Vries.

'You want to talk to Deirdre or me any more?'

'No, sir. Thank you. When I come to the main road, which way do I go for Riebeek-Kasteel?'

'Turn right. When you reach the T-junction, turn left and you'll see it signposted. There's still another hour of light. You'll be there well before nightfall. Just follow me back to the farmhouse and then carry on past me.'

★ ★ ★

De Vries studies the map on top of Thambo's pile of reports, realizes that he is closer to the entrance of the Fineberg olive farm than he had imagined. He shuts off the reading light and looks at his cellphone. There are eight missed calls. The charge is nearly exhausted, but he scrolls down the list, sees that they are all from Don February. He presses the call button and hears Don's phone ringing. The ringing stops and there is the sound of the freeway. 'Don. Can you talk?'

The light on his screen fades and dies; the line goes dead. He has no battery left. He opens the glove compartment, then remembers that he is not in his own car. There is no charger there. He wants to throw the phone down hard, break it into pieces, but he lays it gently on the passenger seat, his hand shaking. He feels his heart beating in his temples. He stays stationary at the junction, engine running, the light beginning to fade around him. He knows that he must return to Riebeek-Kasteel, get in contact with Don February, put together a team, at the least with Ben Thambo. He hears himself breathing above the engine noise, rubs the sweat off his palms with the tips of his fingers, grips the wheel and turns left — towards the Fineberg olive farm.

★ ★ ★

There is no one at the entrance from the main road, and he drives fast and focused onto the track around the olive groves. Already, he needs his full-beam headlights to show him the way. The sun has fallen and the grey dusk of the countryside is blacker than night in the city. He

402

takes the 90-degree turn at the far corner and begins to slow down. He stops the Toyota a hundred metres short of the turn-off down into the wooded dell. He searches the glove compartment and cubby-holes for a torch, finds nothing. He pats his chest for the feel of his gun and realizes that this, too, has been jettisoned back at headquarters.

He gets out of the car, trots towards the turn-off and then jogs down the hill towards the bunker, trying to mask his panting. The moon has barely risen and the canopy of trees block out what there is of dull white light. He ducks under the striped police tape and runs to where he remembers the trapdoor is positioned. It is closed, but not padlocked. He heaves the iron gate up and lowers it as slowly as he can to the ground. He is about to climb down inside when he freezes. In the distance, he hears a horse whinnying. He wonders whether the man calling himself Terry is on the horse or in the bunker, wonders whether to follow the sound of the horse, or let his body lead him where it will. He swallows, descends the ladder and jumps the last few steps, hitting the ground heavily, almost losing his balance. His limbs feel weak and shaky, but he is so charged with adrenalin now that he drives himself on, step after step.

He reaches the green doors at the entrance to the bunker and finds them shut also. He tries to squeeze his fingers between them, but cannot shift them. He picks up the strongest branch he can find on the ground and inserts it into the narrow gap between them. The right-hand door moves a few centimetres, but he cannot gain sufficient purchase to lever it open. He searches the perimeter in the gloom, bent low over the leaves and twigs. His hand hits metal and he brings the object up to his face: a thick rusted blade from what might have been a chisel. He returns to the doors and tries again. Using all his limited strength, he pushes the chisel blade between the gap and uses the left-hand door as purchase. Finally, he swaps it for his fingers, dropping the chisel blade and, grimacing, heaves open the right-hand door. He squeezes inside, leaning his back against the door to keep it open. He uses his left foot to drag the chisel to the base of the left-hand door, lets the right-hand door close, almost completely.

He turns, stares down the corridor that descends to his right, sees only blackness, knows that there will be no light until he passes through the next set of doors and, even then, he doesn't know whether the power has been cut, whether the generator which powered the dull green bulb, the cursed chest freezer, is still running.

He lets his eyes adjust to the blackness and then begins to move down the corridor, his arms held out ahead of him. He senses the walls either side of him, but he cannot see them. The smell infects his nostrils again, damp and mildew-ridden. It brings back the fear and desperation which overcame him, last time he was here. He stops, suddenly paralysed, appalled at the prospect of diving once more into the heavy black air ahead of him. He then pulls himself straight, continues gingerly, step by step.

His fingers hit the double doors at the bottom of the corridor and he swears under his breath. He sees nothing, but he shoulders open the door, which swings forward heavily but silently and then, once he is through, shuts behind him with an almost imperceptible hiss. At the far end, he can just see the low glow of green light that had lit their way only a week previously. Bracing himself, he walks slowly towards the prison block, concentrating on masking his footsteps by walking almost on tiptoe.

Suddenly, he stops. He holds his breath, feels a shiver pass down his back. He hears a voice. It is deep, echoing down the corridor, grasping at his heart like a clenched hand. He cannot hear words, but he knows now that he is not alone. He swallows, becomes aware that his mouth is completely dry. He stifles a cough, retreats until his back hits the wall, rests his stinging fingers against the cold and damp. He stares at the doors to the prison block, but he cannot discern any movement, hear any words. In the stultifying silence, he wonders whether he has imagined the voice; thinks perhaps that he dreamt it, that his senses are shutting down on him just as they did before.

He edges down the corridor, aware of the gradient taking him further underground. When he reaches the doors, he realizes that he has been holding his breath again, and he pauses to stabilize his breathing. He opens one door a crack and peers through. The three dim bulbs are lit in the anteroom, but he cannot see more than a sliver of the space through the gap in the doors. His ears strain, alert for any sound.

Suddenly the voice speaks and de Vries jumps. It is close by, but not in the anteroom. Someone is in the cell area. Then he hears whimpering, a child crying. He knows that this is the missing boy, Joe Pienaar; knows that he has found him, that the man he is seeking has returned to where he is in complete control.

He pushes open the door more fully, hears the hinges creak in the silence . . . but does not think that this is audible inside the cell-block. He slips inside and, keeping low, takes two long steps to the left so that he is not visible from the door to the cells, which is half open. He searches the worktops for something to use as a weapon. He sees a table knife, picks it up, slides it into his jacket pocket. There is nothing else he can see which could be useful.

He hears the voice again; this time it is clear. It strikes such fear into him, he cannot believe how it reverberates through his entire body. He knows that he must move now, or he will become frozen, impotent to act. He steps to the door of the cell-block, sees the back of the man and, inside the middle cell, the boy he recognizes as Joe Pienaar, his torso naked, his face bloodied. He goes to speak but catches himself, swallows, urging moisture to lubricate his throat.

Then he says: 'Trevor.'

The man jumps, flashes around, stares at the doorway. The boy screams, high-pitched and hysterical. Then, just as quickly, he stops, and de Vries hears the thudding silence again. He wills himself to speak.

'Trevor Henderson.'

406

De Vries takes a step inside the doorway, faces the tall man. He seeks confirmation, not from the man, but from his own eyes. He scans his features and he knows that it is true.

'Get back.' The voice, before so deep and calm, is strangled.

'I have no weapon. I am on my own. You are in control.' De Vries is surprised to hear his own voice penetrate the silence, controlled, saying words he had not prepared but which instinctively he knows he must say.

'I know you,' the man states.

'It's Vaughn. It's Vaughn de Vries. And you are Trevor Henderson.'

'I am Terry Hardiman . . . Terry Hardiman.'

De Vries takes another step inside. Henderson darts to his right, grabs a short pistol from the table against the wall, points it at de Vries.

'Stay where you are.'

De Vries stops, shivers with cold fear. He has been so focused on the boy, he has failed to make even a cursory search of his surroundings. His brain is processing the man's voice. He knows that this is — was — Inspector Trevor Henderson, a man with whom he worked for two years; knows that this man has taken three boys and now a fourth; knows that he has taken his own son, locked him away for seven years and abused him beyond understanding. He looks up at Henderson, stares at the barrel of the gun.

'Let the boy go, Trevor. You have me now. Do what you want, but let the boy go. He has his own family waiting for him.'

'No.'

407

'Let the boy go and we can talk about this. We can move forward the way you want.'

'Joe is mine.'

Three words, uttered so calmly, with such total assurance. If de Vries could only be certain that he was not dreaming, he would be so afraid. He struggles to compute what he must say.

'Steven, Toby, Bobby. They were your boys. They were your boys. But Joe — he isn't. Let him go.'

The man's right eye twitches. Vaughn watches every tiny move, tries not to stare at his face directly; knows that all his body language must be subservient. He must keep talking, engage this man, persuade him slowly but consistently, yet make him feel that he is in command. He feels so tired, has so little strength, but the wide-eyed, pleading gaze of the child, now on his knees, drives him on.

'Let me see Joe,' de Vries hears himself saying.

The man turns his back to de Vries for a moment, stares at the child. Then he swivels round, points the gun at de Vries' head and walks towards him.

'I told him,' he snarls. 'I told him that if it was anybody, it would be you.'

'Who?'

The man steps forward, jams the muzzle of the gun into de Vries' ear, grabs his arm, pulls him towards the bars of the cell. His teeth are clenched. He spits, his voice both threatening and pleading.

'Don't ask questions. That's the rule here. No questions.' He twists the gun in de Vries' ear, penetrating it, jabbing it into him. De Vries grimaces from the pain, feels his legs quiver.

'I told him that you were the type never to give up. Where are the others?'

De Vries concentrates on breathing. The gun fucks his ear again.

'The others. *Where are they?*'

Now he feels that the reality is less frightening than the prospect. It is happening; any choice has evaporated. He is calm.

'I told you: I'm alone. They are coming, but we have time to sort this out.'

He senses Henderson gulp. He sees the man's eyes go out of focus for a moment, panic begin to set in. He knows that as the adrenalin hits him, he could do anything.

The man reaches in his pocket with his left hand, struggles to find something. Then he stretches across himself to his right-hand pocket. De Vries hears keys. He slowly lowers his own right hand; out of sight of Henderson, he feels the blunt, cold blade of the table knife in his own jacket pocket.

'Step back,' Henderson commands.

De Vries feels the gun muzzle leave his ear; he staggers back a pace. Henderson glances down at the lock to the cell, then up again to de Vries.

'Joe. Stand at the back by your bed.'

From the corner of his eye, de Vries sees the boy's eyes open wide again.

'Joe! Do as I say!' The man's voice rises with frustration.

De Vries sees Joe Pienaar get up onto shaking

legs, then fall again and crawl towards the back of the cell. He sees Henderson feel for the right key, insert it into the lock, turn it. Henderson points the gun at de Vries and gestures him towards the door.

'Get in.'

Vaughn looks Henderson in the eye, looks down at the gun muzzle. He takes a tiny step forward. Then he stops.

'*Move.*'

Vaughn holds up his hands slowly.

'Trevor . . . Terry. Let Joe go. Let him live. You can do what you like with me, but let him go.' He turns towards the boy, meets his stare, wills the expression in his eyes to resonate with the child.

'I am his father.'

De Vries stands still, watching Henderson. The man glances quickly at Joe Pienaar, and then back to de Vries.

'Get in the cell, de Vries. Move — now.'

Vaughn lowers his arms, turns himself at a slight angle from Henderson and reaches the knife in his pocket. He knows he has only one chance. He stops just in front of Henderson.

'Are you hurt, Joe?' he asks.

He stares again at the child, wills a response from him. Suddenly, Joe Pienaar lets out an ear-piercing scream. Henderson turns to him — and at that moment, de Vries drives both arms down onto Henderson's right arm and then lifts his own right hand and stabs the table knife into the right-angle between the man's neck and shoulder. Henderson screams, drops the pistol and lunges at de Vries, head down with all his weight, driving him away and smashing him against the iron bars of the adjoining cell. De Vries jabs him in the eyes with his fingers, struggles free of the howling man and then jumps on top of him, pinning down his hands with his own, his exhausted body a dead weight on top of him. He looks up and sees Joe Pienaar at the open cell door.

'Run! Just run,' he pants. 'Go up the corridor ahead of you and get out.'

The boy looks startled and deathly pale. He stares at the two men, stumbles across the cell-block, out of the door, then through the anteroom. Over the sound of Henderson's whimpering, de Vries can hear the child's footsteps slow but not stop, and he imagines him trying to run, walking blind up towards the double doors and eventually to the green iron doors and out into the dark, cool night air.

He looks down at Henderson, who has stopped struggling. He feels an unnatural heat against his hands and sees blood oozing out from the man's neck. He does not let up the pressure. He gasps for air, tries to steady himself. When there has been no movement for a minute or so, he releases his weight from one hand and levers himself up. He lets out a deep breath and wonders whether Henderson is unconscious or whether he is dying. He tries to stand up, but feels no strength in his legs; his arms ache as he tries to get upright. Suddenly, he is aware that the body is moving and, before he knows it, he sees Henderson's arm grasp his legs and pull him back down in a vicious rugby tackle. He loses his balance, feels the concrete floor race towards him, the brutal pain as his head hits the rough surface.

Henderson struggles up, kicks de Vries in the stomach, causing him to double up, choke for breath. Henderson then stumbles across the cell-block, finds his pistol, checks it and weaves his way back to de Vries who is now curled up, foetus-like, on the floor. Henderson grabs his collar and drags him towards the cell. At the door, he half picks up de Vries and hauls him inside. He follows him in, turns to lock the cell door, then throws the keys through the bars, until they skid to a stop against two dusty white cabinets by the far wall. Henderson slithers towards de Vries and grabs his hair, forces the gun muzzle into his ear again, hissing, 'We are going to die together, de Vries, you fucking bastard.'

He drops de Vries' head on the floor of the cell, gets up and crosses to the little bed. He picks up Joe Pienaar's rugby shirt and ties it around his neck. The blood has almost stopped flowing. It is not as deep a wound as de Vries had assumed; it is raw, but already healing. Henderson collapses on the bunk. When he sees de Vries stir, he raises the weapon.

'There is nowhere to go, de Vries. Nowhere for either of us now. I condemned us both.'

They sit in silence for five minutes. De Vries begins to come round and tries to lever himself into a sitting position, to face Henderson. He can hear nothing but the sound of his heart

412

throbbing in his head, most especially in his right ear.

Finally, de Vries says, 'Why kill them, Trevor?'

'No questions. No questions!'

De Vries waits ten heartbeats.

'Why kill your boys?'

'I never harmed them. I would never harm them. They were mine. I loved them.'

'So why?'

'I never killed them. *They* killed them. That fucking brother killed them.'

De Vries looks up at Henderson, cannot see through his bloodied eyes.

'What brother?'

'You know who. You know. You tried to arrest him, but he knew you couldn't do that. Knew that could never happen.'

'Why?'

'Why? Why? Why?' Henderson is screaming quietly now, his hands on his temples. 'You keep asking why. Because of *him*.'

De Vries waits, using the time to assess whether he has any strength remaining, whether he can possibly reach the gun, realizing that the keys to the cell are out of reach, knowing that Henderson has no escape plan, no hope, no chance.

'Who is *him*, Trevor?'

When he hears nothing, he looks up again and tries to focus on Trevor Henderson. He cannot make out the expression or even the features on the man's face. His head is bowed, and all he can see is the crown, where his hair is thinning. De Vries waits in silence, until he can hear

Henderson's breath catch and he wonders whether the man is sobbing.

Henderson looks up, muttering, slobbering: 'Toby . . . wasn't . . . my . . . real . . . son. He wasn't mine. I can't have children, so that . . . bitch . . . she screwed some other poor fuck and took his children. She said over and over again that he wasn't mine, that he doesn't belong to me. But he was my son, and I had to have him. And I brought him friends for company, so that we could all be a family . . .'

Now, de Vries hears him crying; wonders whether he can reach him in time to wrest the gun from him, wonders what he would do if he did get it. Suddenly, the crying stops and Henderson lifts his head, focuses on de Vries, and raises the gun shakily.

'It was my family. They killed my family.'

'Who killed them, Trevor? We can leave a message here for the police. We can tell them what you tell me. They can catch whoever killed your family.'

Henderson laughs through his nose, his head heavy on his shoulders.

'The Steinhauers. He gave me my world and then he took it away again.'

'Nicholas Steinhauer? Marc Steinhauer?'

'No questions. No questions. The doctors knew what I wanted and they gave it to me. Do you have any idea what it is like to live one life and be denied your true self?'

De Vries watches him, his own head heavy and wracked with pain. He knows that his only chance is if Henderson is more badly injured

414

than he believes and that suddenly he will go down.

'What doctors?'

'Doctors. Doctors . . . all of them telling me things.'

'Was it . . . ?' De Vries starts. 'Was it Nicholas Steinhauer?' He watches Henderson's bloodied eyes, but he cannot read anything from them or from his silence. Henderson's head begins to fall and then jolts back up.

'Come here,' he says thickly.

De Vries acts — thinks he acts — incapable.

'Come here, de Vries.'

Vaughn shakes his head.

'If you come, I will tell you what you want to know.'

Vaughn looks up at Henderson and sees new light in the man's eyes, new determination, and he knows that his last chance has passed.

'Why die, Trevor? Why not live and tell your story?'

'I'll tell you my story, de Vries . . . if you come here.'

De Vries crawls towards him. His mind searches blankly for options, even for words which might delay what he knows is inevitable. Henderson scrambles towards him, grabs his collar again and pushes the left side of his head against the right side of de Vries' head, their cold, clammy cheeks touching. Then, he places the muzzle of the gun against his own right ear.

'One shot.'

De Vries tries to turn his head.

'You were going to tell me.'

Henderson snorts, teeth gritted, jaw clenched.

'In hell . . . ' He pushes the pistol into his ear, slowly but forcefully begins to squeeze the trigger.

The explosion echoes around the cell-block, reverberating a million times over from bare wall to floor to ceiling, from bar to bar to bar, out through the anteroom and into the dark corridors, fading and growing as each wave hits itself over and over again.

De Vries is aware of intense heat scalding him, agonizing pain in his ears; he feels blood run out of his eyes and nose and mouth and ears . . . But he is breathing — panting. His head is on the floor, his back sends pulses of agony into his neck, his stomach is throbbing and he is dry-retching, his tongue against the dusty concrete floor.

He pulls himself up and stares back across the room, unable to see at all from one eye, but almost focusing with the other. He hears a lock turn, keys jangle against the iron bars. A man walks towards him. He sees the pale palm of his hand reach for his shoulder.

'It's over.'

'Don?'

'Yes.'

'Don?'

'The man is dead. Ben Thambo will be here. There'll be an ambulance. Do not move.'

'What? How . . . ?'

Don February squats down.

'I came here, found the boy at the doors. He could not open them to escape. He told me and I did what I should not do. I came down alone.

I saw you in the cell with that man and I knew I had to take the shot.'

De Vries feels consciousness drifting away from him. He opens his mouth, but he never speaks a word.

PART FOUR

'To conclude,' Henrik du Toit pronounces. 'This has been an exceptionally complicated, disturbing inquiry, with its roots in a terrible crime which shook the entire country seven years ago. However, because of the experience and dedication of the officers leading this inquiry; because of the resources and, above all, because of the structure and freedoms afforded to your Western Cape Special Crimes Department, we have been able to save one young life and resolve many questions which have remained unanswered for so long.'

From the discomfort of his hospital bed, Vaughn de Vries speaks loudly in his empty room. 'What a smooth bastard cunt.'

He watches du Toit sit and General Thulani rise to field questions which are being shrieked and shouted from the audience of journalists and newspeople. He reaches forward with a grimace, wraps his fingers around the remote control and draws it to him. He finds the red button on the top right-hand side and presses it firmly. The foment on the screen implodes.

He sits back, sighing heavily, fumbles for the call button dangling by the bed. He presses it several times.

'After that shit,' he announces to himself, 'I need fucking painkillers.'

421

★ ★ ★

Robert Ledham stretches his back, grimaces at the pains shooting down his neck, stares up at the vaulted roof of his garage. He realizes that he has been stooped over the monitor for almost five hours, observing — rarely contributing to — a profound discussion with fellow members of his group. Never has he witnessed so much debate, so much admiration for a concept. None had heard of Trevor Henderson; none had been privy to the world he had created for himself and — if the police were to be believed — a select few others. Some speculate openly on how they would feel in such an alternative world of freedom; more regret that they have not the contacts nor resources to create such a hiding-place for themselves.

Ledham eventually logs off, edges his way back down the stepladder next to his car in the garage proper. He closes the trapdoor and stows the ladder horizontally on the wall, as if he used it only for DIY. He exits the garage and walks slowly back into his house. He relieves himself gratefully in the bathroom, pours himself a glass of cold water from the jug in the fridge and pads down the corridor to his study, which he unlocks and enters. He sits at his desk, his brain spinning, fingers tingling. He knows that the contacts formed by the abduction will add to his group. Together they will seek further opportunities, and soon he will find a girl to bring him pleasure and relief.

He looks down at the half-finished illustration

422

in front of him. All his life, he reflects, his only desire has been to please children, to make them smile . . .

★ ★ ★

'I think,' du Toit tells him, 'we have all been through enough, especially you and Colonel de Vries, that we can draw a line under certain . . . matters of discipline.'

Don February is sitting in the rectangle of sofas, being offered coffee. He looks up from his cup at du Toit, but he says nothing.

'What is of utmost importance, now that you have been correctly vindicated of any wrongdoing regarding the shooting of Trevor Henderson, is that we tie up what we can, and accept that there will remain unidentified suspects in this case. We can only hope that, one day, we will find matches to the outstanding evidence identified at the Fineberg olive farm bunker. Technology being what it is, it would not surprise me if we subsequently identify perpetrators but, for now, we require closure. I trust that you agree with us here, Warrant Officer?'

Don nods, then decides that du Toit expects something more from him.

'Yes, sir.'

'Naturally, you will need to discuss each element of the conclusion with Colonel de Vries but — and I think this could be most valuable to you personally — I look to you to draw everything together in the closing report.'

'Yes, sir.'

'And finally, I want to commend you again on your loyalty to your commanding officer. However, I would be negligent in my duty if I didn't remind you that Colonel de Vries deliberately ignored my orders and, doubtless, cajoled you — and your colleague, Sergeant Thambo — into supporting him and attempting to obscure his activities. This department has survived this sternest of challenges but, be aware, there are many eyes from above who see much to criticize — and we would do well to resolve to follow procedure and acknowledge chain of command. We fail to do this, and we will lose our remit.'

In the expectant silence, Don February lowers his coffee cup again. He has drunk barely two sips.

'Yes, sir.'

★ ★ ★

'I see the powers-that-be consider you at risk, Vaughn,' John Marantz says, jerking his thumb in the direction of the officer on guard outside de Vries' hospital room before closing the door.

'It's for the protection of the other patients.'

'Huh?'

'It's not to stop people getting in, Johnnie. It's to stop me getting out.'

'Society is probably safer with you incarcerated.'

De Vries snorts. 'There are plenty who believe that.'

Marantz pats him on the shoulder gently; de Vries recoils.

'You got your man.'

'I got a man.'

'You saved the boy, Vaughn. Nothing else matters right now.'

'You think not?'

'I brought you some gifts.' Marantz reaches into a starched paper bag from a smart shop, tips the items onto the foot of the bed. 'Some reading matter, some fruit — and look, some hand-wash.'

De Vries snatches at the hand-wash bottle, his eyes widening.

'Fucking Fineberg olive oil hand foam? For fuck's sake, Johnnie.'

'But,' Marantz continues, 'you really should smell that handwash. Such a lovely soothing scent . . . '

De Vries brings it up to his nose and inhales. He smiles broadly, fiddles with the pump on the top, angles it into his mouth and pushes four times, swallowing the liquid, closing his eyes.

'You got it past those Nazi nurses.'

'Thanks to my training.'

'Single malt?' de Vries says.

'The least you deserve . . . '

★ ★ ★

Don February places his cellphone on de Vries' desk and shuts his eyes. He feels uneasy sitting in his place, exposed to the smirking glances from the squad room. Now he is privy to information he has no right knowing and he is afraid. He wonders about his contact at Vodacom and whether he can be trusted to keep what he has done a secret. He is sweating and shaking. He attributes this to having shot a man in the head, to sleeping so fitfully that he sits awake and be-suited almost in a trance; to being unable even to begin to explain anything to his impatient, concerned wife. In his turmoil, he decides that his contact would be in far more trouble than himself, if the man concerned were ever to reveal that he had passed on this information. Nonetheless, Don knows now who it was who called Ralph Hopkins late in the evening before their attempted arrest of Marc Steinhauer. The question which defeats him is: who can he tell?

★ ★ ★

Vaughn de Vries empties his letter box which he finds surprisingly full; limps slowly up the four stone steps to his front door. He feels like a wounded dog who seeks a hidden nook in which to recover, to lick his wounds. Yet, he cannot relax. He lets himself in, throws the mail on the kitchen table and lowers himself gingerly onto the armchair where he used to sit, heading his family of girls, pronouncing on what would happen in his house. He struggles up again, pours himself a glass of water from the tap, sips it, discards it and lets the tap run for almost a minute, until the water runs cold. Then, he takes it back to the table, borrows a cushion from a side chair and lowers himself again.

Not for one moment has he thought of anything but the exchange with Trevor Henderson. He has found himself half asleep murmuring the man's name, always with a question mark after it.

426

He cannot believe it. He cannot understand how he saw this man, day after day, and did not recognize him to be guilty. It has jolted his belief that he always knows the guilty when he sees them. His mind drifts and he closes his eyes, intent on a precise recollection:

'*That fucking brother killed them . . .*'

The brother? He cannot describe him any other way, and there is only one man to whom Marc Steinhauer can be a brother.

'*The Steinhauers. He gave me my world and then he took it away again.*'

Steinhauers: Marc Steinhauer was incapable of giving anybody anything. Which of the Steinhauers could have given this? All the time he has known, and now he has heard it. But only *he* has heard it, only him. He has asked Don February what he heard, and he tells him: only mumbling, stuttering, did not hear a coherent sentence, recalls no single words. So now, only he knows.

He rubs his eyes and then stops; it hurts. He drinks half the glass of water and looks at the mail. There are bills and flyers, and there is one A4 envelope, slick and stiff. He reaches for it, tears open the seal and shakes the expensive paper out onto the table; a fancy law-firm letterhead embosses his eyeline. Before he spins it around to face him, he knows what it is. He smiles, closes his eyes, and then he begins to laugh. Latin: *Decree Nisi*. At first, he thinks that it is a laughter of despair, of having reached the very bottom, but then, as his brain slowly cogitates, he changes his mind. He feels a tiny weight fall from his shoulders, feels his neck begin to relax. He laughs again, for the timing: it is pure, unadulterated mirth.

★ ★ ★

'I've read your report, Vaughn.'

'I know what you're going to say.'

'It's what anyone in my position would say.'

De Vries stares at Henrik du Toit. 'I hear,' he says wearily, 'that you stood up for me in front of Thulani. That you stood your ground. You must be pleased you did that now.'

Du Toit blanches. 'If I had known that you had departed for your field trip, in direct contravention of my order, I might not have been so keen to defend you. I naively assumed that you would do what you said you would do. From your point of view, you were lucky beyond belief. Think of the alternative outcomes for a moment: at the very least, the end of your career.'

'I think of Joe Pienaar and a desperate, insane man with a gun,' de Vries says bitterly. 'I think that any alternative which involved me sitting at my desk would have been utterly shameful.'

'I — '

'And so do you, Henrik. So do you. And if you don't, you fucking should.'

De Vries gets up from the corner of sofas in du Toit's office and gestures unsteadily around the room. 'That's why we fought for this opportunity; that's why we put up with all this political bullshit because, whilst we are around, there is just a chance we can do things. You think any of

428

that lot would have got off their arses quick enough to save that kid?'

He sits back down, faces his boss. 'Now listen to me, because right now the drugs have made my thinking very clear. I knew a week ago that Nicholas Steinhauer was behind all of this, and everything in my report confirms that.'

'That is debatable.'

'Only by an idiot.' De Vries holds his hands up in surrender, lowers his voice. 'I need one thing from you, sir. I need to know whether Trevor Henderson attended the clinic in Tokai where Nicholas Steinhauer worked, and I need to know whether he was a patient of Steinhauer because, if he was, we may have no direct proof linking him, but we have so much circumstantial evidence that any judge must convict. We have Steinhauer junior, we have Johannes Dyk, and we have four further sets of fingerprints for which we can continue to seek a match, but the one man who is not going to walk away from this is that bastard Dr Steinhauer.'

Du Toit looks at de Vries and smiles wanly.

'It's very clear to you, isn't it?' he says.

'Yes, very.'

'Well, it isn't so simple. Trevor Henderson did attend Tokai First Practice. His commanding officer, Denis Mantabi, sent him there for depression.'

'You *knew* this?'

'Calm down, Vaughn. Mantabi was not privy to which analyst Henderson saw, and the clinic is not obliged to tell us. I believe that they *will* tell us but, honestly, it makes no difference.'

'No difference!'

'I've spoken with Classon. Even if we learn that Henderson was allocated to Steinhauer, it proves nothing.'

'It proves Steinhauer lied to us; at the very least withheld crucial information.'

'It doesn't. For one simple reason: Steinhauer can claim that Henderson never discussed any of this with him and therefore it was irrelevant to the inquiry — then and now.'

'But I know that Steinhauer was influential. How many more times do I have to say it? *I know*. Think about it: someone is controlling everything. It wasn't Marc Steinhauer — he was a sheep, easily led and, according to everyone, incapable of leading or organizing. Trevor Henderson may have been living a lie, but he didn't buy the olive farm. The farmer said he employed him because he had a background with horses and he was English like him, but that he was always depressed and wanted to live on his own, to be isolated. Neither man can speak the name Nicholas Steinhauer because they are afraid — so afraid of him, that they would rather commit suicide than name him and face him.'

'That's a view.'

'I've been there each time.'

'You may know, Vaughn — but you can't prove it. Steinhauer will have destroyed any notes he might have taken, there is no physical evidence linking him to the Fineberg olive farm, and certainly none to any of the abductions.'

'Listen to yourself. You're making excuses for this man.'

'No, Vaughn,' du Toit says sharply. 'You can accuse me of many things, but not that. You know well enough that to prove conspiracy is exceptionally difficult.' He leans forward. 'I am aware that you don't want to hear this, but I am going to say it anyway. I believe every word of your report. I also believe that Nicholas Steinhauer is involved in this case, although I don't pretend to know how. But — and listen to me, Vaughn — *his prints are not at the farm.* You cannot physically link him. That ends it in itself.'

'It delays it.'

'No. Because of the history of this case, because of what happened seven years ago and, frankly, what has been happening now, there will be plenty of people higher up the food chain who will be inclined to disbelieve what you have written here. Not only because of you, your record, but because of what it would mean to the SAPS — and this department — if there is seen to be unfinished business.'

'So that's it, is it?'

'Perhaps, officially, that should be it. Perhaps we will discover matches to the remaining prints and DNA samples, and then we will have a live witness, prepared to testify about Nicholas Steinhauer's involvement. Do you see what I'm saying?'

'Yes.'

'Yes?'

'Yes, I see what you're saying.'

'And are you prepared to follow my guidance?' De Vries says nothing. 'Vaughn?'

'To let a guilty, manipulative monster like

431

Steinhauer walk away?'

'To close the case and wait for evidence that will convict him if he is the ringmaster.'

'You already know my answer.'

'For God's sake, Vaughn. There has to be some compromise. You have, just sometimes, to agree to play it my way. To be expedient. For God's sake!'

'To be expedient — I don't know what that means.'

De Vries feels throbbing in his temples, feels that injustice is the hardest thing to bear. He has always believed that — and, quite simply, that is what makes him do what he does. The pressure builds inside him, even in the seconds of silence which pass, and he knows that he will not bear it.

★ ★ ★

'Give me more time,' de Vries says an hour later, back in du Toit's office. He is calm and ordered. 'I'll write up the reports and, if I can't find any further evidence, then I'll do as you instruct and move on to the next case — on condition that this one is not closed, never closed. There are at least three more men to identify.'

Du Toit looks up at de Vries, standing in front of his desk. Standing, du Toit is convinced, just to prove he can.

'You have the time I have, Vaughn. Twenty-four hours. That's it.'

'It's unreal.' He shakes his head bitterly. 'I need my team.'

'You can have February and Thambo.

432

Everyone else is busy. And leave Dr Dyk alone. Nothing he says can be used, and the man is days from death.'

'Dyk has told us more than he intended anyway. He's shut up shop, just like the rest of them.'

'All right, Vaughn.'

De Vries turns to leave the office, but he twists back to du Toit.

'You can just switch off, can't you? I watched you after the last time. It meant everything to you when you were in the middle of it, but once we called it off, you forgot about it, didn't you, Henrik?'

'Of course not. But you cannot function if you cannot focus.'

'I never forgot them. Not one week went by without me wondering what had happened.'

'You need to discipline your mind to distance yourself. My God, man. How can you live if you have the ghosts of every victim in your head?'

'Why do you think I get up every morning? I have a bond with every victim I encounter. If I don't know my victim, if I don't understand them as if they were my friend in real life, how can I hope to unravel who killed them and why?'

'That sounds untenably stressful.'

'That's why you accepted promotion to a desk and I refuse it, Henrik. You have a second life, don't you? You have your wife. I bet you still go out to dinner parties together, drive out to the countryside to visit your children, polish your car. Don't you?'

'It is important to have a life outside work. I

don't see that as a matter deserving of your scorn.'

'It's not scorn.'

'Envy, then.'

'It's not envy either. It's a different life. I might have chosen that a long time ago, but I didn't. I have my path and it makes my heart beat and makes me feel I still have a place. It's just nothing like yours.'

'How is Suzanne, Vaughn?'

'Divorcing me, sir. Moving on and living her own life.'

'I'm sorry.'

'Don't be. We had over twenty decent years, and now why do I need a wife? My daughters will be married themselves soon. They need a friend, not a father, and they will always have that. This is what you've never understood about me, even after all these years. We started working together about the same time as Suzanne and me, and you still don't see. Nothing charges me like my work: not sex, not the booze, nothing. I like them — I think you know that, and I'll take my best shot at both — but nothing, *nothing*, has ever given me more satisfaction than finding justice for my victim.'

'I've never suggested we were the same.'

'We're not.'

'Don't underestimate my strength or my tenacity, Vaughn.'

'I never would, sir. Because I know your weakness. I always have. You have no passion.'

★ ★ ★

434

'Twenty-four hours,' de Vries tells Don as they walk into his office and close the door. 'If we can't find anything to tie in Steinhauer by then, it's over.'

'Until we identify the remaining prints from the bunker?'

'*If* we ever identify them. I don't hold out much hope. These men are off the radar. Anyway . . . ' He slumps in his chair, gestures for Don to sit. 'What happened when you spoke to Joe Pienaar and his family?'

'I went to his home with a female officer, a white woman, from Durbanville. He was very brave. His parents were with him, and I think he is in good hands. He does not remember anything after he was snatched — the doctor said that he had been concussed — until he woke up and found himself in prison.'

'Does he remember Henderson saying anything?'

'That is what I wanted to know. Not really. Apparently, he told him that he loved him; that he was his child. Joe Pienaar said that he tried to explain that the man was wrong, but he gave up because it seemed to make him angry.'

'Sensible kid.'

'Yes. A mature boy, I think. He asked what happened to you, and I told him that you were injured but alive.'

'Did he ask about Henderson?'

'No. His father told me that they had told their son that the man had been taken away by the police. That he would not be allowed in public ever again.'

'Good.'

'No mention of Steinhauer. I asked him several times and, finally, I used the name myself. But there was no reaction.'

'No.'

'I think he is going to be all right. The Durbanville officer explained about counselling, for the child and also for the parents, but they said that they would see what happened in the coming weeks. They seemed a supportive family, and the boy has two older sisters.'

'Good. Right now, I wouldn't go near a shrink. Not if I needed help.'

Don smiles momentarily, looks out of the office towards the squad room, and then back at de Vries.

'There is one more thing you should know,' he says.

'What?'

'I — I called in a favour from a guy I have worked with before from Vodacom. I gave him Ralph Hopkins' cell number and asked him to give me the numbers which called him between six p.m. on the ninth and six a.m. the next day. Hopkins only received two calls that evening. One was from his own office, but the other . . . Perhaps I made a mistake, because now maybe we cannot use it as evidence.' He swallows. 'It was Julius Mngomezulu's cellphone.'

'What?'

'He called Hopkins at ten forty-five that evening. The call lasted two minutes and . . . ' he glances down at his notepad, flicks two pages back 'two minutes and thirty-six seconds.'

'No other calls?'

'No.'

De Vries sits very still, his eyes unfocused to his right side. Then he says: 'Hopkins told me that Marc Steinhauer called him on his cellphone, near midnight. So, Mngomezulu tipped him off about our surveillance, about the impending arrest?'

'I think so.'

'But why? I know Hopkins met with Thulani. I bumped into him in the corridor. Thulani said that he had negotiated permission for Steinhauer to return to Jo'burg.' He stands up, paces around his desk. 'I don't know what this means, Don.'

'Mngomezulu only acts for General Thulani?'

'As far as I know. You've told no one else?'

'Of course not. I did not know even to tell you.'

De Vries laughs.

'It's just one more piece, Don. One more piece. But for the life of me, I can't see how it fits.'

* * *

Forensic team-leader Steve Ulton says: 'Henderson's cellphone called only one number. Untraceable. Its harder now to hide phones, but this one's old.' He glances at notes. 'The recording setup couldn't have been simpler. Straight out of the box. One piece of proprietary software for a recording device to a portable drive. Nothing else whatsoever. Two very small microphones in the cell area, highly sensitive, voice-activated. Whoever set it up wanted to hear what those boys said.'

'What about the old-fashioned tape machines?'

'If they were used at all, not for a long time. The reel-to-reels are technology from the fifties and sixties, probably left in the bunker as standard equipment. There were only two tape reels in the bunker and they were both fresh out of the box. Fresh as in empty.'

De Vries frowns. 'No prints?'

'Nothing on the tape machines, but a suggestion that they had been wiped some time in the past; on the laptop casing, partial prints matching Marc Steinhauer. Some attempt to clean this surface also.'

'So, who listened to the recordings?'

'Whoever took the external hard drive.'

De Vries holds up his hand. 'Meaning?'

'On the laptop found in the anteroom, there is a computer program for recording audio from the two microphones located in the cell-block. These microphones are voice-activated so that recording only takes place when people, presumably those three boys, are talking.' He looks up at de Vries, who nods. 'Within the program, there are options for where you want to send the recording: to the computer's hard disc or, in this case, to a portable hard drive — that is, in effect, a very high-capacity storage system, a little box which can be disconnected, moved and then reconnected to the computer of whoever wants to listen to the recordings.'

'That sounds complicated. How often would this storage hard drive need to be changed?'

'It's actually pretty simple, and it has the advantage that nothing is stored, or can be retrieved, from the laptop memory itself. That's the clever bit. I thought there would be a copy buried somewhere on the hard drive, but the program bypasses it altogether. Depending on the amount of time in any twenty-four-hour period it was recording, it probably would have to be changed monthly, maybe longer than that. The capacity for these things is enormous if you are recording voice and no video. I guess someone unplugged one device and plugged in a new one. You could record indefinitely with two devices alternated and wiped.'

'Who wants to listen to what they say?' de Vries murmurs, staring past Ulton towards a corner in the ceiling of the lab.

'What?'

He snaps back. 'Nothing. You have one of these hard drive things. We can listen to it?'

'No external hard drive was found connected.'

'I don't understand. You said that was how the voices were recorded?'

Ulton smiles crookedly. 'Er, yes. Kind of. But we haven't found the last device that was used.'

'But the laptop was still operating? It was still on?'

'Yes. I assumed that Marc Steinhauer — if he was the last man to visit the bunker — removed the drive but didn't replace it with a new one. Maybe because the boys were all dead.'

De Vries looks up. 'That's right. Why record empty cells? So, what did he do with it? Was this hard drive found in either of his properties?'

'It's not in the inventory. Having said that, it may have been seen. At the time, we didn't know

439

what we were looking for. If it was amongst other computer things . . . '

'You'll check with your team?'

'I — '

'And if not, send a guy out to both the properties again and let's find it.'

'Vaughn.' De Vries meets his stare. 'I'm not sure I can do that.'

'Why not?'

'Word from above.' Ulton points upwards with both index fingers. 'Orders, no less: move on. There's a backlog here and they told me to bag and tag everything else and start working through the inbox.'

'From above?'

'General Thulani's office, I believe.'

De Vries shakes his head, and Ulton continues, 'I know how you feel, Vaughn, trust me. Three sets of fingerprints unidentified.'

'Every reason to believe that each one is an abuser.' De Vries sighs heavily. 'Six different sets in total?'

'Yes. Marc Steinhauer, Johannes Dyk and now Trevor Henderson.'

'Why weren't Henderson's prints already in the system? Why didn't they show up before?'

'Nothing surprising in that,' Ulton shrugs. 'Files missing, incomplete data. Just the usual.'

'So nothing we have is watertight?' De Vries clenches his jaw. 'Nothing can be relied on?' He turns away. 'Jesus.'

★ ★ ★

Harry Kleinman is wearing long trousers, formal shirt and tie. He sits with de Vries in his office; Don February is seated on the low sofa in the corner, taking notes. His is the only light on; it is as bright as they can bear.

'Bobby Eames was poisoned, using a poison based on amatoxin. He might have been saved if he had been taken to a hospital. Without treatment, his organs would have started to fail one by one and he would be gone within three or four days from the time it was ingested, probably simply through his food or drink. Coma, then death. Very frightening for the victim; very alarming for the two other boys, if they saw what was happening.'

'I bet they did,' de Vries says. 'I bet it was intended for them.'

'Huh?'

'Could it have been accidental?'

Kleinman tries to refocus. 'I can't think how. The poison would have had to have been administered somehow.'

'A deliberate poisoning then?'

'Yes. And one chosen to prolong symptoms and then death over a period of days. I'm trying to tell you, Vaughn. There are easier ways of killing someone: painless ways. But this . . . '

'How long ago?'

'It's impossible to be categoric. Bobby Eames' body was frozen within a few hours of his death. This has allowed his body to remain in reasonable condition, but it obviously distorts all the usual measures by which we would assess a time of death. Working on his physical attributes,

441

I am putting on record that I estimate that he was approximately twelve years old, which would make his death between three and four years ago.'

'Why freeze the body?'

'Why did these people do any of what they did? I don't know. But I will tell you this. Whoever took that course of action showed care and, dare I say it, respect, for the body. There is scarcely a mark on him, and he was wrapped very carefully in a new cotton sheet, like a shroud.'

'Maybe whoever killed him did not bury him.'

De Vries and Kleinman look over at Don.

'Indeed, Warrant February,' Kleinman says kindly. 'The act of poisoning — and the death would not have been swift or without great pain — and the ritual of wrapping and preserving the body seem at odds.' He turns back to de Vries. 'Not, of course, that this is my area. But it is my professional experience that when a body, particularly a child's body, is . . . cherished in such a way, it is the action of someone who loved them and not a mindless killer.'

'Henderson told me he loved them,' de Vries says grimly.

'Did Steve identify prints or DNA from the body?' Kleinman asks. 'Lab work is really your only hope there.'

'Apparently not. And now everything is being scaled down. No time for answers, Harry. No appetite for the truth.'

'I understand how you feel, Vaughn, but do you have any idea how many other deaths I see, in this building alone? This lab was only supposed to operate for your department and as a priority unit for high-profile Metro cases but, frankly, there are bodies on gurneys in the corridors. It's nightmarish.'

They sit in a mourning silence until Kleinman stands, slides his report onto de Vries' desk and walks away, opening the office door and closing it again silently.

De Vries mumbles, 'What to do?'

Don February looks at him, his mind racing. He says quietly, 'I do not know.'

★　★　★

De Vries drinks wine from the cellar of his family's house, wine kept for special occasions, for dinner parties with Suzanne's bosses, for family celebrations of Matric results and university acceptances. He knows that he will not drink to celebrate anything any more.

He starts each evening only with negatives: no new information, no new angle from which to attack the insurmountable peak. Each piece which does not fit into the picture remains unidentifiable. As the time passes, he knows that the answers are moving, not closer, but further from him. As he watches the empty bottles gather at the far end of the mahogany dining table, his frustration festers and builds. When he sleeps, it is only for moments until he jolts awake once more, certain that a new clarity is just within grasp but then, when he is fully conscious, it evaporates. When he finally sleeps for a few hours, he wakes only when he falls from his chair at the head of the table to the floor.

★ ★ ★

'You should know, Vaughn,' du Toit says, 'that I am inclined to agree with those who say this is the act of a desperate man.'

'I don't care.'

'I know you don't — but maybe you should.'

De Vries stares down to the street below. Murmurs, 'Look at them all . . . '

'What do they expect?' du Toit continues, following de Vries' gaze. 'That we'll parade him in through the front doors?'

'At least they know we've arrested him. That alone sends out a warning.'

Du Toit looks up at de Vries.

'Be careful who you say that to. You can't arrest someone simply to publicize your suspicion.' De Vries opens his mouth, but du Toit continues. 'And, for God's sake, whatever happens, I'm telling you this now, don't even *think* about leaking information. Not only could you prejudice future action, but you could unleash a legal hell down on the entire department. And Vaughn — don't leave yourself open to accusations that this is personal.'

'I am fully aware,' de Vries says dryly, 'that this interview can, and will, be used in court. You know that no one wants this man more than me.'

Du Toit steps away from the window, saying, 'He may simply refuse to talk.'

'That is possible. I am banking on him finding it irresistible to debate with me some more. He certainly thinks he won the last round.'

When du Toit is silent, de Vries looks up at him.

'Hopkins arrived here,' du Toit says, 'even before they brought him in. You know that?'

'That is because Ralph Hopkins has an informant from within these walls.'

'Who?'

De Vries appears to ponder for a moment. 'I'm working on it. Hopkins could have known we were arresting Steinhauer even before Steinhauer himself.'

'If there's a leak, I want to know who.'

'When I know, you'll know, sir.'

Du Toit glances at his watch. 'They've been in there almost an hour together. What do they have to discuss that takes them so long?'

'If Steinhauer has found out that we know Trevor Henderson was his patient for nine months, he'll realize that we have a lot of questions.'

'Unless he simply claims that everything is confidential.'

'Of course that's what he'll claim, but he has to answer that he supposedly missed his brother's involvement, and now it turns out that the real perpetrator was one of his patients; either he missed yet another very sick character, in which case he's a lousy shrink, or he was complicit . . . ' De Vries stops, adds forcefully, 'controlling — all this time.'

'I am thinking that he can plead ignorance easily enough.'

'Yes, but will he? I'm not sure that is how he thinks. He's an arrogant son of a bitch.'

'Be careful, Vaughn. Keep in mind what could be used against you by a defence attorney. Your inner conviction of his guilt will not put him behind bars.'

De Vries is about to reply, but he checks himself; knows that he must save the debate for the interview room.

Du Toit turns from the window and sits himself behind his desk, adjusts the angle of the framed photograph of his family, moves it again, then a third time — it is back where it started.

'You are assuming,' he says, 'that Henderson was alone in taking those boys?'

'Henderson was in uniform, driving a marked police car. That would explain why Bobby Eames and Steven Lawson got into the car with him, and why no one saw them. People in this country look away when they see us; they don't want their image to register on the mind of the cop.'

'A cynical view, Vaughn.'

'It's a fact. They're on their cellphones, their exhaust is pumping ten tons of shit out the back of their car, they have a baby standing up in the front seat, there are eleven people in a car with four seats. They don't want to be noticed.'

'That is a state of mind the world over: the more lawless the state, the less people want to condone the authority of the police.'

De Vries sighs. 'I understand your argument, sir.' He chooses his next words carefully. 'And I appreciate the historical difficulties, but we are losing the coloureds and the whites too. This case has significance for everybody.'

Du Toit snorts. 'This isn't the time for your entry into the political fray, Vaughn. You're more educated than you seem, but the real politicians will have you for dinner. Your job is to put something together that gets this man, at the very least, to court.'

'That may be enough for you; nothing short of life behind bars does it for me. I know what Steinhauer has done.'

Du Toit nods. 'Call me when Hopkins says they're ready. Norman and I will be behind the glass.'

De Vries stretches his back, grimaces.

'All right,' he says quietly. 'I'm going down.'

★ ★ ★

Ralph Hopkins does not appear for a further half-hour. When he tells them that he has completed his client conference, they assemble, just as before. Don February faces Hopkins; Attorney Classon and du Toit sit in their same seats in the gallery, each dry-lipped with anticipation. Steinhauer lounges in his upright chair, plays with a gold signet ring on his little finger. De Vries sits down and, while Don February announces those present for the tape recording, de Vries arranges his notes in front of him.

Don gives him the signal to begin.

'Mr Hopkins,' de Vries says. 'You have made clear to your client the legal significance of this interview, compared to the voluntary meeting we had on the nineteenth of this month?'

Hopkins rests his hands on the top of his belly.

'Dr Steinhauer is fully aware of all aspects of this provocative action by the SAPS.'

De Vries smiles. 'Good.' He takes a slow, deep breath, gathering himself. In his head, he knows just what he must say, has anticipated every combination of response he might receive from his suspect, planned how he will build his argument and trap his quarry.

'Dr Steinhauer . . . during the years 2004 to 2009, were you a consultant psychologist at a private clinic called Tokai First Practice?'

Steinhauer smiles minutely, points his chin towards de Vries. Says, 'No comment.'

De Vries swallows. He opens his mouth and shuts it again. He says firmly, 'Have you ever met Inspector Trevor Henderson, formerly of the SAPS?' He waits, watching Steinhauer's eyes examine the surface of the wood-laminate table. Nothing is forthcoming.

'All right, Doctor. We know, as a fact, that you were based at the Tokai Private Practice and that Trevor Henderson was referred to you by the SAPS.' He scrutinizes Steinhauer's expression; observes a stillness and control over muscles and flesh; notices that the man's breathing is shallow and rapid. Nothing but the breath in his body registers any movement, any sound.

'We have already waited some time while you consulted with your legal representative and this is a simple enough question: are you, or have you been, acquainted with, personally or professionally, a man known as Trevor Henderson?'

'No comment.'

'I have asked you a question, Doctor. Please answer it.'

Ralph Hopkins leans forward. 'My client has answered your question, Colonel. He has elected to make no comment.'

'Have you advised your client that to take such action will, whatever the letter of the law, reflect poorly for him in court?' de Vries asks.

Now Hopkins smiles. Replies smoothly, 'Well, that assumes when, rather than if, you charge my client with anything.'

De Vries appreciates Hopkins' guile; an echo of the first interview — Don February's taunting use of one word over the other. He feels his adrenalin ebb.

'Will you be preferring charges at this time?' the lawyer demands.

De Vries glances at Steinhauer, settles back on Hopkins.

'Will your client be prepared to answer any questions at this interview?'

Hopkins shrugs his shoulders. 'There may be topics he is prepared to discuss with you, but you should be aware that I have advised my client to decline to answer your questions.'

'On what grounds?'

'We have discussed at length — as you were so ready to point out to us a moment ago — the coincidental matters which apply to my client regarding this case, and we have considered the information you have presented to us regarding an evidentiary link to the charge of conspiracy on which basis my client has been detained. As you will doubtless have been informed by your legal advisers, to prove a charge of conspiracy is extremely difficult and the level of proof required is, to say the least, demanding. My client has assured me that you can have no evidence directly connecting him with these accusations and therefore he declines to discuss coincidence and arbitrary connection with you at this time.'

'At this time?'

'If you charge my client, and present the basis of your evidence, then naturally we will reconsider our position in the light of your so-called evidence. I ask you again: do you wish to lay charges now?'

De Vries feels all the momentum, all the expectation drain from him. He feels himself flushing.

'Your client will remain in custody while we reflect on his decision not to cooperate with us in interview.'

Hopkins leans over to Steinhauer and whispers something in his ear. Then he says to de Vries, 'Inform me the moment you wish to speak to my client again.'

De Vries turns slowly to Don February.

'Warrant Officer. Take the prisoner back to the cells.' Don dictates the time of the interview termination for the tape recorder, rises and goes to the door of the interview room. An officer enters and, together, they escort Steinhauer away, down the corridor.

Hopkins rises, checks his wristwatch.

'It's make your mind up time, Colonel,' he says to de Vries. 'And time waits for no man.'

Then he leaves the interview room, pulling his cellphone from his jacket pocket. As de Vries listens to his footsteps, he hears Hopkins speaking; the voice and the footsteps moving away from him. De Vries, aware that both camera and gallery are behind him, clenches his fists under the table, bares his teeth and screams silently.

★　★　★

Don knocks tentatively on de Vries' door. He hears nothing, but he has already seen him slumped over his desk, head resting on interlocked fingers. He opens the door, closes it quietly and walks over to the desk. De Vries looks up.

Don says, 'It was always a possibility that he would refuse to talk. It is not our fault.'

De Vries sighs. 'No, Don. It's *my* fault.' He shakes his head. 'I was so certain that the one thing he wouldn't do is clam up. I know this guy. He wants to speak. He wants to take me on, to fight me, to beat me. It's Hopkins. He knows we have nothing concrete and he's not going to let Steinhauer give us anything.'

He sits up, looks out at the almost empty squad room. 'Where is everybody?'

Don glances behind him, even though he has just walked through the room to reach de Vries' office.

'Just out.'

'Three boys, two more men. All dead because of what Nicholas Steinhauer managed to do. No

451

one cares. They're not even here.'

'They care,' Don says quickly, 'but right now, there are another five deaths, just today. And yesterday, there was a mother, father and five-year-old child all burnt alive in their shack in the camp above Hout Bay. Maybe a thousand people within two hundred metres and no witnesses. Not one.'

'All right, Don.'

'I am not trying to play down — '

De Vries snaps: 'Okay!'

Don February stops, waits, sits down in the visitor's chair. Waits some more. In the silence, he hears strides across the squad room, drumming footsteps which herald nothing good. The door opens and du Toit comes in, followed by Norman Classon. Don stands up, and de Vries pulls himself half out of his chair.

Du Toit looks at both of them and then around the office.

'Warrant Officer,' he says quietly to Don. 'Please fetch two more chairs from next door.'

Don February walks out, takes the two chairs nearest to the office and carries them back in. Du Toit motions with his finger.

'Put them around the desk there.' He looks up at de Vries, frozen in his crouch. 'Sit down, Vaughn.' Du Toit and Classon sit opposite de Vries with Don a little way back, lower in the visitor's chair.

'I'm sorry it went like that,' du Toit starts. 'I suppose we should have expected that they might take that route. I am afraid Ralph Hopkins has plenty of experience dealing with clients who

452

do better saying nothing.'

'We can hold him,' de Vries says. 'Maybe we'll see if he feels like talking at two in the morning.'

Du Toit takes a deep breath.

'No, Vaughn. It's over. We have to release Steinhauer, close the case and wait until we get a breakthrough from DNA or some corroboratory witness.'

'Over? We can hold him for another . . . ' he consults his wristwatch ' . . . twenty-two hours.'

'I have received instructions that Nicholas Steinhauer is to be released immediately,' du Toit states. 'That is the position.'

'Instructions? From who?'

Du Toit looks at de Vries darkly, his palms flapping slowly in a calming motion.

'Listen to me. I have orders from the Provincial Commander which, he tells me, emanate straight from the Police Minister's department.'

'On what grounds?'

'There's no debate, no argument,' du Toit snaps. 'We just do it. The case is closed officially and the press will be informed that Nicholas Steinhauer has helped us with our enquiries and that no charges have been laid.' Du Toit looks over at Classon.

'It's revolting,' Classon says. 'But I cannot find a way to lay charges against Steinhauer which have any chance of sticking even before they reach court. Put simply, what we have isn't enough to go to trial. If we are seen to present charges which the press might describe as 'trumped up', and then we go on a fishing trip, we will lose the media high ground and come out of this with nothing.'

'As opposed to what?' de Vries says bitterly.

'As opposed to leaving open the possibility of later action,' Classon temporizes. He lowers his voice. 'I think that we, here in this office, are all agreed that Nicholas Steinhauer is involved in some measure in the conspiracy which led to the events seven years ago, and then again, this month.'

'While the case may be closed officially,' du Toit says, 'unofficially I am sure that time can be found for further forensic work and, in due course we may be able to identify the other three men — we assume men — whose DNA was recovered at the bunker scene.'

De Vries says nothing; he stares at his desk.

Don February says: 'May I ask one question, sir?'

'Of course, Warrant Officer.'

'Is it usual for the Police Ministry to be involved in the investigation of murder cases by the SAPS? I mean, even before a suspect is charged?'

Du Toit smiles. 'What can I say, Warrant Officer? The answer is no.'

'So . . . why . . . ?'

'Because a voice very high up has decreed it. You must judge what his, or her, motives might be. I prefer not to try to double-think these people. Gives you an ulcer.'

Don raises his right hand to ask another question, can see du Toit would prefer that he didn't, asks anyway.

'Is Nicholas Steinhauer being protected?'

Vaughn laughs; du Toit shoots him a look.

'We can't know that.' Du Toit sits up. 'Chances are, this is politics, plain and simple. The Police Department is a department of civilian politicians. They have come to the conclusion — and you may well ask why they should have deliberated on this matter at all — but they have decided that, politically, everyone is best served by the conclusion of this case.'

'You see why I hate politics, Don?'

Du Toit turns to de Vries.

'I know you don't want to hear this, Vaughn, but you have identified the murderer of Bobby Eames and Steven Lawson, you have saved Joe Pienaar from a probable fatal threat, identified Trevor Henderson and . . . dealt with him. Your actions, Warrant Officer,' he says to Don February, 'undoubtedly saved the life of Colonel de Vries and have, though neither of you may see it in such a way, saved the SAPS a great deal of adverse publicity and a further demotion in respect from the general public. The outcome of this case, the past few days, cannot be described as a disaster.'

De Vries sighs again, mutters.

'You may feel,' du Toit continues, addressing de Vries, 'with your personal connection to the case, as I do myself, that there is a major piece missing. However, sometimes not everything is achievable. We have done our best.'

'We have, sir,' de Vries says. 'But it is not enough.'

Ralph Hopkins walks with Nicholas Steinhauer to the front entrance of the building. At the bottom of the concrete and steel staircase at the back of the lobby, they pass du Toit and de Vries. Du Toit steps out in front of them.

'I don't imagine that the people out there will be satisfied by 'no comment'. You wouldn't prefer to leave by the back entrance?'

Nicholas Steinhauer looks down on du Toit, says quietly, 'Get out of my way.'

Hopkins puts his arm on Steinhauer's, but Steinhauer shakes him away.

'Enough now. Enough of my time has been wasted.'

Du Toit steps back; de Vries says, 'Whatever you do say, I'll be listening.'

Steinhauer smiles. 'You will find that *every-body* will be listening to what I have to say. Don't worry about that.'

As he passes him, de Vries says, 'Don't make a mistake.'

Steinhauer stops, turns, smiles calmly at de Vries, totally at ease.

'I haven't yet.'

He and Hopkins walk briskly to the entrance and, as the door opens, the flashguns blaze and the shouted questions form a cacophony like a firework display. De Vries watches the media form an amphitheatre of attention around both men, microphones poised, straining to hear what they have to say. He waits on the spot, totally still, staring but not seeing, the flashes of

456

perfectly white light stinging his eyes until he simply stands there and closes them.

★ ★ ★

General Thulani's office is blizzard-cold. Du Toit wonders whether this is to keep interviews short or merely to penetrate the depths of Thulani's waistline.

'It's over, Henrik,' Thulani says. 'That is the best part of it.'

'Perhaps not in everybody's minds, sir.'

'Then make it clear to Colonel de Vries that this is so.'

'Yes, sir.'

'Good.' Thulani relaxes again. 'You see how it must be. The media: they require a beginning, a middle and an end — and this we have now provided.' He folds his arms. 'I assume that you now have de Vries' mind occupied elsewhere?'

'Vaughn is having some marital difficulties. I suggested a few days' leave to get these matters under control and then, as you know, we have more than enough to keep us all occupied indefinitely.'

'The long-term problem you have with that officer is that he may be motivated and effective, but he is the opposite of the image we in the new SAPS wish to project.'

'But perhaps there is room for some unorthodox methods?'

'No, Henrik, there is not. You retain him at your own peril and you are responsible for policing him but, be aware, you jeopardize your own

457

standing by continuing to support his behaviour.'

Du Toit feels his jaw tighten.

'I support the man, not his behaviour. And whatever you think of him, sir, we need men like de Vries. Not only because there are precious few senior white officers remaining in the force — and we do, supposedly, represent the 'Rainbow Nation' — but because there are now so few who have served in the ranks and have risen on investigative merit.'

'That could be taken as a racial slur.'

'As could any comment which does not unconditionally praise a particular group. We have too much work to play games.'

'We live and die in the media spotlight, Henrik. Watch yourself. As for your implied criticism of some black officers, does that include me?'

'Obviously not, sir.'

'Obviously not?'

'We have worked together for many years, sir. Of your experience and qualifications for your role, there can be no doubt. There remains, however, a question over the experience of some officers, those who have been promoted rapidly . . . '

'There will be time for officers of all races to gain experience. Right now, we have a representative body of men and women. You — and your small group of older officers in your department — would do well to recognize that this is the future. It will be no other way.'

Du Toit smiles wanly back at General Simphiwe Thulani.

★ ★ ★

David Wertner marches briskly to his car, salutes two police officers walking towards the building's underground exit. As he reaches his vehicle, he sees Vaughn de Vries appear from behind a wide concrete pillar.

'You're very predictable,' de Vries says.

Wertner stops. 'What are you doing, de Vries?'

'A few words with you before I go on leave.'

'You know where my office is.'

De Vries saunters towards him. 'But I understood that you favoured private conversations below ground.'

De Vries watches a tiny pulse of pink colour on Wertner's tightly shaved cheeks, rise towards the dirty shaven skull. Wertner makes for the door of his car, but de Vries blocks his way.

'Do you have the special key for this lift too?' de Vries smiles, but does not move.

'I have technical rank, de Vries.'

'You can't bully me, Wertner, and you can't catch me out, however hard you try. I will do what I do and face anything you try to throw at me. And you know what? Whatever you think of me, my men are loyal to me. You want to undermine me to my team, next time do it officially or better still, be a man, and say it to my face . . . '

'Move out of the way.'

' . . . instead of threatening my Warrant Officer, claiming you control the future of his career.'

'Every man in this province is under scrutiny which can make or break him. Without such sanction, there is anarchy.'

459

De Vries laughs. 'There is more anarchy in the new South Africa than you can control. Spend your time rooting out the corrupt and the incompetent, and leave those of us who understand the job alone.'

'The job description's changed — that's what you don't get.'

'Why don't you, just for once, listen to something somebody tells you.'

'Why should I do that? You don't register on my scale. I don't value your outdated opinions and I don't respect your failings. I am sick of reward for failure in this organization.'

De Vries steps still closer to him.

'Ask yourself who has links to the Police Ministry. Ask yourself why they intervened to stop further investigation into Nicholas Steinhauer.'

'Why should I do that?'

'At the very least, question their motivation.'

'All I hear from you is Nicholas Steinhauer. What about Ledham, and your unfinished enquiries there?'

'You know by now that the insert to the original abduction report was just that — inserted later. It was never there.'

'I do *not* know that.'

'But I do, and I'm telling you. Read the full report and you'll see how Robert Ledham was nothing. He had as much to do with this case as Iraq had with Nine/eleven. That was added to the file to discredit me. It was a stupid, blunt instrument, but you bought it long enough to consider delaying me.'

460

Wertner reaches for his door handle, turns back.

'It's over, de Vries. You'll step out of line again and this time you'll leave your footprint, and then you'll be gone. I will personally see to that.'

'Leave some of us to do the job properly. Concentrate on your own people.'

Wertner stretches his neck forward and puts his face in de Vries'.

'My own people? Get the fuck out of my way.'

De Vries braces him for a few seconds, and then he stands back. Wertner opens his car door, sits heavily in the cabin and slams the door shut. He starts the engine and lowers the driver's side window.

'Your people,' he spits, 'don't run the show any more. You don't get to make the rules and you don't get to break them.'

'That's what this has always been about for you, isn't it?'

'It's the future. You people don't get that yet.'

'What people, Wertner? White people?' de Vries laughs. 'You think black Africa is going to embrace you? You think you'll have a place at the table? Whatever you think you've got, you're going to lose it.'

Wertner sticks his hand out of his window and raises his middle finger.

'Fuck off, de Vries.'

Wertner accelerates out of the space, turns hard left and heads towards the small rectangle of daylight at the far corner of the garage.

★ ★ ★

461

He wakes to a bright yellowish light, unnatural and sickly. Above him, slowly coming into focus, narrow white bars enclose him in a tiny cell. He tries to sit up, hits his head, closes his eyes, lies back down. It is cool here; his head is supported and he can breathe cold, fresh air. He struggles into consciousness again, aware that he is afraid, swivels aching eyes, suddenly realizes where he is. He wriggles out of the refrigerator, crawls away from it and turns back to see what he has done. He rests on all fours, his head down and heavy. Around him, scattered on the floor, are half-opened packets and sticky jars which occupied the bottom two shelves of his fridge. One metal shelf is balanced at an angle against the leg of the kitchen table. He has no recollection of this; how he cleared the space, lay on his back, rested his head on the bottom shelf, and fell asleep.

He helps himself into his tall-backed carving chair, feels consciousness slipping again, his right ear flat on the pile of paperwork which cajoles his attention on sight.

Now, he is in a dark tunnel, not walking towards a light, but floating in the blackness. The ability to hover weightlessly calms him, laugh-lines appear around his eyes and mouth; he feels content. And then a fear of the endless yet confining darkness begins to grow, the cold seeps inside his skin, his eyes ache; the ceiling seems lower, the passage narrower. There is no way out for him . . . except the shocking jolt of consciousness.

462

He sits for less than ten minutes in the plush waiting room of the Huguenot Chambers off Company Gardens in the centre of town. He looks at his scuffed shoes, runs his scalded hand tentatively over his raw scalp and spiky tufts of hair, imagines that the pristine secretary has never seen such a figure before.

Hopkins appears at the double doors to his office, relaxed, smiling.

'You've caught me at a lucky moment, Colonel. Come into my office.'

De Vries rises, passes him, and enters the large book-lined room, red-carpeted, high-ceilinged, richly furnished.

'You do all right,' he tells Hopkins.

'You might say, crime does pay.' Hopkins chuckles at his own joke, gestures towards two small armchairs either side of a coffee table by the tall windows. De Vries sits and Hopkins follows him.

'I do, however, only have a short amount of time.'

'I am sure you have been told already,' de Vries starts. 'We have ended the investigation into the triple abduction and, since two of those implicated are dead and Johannes Dyk is not long from joining them, there will be no further arrests at this time.'

Hopkins looks at him, purses his lips. Says, 'Indeed, I have been informed.'

'Will you tell your client?'

'Which one?'

'Nicholas Steinhauer.'

463

Hopkins smiles. 'I think that he has been confident, from the very beginning, that no charges would be brought against him.'

De Vries absorbs both Steinhauer's and his lawyer's self-assurance bitterly; their assumption that he would fail has been vindicated.

'But,' Hopkins continues, 'I am sure that is not why you have come here. What can I do for you, Colonel?'

De Vries hesitates, wonders whether, here in his own space, Hopkins will prove impregnable, but he catches the feckless charm of the lawyer's expression, and it resolves him.

'You lied to me. I need to know why.'

'Lied?'

'To my inquiry. A serious matter.'

'You will have to explain.'

'I know who called you on the night before Marc Steinhauer's death.'

Hopkins shrugs.

'Was it a business arrangement?'

'I have already stated to you the events of that evening.'

'Julius Mngomezulu called you.' De Vries watches Hopkins' eyes narrow, his posture stiffen almost imperceptibly. 'I know this and, if I need to, I can prove it. Marc Steinhauer never called you. I want to know why Mngomezulu did.'

Hopkins produces a pink handkerchief and dabs his lips. He adjusts his position, posits the question to de Vries as if he were conducting a cross-examination.

'Did Mngomezulu tell you?'

'I merely want to know whether this officer is

464

disloyal or corrupt. I'm looking to you to help me. If you do, I might overlook the fact that you deliberately misled me in the middle of a complex murder case.'

'If you try to do that,' Hopkins counters, suddenly more confident, 'your source will have to be beyond reproach.'

'Tell me about Mngomezulu.'

Hopkins places his hands on his stomach, glances about the room. He snorts.

'You won't like what I have to say.'

'Tell me.'

Hopkins reclines; he can offer what is wanted.

'I didn't ask him to call me; I certainly didn't offer payment. I think he did it for his own personal reasons. One might speculate that it was because he wished to ensure justice, but that is not the case here. He did it because he doesn't like you. Possibly for your manner, conceivably for your independence but, most of all, I'm afraid to say, I think because of your colour.'

'To what end?'

'You must ask him that. To undermine you, certainly. Perhaps to create a rift within your team.'

De Vries nods absentmindedly.

'How,' Hopkins says casually, 'will the matter be dealt with?'

'I think,' de Vries replies, trying to phrase his words as du Toit might, 'that understanding your relationship to your colleagues is very important and that sometimes, to know things that people don't know you know can provide . . . insurance.'

Hopkins smiles, sits forward, lowers his voice. 'We may be on opposite sides on occasion, but on this perhaps we are together. Mr Mngome- zulu is a strange and, I suspect, troubled young man, full of anger and blame. He is resentful and unforgiving and, I am afraid to say, there are plenty like him in the law, in business, every- where. If you give these people too much power, they will turn it against us.'

De Vries moves his chair back a fraction, away from Hopkins, says, 'There are people in my team I don't like; I just get on with it.'

'Too true,' Hopkins says. 'I have many a client I don't care for, but one has a job to do.'

De Vries smiles at Hopkins, bends towards him so that they are both leaning in towards each other. Echoing Hopkins' hushed tones, he murmurs: 'Do you like Nicholas Steinhauer?'

Hopkins' smile remains, but de Vries appreci- ates that, as the seconds pass, it falters, just a little. Hopkins affects a shrug.

'He pays my bills.'

* * *

De Vries sits alone at home watching dusk overtaken by night, staring at his garden, the green pool with its intestinal hoses and jellyfish — like cleaner floating dead in its clammy calm and, behind high, faint, scudding clouds, almost a full moon. He thinks again through all the information he has accrued in the last weeks, checking and rechecking every word of testi- mony, each report filed. Always, the man

466

Steinhauer is present. He sits just beyond his field of vision, perhaps somewhere in the corner of the dark yellowwood ceiling beams, almost like a judge on the bench. De Vries feels anger and frustration rise through his body like a cold sweat. It hits his groin and then his stomach, passes up his chest, making him fight for breath, until it reaches his head, when he finds himself panting out loud, fists clenched, teeth gritted, a paroxysm. Then, eyes bulging, he returns to the domesticated pastoral scene until his pulse steadies, muttering to himself to stay calm, his hand to his left pectoral.

He draws the curtains and turns up the light above the dining table and studies the papers, making notes and drinking. It is a table which held his family together for so many years. Another lawyer's letter informs him that Suzanne de Vries wants him to keep this house, at least until the girls have decided where they want to live. She was, her lawyer informed him, earning so much, she could not see the need to force a sale. A gesture of kindness posited as a humiliation. He wonders whether this was her phraseology or just a cheap jibe from a hubristic legal mind.

He questions his every decision and still he cannot see a way to break Steinhauer. He invents and hypothesizes until he sees the moon cross behind Devil's Peak. He has drunk steadily, but his mind seems on automatic: the self-criticism and frustration become self-perpetuating. He is still awake; still conscious of his surroundings, but he knows that he is not in control, his imaginings more bizarre and distorted as the night has deepened. He sees Nicholas Steinhauer standing over him, smiling pitifully at his travail. He wakes momentarily, seemingly halfway through a spoken sentence. His eyes flicker and, as he fades into unconsciousness once more, he hears himself tell his phantom to his face:

'You will not walk away from me.'

★ ★ ★

Just after midnight, de Vries drives carefully up the sharp incline that takes him from Vineyard Street onto Vineyard Heights. The street-lights are out again and, still dazed, he knows that he should not be driving at all, but no Cape Town policeman will dare pull him over. For a few days, he is a hero to all but himself. Alone, he has talked himself hoarse, yet he has no answer, no insight as to how he might ease the pressure that contorts him from within. He is unfit for public consumption, his cheeks scarred, eye-sockets blue and scalp still swollen.

He parks under the tall blue gum opposite Marantz's front wall and leans on the video entryphone. The front gate buzzes, clicks open and he pushes through, crunches across the gravel courtyard and opens the front door. He slams it behind him and begins to descend the steep wooden staircase. He hobbles down the main flight to the mezzanine level, looks down on Marantz's big sitting room, sees the fire lit and the tall windows closed and curtained. It is not home, but it is a sanctuary.

'So,' he says as he shakes Marantz's hand. 'Is this early or late?'

'I was just sitting up reading. Why?'

'No poker?'

'No . . . No stomach for the fight. Luck is a tireless enemy.'

De Vries chooses the position nearest the fire, sits heavily.

'Drinking?' Marantz asks.

'Wine — better be wine.'

Marantz fetches a bottle of Merlot and a saucer of biltong, places them at de Vries' elbow. For a few minutes, they sit silently, almost in meditation, listening to the fire crackle, the wind in the line of trees outside the windows.

Marantz looks up. 'You saw the papers today?'

'No.'

'I'll paraphrase; they like you. Admire how you saved the kid and killed the bad guy.'

De Vries sighs. 'I don't care, John.'

'I know you don't. I wouldn't have told you if you did.'

De Vries empties his glass and refills it to the brim.

'You read all the docket reports?' he asks Marantz.

'Yes. All of them. Several times.'

'For fuck's sake, tell me I missed something. Tell me we fucked up completely and there's a simple way we can make it all come together.'

'Look — if there's no forensics, there's no forensics.'

'There's nothing. Never has been.'

'Unless you make some up.'

De Vries looks up at Marantz, searches his expression for irony, for evidence that he is joking; sees none.

'There are nations,' Marantz continues, 'who build DNA databases, promise to destroy stuff after a few years, never to obtain it illegally, do the opposite, and there's still never a match. It's the way it is, especially with these people. You ask yourself: if you are going to cheat one way, why not cheat in another?'

'Meaning . . . ?'

'Steinhauer will walk. I guess if you can match hubris with ability, you're pretty safe. And he has a sponsor somewhere, because just about everyone but you seems to be giving him a free ride.'

'What do you mean, a sponsor?'

'Someone powerful who watches out for him, perhaps? Influence can flow in both directions.'

De Vries murmurs, 'There's at least one leak; those above wanted to stop the inquiry.'

'These people operate on a different plane from you and me. But we have one advantage: we know they're there.'

De Vries frowns. 'You always talk in riddles.'

Marantz meets de Vries' eye. 'I'm not the one being disingenuous, Vaughn. You're not here for no reason. You want to know what to do, but you'd better understand something: if you've come here, to me, knowing me as you do, then you already know what you want.'

'I don't understand that sentence either.'

'Re-check your motives: coming to me before you decide your reaction?'

De Vries drains his glass and tips the bottle again. Says, 'I came for company.'

'Get a cat.'

'A sounding board.'

'Sound off then.'

'I'm drunk.'

'No mitigation accepted,' Marantz says. 'I know what you want to do, and I agree. You just have to admit it to yourself and comprehend the consequences.'

'And how,' de Vries says bitterly, 'do you know what I want to do?'

Marantz stares at him.

'Because it is what I have dreamed of, awake and asleep, for five long years.'

★ ★ ★

'You know, after all this time, I quite like the name.'

'It is my work name.'

'You don't want me to be Mrs February?'

'No.'

She sits up and leans over the foot-stool, blocking his view of the muted television. 'Because as it is, only our friends know that I am the attractive wife of the hero in the newspapers, Warrant Officer Donald February.'

'There is only one picture, and it is very dark so that you can hardly see me.'

She squeezes herself onto the ottoman and begins to massage his shoulders from the front.

'I can see you.'

'But only because you know that I am there.'

He kisses her quickly on the cheek. 'Anyway, it is safer for me, and it is safer for you, that people do not know me and do not see me. It is best that way.'

'Safer?'

'Safer, and easier. It means they can say my name. Sometimes, in the SAPS, it is better not to reveal everything about yourself. Most of them do not know who I am.'

'Even your Colonel?'

'Even him.'

'But why would you not want to take credit for what you did?'

Don turns away from her, leans back on the sofa, searches for a magazine on the side-table shelf.

'You hate those magazines,' she says, scolding. 'What are you doing?'

He turns back to her fast, sitting forward, holding her by her shoulders. He speaks slowly and marks out the sentences with his grip on her.

'I killed a man. I killed him to save my boss. He is the first man I have killed and I never want to kill another. I am not a hero. There are things to boast about and show off to your friends about, and there are things never to be discussed. You hear me?'

★　★　★

In the time it takes de Vries to shuffle to the bathroom, Marantz descends into melancholy. He feels charged by his involvement with de

Vries' case, but it cannot patch over the pain he suffers. It is the men who took his family against whom he should be plotting: the group in the Russian underworld who planned the destruction of his life — his family, his career, his mind. Dreams of vengeance dominate him; he seeks anything which might mitigate their intensity.

De Vries slumps back into his chair, belches.

'Welcome back.' Marantz stands, fetches a second uncorked bottle of Merlot, places it beside de Vries; forgets his memories and immerses himself in another world, less agonizing.

'You have eliminated going to the press, releasing what you know on the Internet?' he asks.

'Could prejudice later action, that's the official line. It would probably just work as a lonely hearts ad for him.'

'I agree. He outplayed everyone this time. No reason he won't next time too.'

'If there is a next time. Maybe this is the end?'

'Don't be naive, Vaughn. If there's one thing your Dr Matimba should have told you: these people never stop. Especially if they think they're God.'

'He has answers for everything, then no answers for anything. He and his kak lawyer, Hopkins, they worked it perfectly. Then they close it down from above. Police Ministry, no less. SAPS brass couldn't be happier. They're still licking their wounds because it was one of their own who took those boys in the first place. Who'll trust those kind, helpful bobbies ever again?'

'Did you ever have those in South Africa?'

'Maybe not.'

473

The fire spits, sends embers flying onto the flagstones. Marantz gets up, stamps them out, toes them back against the hearth.

'So,' he says. 'What else have you thought?'

'I've thought . . . How justice is an inexact science. How it sickens me to see Steinhauer walk away. I spent most of yesterday daydreaming of ways to trap him, hurt him, maim him, force him into confession, kill him. Pathetic, isn't it?'

'That's what happens when you rely only on twelve good men and true.'

'Three judges for us.'

'You know what I mean.'

'I've always believed that if you give up on that, you're finished,' de Vries states. 'It's stipulated and mandated and it forms the core of what you and I might call civilized society.'

'A reporter asked Mahatma Gandhi what he thought of Western civilization. Do you know what he said?' Marantz smiles.

'What?'

' 'I think it would be a very good idea'. Structures and laws — what are they for? What purpose does it serve to revere them when they patently fail?' Marantz goes on. 'The evening we first met, in Bishopscourt, at that party, the only interesting thing you revealed is something you didn't even tell me, something I read from you. A determination to get to the end. You see the end here, but you can't reach it. How will you ever concentrate on anything else until you do?'

'Your view of the end may be different from mine.'

474

Marantz looks at him. 'But it isn't, is it, Vaughn?'

De Vries listens to the crackle of the fire echo around tall walls and hard stone floor, feels a pocket of heat waft over him.

'You cannot always rely on luck,' Marantz says. 'If you believe that what will be will be, then you are no more than flotsam. You have relinquished all control over your life.' He looks at de Vries' face, meets his eye. 'I had control taken from me, and I drifted for five years. That was a mistake. Now I know what I have to do if I am to make headway. And I think you know that you cannot be passive any more. This is the time in your life you have waited for.'

'I understand your motives, given what you have been through,' de Vries says quietly. 'If you could know, could find those responsible, if there were no other justice . . . But here — how can I know that?'

'But you do know — you are only afraid to admit it. You are at a crossroads. I'm at your side, Vaughn, but I will not help you to make the first step. Once you have made it, whatever you decide, you need not be alone.'

'I'm too tired and too drunk for this conversation.'

'Men like us, we are haunted by injustice,' Marantz says passionately. 'The men who destroyed me loom over me in the dark and they are always out of my reach. Present, but untouchable.'

De Vries looks up at him, wonders how one man's delusion can be so like another's.

475

'And it leads — where?' de Vries asks slowly.

'I can't tell you that.'

'And I can't contemplate it. Not in the middle of the night.'

'Frightening, isn't it?'

De Vries rocks forward, rising on the third arc.

'I'm too pissed to be frightened and too tired to think. I'm going home while I can still focus.'

'Don't be stupid, Vaughn. You'll crash your fucking car before you get to the freeway.'

'I've had practice.'

'Just take the spare room and drive home tomorrow.'

'No.' He looks up at Marantz. 'I have my house all to myself now. Going home is a pleasure I savour.'

'*If* you get home.'

'When,' de Vries says, as he walks proudly to the staircase, 'have you ever known me incapable?'

★ ★ ★

De Vries wakes to hear his cellphone ringing. He is sitting upright, his neck locked; spasms shoot down his back. He reaches sideways to fumble on his bedside table, but his hand hits glass. He peels open sticky eyelids and realizes that he is still in his car. He feels in his pocket and pulls out the phone.

'Yes?'

'In the morning, take a look at the email I just sent you. Transcript of an interview Steinhauer gave tonight. Tell me what you think.'

'What time is it?'

'Two thirty. Where are you?'

'In my car.'

'Still?'

'Ja.'

'Close to home?'

De Vries looks out of the driver's side window and sees his lawn under his tyres and his front door about five metres away.

'Yeah.'

'Well, take care.'

'I'll make it.'

★　★　★

De Vries, bleary-eyed, furry-mouthed, stares agape at his laptop screen, at the frozen picture of Nicholas Steinhauer smiling at the camera. He sits back in his study chair. His head throbs so hard, he feels the blood being sucked from behind his eyes. Only sporadic sleep has obliterated the incessant drumming, the increased heart-rate, the adrenalin of possibility. He has felt his mind re-programmed so that what seemed impossible to him has become a likelihood. He stretches for his cellphone, just out of reach, fumbles with the small buttons, presses the speed-dial, notices the device shaking in his grip. The ring-tone stops. De Vries waits and hears nothing. He says: 'A walk on the Mountain. I need the exercise.'

He listens to a suggested rendezvous, replies: 'Yes,' and then, 'Conversation . . . and resolution.'

He disconnects and places the cellphone neatly at his right hand, contemplates returning to bed, considers a beer. Instead, he sits back in the chair, watches the screensaver send stars. Then he closes his eyes, concentrates only on the pain, feels it coursing through his body to his extremities; understands that the pain charges him, knows that if it leaves him at any time this day, he will lose all resolve.

★ ★ ★

After the weekend, early on Monday morning, his cellphone rings by his ear. He had debated turning it off, disconnecting the home line, waiting until they came for him, but he has been awake for hours already, is grateful for something happening which is outside his brain.

'Vaughn?'

'Ja.'

'Henrik. You need to get in here now.'

'Thought I was on leave. What is it?'

'Not on the phone. Just obey an order, for once. And quickly.'

De Vries hangs up, swings out of bed, takes a long shower. He drives via his local Engen garage, fills up with petrol, buys a large, strong coffee and takes the high road into town. The morning is grey and dark and, although there are streaks of dirty sunshine on the water beyond the harbour, there is cloud over Lion's Head — a sure sign of rain to come. He cuts across the southern end of town, drives in off the main drag and parks under the building in his usual spot, takes the elevator straight up to his floor. He walks towards his office, sees Don standing at his door.

478

'We have to go up,' Don tells him.

'What's happening?'

'Steinhauer. Nicholas Steinhauer is dead. His house was burned down. Body in the wreckage. They've just identified him.'

De Vries tilts his head, deep in thought.

'When?'

Don starts walking towards the stairs.

'Let the Director tell us. I am probably not supposed to know.'

De Vries follows him silently, each step an effort.

Thulani's office is busy. Seated behind his desk, General Thulani is attended by Julius Mngomezulu. Du Toit stands by the door, and behind him, de Vries can see two black men, sharply dressed. Du Toit beckons them in, gestures for them to stand with the be-suited men. As de Vries passes through the doorway, he hears the elevator bell announce its arrival on the top floor. He looks around to see Norman Classon striding up the corridor towards the office. He shakes du Toit's hand and comes in.

Thulani says: 'To those of you standing, this will not take long. We have a serious problem. The body of Dr Nicholas Steinhauer was found in the early hours of this morning in his house in Constantia. His body is seriously burnt and almost beyond recognition, and we must wait for a more detailed post-mortem to establish the actual cause of death. However, we have positive identification now, and the scene is entirely under our control. His house has been razed to the ground, presumed arson. It took the locals

479

several hours to get the situation established and to work out why we should be contacted but, once we knew who the property belonged to, we hastened to establish ID and close down the scene from the press. The time of death has not been established, but the fire was reported at two thirty a.m. by neighbours.'

'Accident?' du Toit asks.

'That,' Thulani pronounces gravely, 'is the question which I will be asked. We need to be able to provide answers.'

'And, if not, what motive?' du Toit says.

Thulani frowns at him.

'The inquiry is just beginning. Until we can speak to others who knew the property, it is difficult to ascertain what might be missing. If robbery was the motive, doubtless we will find high-value items missing. This is why we have closed the scene tightly and we are making access to the public — and the press — impossible. Besides, access to the property is difficult even for the professionals as the structure has partially collapsed.'

'Was he alone?'

Thulani looks over to de Vries.

'It appears so, Colonel. Did you expect otherwise?'

'Nicholas Steinhauer kept his lawyers close.'

Thulani smiles fleetingly. 'You may be disappointed to hear that no lawyers have been found on site.'

De Vries widens his jaw on reflex, checks himself, coughs.

Thulani lowers his voice. 'Let me be clear: I

am separating this enquiry from your department, from this building entirely. In the light of the media interest there will be, I have asked Major Mhlawuli and Warrant Officer Qhwalela to be present here this morning' — he indicates the suited duo — 'to speak to each of you: Brigadier du Toit, Colonel de Vries and Warrant Officer February. When we are asked the inevitable questions, I want everything covered. You understand?' He looks to du Toit and de Vries. They remain impassive. 'I want total deniability,' Thulani continues. 'To be able to say that we have talked to the officers in charge of the Steinhauer inquiry and that they have no part in this — in any way.'

'Part in it?' de Vries blurts out.

'We are cast as suspects?' du Toit says.

'You are eliminated before any suspicion even arises.'

'Is there a suggestion of lack of confidence here?'

'No, Henrik,' Thulani replies quickly. 'You, of all people, should be aware of the need for answers to questions before they are asked. Don't make this a personal matter.' He waits for du Toit, who looks away from him.

He continues: 'This will take place immediately. Following your . . . debriefing . . . none of you will have any involvement whatsoever. Is that clear?'

Everyone nods; even those with no reason to do so.

'Colonel de Vries and Warrant Officer February are booked out on leave. On

481

conclusion here, you will take it. Leave the city and speak to no one. You understand me?'

February nods. De Vries smiles.

'Major Mhlawuli will arrange official interviews with you now. There is to be no word to the media. All such activities will be coordinated through me.' He points at the group in front of him. 'You five will go now. When you are finished, go home, ignore the press, and refrain from any comment whatsoever. That is a direct order. 'No comment' is the only acceptable response.'

Thulani gets up and Mhlawuli, the shorter of the two black officers, moves to the door, opens it, and gestures du Toit, de Vries and Don February out of the office. Qhwalela protects their rear flank.

When they have reached the elevators, Mhlawuli pronounces: 'Director du Toit, you will come with us now. Warrant Officer February, you will wait in Interview Room Two. Colonel, wait in your office and we will send for you after we have finished with Director du Toit.'

The elevator doors open and they enter the lift. Mhlawuli stands facing de Vries, who is still on the landing.

'You, Colonel,' he says, 'can take the stairs.'

★　★　★

'The Police Minister has asked for an interim report immediately,' Thulani tells Classon. 'I was under the impression that he was greatly displeased by this turn of events.'

482

'Why should that be?'

'A prominent man murdered; further complication to this long-running affair. It casts only more darkness on what is already a grey cloud hanging over every one of us.'

'Does the Police Ministry have a special interest in Nicholas Steinhauer?' Classon asks. 'This is the second time they have intervened.'

Thulani sits back down behind his desk.

'Steinhauer acted as a consultant to them seven years ago. They may have been in touch with him now, since he returned to the country. I assume that this is a matter of loyalty.'

'Blind loyalty can be dangerous,' Classon says.

Thulani smiles. 'I know what you think, Mr Classon, but it has always been so. Influence in this country is cherished, closely guarded, and used without shame or apprehension.'

'Weren't we promised better?' Classon mutters.

Thulani looks down at him, closes his eyes slowly, nods.

'Africa is a continent of broken promises. None of us should expect that to change any time soon.'

★　★　★

The interviews last no more than twenty minutes. In the elevator, Don February reflects that the case has not ended as he hoped; would not reflect as well on him as if Steinhauer had been proven guilty. He travels back up to the eighth floor to see if de Vries is still there, to

483

check that he can go.

He is almost at the door of de Vries' office when he realizes that Director du Toit is sitting in the visitor's chair; de Vries with his head in his hands at his desk. He knocks on the door and is waved in by du Toit.

'All all right, Warrant February?'

'Yes, sir.'

'No awkward questions?'

'No, sir. I was treated respectfully. They wished to know my whereabouts on Sunday evening. I was able to tell them that I was at a friend's house until late and with my wife at all times.'

Du Toit nods. 'Good.'

Don looks at de Vries, who raises his head, tortoise-like, morose.

'Go home, Don. They're covering their backs in case one of us has gone rogue. It's shit and they know it, but it has to be seen to be done . . . ' He tails off, glances at du Toit, sits up. 'I'll say it, if no one else will. Fucking good riddance to Nicholas Steinhauer.'

Du Toit nods his head in agreement, but Vaughn sees Don February out of the corner of his eye; there is no reaction from his Warrant Officer.

'We all drink to that — but I think,' du Toit says, 'that should be the last time you say that.'

De Vries laughs, holds up his hands in surrender.

Du Toit turns to face Don. 'You're taking some leave, I understand?'

'Yes, sir. As you proposed. Seven days, starting today.'

'Seems you are already owed another morning then. Enjoy it. Try to forget about the job for a few days — and don't worry about this. Answers will be found.'

Don nods, looks at de Vries. De Vries looks back at him seriously, unmoving.

Don turns smartly and leaves the office, walks through the squad room to the corridor beyond, does not look back.

Du Toit turns round to de Vries. Says: 'Solid officer.'

'He is.'

'Trustworthy.'

'Probably the best black officer I've worked with.'

Du Toit frowns, considers challenging him. Instead, he says: 'Good. I hope you communicate your satisfaction with him?'

'In my own way. He works well, but I think he keeps secrets.'

Du Toit sniffs. 'Can't you just accept that some people are on your side, Vaughn?'

'No.'

'Well, that's your problem. You don't know who to trust. It's a big part of the job.'

'Big part of life. Best not to trust anyone. Then you don't get disappointed.'

'You inhabit a dark and lonely place. No wonder you find the going so tough.'

'You think that, do you?'

Du Toit raises an eyebrow; de Vries is not looking.

'Why do you think Thulani said it was 'a problem'?' de Vries asks.

'Steinhauer is dead.'

'Dozens of people die in the Cape every day. Besides, according to him, Steinhauer was no longer part of this inquiry. So why should it be a problem?'

'He's covering his back, I guess.'

'You don't find Thulani's choice of words interesting?' de Vries persists.

'It's clear that he has little trust in us.'

'It's not us he's worried about though, is it?'

'Not Warrant Officer February.'

De Vries is about to reply, realizes that du Toit is on an alternate plane of thinking, suddenly feels it is not worth explaining that what lurks above him is more dangerous than the threat at street-level. Instead he says: 'They tell you what they were thinking?'

'They don't have anything yet,' du Toit says. 'Crimes like this: often no evidence.'

'No.'

'So Vaughn, where were *you* late last night?'

De Vries looks up, chuckles. 'Watching British football, drinking beer, eating nachos, inadequately flirting with women. Mexican restaurant in West-lake — forty witnesses, there from eight p.m. until about one a.m. — and yes, I took a cab.'

'Much better than sitting at home with just a selection of bottles for company.'

'That has its charms.'

'I'm sure it does. Aren't you going to ask me what *I* was doing?'

De Vries smirks, replies very quietly, 'I know where you were.'

'How's that?'

De Vries looks at him askance. 'For God's sake, Henrik. I don't really know what you were doing. I just know where you were: a long way from this case. Because that's your talent, that's what you can do.'

'Very cryptic, Vaughn. You're so erudite these days. Perhaps you've been spending too much time with that friend of yours?'

'I don't have any friends.'

Du Toit gets up from his chair. 'Be careful that cynical little aphorism doesn't come true.'

De Vries gets up, too, and not out of deference. 'Did you doubt me just a little, Henrik?'

'Doubt you?'

'Last night, around midnight?'

'Of course not.' Director du Toit turns towards the door, opens it. 'You may not trust anyone, but I trust you. We go way too far back for that. I may not know who you are after all these years — but I know what you're not.'

★ ★ ★

De Vries drives out of the city on the N2, past the airport, over Sir Lowry's Pass and across the Overberg. On the other side, he pushes on at a steady 140kph for 250 kilometres. Just short of Heidelberg, he pulls left into the Blue Crane farm shop, drives past the farm-stall itself and parks under cover at the back of the gravel car park. He eases out of the car, stretches his shoulders and arms, hobbles back towards the shop. Even in the mid-afternoon, the air here is hot and thick; he misses his air conditioning after

487

only a few steps. He scans the car park, sees only five cars and none seem familiar. You start at one farm-stall, he thinks, and end in another.

He trudges up the gravel path, passing a mother and two children eating cream cakes on the scrubby lawn, through the cool shop and into the dining area, under a giant naive mural of the mountain ranges which shadow the freeway all the way to Plettenberg Bay. In the far corner, behind a magazine, he sees him.

Marantz lowers the magazine and smiles at him. Says, 'It's a small world for a vast country.'

'How do you know this place?'

'It's one hundred metres from the turn-off to Vermaaklikheid; the most efficient turning to Vermaaklikheid. Why take you out of your way?'

'Where are you going?'

'There's a poker event at the casino in Port Elizabeth. Good to get out of the house sometimes.'

De Vries orders coffee and cake from the waitress; waits for her to back away towards the kitchen.

'What happened?'

Marantz looks past him, down the length of the dining room. Only one other couple are eating at the far end. They are silent, chewing, watching each other eat.

'Happened?'

De Vries stares at him.

Marantz shrugs. 'I couldn't tell you.'

De Vries whispers, 'Steinhauer is burnt to a frazzle, his place razed to the ground. Not subtle, is it?'

'We don't live in a subtle country.'

De Vries feels the frustration gather inside him. He knows now: it is when he is not in control.

'What was learnt?'

'The doctor was resistant, but he was overcome. The audio files from the bunker exist, in a safe, in his Constantia house. There's a combination in an email you received from a junk mail company. You'll find it if you look. But . . . I doubt it can be used. You could never explain how it was obtained. But I don't know. Maybe you'll find a way.'

'He confessed?'

'There are names too — three names. Others involved. Perhaps they will match the prints you found?'

Marantz sits back, and de Vries does the same. It is subconscious — you want something from somebody, you echo their physical movements; flatter them that they are leading and you are following, subservient. He sees Marantz's eyes focused on the doorway from the kitchen. He hears light footsteps on the terracotta tiles. The waitress reappears, presents him with his coffee and cake, retreats again.

'He was guilty, Vaughn. Just as you said. You don't need the detail.'

'How?'

Marantz drains his glass of what might be orange juice.

'As a policeman, you do everything you can to find justice for the victim. That's your *modus operandi*, your reputation. Consider yourself righteous, because you were right, what you said about what you will do and what you won't. It is the only thing that stops society imploding. But society operates to the lowest common denominator, and sometimes, there's a perpetrator who plays on that, and then he has the advantage only because you will not fall to his level . . . But I will. I only stepped in because everything you could do wasn't enough. My boundary is closer to the darkness than yours.'

'Just make sure you step back from that boundary now.'

'Special circumstances. He would have walked away.'

De Vries nods. He is staring at the table, food and cup and Marantz out of focus. He snaps to, looks slowly up at him.

'I hope I can trust you?'

Marantz laughs, loudly enough that it echoes down the dining room and causes the couple at the far end to look up at them.

'That is quite a stupid question.'

'It is an important one. To me.'

'What have you ever seen that makes you think people change, Vaughn? We're born and we're formed. We can fight it but, at some point, you accept what you are, and you know what it takes to get you up in the morning, get you through the day. The first rule of survival — stay alive.'

He gets up, swings his car keys on their fob.

'Long way to go, Vaughn. No time to lose.'

Vaughn catches his eye for a moment; sees nothing but assurance.

Marantz strides away across the restaurant. De

Vries does not watch him leave; picks up the cream cake, bites roughly into it.

★ ★ ★

He crosses over the freeway and heads south towards the sea, leaves the black-top and motors over dirt track, cross-country, cruising at only 50kph, steering around the potholes and avoiding the ruts which pepper the gravel tracks in the countryside. He sees ostriches on the horizon; ewes and their lambs recoil from fences as he accelerates past them, leaving a wake of drifting deep-red dust. He passes through kilometres of burnt-out arable land, marks the distance by the telegraph poles and the birds of prey that occupy them, each a sentinel, each readying itself for the dusk hunt. There are cows too, and the occasional buck. He stutters and chokes as he passes through a eucalyptus-bounded farmyard on a hairpin bend, the heavy odour of manure filling the cabin of his car; the remembrance that smell may be invisible, but it is all particulate.

Away from the farm, he opens all four electric windows, feels the constant heat of heavy afternoon air blowing across him, warmed for kilometres over the bleached, scalding soil. He slows down momentarily to frame a windmill pump before a stand of gum trees, in front of a range of purple mountains. He leans out of his window, stares through the passenger side, behind him in the mirror: everywhere, the land stretches out, wide and high, up to the mountain ranges behind him and distant horizons on the other three sides. There is a sky as big as he has ever seen, curving at its edges, the horizon no more than a pixel point.

He descends a narrow pass on a sandy track, crosses a dry ford in the valley and scrambles his vehicle back up the other side, freewheeling down towards the quiet village, consisting only of farmers' and fishermen's houses, simple shacks, their stoeps draped with washing. From sand track to loose gravel, suddenly there is tarmac. A blessed smoothness and silence may be enjoyed past the village bus stop, for a whole 100 metres, until the gravel track begins again. De Vries smiles, as he always does, when he passes over that 100 metres of civilization and modernity.

Ahead, the road forks, and he takes the sharp left turn uphill again, and then begins to fall gently down towards the Duiwenhoks River. He turns off the road, onto a rutted grass track. Opening a gate, he drives between rocky outcrops of aloes and cacti until he reaches a small thatched cottage.

He parks his car under a diagonally leaning car-port, unloads a single small suitcase from the boot, drops it on the stone doorstep of the cottage. He limps back to his car, takes a case of red wine from the back seat, and places that also on the doorstep. He nudges open the unlocked door, releases the group of flies at the kitchen window into the cooling evening air. He pulls a pair of navy shorts from his case, levers off his shoes and pulls away sticky socks from his tired feet, drops his trousers and switches into the shorts. Then, between three-metre-high reeds, he hobbles down the slatted wooden jetty to the boarded dock where a kayak and an old traditional rowing boat are moored. He sits down on the end of the dock, lowers his feet into the tea-coloured water. He takes a deep breath, listens to the silence.

Occasionally, there is a bird-call, a whirring of a passing insect, even the occasional muted splash as a fish breaches the mirrored surface. The tide is on the turn and there is not a breath of wind. In his brain, apart from the distant echoes of road noise from his journey, there is silence. No beating, no pulsing ache. He ducks his head and stares down at the water, but he cannot see the bottom.

★ ★ ★

On Sunday nights, the Casa Mexicana is busy with locals and regulars, soccer fans and students, who drink South American beer, eat sticky nachos and watch the English Premier League. In summer, the outside terrace is full of revelry but, this evening, the windows are steamed up, and the open fire is lit. De Vries sits at the bar with two drinking buddies whose names he does not know, watches the game, watches the girls, watches the waitress, watches the guy in the kitchen wipe his nose with the back of the hand with which he wraps enchiladas. De Vries watches women avert their eyes from him as they come through the door. He whoops when one team scores; he cheers when the other team scores. Later, he asks the greeter to book a taxi for him, specifically naming one company. Vaughn de Vries spends the whole evening there until everyone but himself is convinced that he is drunk.

★ ★ ★

It is strange, John Marantz reflects, that a process banned should be learnt in such detail. As if not knowing of it would make it more, not less, likely that you might unknowingly practise it. The speaker in the featureless room is a pale, bland man, an expert on torture and the effects of torture on its victims. The class of nine men and one woman sit silently, their pens hovering over notebooks, yet unmoving. That which should not be known should not be recorded lest it be known. Yet it must be remembered.

Dr Vincent Dayton speaks in a monotone, a transatlantic drawl, which both bores and mesmerizes at once. Terrible fact rendered banal.

'Your colleagues may have faced death. By that, I mean known that death was inevitable. Even if they survived, they will not be able to describe it to you, because it is indescribably terrible, the ultimate personal tragedy, individual remembrance, peppered with fear so intense that it may kill you first: it is the most terrifying feeling you can imagine. To simulate imminent death, therefore, is torture, pure and simple.'

He takes a sip of water from a plain glass on the empty desk.

'This action is deemed by some to be

494

acceptable, used in short phases. But, as you will hear, whilst the physical damage may prove to be minimal, even over time, the psychological effects can insinuate themselves after the first administration. I have witnessed panic attacks, intense Post Traumatic Stress Disorder, permanent chronic depression of the most severe nature. These indications begin quickly and, years later, show no sign of abating.'

He drinks again, contemplates the glass afterwards. Marantz knows that this is as much to punctuate his speech as to cool his throat. It is a psychological test also. Marantz can see that the speaker watches all of them as he drinks.

'It is well documented that for some victims, it becomes impossible to shower or bathe or swim. For others, the mere sound of rainfall can induce panic, shortness of breath, and inability to breathe normally. These are facts, ladies and gentlemen. They are denied, but they are true.'

★   ★   ★

All the time, the man is unconscious. He is laid on a dusty green velvet couch in a small back room, parquet-floored but sound-deadened by textile hangings on the walls, double-glazed windows overlaid with heavy drapes. The only light is from a small brass reading lamp with a green glass shade which stands at the far edge of the wide leather-topped desk.

The long plastic ties loop around his arms and wrists, separated from skin by his shirt and thick tweed jacket, under the couch and back again, a

495

tight circle in which no movement is possible. The evenings are cooler now and an open fire is lit, the small grate piled high with eucalyptus logs, each cut evenly and to the same length to fit perfectly in the narrow fireplace. The unconscious man is unaware of it, would be unable to twist his head to see the crackling fuel. A band of plastic runs across his forehead, over two wooden wedges either side of him placed behind his ears, under the couch.

His ankles are bound also with plastic ties, one to each corner leg of the couch. At the end where his feet mark the corners, the couch is raised. A foot nudges a book in place beneath the first leg, then the second. The chaise-longue end rises again, and another hardback volume, similarly thick, is pushed on top of the first, both left and right, and the incline increases. Blood begins to pour towards his head.

The man takes the spectacles from the prone body's face, places them gently on the desk next to two plastic syringes, two small glass bottles. He selects a syringe with a green label, inserts it into the man's neck, slowly plunges the piston between thumb and first two fingers, and watches the liquid empty from the plastic reservoir into the man. In less than a minute, the man stirs, his eyes begin to flutter and try to focus, he half-heartedly tries to stretch, finds himself unable to move, groans, swallows hard, begins to pant as panic overtakes him.

The other man takes a thin cloth, a tea-towel bearing a faded picture of Table Mountain, places it gently over the prisoner's face. He

496

turns, picks up a clear glass jug of water, holds it some three or four inches above the man's nose and mouth and begins to pour. After three or four seconds, the man gags. He is drowning. The trickle continues and the man begins to splutter, to scream hideously, to jerk in his shackles and try to shake his head. Water enters his sinuses, his pharynx, his larynx, his trachea. His eyes squeeze shut, yet beneath their lids they bulge in terror. Tachycardia is almost instant, the heart's response to the threat of its stilling. Death confronts him and, in this form, there is no doubt.

★ ★ ★

'Ironically, this process is unlikely to cause drowning. However, even a victim who understands this to be fact, who is convinced of this, will not believe it, and the time taken for his belief to ebb will be, not minutes, but mere seconds. As the victim fails to exhale air, or cough up water, his trachea and sinuses will fill with water, and his lungs will slowly, and appreciably to the victim — can you imagine that — collapse. Since chest and lungs are kept higher than the head, the coughing mechanism serves only to draw water up and into the lungs whilst avoiding terminal suffocation. In short, this is a prolonged prelude to death. It is now in the hands of the dispenser to end this sequence . . . Only knowing that it will be repeated minutes later.'

★ ★ ★

'Dr Nicholas Steinhauer. In the minutes before you return to where you were, you have a chance to speak.'

Steinhauer sputters, chokes — says nothing.

'A final chance.'

The man waits until he is certain that Steinhauer can speak. When he does not utter, he slowly folds the tea-towel back down over the captive's mouth. From beneath the shroud, he hears one word.

'No.'

The man takes the refilled jug, raises it above Steinhauer's head and begins again to pour.

★ ★ ★

'Even though this technique is designed to mimic drowning psychologically, rapidly bringing the victim to a perceived state of moving away from life and towards death, there are accounts of victims drowning, suffering heart attack, or permanent damage to the lungs so as to make normal respiratory function all but impossible. The threat of loss of consciousness, and therefore control over his fate, is constant, and, once unconsciousness occurs within the procedure, the likelihood of death is significantly increased. Remaining conscious, however, may lead to physical breakdown or a physiological resignation to die. It may be argued that skilled operators can predict such sequences and effectively halt the procedure just short of a fatal outcome. But note: the halt will merely be temporary, until the victim recovers enough strength to be able fully to experience further treatment.'

★　★　★

After the second phase, when the tea-towel is moved away from his nose, Steinhauer speaks.

'I — I brought him out — Henderson. I recognized his need and set him within my experiment.'

His lips move, and the sounds form words, deep and croaking once, strained and falsetto the next. His eyes remain covered by the tea-towel, his nose drools liquid mucus over his upper lip and into his mouth, down his chin. In the silence between his words, he can hear drops of water hit the puddles on the wooden floor beneath, before his fractured breath drowns out the water.

'Who else visited the site?'

'I cannot say . . .'

'You will say. This never ends. There is never respite. You have one chance only.'

' . . . Dyk. Johannes Dyk . . . Ralph Kierson . . . Van Leuren . . .'

'Good.'

'Untie me.'

'The audio tapes and files. You kept them. Where are they?'

'No.'

'*Where are they?*'

Coughs, snorts and spits, shakes and quivers.

'The safe in my office.'

499

'Combination or key?'

'Both.'

'Where is the key?'

'On my . . . key-ring.'

'Combination?'

Burning lungs, intense pain in his temples, behind his ears.

'Thirty-seven . . . ten . . . nine . . . sixty . . . eight . . . thirteen.'

'What is the significance of those numbers?'

'What?'

'What do they mean?'

'How do you know?'

'Because you are the same.'

'The same?'

'You are not unique. The numbers?'

'My father's birthday . . . my birthday.'

The man nods. 'Inverted.' He smiles thinly, looks down at the body prone. 'Then this is done.'

He moves away from the couch, back to the desk. He takes the syringe marked with red, injects the liquid into Steinhauer's neck, and watches consciousness leave him. He pulls away the tea-towel and stares at the man's eyes.

He overloads the fire with fuel. He cuts the plastic ties, takes them, the tea-towel, the empty syringes and un-needed tiny bottles, places them all at the top of a small black rucksack. Beneath them lie jewellery and silverware, some foreign objets d'art, and a small, very old, wooden tribal mask.

He places a full glass of brandy on the couch next to Steinhauer, tips the open bottle over the table, where it runs onto the parquet flooring. Using the tongs beside the fire, he pokes the white-hot embers beyond the hearth, moving one large glowing chunk of wood beneath the African textile on the wall beside the curtains to the side windows. Even as he takes a final look about the room, a last glance at Nicholas Steinhauer, prone and beyond knowing, the flames begin the rise up the wall, engulfing the grassy textile, towards the wooden beams and the yellowwood ceiling.

He closes the door, retraces his steps to the back door of the house, lets himself out into the night, across the garden, and towards the common land of Constantia. No alarm sounds. By the time the flames appear at the side window, still unseen from the distant neighbours' homes, he is already half a kilometre away, walking up to a dark anonymous motorcycle, parked on an unlit road, overlooked by nothing but an empty house, surrounded by tall trees, heavy with dry autumn leaf and abundant with fruit.

★ ★ ★

Vaughn de Vries is sober. He has been drinking all evening, but his head is clear and calm. After his braai, he has lain on his back on the jetty, looking up at the Milky Way, a splash of sparkling white across the blue-black of night. An occasional bird-call, a passing insect; only these have broken the near-perfect silence.

He slowly struggles up, his body heavy, aching, resisting each movement which brings him to his feet. He moves cautiously in the near-blackness, drawn only to the candle he has lit and placed on the kitchen table. Its light seems very dim beyond the tall reeds. From the jetty, he hears the breeze in the reeds, whispering. He stops and looks ahead. He is different; unexpectedly clear of thought, organized. He has remembered a pillow and bedding, so there are clean sheets on the bed. He has packed soap and towels; sufficient food for several days. He has everything he wants.

He steps into the kitchen, picks up the candle and walks it up a rickety wooden staircase to his bedroom in the eaves of the boathouse to the side of the main building. 'Any time,' this long-held acquaintance has told him, 'this room is yours.'

He sits on the edge of the bed, deep in thought, yet strangely relaxed. To find some comfort from the interminable ache of his bruises, he lies on his back with his legs drawn up. He places a spare cushion under his legs and lets his head sink into the pillow. In the vaulted-roof room he is sweating already and he regrets pulling the curtains over the windows. He considers getting up to open them, to sleep with the cool night-time breeze on him, but he decides to stay where he is. He returns to his thoughts: what has he countenanced; what has he condoned? A tiny wave of panic passes over him; he does not know whether he will sleep.

Within moments, he is asleep.

Acknowledgements

I have received transformatory advice and guidance from Krystyna Green, Martin Fletcher, and much support from Duncan Proudfoot at Constable & Robinson.

The initial critique, and consistent support from my partner, Gareth Hughes, helped me to move forward logically. I would also like to thank Philip G., Erica, and my wonderful, ever-supportive parents.

Everything that is procedurally correct is down to my wonderful police adviser, SAPS Warrant Officer Marianne Steyn; everything else is my doing and, basically, fictional.

I have asked all my Cape Town friends endless questions. Thank you to the Birch clan: Arch, Tas, Simon, Jane, Lannie, Peter, Kate and Lindsay; also to Johan, Eben, Robert, Tania and Matthew K.

During the course of writing this book, I consulted many links online; to those writers and bloggers who have mainly subconsciously influenced me, many thanks.

Other titles published by Ulverscroft:

PRESERVE THE DEAD

Brian McGilloway

On a humid evening in County Derry, Detective Sergeant Lucy Black is visiting her father, a patient in a secure unit in Gransha Hospital on the banks of the River Foyle. He's been hurt badly in a suspicious accident, and Lucy is shocked to discover him chained to the bed for safety. But she barely has time to take it all in before an orderly raises the alarm — a body has been spotted floating in the river below. An elderly man in a grey suit is hauled ashore: he has been cold dead for several days. A full-scale investigation is launched — could this really be the suicide they at first assumed? As Lucy and her colleagues probe more deeply, they find the truth is more bizarre than they could have imagined . . .

THE GOOD LIFE

Martina Cole

Cain Moran wants Jenny Riley more than he has ever wanted anything before in his life. But he is not a free man . . . and Jenny is not just any girl. She cares nothing for Cain's hard-man reputation; she just wants to be with him. But Cain is about to find out that when his wife Caroline said 'Til *death do us part*, she meant it. When Cain is sentenced to life in prison, it seems that Caroline might have got her wish. All Cain and Jenny know is that if their love can survive such separation, then one day they will have a chance at the good life together. But there are greater trials ahead than either can foresee. They're about to learn the hardest lesson of all: live the good life . . . pay the price.

IN A DARK, DARK WOOD

Ruth Ware

Nora is a reclusive crime writer, content with the routine of life in her apartment in London. She hasn't seen her friend Clare in years — not since Nora walked out of school one day and never went back. So she's surprised to receive an invitation to Clare's hen do. Perhaps it's a chance to reconnect with her best friend. But something goes terribly wrong in the eerie glass house deep in the English countryside . . . Then Nora wakes up with her head bandaged and a police guard outside her door. Are they there to protect her – or arrest her? Nora is scared. Scared because while she can remember the broken glass, the gun, the blood, she's not sure if she can bear the full truth of what happened . . .

THE BURNING ROOM

Michael Connelly

In the LAPD's Open-Unsolved Unit, not many murder victims die a decade after the crime. So when mariachi musician Orlando Merced finally succumbs to complications from being shot ten years earlier, Bosch catches a case in which the body is still fresh, but any other evidence is virtually nonexistent. Partnered with rookie detective Lucia Soto, Bosch begins to see political dimensions to the case. Soto soon reveals a burning obsession that could make her a loose cannon, while the one piece of evidence they have on the Merced shooting points in a shocking and unexpected direction that could unsettle the very people who want Bosch to close out the case. It's looking like Orlando Merced may not be the investigation's only victim . . .